A LOVE LIKE NO OTHER

Morgana opened her eyes and saw the man she had loved as no other hovering over her, his hair wet and clinging to the beloved lines of his clean-cut jaw and chin, his proud forehead.

How could she deny this when her heart and mind and body wanted a union of their souls more than anything, and to deny it would have been like trying to deny the tide of life that flowed through her with every pulse beat.

You don't have to deny it, whispered her heart. *Who will ever know beside the two of you?*

Tears of joy spilled from her eyes as any remaining reservations evaporated. "Love me, Leif," she whispered on a sweet, soft sob of adoration. "I've missed you so . . . need you so . . ."

"Morgana, Morgana, *ást mín,*" he whispered against her eyes, her brow, her lips . . .

LINDA LANG BARTELL

TENDER MARAUDER

ZEBRA BOOKS
KENSINGTON PUBLISHING CORP.

ZEBRA BOOKS are published by

Kensington Publishing Corp.
475 Park Avenue South
New York, NY 10016

Zebra, the Z logo Reg. U.S. Pat & TM Off. The Lovegram logo is a trademark of Kensington Publishing Corp.

First Printing: January, 1994

Printed in the United States of America

Don't look now, Judith E. French, but this one's for you, too. And for Gail Oust (aka Elizabeth Turner), and for Linda Ladd, and Maria Green—wonderful friends, the most talented of peers . . . and always there when I need them.

Anger is a short madness.
Horace

Prologue

Norvegia, March—A.D. 907

Expectation hung heavy in the air.

Waist deep in the icy water, a half score of somber young warriors heaved in unison against the hand-hewn oaken hull of the great longship. The vessel, with its long but shallow keel, scraped softly against the sand as it slowly moved forward and onto the ocean's gently-heaving bosom.

A dozen archers nocked their fiery arrows and took aim, their bowstrings as taut as the quivering quiet. At a silent signal, they loosed their burning brands toward the ship. Like shooting stars they arced through the air toward their target, catching quickly, as they were meant to. Fingers of flame leapt upward toward the seething skies. The tent sheltering the body of the dead jarl was quickly consumed, swiftly sending its exalted voyager heavenward.

Morgana watched as marauding clouds swept overhead in the quickening wind, obliterating the last gold and mauve striations just above the horizon. The encroaching darkness and growing cacophony of the elements was the perfect background for this unexpected—and unwelcome—event, she thought.

The crowd of people around her began to cheer as the graceful longship eased forward ever farther, its great square sail catching the breeze and filling with a low, whooshing sound.

"Hail Harald!" they shouted all around her. *"To the realm of Asgard! To the halls of Valhalla!"*

Aye, Morgana thought bitterly as she watched the flames climb the single mast and reach greedily for the bloodred sail. Valhalla, where, no doubt, dwelt her husband of only six months, Leif Haraldsson.

And now father joins son.

An acrid grief rose within her, pushing with burning talons against her breast . . . white-hot, stringent. She wanted to weep. She wanted to shriek at the gods in rage.

And also at Leif, for he had been eager enough to join the latest expedition of warriors answering the call of the sea . . . to up and leave his new young bride in impetuous answer to the call of excitement and adventure. Even though he'd promised Morgana he would not go a-viking across the wild northern waters, that he would stay closer to home at least until the birth of their first child, he'd left after only a few months, telling her he'd lost a wager; telling her that he was bound to uphold his end of the bargain, whether winner or loser. And the voyage was important for them all . . . exploring uncharted waters for new lands. Exactly *where* they were going had remained rather nebulous, which did nothing to reassure Morgana. Not even when Leif had said simply, "Trust me."

But Morgana knew that Earl Harald, too, had had misgivings about his firstborn going on any voyages into the virtual unknown. The leader would never admit to it, but Morgana had suspected that he would rather have had his beloved son's safety a bit more ensured, if only long enough to see Leif's children before Harald himself died.

"Hail Harald!" she cried with the others, and raised her fists heavenward, her eyes brimming, for she really blamed Leif for his own death, and not Odin.

And so, as Morgana hailed the passing of the respected

and esteemed Harald Estrithsson, she raged at the memory of his beautiful, strapping son . . . who had broken his promise and left her for the lure of uncharted waters.

With his child growing within her.

Chapter One

Spring, A.D. 909
Home.

Leif Haraldsson felt the unwelcome pressure of emotion behind his eyes. He lowered his sun-bleached lashes to hide the alien feeling.

Home.

And Morgana . . . The name whispered across his soul.

Despite his fierce resolve, his heart punched up against his sternum, shattering the pattern of its strong and steady cadence. The fingers of one hand clenched around the small filigreed cross suspended from a fine chain about his neck. It was an unconscious movement, somehow comforting, touching this one token passed on to him from the mother he never knew.

Sporadic cries of "Home!" burst out here and there in the awed silence that had, up until now, been punctuated only by the splash of the oars and the whine of the wind in the singular, faded blue and green sail, as the Norwegian coastline came into view. It loomed steadily larger as the *hafskip* skimmed over the crystal-bright waters. The shouts began to meld into a triumphant roar as the Norsemen's homeland materialized with magical clarity from the dissipating morning mists.

Like magnet to metal, Leif's gaze was drawn once more

10

to the sheer, craggy cliffs with their snow-tipped peaks, and their spattering of verdant green patches beneath the spring sun, intruding like carelessly-strewn, glittering emeralds.

Every man aboard the *knarr* knew the network of fjords like the back of his hand . . . familiar, comforting, welcoming, even as they could be forbidding to the stranger.

Part of Leif wanted the ship to fly over the water, to speed them on their way to the settlement. Yet another part of him wanted to savor the endless-seeming moments as the vessel made its way toward the steadily-approaching, beckoning shoreline.

Its square sail tattered, its once-decorated oaken hull bruised and beaten, the dependable *hafskip Wave Rider*— not as sleek and long as the fighting *langskip,* but sturdier for navigating the vicious northern seas—was still seaworthy enough to limp lightly through the glassy swells with little enough difficulty, considering what she'd been through.

Leif suspected now, with a seasoned man's wisdom as opposed to the ignorance of untried youth, that he would never forget this homecoming; that none he would ever experience in his lifetime would be equal to it.

Morgana. Her image came between the nearing shoreline and his mind's eye . . .

Her hair, a silken mass of curls, was the hue of a silvered moon on a clear, crisp night. Her brows were several shades darker, and the shadowed sweep of her umber lashes contrasted vividly with her fair skin. And her eyes . . . a clear, crystal blue like the spangled waters of the fjord beneath the spring sun. In the brief Scandinavian summers, when the sun kissed Morgana's alabaster skin, it tinted her high cheekbones and small straight nose a lovely and delicate pink.

Sweet and normally soft-spoken, she also possessed a quiet courage and an occasional inclination to impulsiveness that had often surprised, yet pleased him. She'd been

11

young—fifteen winters—when he'd left. What would she look like now? he wondered as familiar and welcome stirrings moved within him.

The chill salt spray tingled on his skin, but he ignored the cold sting, his mind focused intently on the woman he'd left behind. The woman he'd literally abandoned in the wake of his solemn promise to her.

Solemn? jeered a voice in his head.

Já. As solemn as he could have been three winters past . . . full of fire and zeal; in love with life and the prospect of adventure. And more excited about exploring where only a handful had gone before than nurturing his fledging marriage to his young and inexperienced bride.

And why not? he thought as he lowered his gaze to the deck again. Morgana had been his since childhood, their love growing with each passing year. Morgana would always be there for him; no matter where he went or what he did, she would still be his sweet, silver-maned Morgana—named after a Celtic slave by her whimsical mother, and just as patient and forgiving and whimsical, too, as the beauty who'd borne her.

Well, he thought with rue . . . usually.

He was a lucky man, lucky in many things, and luck was that most precious and prestigious commodity in Norse society . . . more important than skill or virtue or intelligence.

He ran his tongue over dry, wind-roughened lips, oblivious to the briny taste, as he thought just how lucky he was. Odin had spared him, although 'twas no small thing to be chosen to join the warriors who fought and feasted in Valhalla. But one part of Leif Haraldsson had been awakened to the joys of the here and now, and although he wouldn't readily admit it to a comrade, Morgana and the family they would eventually have were more important to him now than any lure of the unknown. For it was only in almost losing his life and, therefore, Morgana, that Leif had suddenly and swiftly matured and, in the process, realized just how precious she was. Would always be . . .

A hand slapped him solidly on the back and a voice boomed in his ear, "Home, Haraldsson . . . home! 'Tis enough to make any man smile!"

His brief introspection disrupted, Leif raised his regard to meet that of his fellow Norseman, Ragnar the Red. An automatic smile curved Leif's mouth, and caused him to wince inwardly as several minute lacerations in his lower lip split fractionally with the movement and stung from the sea spray.

"Indeed 'tis," Leif agreed over the soft song of the wind. "And if not for you, Ragnar, we'd yet be stranded on that damned island."

And it was no exaggeration. Leif recalled the fierce storm they had encountered just south of Greenland. Nearly half the crew had been lost in the boiling sea, and the *knarr* then hurled like a toy against the half-hidden, treacherous rocks that lined what turned out to be nearby land. Those who survived the catastrophe had managed to coax the crippled and leaking *Wave Rider* to solid ground. They discovered an uninhabited island with little enough for food, but plenty of trees for a new pine mast, replacements for split and crushed planks in the hull, a snapped tiller, and an all but useless keel.

What had been a grim situation was compounded by the arrival of a band of Skraelings—copper-skinned and sloe-eyed natives. Fortunately, they were more curious than hostile, claiming they'd come from the 'big land' to the west; the very land, Leif suspected, that a few other brave souls had discovered and lived to tell about. They'd traded on several occasions with the Norsemen, the latter having discovered the Skraelings' keen interest in the blue and green wool on board. Leif sparingly traded strips of the material for valuable furs to keep his men warm. He was

13

even persuaded, in the face of near-starvation, to trade the swords of several of their deceased for food.

As wise sailors always did, Leif and his band had carried more than two hundred ells of extra wool for sail repairs, an assortment of needles, thread and cord, nails of varying sizes, broadaxes, hooks, gouges, augers, and other appropriate tools for repair and maintenance of a vessel. Although enough of those tools had been lost so as to seriously impede their progress, those remaining supplies along with every man's contributed knowledge of shipbuilding and survival had saved their lives, eventually restored their *knarr*, and seen them successfully launched homeward after three endless, bitter winters.

Yet it had been Ragnar who was the skilled shipwright, a master at it, as were his father and grandfather before him; Ragnar who had kept up their spirits when they would flag, who had solved their thorniest problems having to do with refitting *Wave Rider*.

And Matiassu. Matiassu, the red man whom Leif had stumbled upon as the Skraeling had sat, transfixed, upon the beach. Matiassu, who'd used his survival skills and shown the Norsemen how to stretch their supplies to the maximum . . . Matiassu, who, it seemed, would defend Leif with his very life. Or follow the Northman to his death if necessary, he mused as he allowed his thoughts to drift further . . .

". . . look!" Ragnar had said, pointing to a dark speck on the western horizon. "I'd wager 'tis the Skraeling, by Mjolnir! The man is addled to attempt such a thing in that fragile skin boat."

Leif strained to make out the tiny form following them, his eyes narrowed against the glare of the morning sun upon the water. He was thoughtfully silent for long moments. Should he have the sail lowered? he wondered. No, that would only encourage the red man's madness. "I'd not have thought him foolish enough to attempt such a thing,"

14

he said with annoyance. "I told him to return to his own people, his own land."

"He has a mind of his own, that one," Ragnar answered, "but he'll learn quick enough if he continues his folly. He won't last long in these seas with that puny boat."

Leif determinedly turned his back upon the man following *Wave Rider*. Surely he would give up and go back to where he came from. He couldn't possibly keep up with the *knarr*, nor could he hope to survive a voyage all the way to Norvegia.

And, of course, in spite of the Skraeling's strange ideas, he belonged with his own kind, not with Leif.

Yet the next morning the speck was still well to the west of them, barely discernable, an insignificant scrap of life upon the endless and unpredictable expanse of the sea. Leif was amazed that the man had managed to remain within sight of *Wave Rider*.

As the day progressed, the air thickened, and dark clouds swept across the sky. They were heading into a storm. Leif knew *Wave Rider* could weather it, in spite of her recent repairs—Ragnar had assured him to that effect—but what of the man so stubbornly following them? He hadn't a chance.

But he wasn't Leif's responsibility. If the Skraeling had attached himself to Leif, believed for some strange reason that Leif had come upon him that day by design of the red man's gods, that was his affair, not Leif's.

The wind continued to build. "Lower the sail," Leif ordered, not out of any consideration for the man so doggedly following *Wave Rider*, but rather to facilitate their weathering the squall.

The Skraeling slowly gained on them. " 'Tis impossible," Ragnar said to Leif, as they stood side by side on the dipping, bucking *knarr*. "His strength must be that of ten."

Leif suddenly grinned. "Skraeling doesn't fit him, for

he's strong as Thor," he said, "despite his size. A little Thor."

Ragnar nodded, for Skraeling meant, among other things, "wretch" or "weakling." "It suits him. Yet he'll soon be a dead little Thor." He obviously found no humor in his words, however, for he didn't laugh. Surely he was thinking of how much Matiassu had helped them, Leif surmised. The red man had no place among their kind in Norvegia, yet they owed him more than letting him drown before their eyes.

And who are you to tell him where his place is?

The storm intensified, until the crashing waves and sheeting rain obscured their view in all directions. Leif's concern increased. Surely the Skraeling had capsized and been swallowed by the sea. He turned his back to the west, trying to dismiss the man from his mind as the dependable vessel cut through the churning seas, as it was designed to do.

Then, just as quickly as the storm had materialized, it was over, leaving a rough sea, but a clearing blue sky with only a few fat-cheeked, pristine clouds sailing overhead.

"No damage to our patched sail or mended hull," Ragnar told him. "We've only taken on a little water." He lowered his voice. "And I see no sign of the Skraeling. I suppose we are well rid of him." But his eyes didn't meet Leif's for once, and guilt rose in Leif.

He shielded his eyes with one hand and swung his gaze to the west. There was no sign of the red man or his skin boat.

You sent to me by Great Spirit, Kiisku-Liinu . . . *Sun-Man. My life now.*

Matiassu's halting Norse, and a gesture that had looked disconcertingly like "forever," came back to Leif now. Although some parts of the Skraeling's attempt to explain things to Leif were clearer than others, he'd gathered that the man believed Leif had been sent to him by his god. And that his place in life now was beside Leif.

Leif had turned his head at the time, and resisted rolling his eyes toward the skies. He certainly didn't need a fierce and zealous Skraeling in his life in Norvegia. The red man would be the butt of jokes, of ridicule, and the gods knew what else. Leif would end up being *his* protector . . .

"Look! The Skraeling!" someone shouted as two men hoisted the sail. Leif, Ragnar, Egil and the man who worked the tiller, Olaf, leaned over the side and turned their heads back toward the west. Bobbing among the spume-crested waves was a man . . . the Skraeling, from his light copper skin and his long, ebony hair floating about him like seaweed in the water. He clung to a paddle and appeared either unconscious, or utterly exhausted.

"Damn him," Leif muttered under his breath as he spotted a menacing fin off to the left of the red man. "Get me a rope," he ordered, thinking that he might easily end up a meal for a hungry shark in the act of rescuing a mad Skraeling.

Leif pointed to the fin. "Watch it," he shouted to the men as a rope was passed to him. He secured the line about his waist, his dagger gripped between his teeth, then balanced upon the side of the hull and dove into the water, all the while cursing the strange savage who'd stubbornly determined to become a part of his life . . .

Leif's attention was pulled from the past as Ragnar shrugged off his leader's earlier praise with a movement of his great shoulders, his own grin widening. " 'Twasn't entirely my doing. Everyone pitched in. And—the gods be praised!—we managed to save a good many of our carpentry tools. Yet if Odin hadn't given us trees in the wake of our mishap, we'd still be there." He leaned closer, his voice lowering conspiratorially, one auburn-lashed eyelid dipping in jest, "Although our jarl's son, with his renowned victory-luck, would have seen us safely home." The huge, fiery-haired Ragnar straightened and raised his face to receive the kiss of the rising sun. "Now, if only our women have remained faithful in our absence!" He threw back his shaggy head even farther and laughed heartily.

As his words echoed across the waters, as men turned to him, their expressions mirroring his jubilation, an alien chill unexpectedly feathered down Leif's spine. It was like a premonition.

Morgana would never look at another, he assured himself. Yet, he had broken his promise and gone a-viking where few of his kind had ventured . . .

And if she thinks you dead? came a faint echo in answer. *She could have taken another husband.*

Ragnar smacked Leif's shoulder again, scattering his dark ruminations . . . and dispelling the portent that had briefly wafted over his heart like a puff of frosted breath. " 'Twas but a jest, Haraldsson! Surely you're not concerned about your comely new bride? We've only been gone three winters. 'Tis not unheard of, eh?"

Leif shook his head and watched as two men readjusted the patched sail. The mast itself served as a grim reminder of how close they'd come to perishing on that accursed island, for its great height was marred by an unmajestic curve: the result of having used unseasoned pine. As a result, the sail required close attention and constant adjustment to compensate for the mast's slight skew.

He glanced over at Little Thor, who sat cross-legged behind Olaf at the tiller, calmly surveying the aquamarine waters over which *Wave Rider* swiftly moved. However, Leif refused to be distracted just now by the Skraeling's presence.

Seagulls spiraled lazily overhead, a few swooping toward the ship, then soaring upward into the sky as they shrieked in raucous greeting. The ship rocked gently as it sliced through the glassy, foam-tipped swells; the breeze sighed against his ear, *Morgana, Morgana* . . .

Nei, he thought. Nearly three winters (and six moons) wasn't so very long. Yet his lightly-given promise to Morgana loomed over him suddenly like a heavy black cloud. Morgana had lost her father and three brothers to the sea. She had understandably feared for Leif, hence the required oath from him on their wedding day: *Until the birth of our first child, no farther west than the Faroe Islands, swear to me,* ást mín . . .

Swear to me, my love.

There are things a man must do, wife or no, a voice reminded him.

Ragnar had moved away, obviously on to someone in a more jocular mood, leaving Leif alone with his thoughts . . . and the whispered warnings of the wind.

From high up in the crude-built, wooden lookout tower, a horn bellowed.

Morgana lifted her head and tipped it toward the familiar and welcome sound. For the briefest of moments her heartbeat was jarred from its steady rhythm.

When would she learn not to be so affected by that sound? She shook her head, and the long length of curly hair that was secured at the base of her neck before it cascaded halfway down her back in a thick, pale rope, switched slightly with the movement. With vigorous strokes, Morgana continued kneading the bread dough in the hip-level trough before her.

Probably never, she thought with an inward sigh. A Norsewoman's life was too intricately entwined with the comings and goings of the great dragon ships and the men who sailed them to ever leave her unaffected.

Yet it wasn't the time of year for a vessel to be returning from anywhere. It was early spring, and the men were readying their ships for their spring voyages after planting.

Unless . . .

Morgana stilled and raised her head, concentrating on the second blast of the horn. Unless it was a ship that had been missing . . . a ship that was several winters (three to be exact) overdue, and its crew presumed dead.

Impossible, impossible . . . one part of her thought.

Nothing is impossible, insisted another.

But no ships had failed to return since . . .

Her hands began to tremble. A debilitating weakness invaded her limbs. Her heart skipped a beat, then began to rap against her ribs, like a bird imprisoned in a cage and beating against the bars. She stood rooted for a long moment, and willed herself to calmness, her eyes downcast, her long, dusky lashes resting against her fine cheekbones like a gently curling fringe.

Something tugged on her skirts. Morgana looked down at her son. His small fair head was thrown back as he gazed questioningly into her face, his lower lip gripped beneath his tiny front teeth, his blue eyes shining with excitement. "Sip, Mamma. Sip, *já?*"

Morgana bent to lift the toddler. *"Já.* Ship." She hugged him to her fiercely and murmured into his hair, putting her thoughts into one word before she could catch herself. "Leif," she said on a wisp of breath. "Leif."

Eirik squirmed in her arms and she set him down. Morgana turned slowly toward the door at one end of the longhouse just as the child pushed it open and ran out into the April sunlight. Anticipation and fear warred within her breast. She'd dreamt of this moment a hundred times, at first with longing, then later with anger and a sense of perverse satisfaction.

'Tis mayhap a visiting ship.

But the signal was not that for a visitor . . . or an enemy.

The door burst open again, this time admitting Britta, Morgana's younger step sister. "Morgana?" she said, pausing in the doorway to allow her eyes to adjust to the dimness. "Come and see! Everyone is down by the water!"

20

She turned and disappeared back through the doorway, obviously unaware of the roiling feelings paralyzing Morgana . . . and the import of the ship's arrival if it had a green and blue, diamond-patterned sail.

And if its markings, the design of its prow, identified it as *Wave Rider*.

" 'Tis *Wave Rider* . . ."

"Earl Harald's son returns . . ."

"Nei!"

"Já!"

Morgana watched as the *knarr* rounded the bend and glided into the welcoming embrace of the fjord. As it steadily approached the settlement over the deep blue waters, myriad thoughts chased through her mind, myriad feelings through her heart.

The voices around her dimly penetrated her concentration, but she remained statue-still, her fingers rigidly clenched about her son's small hand. Eirik wimpered softly and raised puzzled azure eyes to her face.

As the child's distress registered on the periphery of her inner agitation, she released the unnaturally tight grip. Eirik immediately scampered away, closer to the water. Morgana opened her mouth to call him just as more snatches of conversation came to her:

". . . the ship, but not necessarily Haraldsson . . ."

New shock zigzagged like white-hot lightning through Morgana's breast. She hadn't even considered that Leif might not be on the ship. True, one tiny part of her had half-hoped the approaching vessel would be without its leader for, after almost three winters, life had settled into a new pattern, with broken heart and bitter memories pushed into the dim recesses of her consciousness with a grim determination. But another, stronger, part of her

21

hoped with urgent desperation that Leif Haraldsson was aboard the nearing *knarr*.

To play havoc with your new life? taunted the part of her that had deliberately and purposefully severed her ties to him after he'd broken his vow to her.

All ties, that is, except their son.

The mid-morning sun had chased away the mists. It now scintillated on the water and caused the sudden moisture quivering along her lower lashes to shimmer, to distort her vision. One telltale tear spilled over and onto her cheek, winking in the sunlight until she flicked it away with the back of one hand in irritation.

She dragged her gaze from the *hafskip* and looked in the direction of the men working on the overturned hull of another ship. She couldn't hear the pounding of the axes or the scraping of the gouges for the sudden buzzing in her ears. "Allfather help me," she entreated silently.

As she willed away her traitorous emotion, Morgana tried to pick out Hakon from the men ceasing their work, one by one, and moving toward the water. But her eyes would not clear, would not focus. Instead, they were drawn back to *Wave Rider* as it moved toward the beach, an undulating blur, now, of blue and green and varying shades of oak along the refurbished, partly unpainted hull. Even the mast seemed to bow before her, mocking, throwing back in her face a hint of the damning consequences she would now face as a result of her angry and vengeful actions three winters ago. She ignored that hint, nevertheless, and strained to get a glimpse of one beloved and only too-well-remembered face among the crew of the *knarr*.

Instead of picking out Leif Haraldsson, however, Morgana found her line of vision interrupted by the figure of Hakon Sweynsson as he positioned himself, straddle-stanced and knuckles resting against his hips, immediately before the mooring area at the water's edge.

The ship eased closer, shouts from its crew bouncing off

the rocky cliffs of the fjord, even above the song of the waterfalls across the inlet, as the men aboard scrambled to lower the sail.

" 'Tis Haraldsson!" shouted a familiar voice that Morgana didn't bother to identify. "Thor's hammer, will you look at that? Leif the Lucky returns!"

Hakon turned to watch Morgana as she stood unmoving on the slope above him. He frowned as his eyes met hers, tossed his head as if in mute challenge, and swung toward the fjord. He threw back his impressive shoulders, his spine straighter than *Wave Rider*'s mast, his stance visibly stiffened with what could only have been grim purpose.

A sense of doom filtered through Morgana, weighting her limbs, numbing her ability to think clearly. She couldn't move. Nor could her suddenly sluggish brain seem to function. She was pinned to the spot, as effectively shackled emotionally as a captive about to be put to death. Yet feelings began bubbling inside her, clamoring to be heard: disbelief and uncertainty and dread . . . and a distant and incongruous, but very real, echo of joy.

The ship scraped against the pebbly bottom of the mooring strip. The scene was sudden pandemonium as men rushed forward to aid the returning crew as they leaped down from the sides of the *knarr* to secure it. Loved ones and friends were recognized, their names shouted with exaltation. Here and there, cries of dismay could be heard as the eight men who would never return were discovered missing.

Morgana watched, standing literally alone above the joyous scene, as one man—the last man—stood poised at the prow nearest them, one foot braced against the edge of the hull, and surveyed the scene. His long hair blew about his face, in spite of the band around his forehead. He was leaner than she remembered, and something about his mien was different . . . more somber. Even from a distance, from the depths of her mental maelstrom, Morgana could tell.

What had he been through? she suddenly had the presence of mind to think. What had they all been through, she wondered, as it registered in her mind that the returning crew was fewer in number than the original . . .

Leif caught sight of Morgana, standing apart from the others, her moon-bright hair shining out like a beacon among the many heads ranging from gold to sand-hued, flaming red to light auburn, dun-shaded to loam brown. And suddenly, as his gaze clung to her for a moment, as he savored the sight and willed his insides to cease their quaking, he momentarily forgot about Matiassu, standing like a shadow within the greater shadow of the mast.

He placed one hand on the ship's side and vaulted over it, dropping lightly into the shallow water, flexed knees absorbing the landing, even though they felt as soft as melted tallow. Looking neither left nor right, he strode up the rock-strewn slope toward her, shouldering his way though the crowd, giving only cursory nods and half-smiles to those who were slapping him on the shoulder, welcoming him back with words of praise.

Morgana watched, unable to mobilize her feet . . . her thoughts . . . her tongue.

When he stood at last before her, he said simply, earnestly, "Forgive me, *ást mín.*"

He didn't move to take her in his arms, the natural thing to do, but rather stood calmly before her in the middle of the celebration around them, and quietly entreated her. In those moments, a score of details came to her . . . how the elements had bleached his brows and lashes, how they had lightened his auburn hair to a beautiful shade of red-gold. The lines about his gem-gold eyes were etched deeper into his tanned skin, his beloved face now leaner.

"Morgana?" The softly-uttered word twined about her heart and squeezed.

24

He held out his hand to her, obviously uncertain. Never had Morgana known Leif Haraldsson to be uncertain. Her chest felt suddenly banded, her heart crying out to him. She raised her own hand and slowly extended it toward his. Their fingertips touched, tentatively, their eyes locked for a brief eternity. No one else existed. Nothing else mattered in those ephemeral moments as warm flesh met warm flesh . . .

Until a small voice shattered the moment. "Mamma? Who—?" Eirik gazed up at Leif, his brow creased.

The child's query, his immediate presence, pulled Morgana from her trance. Before she could answer, however, a male voice from behind Leif answered the little one's question. "This is the old jarl's son, Eirik. Leif Haraldsson."

Eirik's frown deepened as Leif swung to face Hakon. "Earw Sweyn, Papa?" the toddler asked in his sweet voice, grabbing Hakon's hand, the thumb of his other hand popping into his mouth.

Old jarl? An icy finger of fear touched the back of Leif's neck, and the feeling of premonition he'd experienced when talking to Ragnar returned. "Where is my father?" he asked suddenly, half-dreading the answer in light of Hakon's words. *And what kind of welcome is this?* he added silently. *No embrace from my wife? Or a man I thought was my friend?*

Tension began to build, changing the scene from one of happy expectation to suspicion.

"Dead. Hunting accident," Hakon apprised him in clipped tones, his blue eyes cold. "Two winters ago. Your name was the last word he spoke as they placed his sword in his hands."

Were they blaming him for Harald's death? Leif wondered. He looked at Morgana for confirmation, his fingers tightening on hers.

"*Já.* 'Tis true."

25

He moved to take her into his arms. She took a short, stiff step backward and he checked himself. "Then who . . . ?" His look of consternation was not so much at the news of his father's death, but rather at Morgana's obvious reluctance to do more than touch hands.

She's angry still. Can you blame her?

"His brother and my sire Sweyn, is jarl now," Hakon said in a hard voice. He stared down at their clasped hands. Leif did the same. Morgana tried to extricate hers, but he would not release it.

"And Astrid?"

"She is wed to Sweyn now, Leif," Morgana answered, struggling to keep the tremor out of her voice.

Leif frowned, fighting to absorb the news, and wanting, in spite of the unease that now hovered over them, in spite of the astonishing news and the sudden quiet that had befallen those around them, to fold Morgana into his embrace and make up for three long winters of absence, everything and everyone else be damned.

"Papa?" Eirik insisted, pointing to the water and the newly arrived ship.

Leif's gaze was drawn to the child. Hakon's son? he wondered as he noted the child's golden hair and beautiful features. Envy moved through him, for he and Morgana could have had a child like this one by now . . .

He watched through his lashes—like a stranger on the outside looking in, he thought—as Hakon and Morgana exchanged glances, then man and child turned and walked down to the newly-arrived *knarr*.

This was a far cry from the homecoming he'd envisioned. It was like returning to a different settlement.

He looked back at Morgana, who was watching him silently. Others had turned away and were gathering into smaller groups. They spoke in hushed tones, with curious looks thrown his way, some guilty, some pitying, obviously explaining the situation to their newly-returned cohorts.

"Welcome home, Leif," said a friendly voice, like a stone dropping into a still pond.

Leif glanced away from his wife to a young man about the same age as his five and twenty winters. Gunnar limped toward him, his arms wide, a grin spread across his even features. The two men embraced, and some of Leif's tension ebbed briefly. There was no reservation in his friend's greeting.

"I've missed you," Gunnar said quietly, emotion edging his voice. He held Leif at arm's length, his hazel eyes grave as they delved into his friend's. "They thought you dead all this time, but I expected more from you."

In spite of everything, Leif flashed a grin at Gunnar. "You always did expect godlike behavior of me, Gunnar. But luck only goes so far." His gaze returned to Morgana. "She has not forgiven me for breaking my promise . . . and they say Harald is dead," he added in a lower voice, his grin fading as quickly as it had appeared. "How can he be gone? And where is everyone else?"

As he fired the questions at Gunnar, what appeared to be a combination of pain and anger flickered in the latter's eyes, then was gone. "There is much I would tell you . . . ." He reached to drape an arm over his friend's shoulders, and with seeming nonchalance—which Leif could tell was feigned by the tension in Gunnar's arm—drew Leif's ear toward his mouth. "First, you must know before you look the fool," he murmured for Leif alone, "that Morgana dissolved your marriage two winters past. She is Hakon's wife now."

Chapter Two

Leif pulled away, his head snapping up. His stunned gaze went to Morgana as the words registered. Disbelief shaded his eyes. "That cannot be," he said softly. "You are *my* wife."

The tone of his voice pushed aside some of the guilt and pain Morgana was feeling, making room for a gleam of remembered anger and renewed memories of betrayal.

"You broke your vow to me. What of *that?*"

The silence swirled around them. Of course he'd broken his vow to her. He'd been young and rash and had had life by the tail. He had thought he could do anything . . . that he was invincible, the stuff of legends.

"But you didn't even wait to see if I would return? How could you have been certain? We could have encountered disaster . . . anywhere!" The questions spewed forth, and suddenly the vow paled in significance in the face of her actually sundering the bonds of marriage, and then wedding another. Hakon, who had always stood in Leif's shadow. Hakon, handsome as Frey and pure Norse— golden blond and blue-eyed. Handsome and vain and not-so-secretly covetous of Morgana, although Leif had never been concerned about it. Now, however, with his world being rocked by upheaval, and his self-image unexpectedly and uncharacteristically faltering because his mother had been a slave, mayhap he should have guessed that Hakon would be the one to whom Morgana would turn.

He sought to absorb the events that had transpired in his absence, but his mind could not grasp everything immediately . . . would not grasp it. It couldn't be true.

Gunnar's hand on his arm brought Leif's thoughts up short. He wouldn't make a scene . . . wouldn't discuss something like this before the entire village, no matter how great his sense of betrayal, his sudden urge to murder Hakon and—

Before you look the fool, rang through in his mind, like the blast of a horn. His fists clenched at his sides, his jaw tightened, his eyes turned deep topaz with anger as he stared at Morgana. Hakon's wife.

And they have a son . . .

In the midst of his ire, one part of him suddenly felt lost, foundering in a village of somber—if not hostile—faces. By Thor's silver hammer, where did he even *live* now? His father was dead, his step mother wed to another. Would he abide with them? Or with his traitorous wife—*former* wife—who had wed another?

After all, he'd been born out of wedlock, son of a Byzantine slave, and the only son of Harald Estrithsson, who had adopted him. With his father gone, and his uncle established as jarl, (Leif wondered how many men Sweyn had had to banish—or worse—in order to establish his dominance), it would stand to reason that Hakon, Sweyn's eldest son, would covet his father's status upon his death. Leif had been unexpectedly robbed of the chance to succeed his father, whether through physical prowess or acceptance by the others. Harald, Morgana, his favored position as the jarl's only son . . .

Hakon and the little boy were returning from the water's edge. Leif narrowed his eyes at his former friend. "Hiding behind your skirts, is he, Morgana?" he said in a low,

29

rough voice. "Why didn't he tell me himself that he stole my wife and——"

Morgana moved closer to him and put an appealing hand on his arm. "Hakon is not to blame. If you won't take any blame for your actions, Leif Haraldsson, don't lay that burden at Hakon's door. *I* dissolved the marriage. A purpose. He didn't pressure me——"

"Didn't he?" Leif said sharply.

"Who's that creature skulking in the shadow of the mast?" Hakon demanded, squinting at *Wave Rider*. "He frightened Eirik and looks about to slit the throat of anyone who comes near him!"

"Fear not, Hakon," Leif said dryly. "He's a stray Skraeling we found——"

"You brought home a *Skraeling?*" asked a boy of about twelve, his eyes round with wonder and fear.

As all eyes went to the ship, Egil quickly stepped forward and put his wit to work. "He'll not harm anyone," he assured them. "Leif the Lucky saved his life . . . twice. The second time Leif plucked him from shark infested waters in the aftermath of a storm. He's obviously pledged his life to Leif, but only time will tell if that is good or bad!"

Laughter sounded here and there, as if there were still doubts in the minds of some.

"Then why is he hiding from us?" asked a woman. "Mayhap he knows a Norseman is fiercer even than any Skraeling, eh?"

The laughter spread. "He'll come forth when he's ready," Leif defended the man.

"Or if someone raises a hand to Leif," shouted Olaf as he waved a warning finger. "He moves like lightning."

"I didn't know Haraldsson needed a protector," Hakon observed.

"Leif!" Leif's attention was caught by Sweyn Estrithsson, who came up to them at that moment and heartily embraced his nephew. Leif remained stiff and aloof. "Welcome, son of my brother," Estrithsson added. He held Leif away from him, his shrewd eyes taking him in from head to toe before pausing to linger on his face. He was an older version of Hakon, with long blond hair and a thick, braided beard streaked with gray. He was still strapping, a formidable opponent in spite of his age, Leif knew. And, obviously, he was even shrewder than Leif had given him credit for.

That, among other things which were apparent now, had been a mistake.

"Not welcome *home*, Uncle?" Leif answered in greeting, his expression stony. 'Tis not my home now, is it? There is no place for me here . . . say it and have done with it."

Sweyn didn't seem the least taken aback by Leif's words. *Of course. He's had a long time to prepare for this.*

". . . regret the passing of my brother, but he died with his sword in his hand, as was fitting. And you, nephew—in spite of the changes in Oslof—will always have a home here."

Leif could detect no insincerity in his uncle's words or tone, but his blue eyes held a subtle warning.

Leif glanced at Astrid, who stood several paces behind Sweyn. She nodded at him as their eyes met, but there was no warmth in her gaze. Leif knew only too well how much she'd resented him and the woman who had borne him. Barren herself, Astrid had not only hated Leif's foreign mother but, Leif had always suspected, him as well, although he never spoke of it to his father. Harald had seemed unaware of Astrid's buried animosity. Or else he'd chosen to leave it unacknowledged. The fact that he'd remained married to Astrid was more than proof of his esteem for her. And no one could blame a man for siring a child by his concubine when his wife couldn't give him sons and daughters.

Leif nodded automatically at Sweyn's words, but the shock was beginning to wear off, and in its place a seething

31

anger was beginning to build, feeding off the first stirrings of stunned disbelief and betrayal. He wanted to drag Morgana off somewhere and shake some sense into her, make her realize what a mistake she'd made—realize that she still loved him and he her.

Does she? asked a nasty imp. *No matter how angry she was, she would never have ended your marriage if she loved you.*

He stared at Morgana as Hakon came to stand beside her, the child between them. A barrage of emotions assaulted Leif, seething, churning, threatening his control. He opened his mouth to vent his anger on Hakon, who was glaring right back at him, a cold, hostile stranger, not one of the friends among whom Leif had grown to manhood.

"You, indeed, have little reason to celebrate my return," Leif said with soft menace. "Yet it seems to me that I have more reason for outrage than you, Sweynsson—"

"Leif," Gunnar said from somewhere behind him, the quiet urgency in his voice acting to stem Leif's words. "Come with me."

Leif slowly turned his head to take in the others gathered around. A sense of unreality passed over him. These men who'd returned with him had accomplished nothing short of the miraculous. They'd lost valued comrades and survived months of hardship and deprivation, clinging to thoughts of their loved ones back here in Oslof. They had combined their skill and determination to deal with what the gods had thrown their way. And, ultimately, they had prevailed.

Their accomplishment, their triumphant return, merited the attention and celebration of all. His own problems, important as they were to him, should be secondary to the accomplishments of the group; to their victory overall.

Leif deliberately avoided looking at the threesome standing so near him—man, woman, and child—and turned his gaze upon each of his crew members, one by one, as they stood among their friends and families in what should never have been an awkward, tense atmosphere; one of grieving, to be sure, for the relatives of those who'd been lost at sea. But never *this* for his courageous comrades. He may have lost his wife and father; he may have lost his chance to become jarl; but Leif Haraldsson hadn't lost his innate sense of fair play and priority, of leadership . . . of what was of primary importance to the people of Oslof.

Setting aside his own problems for the moment, he cut his gaze to Sweyn as he said in subtle challenge, "Do you not wish to know what befell us? Surely our jarl wishes to honor the return of so many with a celebration . . . with proper lauding from our *skald*. Egil has much to tell tonight . . . much to do if he's to extoll our exploits properly, for we've much to recount."

He caught the flash of Ragnar Thorsson's red head and looked over at him. The fiery-maned Norseman thrust a fist skyward and shouted, "Hail, Haraldsson! Hail the one who led us home!" Others joined his laudatory salute, and soon their cries of jubilation reverberated around the rocky walls of the fjord.

"Ragnar can tell you what happened, Uncle. Any of the others can. For now, I have other . . . matters that need attending," Leif told Sweyn when the din had died down.

Then out of the corner of his eye he noticed a figure moving on *Wave Rider*'s deck. He looked up and saw Little Thor standing beside the freeboard closest to the shore, in full view of everyone.

Of course. In his attempts to absorb the drastically changed situation around him, Leif had forgotten the red man. He raised his hand high in a beckoning gesture and watched as Little Thor dropped effortlessly to the beach below and waded through the shallow water. Leif wondered if the Skraeling had noticed the undercurrent of hostility in this homecoming, then dismissed it as impossible. The man had been too far away to discern any distinct voices or attitudes.

Others followed Leif's gaze, and the babble of voices rose again. People pointed, many looked outright suspicious and hostile. Some, especially the children, could only stare in wonderment.

Leif had to admire the way the red man walked into their midst. He was almost a head shorter than Leif, his bone structure smaller, yet his build was solid and compact beneath his borrowed tunic. His long black hair hung down his back in two thick plaits secured with leather thongs. An ornamental beaded band encircled his forehead, not unlike that which many Norsemen wore to keep their hair from their eyes . . . except for several seagull feathers. He wore breeches and tanned-skin calf-high boots, also decorated with beads.

He returned the looks of those about him with all the regalness of a king, yet didn't stare as they did. His dark sloe eyes finally met Leif's as he slowed and stopped before him. Then he looked at Morgana.

Only then did he show any reaction. His eyes widened fractionally as they came to rest on her hair, then narrowed as if against its brightness in the morning sun. For long moments, silence gathered around them.

This is your woman, he signed to Leif. It was a statement rather than a question, and the fact that he used sign language told Leif that Little Thor had uncannily discerned trouble, and wouldn't exacerbate it by using his halting Norse.

Leif watched Morgana return the Skraeling's gaze steadily. Of course she wouldn't show fear, he thought. She possessed an inner strength, a fearlessness, that her sweet demeanor belied. And she was too kind to reject the stranger outright.

She was my woman before I left. Now . . . His hands stilled in midair. He couldn't finish his sentence. *Come with me*, he signed then, and without another word, turned and followed a frowning Gunnar.

"Sweyn is probably furious," Gunnar told his friend as Ingrid, his wife, served them horns of mead.

Leif threw him a sharp glance, but said nothing at first. He only shrugged.

"Are you hungry?" Gunnar asked.

"I've more a need for drink . . . *strong* drink," Leif said darkly as he raised the horn to his lips. He let the potent liquid sear its way down his throat, having been without it for most of the last three years. When he'd greeted her, he'd noticed that Ingrid was with child. Now he saw that a boy-child was napping at one end of the benches along the walls that served as seats during the day and beds at night.

Little Thor was seated cross-legged upon the floor near the door, a bowl of food and a tankard of mead before him. Both were as yet untouched as the Skraeling silently watched Leif.

"Does he speak Norse?" Gunnar asked.

Leif nodded. "Some. He seems to prefer hand signals, of which he has taught me many. I suspect he understands much more Norse than he lets on."

"What happened to *Wave Rider*? To all of you?" Gunnar pressed.

"A storm. A bad storm, just southwest of Greenland as we entered the frigid currents from the north." Ingrid placed a steaming bowl of rich stew before Leif, in spite of his denial of hunger, and topped off the mead in his horn. Despite his inner turmoil, he felt his stomach rumble. "We lost eight of our men—as you saw. The *knarr* took a beating before Aegir and Ran were satisfied with what they'd wrought." He paused, suddenly lost in thought as he relived those helpless moments when he thought for cer-

35

tain that the gods of the sea would allow them to be sucked into its icy depths, vessel and all.

"We were forced to remain on that island for two winters while we repaired the damage to *Wave Rider*. If not for a band of friendly Skraelings—and Little Thor here—we would more than likely have perished. A man's body functions only when his belly is full, no matter how courageous or enterprising he may be."

He stood suddenly, clutching his horn, and began to pace the longhouse in agitation. "But what of things in Oslof?" he demanded of Gunnar, who was watching him. "What happened here?"

He was hungry, after all, Leif decided, and tired physically as well as mentally. His spirits had taken a beating since *Wave Rider* had touched shore, too, but he'd never sleep, he'd never be able to eat a morsel, until Harald's death and Morgana's betrayal had been satisfactorily explained to him.

Such a thing can never happen.

He came to a halt before the sleeping child, looked down at the boy for a long moment, then spun away. "Your son?" he asked, his voice lowering, then looked over at the flaxen-haired Ingrid, who stood quietly near Gunnar.

"*Já*. His name is Harald, after your father." She paused, then added, "We are to have another child at summer's end."

It was almost too much to take in at once. Had it been what seemed only a few winters before his marriage to Morgana that they had all been childhood friends? Morgana and Ingrid, Leif and Gunnar. Ragnar and Hakon . . .

Hakon. His heartbeat stuttered, then steadied as he forced himself to think of other things. Other memories assaulted him . . . Gunnar planning to wed his Ingrid, and Leif Morgana. Then Gunnar's lower leg being crushed by a great wooden roller as a newly-built ship was eased into the waters of the fjord. The near loss of his life as he lay fevered, his wound seeming to drain the lifeblood from him. And the never wavering love of Ingrid; the support of his friends and family . . .

He can never go a-viking, my son . . . Harald's voice. *He would be a liability, even if he walks again* . . .

Gunnar the good-natured, the lover of ships and the sea. The strong, athletic Gunnar . . .

The object of his thoughts spoke, breaking into his remembrances: "Harald was killed hunting . . . was thrown from Geri and died of a broken neck."

Leif's eyes darkened with pain and suspicion. "You know my father was a good rider. He was equally at ease on Geri as any ship."

Gunnar absently massaged his mangled left leg beneath his breeches as he stared at the rush-covered floor. "There are some who speak of treachery." He looked up at Leif. "Others have left Oslof, unhappy with your disappearance—they took it as an omen—and the death of Harald. They wanted naught to do with Sweyn, for 'tis said that he's made a secret bargain with—even taken silver from—Harald Fairhair."

Leif nodded, a scowl moving across his face. "The man who would be king of all Norvegia." He walked to the partially open door and looked out into the cool, sunlit day. His quiet but tense words revealed exactly what was uppermost on his mind. "What am I to do, Gunnar?" The next words surprised Leif as they were wrenched from his soul. "Morgana . . . Morgana is my world."

The silence that followed was sepulchral. Little Thor stared straight ahead into the middle distance, as if deep in thought from his place near the door.

Then Ingrid declared, "Win her back, Leif." Her words fell into the quiet like stones into a placid pond, as if they'd been poised on the tip of her tongue.

37

Ingrid the steady, he thought suddenly. Always. Steady as a rock to Morgana's occasional unpredictability.

Gunnar threw her a meaningful look, shaking his head in obvious warning.

"Win her back?" Leif said over his shoulder, his tone edged with irony.

"*Já!* She believed you broke your vow to her . . . everyone knew that when she declared her intentions to divorce before witnesses," Ingrid said, moving toward Leif. He swung from the door to face her, a combination of half-hopeful expectation, bleakness, and disbelief etched on his features. "And the worst of it was—"

"Ingrid!"

She looked at Gunnar. A silent war waged between them; Leif could feel the sudden tension.

"What was the worst of it, Ingrid?" Leif said, moving toward her, ignoring Gunnar's obvious annoyance with her. "Surely it was the fact that she wed Hakon without knowing aught of our fate?"

She turned her head to meet his gaze, a troubled look in her eyes.

"That is for Morgana to tell you," Gunnar answered for her. He heaved himself from his seat and moved to put a hand on Leif's shoulder. "I would speak of most anything you wish, my friend. But 'tis not my place—nor Ingrid's—to divulge certain things. Morgana's reason for ending your marriage is between the two of you."

Leif's eyes narrowed. There was more than a violated oath? What could he ever have done besides break the vow—or so Morgana believed—he'd made to her?

'Twas bad enough.

He ignored his conscience, for he loved her deeply, thought he'd known her better than anyone else. If he never quite trusted Hakon, he was dead certain about Morgana. He would have wagered his life on her love and constancy.

"Morgana has changed," Ingrid said gently. "She's a woman now. *You* made her a woman . . . and through your affection and commitment ultimately brought out the strength in her."

Their eyes met before Ingrid looked down.

"Then I did a foolish thing," he answered, bitterness curdling his tone. He realized the double meaning of his words and added, "In wedding her."

"Nay," Ingrid said, looking directly at him again. "That wasn't your mistake."

"Tell us how you found him," Gunnar said, inclining his head toward Little Thor. Leif complied, but all the while he spoke, Ingrid's words echoed over and over in the back of his mind.

"I must speak to him, at least. I owe him that much."

Hakon's mouth tightened as he stood before Morgana in their partitioned sleeping room. "You owe him naught! He broke his vow and you chose to leave him. You made your decision, Morgana, and I won't have you trailing after him like a lost puppy."

Morgana's head snapped up, her eyes darkening with ire. "What? A lost puppy?" Color rose in her cheeks. "He was my husband . . . he deserves an explanation—"

" 'Tis not what you said when you declared your intentions to divorce him," he cut across her words. His eyes bored into hers. "Are you regretting your decision? Now that you have seen him in the flesh again, are you having second thoughts about what you did? Your marriage to me?"

Morgana's look turned bemused. This was not the Hakon she'd wed. This man was suddenly too stern, too insecure, obviously in light of Leif Haraldsson's return . . . an insecurity he was covering with anger and bluster.

39

And that was absurd. She was his wife now, and had no regrets.

No regrets? taunted a tiny part of her. *How can you truly blame him? Now that your anger has cooled with the passing of time? Now that Leif has indeed returned? What if the shoe had been on the other foot? How would you have felt?*

Several emotions flickered across her fine features, subtly altering her expression as the questions hurtled through her mind like Thor's thunderbolts. Then, summoning her patience and understanding, she said with quiet emphasis, "I am your wife, Hakon. Eirik regards you as his father. He has known no other. I would never hurt either one of you."

But Hakon, obviously greatly disturbed by the arrival of his childhood friend—now possibly his rival for Morgana's affection—wasn't convinced. "Show me, Morgana," he growled, and dropped down beside her on the square wood-frame bed. His lips met hers, hard and demanding, as he pushed her onto her back. "Show me your love, Morgana," he muttered harshly against her mouth. "Prove it!"

She was dismayed by his unexpected aggression. He'd never been a coward, to be sure, but neither had he ever been in the forefront when Leif or Gunnar had been around. He had always been a follower, perhaps, Morgana suspected, to spare his fair countenance—he'd been nicknamed "Pretty Face"—from being marred, for he'd been vain. He wasn't as tall as many of his fellow Northmen, but his looks and well-formed body had caught every woman's eye in Oslof. Except Morgana and Ingrid, of course, for they had been in love with Leif and Gunnar, respectively, ever since Morgana could remember.

She had suspected when she was twelve winters that Hakon loved her, and he had confirmed her suspicions when he'd pursued her after she had declared for an end to her marriage to Leif. "I've always loved you," he'd told her.

Yet his affection had lacked the depth and passion of Leif Haraldsson's—or had it been Morgana's response to him that lacked depth and true passion? Morgana had no doubt that he loved her as much as he was capable of, but Hakon Sweynsson would always love himself more; would always put himself first. And she had accepted that. She had even convinced herself that she loved him, although in a different way than she had loved Leif.

Until now. Until she had seen Leif Haraldsson striding up the beach toward her, tall and commanding. And oddly, endearingly, vulnerable.

"Nay!" she said, and pushed against Hakon's chest. Wrenching herself from his embrace, she sat up. "Don't be absurd," she began, then softened her tone. "I need not prove anything, Hakon. I wed you and—"

"We need a son, Morgana," he cut her off fervently. *"Our* son . . . *my* flesh and blood as well as yours. My father longs for a grandson . . . and 'twill bind us more—"

"Hakon?"

His father's voice right outside the sleeping chamber curtain interrupted Hakon's words, and deflected his intentions.

"Já, I'm coming," he said, and stood. "I'm—I'm sorry, Morgana," he said softly, but the look on his face was anything but remorseful, his stance anything but humble, his arms held stiffly at his sides.

She knew, suddenly, that he was afraid; by his last words as well as his behavior. Perhaps not as frightened by the threat of Leif Haraldsson's effect on her as by the impact his half-cousin's appearance would have on his own image in the eyes of others. Once more, he would live in Leif's shadow—as would they all; as they had in Harald's shadow as well—and Morgana knew somehow that now Hakon would not accept that.

But at least he'd uttered words of apology . . .

Morgana nodded as she looked up at him. "Go," she

41

said, "you need have no fears." She gave him a weak smile.

His look only darkened, as if he resented the lack of depth in what was normally a warm and freely-given curving of her lips. He didn't reciprocate before he turned and quit the chamber.

Morgana stood then, straightened her clothing and followed him. She heard Eirik's giggle and Britta's remonstrance as the door to the longhouse opened and, assured of the child's proximity, turned her attention to the matter at hand, preparing for the feast in honor of the return of *Wave Rider*.

Without even consulting Astrid, who was busy removing and stacking silver jugs for wine and mead from one cupboard, Morgana knew exactly what she had to do. She stoked the oven at the far end of the longhouse, and assigned a young thrall, Ana, to finish the white wheaten bread she'd been making when the horn had sounded. Essaying to keep her whirling thoughts at bay, Morgana fetched several white linen embroidered tablecloths and laid them over the length of the great board that served as a table.

Just as she smoothed the last fold from the table linen, another slave entered the longhouse carrying a basket of wild greens and dried onions to add to the cooking pot hanging from its tripod, its rich stew already simmering over the fire. Britta and Eirik followed, Eirik clutching a feather-stuffed leather ball and Britta what appeared to be several wrapped bricks of butter and cheese.

"From Ingrid," she explained to Astrid as the latter turned to her. Astrid nodded and accepted the offerings. "Start another pot of stew," she instructed Gerd, the girl carrying the vegetables. Her eyes, however, narrowed slightly and cut to Morgana, a question in them; for she knew that Ingrid was Morgana's closest friend. And, too, that Leif was staying with Ingrid and Gunnar.

"And Mamma comes with mead and ham," Britta

added, then moved over to her half sister. "Can Eirik come with me to help her?" she asked.

Morgana looked down at her sister and mustered a smile. "Just be sure to give him something he can manage, won't you?" She ruffled Britta's fine hair and then watched her take Eirik by the hand.

"Come, Eirik," the little girl bade him. "Let's help your *amma, já?* There's to be a feast tonight."

The leather ball dropped softly to the floor, forgotten, as Eirik gripped Britta's hand, a ready smile revealing his tiny, perfect teeth. "Put your ball away, Eirik," Morgana reminded him, "before someone trips over it."

With obvious reluctance, Eirik released Britta's hand and squatted to grab the ball. He toddled over to a small wooden chest against one wall and deposited the toy therein. "Bawh," he said, then slipped one finger into his mouth and looked up at Morgana for obvious approval.

"Good boy!" Britta praised him before Morgana could say a word. "Come." She held out her hand to him. He tripped over to her on his short little legs and clutched her hand once more.

"Fehki?" he asked.

"We'll find Freki, too," Britta assured him, and led him through the door.

Morgana spun around sharply, away from Astrid's probing gaze. A sliver of pain speared her chest. Freki, the dog Leif had given her before he'd left. A young wolfhound brought back from a raid. Surely Freki wouldn't remember Leif, for the dog had been but a pup when *Wave Rider* had last departed. Not only did Morgana love the huge, shaggy dog, but Eirik did as well.

He'll protect you, my love, in my absences . . .

Well, the animal hadn't protected Morgana from her own actions, nor was he ever meant to . . .

She closed her eyes briefly and drew in a deep, sustaining breath. She had to think about other things, *anything,* or all those feelings she had kept shut tightly away in her heart would come bursting out. All the old questions, the rancor and the outrage . . . and the disconcertingly real echoes of love. She knew not whether she could deal with them now, with Leif Haraldsson returned to Oslof. To her life.

"Morgana?" Britta asked, sticking her head through the door. Morgana lifted her gaze and looked at the girl. "Mamma needs help—"

Ana moved to comply from the trough of bread dough, but Morgana held up her hand. "I'll go, Ana."

Without glancing Astrid's way, she moved to the door, up the three steps, and out into the bright sunlight. After the dim, smoky interior of the longhouse, the brightness of the outdoors struck Morgana like a physical force, yet it was welcome. The breeze from the fjord was brisk, but pure and refreshing. It dipped beneath her skirts, making them billow about her ankles. It lifted the tendrils of hair that hung against her neck and caused a shiver to dance down her spine after the stifling warmth of the hall.

Tyra was carrying a small keg of what Morgana knew was her specially spiced mead. She was known for the best in Oslof.

Morgana reached her mother and moved to take the keg. "Why didn't you send a thrall?"

Tyra, an exact replica of her daughter, but a little shorter, a little stouter, slanted her a look as she continued to trudge toward Sweyn's longhouse. It seemed to say, *You know why*, but she merely replied, "They are out planting."

"Are you come to see my reaction, then? Or to remind me of what you consider my folly?" Morgana asked, lowering her voice. "Even if I said you were right, Mother, it changes nothing now."

She should have known. Tyra had always loved Leif; like one of the three sons by Morgana's father she'd lost to the sea.

A blur of gray appeared just then, from behind the

bathhouse. Freki. He came at Morgana with his long-legged, graceful lope. Eirik followed behind in a futile attempt to keep up. Morgana bent to greet the dog, holding out her hands against the inevitable collision and burying her face in his coarse gray coat. She regretted her sharpness with Tyra. After all, Tyra was her mother, and had what she obviously considered Morgana's best interests at heart. Yet Morgana had shrilled at her like a whining old shrew.

Tyra slowed her steps. When Morgana rose, her mother looked deeply into her eyes. "You would have gotten over Leif's broken promise, Morgana, and you could have waited longer . . . 'tis not so very unusual for a Northman to be at sea for long stretches."

Wordlessly, Morgana took the cask from Tyra and swung toward the longhouse, her beautiful mouth set in a mutinous line. "There was more to it than that, Mother, and well you know it. We've spoken of this many times."

Tyra's hand on her arm arrested her as she moved to step away. "And now you reap the harvest of your burst of anger, daughter of mine. Now your troubles begin in earnest."

Chapter Three

"Get rid of him."

Laughter and raucous badinage swirled all around them, celebratory sounds and mouth-watering smells filled the close, smoky air of the longhouse. But Leif and Morgana were isolated in their own small world for long moments, the tension between them tangible as they stood at one end of the hall, apart from most of the others.

"I'm alive and well. And *I* am your husband, Morgana. Dissolve your marriage to him. You're *my* wife . . . will always be mine, in this life and the next."

Morgana couldn't drag her gaze away from the intensity of his. There, in his beautiful golden eyes, was frustration and anger . . . and yearning. A yearning so powerful she could feel it pulling her soul to his.

He broke his vow.

Aye. He had broken his vow; broken it as easily and carelessly as an ignorant child might dash a fragile treasure upon the ground. For that, she couldn't forgive him.

Or have you already? Have you come to your senses now that he stands before you? Now that 'tis too late?

No!

"I sundered the bond," she told him, tearing her eyes from the potent pull of his and mobilizing her tongue.

"Deliberately. Don't you understand? Have you learned nothing while you were off . . . conquering the world?"

The bitterness in those last three words struck Leif powerfully, revealing, however subtly, the previously hidden extent of her anger with him.

He opened his mouth to respond, but she spoke first.

" 'Twas a promise, Leif. A *promise*. And had you not been so eager to break it, you would have given me the chance to tell you that I was with child—*your* child—and needed not to hear of frivolous plans to desert me at such a time."

He looked as if someone had struck him. His whole body tautened visibly, his eyes widened fractionally in surprise. He opened his mouth slightly, as if he would question or deny her. Then his lips came together again in a tight, white line.

"You lie," he said through set teeth. He took her arm and pulled her toward the door of the longhouse. "You'll not use that ploy to increase my guilt and excuse your actions."

"Leave her be."

Hakon suddenly stood before Leif, blocking the way. Morgana couldn't see his shadowed features for the bright rushlight in the wall behind him, but she could tell by his voice, his stance, that he was furious. Bolstered by a prodigious amount of ale, she guessed, he was ready to take on Leif Haraldsson.

Without releasing Morgana's arm, Leif stood his ground, his gaze locked with that of his half-cousin . . . and felt the tip of the dagger Hakon pressed to his belly.

"Go ahead, wife-stealer!" he snarled softly. "Skewer me! What are you waiting for?"

Morgana put a hand on her husband's arm and squeezed. "No, Hakon. I will talk to him . . . outside. Please—"

"There's no need for talking. He broke a vow. You

47

divorced him and married me! What's done is done . . . what can you say in private that we can't all hear?"

He was being completely unreasonable, Morgana thought, all his doubts and old jealousies surfacing in light of this unexpected, and what he obviously considered very real, threat.

She looked into his eyes, trying to will him to calmness. In the two winters they'd been wed, she'd never had to stand up to him—perhaps because of her gentle nature, perhaps because Hakon was normally fairly compliant where she was concerned. But this was different; and only a fool would be unaware of the dangers of the very object of their sudden and ferocious feud acting as intermediary to these two men.

She was placing herself in the thick of things, into the heart of the flames; but Morgana was no coward. She felt that she owed them both that much, and that consideration came before all others.

"Afraid she'll choose me, Sweynsson?" Leif challenged softly, an ugly twist to his mouth.

The brief flicker of something akin to uncertainty in Hakon's expression was answer enough.

"Never! Morgana is mine. Eirik is mine." His voice lowered to a snarl. "There is no place in Oslof for you anymore, Haraldsson."

"Oh, aye. 'Tis not the real Hakon who speaks now," Leif said in a derisive drawl. "Rather 'tis the coward who stole my wife . . . the boy who hides behind the new jarl's breeches. The new jarl who, most conveniently, is that boy's father."

Hakon stepped forward, right in Leif's face—or almost, for the difference in height wouldn't quite allow it. He tried to fling Morgana's arm away, but she wouldn't be put aside.

"Let me speak to him," Morgana entreated her husband. "Just—"

Hakon flung out his arm again, this time dislodging Morgana and causing her to stagger backwards.

Leif shoved Hakon aside and caught Morgana around the waist, steadying her. He spun to face Hakon, his expression murderous. "You ever touch her again in such a manner and I'll kill you. As Odin is my witness, Hakon, *I'll kill you*. Do you understand?"

Hakon looked at Morgana, as if gauging her reaction to Leif's words. Some of the anger in his eyes faded as he regarded her, as if he regretted his roughness.

Or was he regretting, just the smallest bit, having provoked a man who normally did not back down from anything? wondered the silent, unacknowledged part of her that had never considered Hakon Leif Haraldsson's equal. In any way.

Morgana stepped away from Leif's sheltering arm and touched her husband again. This time, on the cheek. "I ask you once more, husband. Just a few moments outside the hall?"

She didn't see Leif's reaction to her choice of words, but Hakon looked about to relent.

Just as he opened his mouth to speak, however, someone at the board thumped it solidly with an open palm, catching Hakon's attention.

Sweyn, seated in the high chair at the center of the board, and the men immediately around him, had been growing more boisterous by the moment. As her eyes followed Hakon's, Morgana saw it was Ragnar who'd pounded the board and set the wooden platters, tankards, and eating implements a-dancing. "Ask Haraldsson!" the flame-haired Northman roared, his gaze searching the smoky hall, obviously for Leif.

"Tell us yourself!" challenged Gunnar. "You've never been at a loss for words." He threw a glance over his shoulder and briefly met Leif's eyes as the assembly roared with laughter. When the merriment began to subside, he added over the babble of voices, "Leif tends to other matters just now." Gunnar turned and looked at a man known as Egil the Tall, a dark-haired, short and wiry fellow, with a quick wit and sense of humor, a flare for the dramatic, and a tongue as nimble as a hare before the hounds. He was well-suited for his job as *skald*, or storyteller. "Better yet, 'tis time to begin your story, Egil," Gunnar added. "Leif—and any of the others—can embellish it if your memory is too sodden with brine from all that time at sea."

Again, laughter broke out, and Ottar, Morgana's stepfather, slapped the younger man on the shoulder with approval. "Aye. Let's see if the old jarl's trust was well-placed when he sent you along with *Wave Rider*. What can you tell us of his son's exploits, Egil?"

Suddenly there was absolute silence. Sweyn Estrithsson's face turned an even ruddier shade than it was from drink.

Leif seized the moment and took Morgana's hand. " 'Twill definitely ease an awkward situation," he told Hakon with heavy irony in a low voice. "All of the men were courageous—Egil knows. Tell him to start at the beginning."

Before Hakon could react, Leif drew Morgana away and out into the night.

"How could you have said such a thing? You put yourself in grave danger," Morgana told Leif, distress in her voice.

Leif let out a soft laugh that had nothing to do with humor. "Then he's much changed . . . or he'll have to resort to underhanded means, as some say he did with my father."

He watched the moonbeams play about her hair, starshine sparkle in her striking eyes, and felt something tug at his heart. Suddenly he didn't want to discuss anything that had to do with perfidy, or betrayal, or struggle. Here, before him, as real as real could be, stood his Morgana. More alive, infinitely more vivid in every way, than in his dreams.

He reached out to brush back a loose strand of her hair, curling silver gossamer stirring gently with the breeze. His anger receded as more tender emotions took over. "Morgana," he whispered, and moved to take her into his arms.

She shook her head and put her palms against his chest, suddenly reluctant and eager at the same time to touch him. The feel of his body beneath her hands, warm and solid, his unique scent, sent a sweet and familiar giddiness sliding through her like quicksilver.

Desire flared deep within her.

"Nay?" he whispered against her ear. His tongue skimmed around that delicate area, teasing, inviting, luring shamelessly.

She tried to shake her head again, pushing against him with dwindling determination. "I am wed to—"

"Me," he breathed, and dipped his tongue with gentle but deft expertise into her ear.

Someone quietly moved past them with a whisper of sound, but neither heeded. The door to the longhouse opened and let a burst of noise escape into the night before it closed and sealed off the sounds of revelry.

Morgana felt a shudder sift through her, setting her body atremble with growing urgency . . .

Leif felt weak for want of her . . .

This felt so right, one part of Morgana thought. But it was so wrong now . . .

She's mine, still, Leif exulted silently, succumbing to the aphrodisiac of her body against his, the essence of her saturating his senses . . .

She wrenched away from his questing tongue. "I didn't agree to come outside with you for . . . this!"

But if he so desired, Morgana wondered if her heart

51

wouldn't have allowed him to take her there and then, encountering only token resistance. She still loved him. Still wanted him. Perhaps, had even forgiven him . . .

No.

"You still love me, Morgana," he said softly. "Leave him. Come back to me, where you belong."

She closed her eyes for a moment, trying to conjure up some of her old anger, but it was difficult from within the circle of his arms. She closed her eyes and thought of Hakon . . . of Eirik . . .

"If I give in to you now, that would mean I made a mistake . . . that I used bad judgment, and I—"

And that, you could never admit to. Would never admit to, taunted stubborn pride.

"You would remain apart from me because of pride, Morgana?" He held her by her upper arms now. His grip tightened.

The anger in his voice—he, who had always been one of the proudest men she'd known—served her purpose more than his. "I didn't say that. But surely you of all people would understand, Leif Haraldsson. 'Leif the Proud' would have been equally as appropriate as 'Leif the Lucky.' " Bitterness crept into her voice.

She felt him stiffen. " 'Lucky' no longer applies when I come home after three winters of hell to find I have no home at all. No father . . . no wife . . . 'tis a nightmare."

"If so, 'tis of your own making."

His brows lifted at her words. She saw this, in spite of the moon behind him forming a nimbus around his head and shrouding his features in shadow. She could feel the tension build within him through his fingers on her arms. "I never knew you to be so stubborn, so unrelenting. You've changed."

"That is because of you, as well. I am not the gullible girl you so blithely deserted."

He released her and whirled away, plowing the fingers

52

of both hands through his shoulder-length hair. His head-band went flying with the agitated movement. After a moment he turned his head aside, giving her his profile, his voice strained with frustration. "I did not desert you, Morgana! Going a-viking is part of a Northman's way of life. Increasing our coffers . . . finding new lands . . ."

Fighting pity and regret and love, Morgana delved into her shadowed side. "And you didn't do either, did you? In fact, you very near lost your entire crew and ship."

He swung back to her, his brows flattened in a fierce frown. "Think you I don't know that? Think you that I do not regret their loss every moment of every day? How can you be so insensitive?"

An insidious guilt uncoiled within her in the wake of his accusation; but Morgana stood firm, a subtle yet intrepid spirit and a quiet inner strength coming to her aid. "And why did you give me your solemn word that you wouldn't hie yourself off farther than the Faroes until after the birth of our first child?" She stepped closer to him, her voice lowering with intensity. "You knew of my fears—of my family's losses to the sea. Perhaps I shouldn't have expected so much of you . . . perhaps 'twas unfair, but you *agreed*. And a promise is a promise. A man is only as good as his word."

He stared at her in the moonlight. She was right. He knew that now. He'd had plenty of time to think while he'd been away. He'd not taken life and its ordinary joys seriously enough, he'd admitted to himself after almost perishing. He thought again of how intoxicated with youth he'd been, feeling invincible, certain of Morgana's undying devotion to him, no matter what he did. What young, healthy man wouldn't feel so?

Yet it had all came down to this: He'd carelessly broken his word. It hadn't meant as much to him at the time as it had to Morgana. And now he knew, from the side of maturity and experience, that the basic things in life, the simple things, were the most important. And certainly among those fundamentals was the value of a man's word.

"I made a mistake," he admitted. "I was wrong."

Every doubt she'd ever entertained about her dissolution of their marriage came back to her, like a scolding echo bouncing off the walls of the fjord and ricocheting with scarifying pain through her breast. Tears formed in her eyes, glistened along her lower lashes before she dropped her gaze to the ground between them. She couldn't answer for the sudden tightening of her throat.

"But what of *your* word? You exchanged a vow of wedlock with me, then betrayed me," he continued, unwittingly doing himself more harm now than good. "And you never gave me the benefit of the doubt, did you? We could have been stranded off the coast of Norvegia itself! Admit it, Morgana. You made a mistake, as well."

The censure in his words, the righteousness, brought a flood of cleansing anger surging through her, washing away the debilitating regret. Her head reared up. "Again you sound like the arrogant and selfish man who made that first mistake by leaving his wife with child to go in search of glory! Adventure! Even death!"

"What is this?" he demanded. "Why do you resort to—"

" 'Tis no ploy, Leif Haraldsson!" she cut him off. "Did you not hear me tell you of your son? Could you not tell by looking at Eirik that he is yours? Yet you dare to name my revelation a ploy to increase your guilt and excuse my actions? How can you have ever wished to take me to wife if your opinion of me was—is!—so low?"

She fisted one hand and held it to her mouth, fighting the feelings colliding within her once more.

"What have they done to you?" he asked, his voice softer.

Her gaze clung to his in the moonglow as she answered, "No one has done aught to me, Leif, except you. You wed

54

an innocent . . . a sweet, gullible innocent who looked up to you as her hero. I trusted you completely, for you were beautiful as Frey, strong as Thor, and wise as Odin. No other could compare to you in my eyes. Until you hurt me beyond anything I'd experienced in my life."

He reached out his hand to her. "Morgana . . ."

She shook her head and pushed it aside. "Nay. I had to reach deep within after that to find the strength to accept what you did. When *Wave Rider* left, I told myself that you were dead to me. Then, after your father died, I decided to divorce you—if you hadn't already perished and made me a widow—and find a father for your child."

The child again. *His* child. For the first time, the implication of those words hit him. Morgana had actually been carrying his child when he'd broken his word and left her?

'Tis not my place—or Ingrid's—to divulge certain things . . .

Morgana's reason for ending your marriage is between the two of you . . .

"Haraldsson! Haraldsson!"

Quickly the lone, faint voice from within the hall became a chorus. The din grew so loud, even through the thick walls of the longhouse, that it was distracting.

The door swung open and Gunnar stepped out into the night. "Leif? Morgana?" he called, then limped forward as he caught sight of them standing close by. "They wish to hear your side of the tale." He shrugged his shoulders and smiled faintly. "After all, you are Harald's son, they say. Leif the Lucky, who led them home and—"

"But first led eight of them to their deaths," Leif replied tonelessly. "And what of Sweyn? This, no doubt, will stick in his craw if he hopes to keep their favor to pass on to Hakon." The name emerged as something foul on his tongue.

"He cannot voice an effective objection now without appearing churlish, so he'll go along with this, at least. Nor can he take this one thing away from you. Or deny your gilded tongue." Gunnar motioned him forward with one hand. "Come and quiet them . . . tell them of your narrow escape from the Skraelings, eh?" He raised one eyebrow. "I hear the savages are enough to make the heartiest quake at the sight."

He swung away, then paused and said over his shoulder, a smile in his voice, "Eirik searches for you, Morgana. He and our Harald have wrapped bird feathers in their hair in imitation of Leif's fierce Skraeling."

A thrall served Leif a foaming tankard of Tyra's mead. He tasted it, nodded in approval, then held it up in salute to Tyra as he spotted her. "Always the best," he said softly, knowing she could read his lips from where she stood down the board.

She nodded at him in answer, a message of some kind in her eyes, just as Ottar grabbed Leif's shoulder with his huge smithy's hand. "Out with it!" he thundered, his cheeks ruddy, his blue eyes bright with drink and laughter.

"Let me give a fit introduction," Egil demanded with a frown of indignation that fooled no one.

Laughter followed, and Ragnar smacked the *skald* on the back, making his head jerk like a boneless puppet.

"You've already given *three* introductions!" shouted another man, causing the laughter to increase in volume.

"He had naught better to do than practice on us for the last three winters!" added Ragnar, who then howled with hilarity.

"Rest your tongue and wet your whistle with Tyra's mead!" added the first man.

Leif felt like an outsider looking in, merely a detached observer. In an attempt to chase away his black mood, he drained his tankard and held it out to a thrall for more. Ana emptied the contents of one of Astrid's silver pitchers into his mug, then grabbed the handle of another that lay upon its side, a ruby thread of imported wine wending its way over Astrid's white tablecloth to settle into what looked like a bloodstain.

"Welcome home, Leif," Ana greeted him with a tentative smile.

"*Já.* Ana," he answered with a nod at the comely redhaired slave his father had brought back from a raid on Tara. He couldn't bring himself to smile, or to lie about how good it was to be home. He felt out of place here.

Ana could undoubtedly empathize, he thought, as a slave in a foreign land. Or Little Thor, dozing near the door, chin on his chest, in spite of all the noise and commotion. Either the indefatigable red man had succumbed to exhaustion, or—more likely—ale.

Ana swung away and headed toward the wooden vat of barley ale near one wall, with its long-handled wooden ladle. Beside it rested several casks of mead and wine.

Leif watched as she suddenly collided with little Eirik. The child popped out from beneath the board, his face streaked with soot, two drooping feathers stuck in a narrow cloth tied crudely about his head, and his attention on a huge wolfhound at his heels.

Freki. For an instant Leif could only stare at the dog he'd given Morgana when it had been no more than eight or ten months old. Of course it would be full grown by now. By all the gods, time seemed to have passed him by . . .

Eirik cried out in surprise as Ana made a valiant attempt to avoid falling directly atop him. Both silver pitchers went rolling, one almost tripping Gunnar's young Harald, who had followed his friend from beneath the board, the other thudding to a halt against the trestle table support.

From out of nowhere Hakon appeared and hauled Ana up by the back of her gown. "Careless wench," he growled. "You could have hurt my son." He released her with a push backwards, but not before Leif saw the fear flash in her eyes.

"I—I'm s-sorry," she stuttered, fighting once more to regain her balance in the wake of his ungentle shove.

"My good pitchers, you stupid girl!" Astrid cried from behind Hakon as he bent to retrieve Eirik.

Before he realized what he was doing, Leif jumped up and leapt over the board, moving to stand protectively before Ana.

He noted peripherally that the hall was suddenly quiet.

"Ottar can repair any damage, Astrid," he told the woman. "The boy darted into Ana's path without warning," he added to Hakon, a subtle glint of challenge in his golden eyes.

"Ottar's a blacksmith, not a . . ." She trailed off as she looked into his set features.

"Then surely old Orm can repair them . . . or is he dead, too?"

He heard Hakon's hiss of indrawn breath, for the man would have had to be an utter fool to miss the accusatory edge to Leif's question. Orm had been Harald Estrithsson's half brother . . . and Leif hadn't seen him since *Wave Rider*'s return.

"What do you mean by that?" Hakon asked, lifting Eirik into his arms and scowling at Leif.

The child peered at Leif from the shelter of his stepfather's arms, his silver-blue eyes suddenly endearingly familiar to Leif.

Could you not tell by looking at Eirik that he is yours?

His attention was riveted suddenly to the child. This beautiful little boy was his and not Hakon's? His and Morgana's? With a will of its own, his hand reached out toward Eirik, half in wonderment, half in disbelief.

The toddler buried his head in Hakon's shoulder and clung tightly.

If so, then obviously Hakon had usurped the affections of Leif's child, as well as his wife.

Leif's gaze narrowed. "Just what I said, Sweynson. It

58

seems that many of my father's family are strangely missing from Oslof."

Hakon shrugged. " 'Twas becoming crowded here. Mayhap they moved elsewhere . . . or mayhap they hide in their longhouses, reluctant to attend your welcome home celebration."

"And why could that be?" Leif asked, his gaze narrowing, "unless they feared reprisal for welcoming the former jarl's son home."

"Enough, Leif," Gunnar warned low, in his ear. "Orm is at home, old and ill, not dead. Let the festivities continue for now."

Leif watched as Morgana came to take Eirik from Hakon. Her eyes met Leif's briefly over the child's fair head. The look in them was imploring before she turned away.

"Leif?"

Gunnar's voice came to him, catching his attention. Gunnar was right. The newly-returned men needed and deserved this release, this attention, this honor. How selfish of him, however unintentionally, to rob them of it.

And Leif needed more time to take stock of things, assess the entire situation. He had no doubt of Sweyn Estrithsson's strength of purpose . . . after all, the same blood that had run through Harald's veins still ran through Sweyn's, even if the same sense of honor and fair play didn't. Which made his uncle all the more dangerous.

A cool wet nose pressed against his hip drew Leif's gaze downward. The wolfhound was sniffing him with a vengeance, the hair on his neck raised. *Oh, you too, Freki,* Leif thought bleakly, self-pity flaring within him. *Bite the hand that nursed you to good health and brought you to a better home.*

Commiserating with a cur, Haraldsson? Mayhap you should have succumbed to the sea with those others, for your father would not have acknowledged such behavior from his son.

59

Freki raised his head. He whined once, then his tail began to move tentatively.

"Can you possibly remember me, eh?" Leif asked the dog, reaching out one hand to stroke the animal beneath his chin.

Freki responded, his tail swishing with more enthusiasm now.

Leif bent over, almost nose to nose with the dog. " 'Tis good that you remember me, Freki, else I would have regretted naming you after one of Odin's wolves."

"And how could a cur remember you after three winters?" Hakon said sourly. "He was but a half-grown pup when you left."

" 'Twould appear marriage does not agree with you," Leif replied without taking his eyes off the dog. "All you do is complain and carp like a shrew. 'Tis most certainly an insult to Morgana."

He stood then, and Freki stood, too. On his hind legs. His great paws draped over Leif's shoulders, he began to nuzzle Leif's face and neck. In spite of everything that had happened since his return, for the first time Leif threw back his head and laughed. By the gods, this was too much. After month upon month of hardship, of facing the unknown and impending death, to return to Oslof and receive the warmest welcome from a dog . . .

As his laughter faded, Leif lowered his head and met Freki's solemn regard. The dog was exactly on a level with his old master, and Leif had to dodge his swiping tongue twice before he was able to answer Hakon's question.

"Mayhap he doesn't remember me, Sweynsson, but at least he knows how to accord a returning warrior an appropriate welcome."

He laughed again, and others nearby joined in this time. The celebration was rejoined.

Chapter Four

Morgana had put Eirik to bed, and was sitting to one side of the hall, watching Leif Haraldsson hold the crowd in the palm of his hand with his storytelling abilities. In her mind he rivaled Egil, who added an embellishment now and then, or offered a metaphor or *kenning*, just, Morgana suspected, to reaffirm his skills and his place as *skald* in Oslof.

The sight of Leif, the sound of his voice after all this time, was oddly soothing and unsettling to her at the same time. An ineffible yearning slowly blossomed within her and grew with the passing moments. Morgana discovered she was torn between the need to flee to the bedchamber she shared with her husband and son against the power Leif Haraldsson still unwittingly wielded over her, and the need to remain where she was, taking in the very essence of the man like a child soaking up the first, welcome rays of the spring sun after a long, dreary winter.

Very obviously, the sweet and forgiving side of her was in control once more; much more dominant than the side capable of the outrage she'd once felt at Leif's leaving in light of his promise, and then his failure to return.

She should have stayed in the sleeping chamber.

And shown everyone what a coward you are?

Morgana let out a soft sigh. She'd had little choice. The night was still too young for the festivities to end.

And she couldn't avoid Leif, couldn't hide in a bed-chamber, for there would always be the next morn. And the day following, and the night following that. As long as they lived in the same settlement, there was no helping coming in contact with him.

Forgive me. Without warning, those quietly uttered words tiptoed through her mind.

She tried to ignore them, for she couldn't yet bring herself to admit that she'd made a tragic mistake. That would have been tantamount to condoning Leif's thought-less behavior; and she would never do that. Her pride, her strong convictions about right and wrong, would never allow her to do such a thing.

". . . silent as shadows," Leif was saying, "most fearsome were they, with light copper-hued skin, hair and eyes as black as midnight. They were compact warriors, not nearly as tall as Norsemen, but fine physical specimens with well-muscled bodies, like Little Thor there."

"Scrawny Skraelings, by Odin!" shouted a man called Godi, who was obviously well in his cups.

"Hardly that," Leif answered, before continuing. "A Norseman should know better than to ever underestimate an enemy, Godi. They were upon us in the dead of night before we knew what was happening. Only Little Thor's warning saved us from total humiliation."

Morgana could tell he hated admitting such a thing—any warrior would—but it was a subtle warning to the others. "Most fearsome were they, in spite of their size, with partly-shaved scalps, or long braids and bird feathers in their hair—"

Someone laughed. It was Hakon. "Fearsome as birds!" he said with contempt.

It was Ragnar who responded this time. "You were not with us, Hakon." He paused, as if for effect, Morgana thought, for Hakon had turned down the invitation to participate in the venture—unusual behavior for an unmarried man—and his nebulous reasons had been a matter of some speculation.

Even as the last thought formed, another, more insidious and destructive one, crept into her mind: Hakon remained behind deliberately to take advantage of Leif's absence in every way he could.

No! That was absurd . . .

Then what of the rumors of Sweyn's part in Harald's death? Couldn't they both have plotted against the old jarl and his son? One for control of Oslof, the other for Morgana?

". . . fearless, with an utter disregard for death—"

"Mayhap they go to Valhalla, too!" The tipsy Godi's theory was taken in the same vein that it was given—as a good-natured jest.

Leif threw back his head and laughed. The others followed suit, breaking any tension caused by Hakon's acerbic comment.

The sight and sound of Leif's amusement warmed Morgana's heart, for he'd had little to laugh about since his return.

"After fighting the sea gods, I should think a few savages would have posed little threat." Hakon was speaking again.

Morgana glanced at him. He stood with one foot upon the bench, his arm over his bent knee. In his other hand he held a tankard, which he raised to his lips to drink. His words were for Leif, but as he lowered the tankard, his gaze suddenly met Morgana's in silent challenge.

In spite of her better judgment, she looked away from her husband and at Leif Haraldsson. Apprehension pricked her, for she knew now that Hakon was seeking to provoke Leif. No doubt it had much to do with Tyra's mead.

Leif opened his mouth to retort, then looked at Morgana. He caught the arrested look in her eyes. Was she afraid for him or for Hakon? he wondered, feeling his sudden anger at Hakon diluting in the wake of his natural concern for her.

Gunnar stepped in. "One does not fight Aegir and Ran, Hakon. And if you will hold your tongue long enough for Leif to finish, you'll discover that 'twas wiser, in the end, to bargain with the Skraelings than to battle them."

"Look at him," Hakon challenged, jerking his chin toward Little Thor. "He cannot hold his eyes open. How ferocious an opponent!"

"He's unused to ale," Leif answered. "He knows naught of swords, but put a bow in his hands and he'll outshoot any of us."

Hakon snorted, and several others also made sounds of disbelief. "I'll believe it when I see it with my own eyes."

Morgana looked quickly at Sweyn where he sat at the center of the board, on the high seat facing the east wall of the longhouse, as was customary for the jarl. He didn't look any too pleased with the exchange, yet Morgana knew it would have been unwise of him to show excessive bias against Leif Haraldsson. Even though some had left Oslof, many who remained were still unsure of Sweyn Estrithsson, and some secretly harbored suspicions about the "accidental" death of the late jarl; some who would have lain the deed at Sweyn's door had they any substantial proof.

Morgana had been too caught up in her own anger and grief, and then with the perverse need for a gesture to punish Leif, to concern herself with the politics of the men. Her first priority had been remedying her position as a widow with a young son to raise.

Hakon Sweynsson had been ready to step in and sympathize with her anger at her errant husband while demonstrating his own attributes; to soothe her smarting pride; to apply his charm; and, finally, to appeal to everything within her that was female and vulnerable at that highly emotional and uncertain time.

Leif lifted the tankard in his hand and drank deeply. He thought of his next words, controlling his urge to fling his drink at Hakon and then throttle him. Ana placed the replenished pitcher near him, and he grabbed it like a lifeline, pouring himself another draught of mead with a quiet desperation. Perhaps, he reasoned, the drink could help him hold his temper in the face of Hakon's baiting; ease the sense of loss in the wake of the unexpected news of his father's death; numb the renewed ache in his breast whenever his eyes alighted on the woman he loved sitting so close to him, yet a world apart.

Perhaps it could help him find the clever, poetic words that would allow him to continue his story, even as he wanted nothing more than to stop and set things aright in this topsy-turvy world to which he'd so unsuspectingly and eagerly returned.

"The swords, Leif," Ragnar said to him. "Tell them about the trading of the swords of the dead to benefit the survivors, eh?"

Leif nodded and wiped his mouth. "If 'tis any consolation," he said, desolation rising in his eyes, "the eight men we lost did not die in vain."

All eyes turned to him.

"They valiantly battled the sea gods like true Norsemen, and surely they reside in Valhalla now, feasting and fighting with the best. Several of their swords were saved and traded, along with spare sailcloth, for warm furs and badly-needed food."

"How can the Valkyries accompany a warrior to Valhalla without his sword?" Hakon challenged.

A few voices rose in agreement; not, by any means, the majority. Yet even those few were silenced by Leif's abrupt leap to his feet, his eyes slitting with tightly-leashed outrage at Hakon. "Do you imply my men died disgraceful deaths?" He slammed his fist against the board. "If so, you know not of what you speak, Sweynsson."

Hakon stood and glared back. "I hear only what you say. Everyone here knows a warrior cannot enter the realm of Asgard without his sword. You led a score of men into uncharted waters, and then lived to return and tell us of their ignominious death by drowning?"

It was an open and unjust accusation, yet quiet prevailed within the hall once more.

"And you were conspicuously absent from that voyage. Everyone here also knows that our way of life includes trading, raiding, and exploring new territory for the benefit of all." He leaned forward for emphasis, his eyes boring into Hakon's. "What did *you* accomplish in our absence to justify your remaining behind? Aside from instigating the death of my father?"

One part of Leif anticipated Sweyn's jumping to the defense of his son. Instead, he felt Sweyn's eyes on him, like a snake sizing up its potential prey, all the while he was speaking. The jarl said nothing but, rather, seemed to be waiting for his son to form his own defense. Leif also knew that the men who'd been with him aboard *Wave Rider* would defend him to the death, no matter what Sweyn Estrithsson might think or say, no matter what any other possible allies of Leif might or might not do. And there was always Little Thor. If he ever woke up . . .

But then, Leif thought as he watched Ottar grab Hakon's arm as if to prevent him from going for Leif, Sweyn had always been cowardly compared to his brother Harald. Leif had noticed it long ago, even as a young boy, and although Hakon might make a great show of coming after Leif, it would be the drink that would ultimately give him the final push. Hakon Sweynsson was all show and false bravado, much like—if not worse than—his sire.

The silence swirled around them, bonding the two men in antagonism. No one moved.

"I say there is no need for this," Gunnar said into the taut silence. "If there is aught to be settled between Leif and Hakon, let it be done privately, outside the hall. We have gathered here to celebrate the return of twelve men, not to air individual grievances."

Leif looked at his friend. Gunnar was right, his words wiser by far than Sweyn's silence. Yet there was accusation in Leif's expression as his gaze met Gunnar's. *Whose side are you on?* he asked silently . . .

Ottar released Hakon's arm and made a great show of lifting one of Astrid's silver pitchers. He held it high and threw back his head. His mouth opened wide and he deliberately poured the contents of the pitcher directly onto his face and into his gaping mouth until the men began to laugh at his antics.

"If a man must drown," Ragnar shouted, taking his cue from Ottar. "then let it be thus!" He pushed the young slave Gerd toward Ottar. "With a young wench in his arms too!" Ottar grabbed Gerd, pulled her head back, planted a wet sticky kiss upon her mouth, and proceeded to pour the mead over her face as well.

"A double insult, Ragnar the Red," Tyra cried, but there was laughter in her eyes and in her voice. "Not only do you imply that I'm old, but you encourage the wasting of my mead!" Her laughter joined the masculine merriment that echoed around the longhouse.

Morgana looked askance at her mother. Tyra had once been a whimsical, merry soul, with a ready smile and a sweet nature. The death of Magnus Longbeard, Morgana's father, and her three brothers had wrought an abrupt change in Tyra. Even though her eventual marriage to Ottar seemed to ease her heartache over the years, it warmed Morgana inside to see her laugh, for Tyra had never recovered her earlier gaiety and easy nature in full measure.

As Morgana's attention was diverted for a moment from

the man across the board from her, Leif did not miss the opportunity to look upon her fully. He watched her cheeks pinken with pleasure, her blue eyes, accented by the bright blue silk of her overgown, glow with a vibrancy that caused his pulse to jump to his throat, that set his loins churning.

It came to him like an unexpected and searing bite of a battleax that, for the moment, and possibly forevermore, Morgana was out of his reach.

He should have been beside her, making up for three winters' worth of absence, but she was Hakon's wife now. Had she not divorced him, she would still have been his, for his appearance would have annulled any union with Sweynsson.

Anger surged through him. Anger at Morgana. Anger at Hakon. Anger at Sweyn. Anger at them all. Unreasonable anger, that he allowed to seep through him, nulling any effects of the wine and mead he'd drunk, until he wanted to do violence.

He suddenly needed desperately to quit the longhouse. He needed fresh air to clear his head . . . and most certainly something to divert his whirling thoughts and feelings.

Egil, as if reading his thoughts, stood and jumped onto the board. "Give the man a respite! His sword arm may be tireless, but his tongue isn't." He spun around in a crouch, his eyes going from man to man at the board. "No one in Oslof can match the verbal stamina of Egil the Tall!" He glanced over his shoulder at Leif with a broad wink.

Leif nodded and pushed away from the table. With swift, impatient strides, he headed through the smoky haze and toward the door. Aye, that was what he needed. A bracing breath of air. And a diversion.

He spotted Ana as he neared the door and grabbed her around the waist, pulling her with him. In her obvious surprise, she offered little resistance, her fiery braids flying, her eyes widening.

Let them think what they would, he reasoned grimly.

Let Morgana think what she would. He'd been without a woman for more time than any man ought, only to discover his wife had wed another. He was free. If he wanted to take every willing female in Oslof, he could.

Let her feel some small measure of the pain he was feeling, if she still cared. And damn them all! he thought as he pulled Ana past the dozing Little Thor, through the door and out into the night.

Morgana lay in bed, unable to sleep. It was nearing dawn, yet dark still. Her eyes burned from smoke, from fatigue, yet sleep eluded her.

And she found herself dreading the new day.

While Hakon snored softly beside her, his heavy sleep a result of his overimbibing, her thoughts were tortured by images of Leif and Ana.

What do you care?

Of Leif kissing the pretty thrall . . .

You divorced him.

Of Leif lifting her skirts, his hands skimming over the skin of her thighs . . . and further . . .

You wed Hakon.

Of Leif moving over Ana, loosening his breeches in his burgeoning need . . .

You have no right to be jealous, foolish one. You renounced all rights to fidelity . . . to anger and jealousy.

The images were unbearable. Morgana sat up and flung the covers aside. She glanced over at Eirik in his small bed. The child was sound asleep. Heedless of her tumbled hair, her bare feet in the chill April air, she ignored her wool dress from the night before and, instead, slipped into her sleeveless linen shift. She grabbed her shawl from a hook on the wall and peered from behind the heavy curtain into the hall. The glowing embers from the central firepit gave off a pale glow, and Morgana could discern that the household and any celebrants who couldn't stumble home after the revelry, were asleep. It was yet too early to rise and continue spring planting.

She strained her eyes against the dimness . . . and could not make out Ana resting in her usual sleeping place. The hollow feeling that twisted through Morgana propelled her silently through the length of the longhouse, up the three steps, and out into the darkness before the dawn. The cold hit her like a slap, and suddenly Morgana knew what she needed. She wished she had thought to take clean underwear at least, but there was no turning back now.

She headed toward the closest communal bathhouse, needing to rid herself of stale sweat and the stink of smoke and cooking food; to relax and clear her mind. As Morgana hurried forward, the small split log building loomed before her in the scant illumination from the skies, a beckoning shadow. She stepped inside . . . and immediately knew that someone had been there before her. The room was still warm and excessively humid for that hour of the morn. The stone-flagged floor was slick beneath her bare feet, the stones in the firepit still red-hot from the peat fire glowing beneath them.

Morgana's gaze searched the room, her eyes adjusting quickly to the dimness after the deeper darkness outside. The platform built around the walls was for bathers to recline upon for greater warmth if they so chose. It was vacant. There was no sign of anyone, save the recently-warmed and humidity-laden air—no rushlights in the wall brackets, no articles of clothing, nothing.

Sweat sheened her forehead, began to form beneath her clothing, reminding her that she was still fully clothed, and hadn't come here to contemplate who'd been here before her. Slowly she removed her shawl, folded it and laid it aside on a small bench for that purpose. She slipped her gown over her head, then shimmied out of her linen drawers and placed them likewise aside.

The humidity enveloped her nude body like a caress, and Morgana let her head fall back and leisurely reached her palms toward the ceiling, like a graceful feline stretching the kinks from her body. Attempting to clear her mind, she raked her fingers through her loose hair as it cascaded down her back like the silvery cataract across the fjord. She shook her head, then walked over to fetch a pail of water from among several sitting near the door. They were kept full by thralls for either making steam or dousing the body afterwards.

She lifted a brimming, metal-banded wooden bucket and, with a heave, flung its contents onto the hot stones, producing an instantaneous cacophony of spitting and hissing that filled her ears and blocked out all other sound for a time. A heavy shroud of fresh steam rose from the stones and drifted upward. Misty tendrils of vapor twined about Morgana and reached into every corner of the room like searching fingers. The moist air became even warmer, denser. She turned toward the platform along the nearest wall . . .

And came up against a solid bulk. Arms encircled her, and her breasts brushed against the muscled planes of a man's broad chest.

She drew in her breath with a soft gasp of surprise; yet, in her heart, she wasn't really surprised. His being here was as natural as breathing, just as she had once believed that their being together had been ordained by the gods literally since birth. Perhaps, one part of her thought wildly in an attempt to defend her rash and angry actions of months before, that was exactly why she'd been so outraged when he'd left her . . . outraged enough to push aside her grief and concentrate on avenging the loss. For Leif Haraldsson had taken a part of her with him, a part of her that could never be recovered. And for that, she could never forgive him.

"Morgana, my love," he murmured, his mouth a heartbeat away from hers. "I knew you would come."

Before she could answer, his mouth closed over hers, the urgency in his grip as his naked body pressed to hers matching the rising need in her. She'd dreamed of this scores of times . . . nay, as many times as there were stars in the sky, even after her marriage to Hakon.

Hakon. Eirik. She tried to conjure up their images in a feeble attempt to break his hold on her, but with little success. *Allfather help me,* she pleaded silently, for her body flush against his felt right and beautiful . . . as if it had been decreed for all eternity.

Liquid fire spilled through her, flaring along her veins, wreaking havoc with her senses. Desire penetrated every pore like a summer cloudburst being soaked up by the parched earth.

There was no time for excess tenderness, only primal need, with distant echoes of restraint receding until they all but disappeared. With lightning swiftness, all rational thought melted away for Morgana. Mouth to mouth, breast to chest, thigh to thigh, three years of absence slipped away for her, leaving a love and a need that had previously transcended all other concerns, and did again in those moments.

For Leif, the months between disappeared as well as he absorbed the very essence of her. She tasted of honey and wildflowers and woman. Her body up against his, her soft curves molded to his solid contours, made his dreams and remembrances smoke on the wind by comparison. Her mouth beneath his, open and giving like a blossom beneath the kiss of the sun, brought his sorely-tried self-control to the brink of destruction.

He pulled his mouth away from hers, holding her tightly, his chin resting atop her head as he closed his eyes and fought for reason, for control. He wouldn't take her like a wench-starved wildman, for showing her how much he loved her, reminding her of what they had once shared, was too important to him.

If he could make her see things as he did, if he could make her . . .

She raised her head, and their eyes met, a question in the smoky, silver-blue depths of hers. Her lips were parted, moist and rosy and full. Then her lids lowered halfway, the spray of her lashes sweeping down to hover just above her cheeks. She moaned softly . . . dissolving any lingering fragments of restraint for Leif.

He lifted her into his arms and carried her to the platform, then laid her down like something cherished, in spite of the desire that made him tremble.

The wood beneath her was hard and smooth, but if it had been a bed of hot coals, Morgana wouldn't have noticed. The steam surrounded them, caressed them, sheened their bodies, adding external eroticism to their fulsome inner rapture.

Morgana opened her eyes and saw the man she had loved as no other hovering over her, his hair wet and clinging to the beloved lines of his clean-cut jaw and chin, his proud forehead. His eyes were brimming with emotion and shone gleaming topaz in the pellucid light of the room. And he seemed to be waiting for some sign from her.

How could she deny this when her heart and mind and body wanted a union of their souls more than anything, and to deny it would have been like trying to deny the tide of life that flowed through her with every pulse beat.

You don't have to deny it, whispered her heart. *Who will ever know beside the two of you?*

Tears of joy spilled from her eyes as any remaining reservations evaporated; as she pushed any thought of repercussions to the back of her mind. "Love me, Leif," she whispered on a sweet, soft sob of adoration. "I've missed you so . . . need you so . . ."

"Morgana, Morgana, *ást mín,*" he whispered against her

eyes, her brow, her lips. One hand moved between their straining bodies, stroking her belly, her thighs, like fingers of flame. He seared her skin wherever he touched her.

She moaned again, the sweet, alluring sound sending Leif's spiraling need ever upward. In an effort to hold onto his rampant desire, he bit his lip until the skin split. Then, as he tasted his own blood, he lowered his mouth to one breast, suckling gently, then greedily, as if he couldn't get enough.

Morgana wrapped her legs about his thighs, arching against him insistently and murmuring encouraging words of love to him.

He positioned himself between her thighs, his swollen staff quivering at the moist and beckoning entrance of the very center of her femininity. He lifted his head and looked into her eyes. "This was meant to be, Morgana," he whispered with a low fierceness. "Naught can ever change that, for my love goes beyond all else."

He didn't wait for her to answer. With a lithe twist of his hips he drove deep within her, reveling in the satin sheath of her as she took all of him, closing around him until he suddenly knew that he wouldn't last more than a few strokes. Their eyes locked, heavy-lidded with passion, communicating a deep and abiding love even as did the blissful union of their bodies.

Suddenly helpless in the powerful throes of ecstasy, Leif drew in a shuddering breath. The frisson moved through his entire body with the force of his climax. He cried out her name, his head thrown back, and she did likewise, feeling the world tilt, then release them both from the bonds of human concerns, of mortality itself.

Drawn out and sweetened by the months of being apart, their surcease was complete in every way. They lay there, moments later, replete. Leif shifted slightly to one side to relieve her of his weight, their hearts beating a single cadence, the blood churning through their veins in perfect synchronization.

"I love you, my sweet Morgana," he whispered against her ear, her hair tickling the tip of his nose. "I'll never let you go again. I'll spend the rest of my life making up—"

"Get off my wife!" snarled a voice.

Before either of them could move, a wave of icy water slammed over their heated bodies, shocking them both like an unexpected plunge into the frigid fjord.

Chapter Five

Morgana let out a soft exclamation of shock, stunned for a moment by the sudden, freezing deluge. She heard Leif's low grunt of surprise, then felt him stiffen beside her. He swiftly sat up, pushing her behind him protectively.

With a clatter that set Morgana's teeth on edge, an empty pail went bouncing to the stone floor and rolled off to the side.

"Who's there?" Leif growled.

A torch flared, then lit the hazy chamber to reveal Hakon standing before them. Ignoring Leif's question, he said to Morgana, "So the wandering hero comes home, and you throw yourself at him like a bitch in heat."

Leif's right hand fisted as he slipped from the platform to stand before Hakon. "No, Leif," Morgana urged. "Please—"

She stopped mid-sentence as Hakon produced a dagger from beneath his shirt. Now he had a torch and a knife against a naked, unarmed man. Fear overcame her guilt and embarrassment.

"I—listen to me, Hakon, I swear on my son's—"

Leif heard the confusion in her voice, the concern for Eirik, and it was all he could do to remain unmoving before Hakon Sweynsson.

Hakon's gaze took in Morgana's nakedness, the contempt in his eyes making her feel cheapened and soiled. "Do not swear upon one hair of his head, for 'twill damn you ever further . . . you'll sink ever deeper in the morass of your lie, whore."

With a blurred movement, Leif lashed out at the torch, sending it skittering across the floor.

The smell of singed hair came to Morgana as Hakon allowed the brand to roll away, jumping back out of Leif's reach.

"Take your weapons and your slurs and get out of here," Leif told Hakon. "At least afford Morgana some decency . . . let her get dressed—"

"Decency?" Hakon let out a bark of laughter, the dagger still gripped tightly in his hand, and pointed directly at Leif's bare chest. The mirth in that sound, however—if that was what it could be called—was cold and hollow. "What is decent about *this?* What is decent about my wife sneaking off in the night and coupling like a cur with you?"

Leif moved closer, his body taut as wire, his look turning murderous.

"Ah, ah, ah, hero. I might have to carve up that unblemished chest." Hakon glanced at Morgana, the corners of his handsome mouth turning down. "And you really believe that he joined with you because of some lost love he feels?" he jeered. "You are twice a fool if you think 'tis so, for he was with Ana only a while ago. Surely he'd been sated, and only planned for you to be caught. He but offers me grounds to divorce you, wife, so you can return to him and soothe his wounded but immense pride."

Morgana shook her head, the hectic color in her cheeks intensifying.

"You know not what you speak, Sweynsson. Get out of here, I warn you . . ." Leif growled.

"So Leif Haraldsson, the bastard issue of the late, great jarl—the son of a slave—returns to Oslof and finds things not to his liking. He breaks a vow and deserts his wife,

77

throws eight men to the tender mercies of the sea gods, then expects to return to glory and adulation. And he cannot abide the thought that his wife might have dissolved their marriage. So he lures her into the bathhouse and—"

Leif's fist streaked out and slammed into Hakon's face; but not soon enough to avoid the kiss of the knife as Hakon anticipated his move and slashed the blade across Leif's chest. Blood began to trickle down his torso even as he launched forward and wrestled with Hakon for the weapon. They grappled, shreds of steam eerily whorling about them like clinging tatters.

It was a nightmare to Morgana. She edged off the platform, her legs feeling suddenly weak, and grabbed her shift. Clutching it to her, she moved toward the two men. In the rushlight from the torch lying to the side, she caught the flash of the dagger as it went spinning into the firepit and landed with a clink among the hot stones.

Both men were poised at the edge of the hole; Morgana froze in mid-step, torn between wanting to stop them and the thought that any movement on her part could send them both plunging into the pit.

Knowing that she couldn't match the strength of two able and angry men, she did something utterly uncharacteristic, yet the only thing that might have any effect under the circumstances. *"Nei!"* she cried at the top of her lungs. *"Stop* it!"

Leif seemed to get hold of himself in the wake of her panicked shriek. He released Hakon and leapt backward to stand immediately before her, once again shielding her. She could hear his harsh breathing, see his back and shoulders heave with exertion. He maintained a half-crouch, every muscle tensed, arms spread and fingers still half-curled, as if in anticipation of an attack by Hakon.

"What goes on here?" asked a deep voice from the doorway. It was Sweyn. He stood there like a king, with only a mantle swung about his shoulders. His face contorted with anger as he took in the scene before him. "You rouse the entire village to witness your bickering and scrapping over a wench?" he charged. "You do dishonor to my name!" he accused Hakon, ignoring Leif as if he weren't even there. "And *you*, obviously, do dishonor to my son!" he said to Morgana.

"Leif?" asked Gunnar from outside the door.

"Aye, what—?" came yet another voice.

"Begone!" Sweyn roared. " 'Tis naught to concern yourselves about. The fields stand in more need of attention than the goings-on in the bathhouse!"

No one appeared through the door, but Gunnar called, "Leif? Are you in there?"

"See how Gunnar knows exactly where to find you?" Hakon said to Leif. "Scream or no scream, he knew where to find two mating dogs. And where's your fierce Skraeling now? No doubt nursing his—"

"Insult Morgana again, Sweynsson," Leif cut him off as he slowly straightened, "and you won't live to utter another word."

"Tsk, tsk, tsk . . . such threats," Hakon said with a derisive movement of his lips as he shook his head in feigned disapproval. "And in the presence of the new jarl."

"The only reason you show no fear."

Hakon threw Leif a look of pure hatred, then bent to retrieve the discarded torch. He looked at Morgana. " 'Twas a plan, wife. And you took the bait like a hungry herring."

"Take her back to the longhouse," Sweyn directed his son. To Leif, he finally said, "And get yourself back to Gunnar's hall. If you cause such a commotion again, we'll put your grievances before the *thing* in a moon's time and see just how much support you'll receive."

"A council greatly influenced by Harald Fairhair?" Leif asked boldly, employing offense as defense. "Who seeks to be king of all Norvegia? Who, 'tis said, has already bought your loyalty?"

He knew his words were audacious, especially considering his very precarious position in the new order of Oslof. Yet he was fairly certain that neither Sweyn nor Hakon would dare do anything outright to harm him. That they might resort to subterfuge, however, as in the case of the late Harald, was another matter.

Leif stood his ground, his gaze locked with Sweyn's, silently answering the jarl's challenge.

Hakon, however, was the one to slice through the quivering quiet. He looked at Morgana, standing silently, still holding her shift to her breasts. "Put on your shift," he said tersely. Then to Leif, "If I ever catch you near my wife again I'll castrate you . . . *then* I'll kill you. Do you understand?"

" 'Twill be impossible to avoid Morgana while living in the same settlement, and you know it," Leif replied, ignoring the threat. "Just how am I to accomplish this, Sweynsson, even if I decide to abide by your . . . dictates?" He spoke calmly, his words laced with irony, as if he were baiting Hakon.

"Leave Oslof. 'Tis as simple as that," Sweyn answered.

"Nay!" Morgana protested. "How unfair to him . . . to *anyone* who returns to what had been their home! What kind of welcome has he received?"

Sweyn stared hard at her, obviously assessing. His scrutiny made her feel guilty and uncomfortable, as if she were somehow being disloyal to Hakon . . . as if she'd committed a crime against him. Even against Sweyn, against the entire village.

Well, fool, did you not? At least against your husband?

Then, realizing how ridiculous she must sound in light of what she had just done, Morgana turned her back, feeling a hot blush creep from her toes to the top of her head. Not so much from her state of undress but, rather, from the absurdity of her words. She closed her eyes, for there was no excuse for what she'd allowed to happen.

Except the truth . . . her heart whispered.

She pulled the shift down over her head.

"He couldn't have received a warmer welcome from anyone than he did from you, could he, Morgana?" Hakon said with soft virulence as three pairs of eyes watched the linen chemise settle over the sweet curves of her form. "Did you take it upon yourself to welcome him on behalf of the entire settlement?" He strode up to her and pulled her ungently around to face him.

He'd never been rough with her before, and Morgana suspected that he was deliberately trying to provoke Leif.

As she looked up into his eyes, for the first time Morgana suddenly wondered why she'd ever wed him. There shone a strange, feral light in the depths of those azure orbs that she'd not seen there before. Half-hidden, sinister shadows lurked in the contours of his face in the play of the torchlight. Perhaps she'd never taken the time or cared to notice. Now it was like looking into the eyes of a stranger.

Morgana deliberately swallowed a grunt of pain at his roughness as she heard Leif draw in a sharp, hissing breath.

" 'Twasn't her fault," he stated bluntly, making no move to retrieve his clothing, his eyes riveted to Hakon's hand on Morgana's arm. "You just said it was a plan, Sweynsson. I came in while she was undressing. When she tried to refuse me, I ignored her pleas."

With an angry flourish, Sweyn bent to retrieve Leif's tunic and threw it at him. He retreated, his expression full of menace, and stalked from the room.

Hakon said with heavy irony, "I see no signs of rape." One hand remained on Morgana's forearm. The fingers dug into her flesh.

"Unhand her," Leif commanded softly. "Your father can't shield you now, Pretty Face."

"Please!" Morgana intervened in growing desperation,

81

knowing how much Hakon detested the childhood name. She looked up at Hakon. "Leave with me now, Hakon, I beg of you. I'll do . . . anything you say." The last three words emerged as a ragged whisper.

Leif couldn't believe his hears. Morgana had never begged for anything in her life. Could it be that she was so concerned for Hakon? Was she actually afraid that he, Leif, would do Hakon bodily harm?

And why would she have any doubts about your ability to best him?

Then why, also, had she given herself to Leif so eagerly? No doubt because she still had no intention of leaving Hakon—would settle for a tryst now and again with Leif, but naught more.

Renewed disappointment and frustration sprouted within Leif and spread like wildfire. He'd be damned, however, if he would scramble to don his clothing, like a guilty youth caught in the act of wrongdoing. Ignoring Hakon, he stared at Morgana, trying to bring the emotions raging through his blood under control.

Morgana, too, was frustrated, and as her gaze clung to Leif's, she felt something deep within her wither and die. The joy, the unabashed exuberance she'd seen in his eyes since that previous morn was utterly distinguished now; as if he truly understood that, no matter what, she wouldn't leave Hakon. Wouldn't tear Eirik away from the man he considered his father. Wouldn't admit she'd been wrong when, in the short madness of anger, she'd followed a childish impulse to pay back his betrayal of her trust by leaving him and wedding another.

"Aye," Leif drawled to hide the pain behind the words, "take your wife, Sweynsson, before *I* take her . . . again."

"What am I to do?" Leif asked Gunnar. "Just leave and admit defeat? This is my home . . . or is it?" He stood on the rocky beach, one hand shielding his eyes from the morning sun as he studied *Wave Rider*. Several men had already removed the bent mast and were lowering it from the *knarr* to the ground. "Mayhap I'll just take any volunteers I can gather after planting and sail south toward Francia," he answered himself. "They say Hrolf the Walker is determined to bite out a chunk of the Frankish king's domain."

Gunnar shook his head and watched Harald and Eirik, fair heads bent together as they sorted stones and pebbles according to size nearby. Britta kept a watchful eye on them as Freki romped about, now and then nosing curiously at the piles of stones and sending them scattering. Little Thor sat on a boulder to their other side, whittling what looked like a tiny bow. "Give it some time. Surely Morgana will relent—"

Leif looked at his friend with a frown. "Relent?" He'd been deliberately keeping his gaze from the two small boys playing on the beach, avoiding any reminder of his broken vow. Now his eyes briefly touched Gunnar, then moved to Eirik and fixed upon the child like metal to magnet. "I'll not beg. She gave herself to him . . . gave Eirik to him."

"Mayhap you should consider a plea, if you truly want her and your son back," Gunnar said quietly. "Pride has naught to do with love."

The remark took Leif completely by surprise and brought his gaze whipping back to Gunnar. "And you are of a sudden an expert in love? Thor's hammer, but that roller did something to your head as well as your leg!"

Gunnar took no outward offense at his words. He shrugged and bent slightly to massage his thigh. Leif suddenly realized that his friend had changed. He was calmer, more mature.

And you haven't.

The thought only irritated him further. "I remember a time when you would have said such sentiments were only for women . . . or the tales of the *skalds*."

"All has not been well since you left, Leif. I've seen Ingrid give birth to a dead babe, and learned of the real closeness between two people in times of tragedy. After an accident such as mine, one has much to contemplate. Then when you were presumed dead—and if it weren't for my leg, I would have been at your side—I had more time to ponder the ways of the gods." He paused and looked over at his son, who was scolding Freki for destroying their carefully piled pebbles.

Leif was silent, pretending to be absorbed in the work of the men lowering the mast. Others were rolling logs to the water's edge to remove the *knarr* from the fjord for further repairs.

"Win her back in subtle ways then, as Ingrid suggested," Gunnar continued in the face of his friend's silence. "Your very presence is a powerful reminder . . . a powerful advantage. Win her back, then take her and Eirik away if you find things intolerable here. You know Morgana still harbors strong feelings for you, and I've never known you to back down in the face of a challenge." He paused, then added, "This challenge is the most important of your life."

Leif looked at him then, his thoughts shifting to his friend's situation. "And what of you, Gunnar? Surely you cannot find things to your liking here now."

"*Já.* Many among Ingrid's family and my own are unhappy. No one would blame me for seeking a new home. I think I could do my part aboard a vessel if I had enough men to help me." But there was a wistfulness in his words, a tinge of doubt, that Leif caught. Was Gunnar's confidence in himself so lacking that he'd changed even more in the last few winters? Did he fear he could do nothing to help his family find a better life?

"You know you can count on me, friend," Leif told him. "I am not so rash and irresponsible as when I left Oslof. I can do my share and be your good leg, as well, in any venture." He held out one hand, palm up.

84

Gunnar stared at it for a moment, then grinned as his eyes met Leif's. He slapped his hand down upon his friend's. "I believe you could, too, by Odin." He sobered. "Ingrid is unhappy here, but pretends otherwise. She would die before she would admit it, but I know she thinks leaving here and starting a new life with her and Harald would be too difficult for me . . ."

"Then she is wrong."

Gunnar nodded, his eyes lighting with hope. "You spoke of Hrolf the Walker. Grandfather says he is nipping at the heels of Charles the Simple of Francia. He is relentless and seeks to carve himself a domain in northwestern Francia . . . the old Neustria." Obviously warming to his subject, he cast a glance about before he continued in a lowered, but no less excited, voice, "While you were gone, some of the men left for England, where Hrolf and his followers are based. They meant to serve him and thus gain lands of their own."

Leif's eyebrows raised. "Aye, I remember Hrolf. Who wouldn't? A giant of a man . . . and outlawed from Norvegia. He's ambitious . . . a leader to follow, perhaps . . ."

" 'Tis something to think about, if things become intolerable here."

Leif nodded thoughtfully. One corner of his mouth curved with irony. "Things aren't exactly tolerable now, but your suggestion has bolstered me."

Gunnar grinned back. " 'Tis what friends are for . . . although I also suggested you go in search of Hrolf . . . which might not be such a good idea." His eyes twinkled, even as his grin faded. "You never could abide Danes, and most of his followers are Danes."

Leif sighed in exaggerated resignation. "If the giant can tolerate them, so can I. And let's hope the men from Oslof met up with Hrolf . . . familiar faces will ease things." He put a hand on Gunnar's shoulder with a soft laugh. "But, friend, I'm not gone yet—"

Their brief bit of levity was cut short by Freki's warning growl. Leif turned to see Little Thor on his haunches before Eirik and Harald. He was holding out the bow to Eirik . . . and Freki was poised to pounce upon the Skraeling.

Leif opened his mouth to call the dog, but then thought better of it as Little Thor lowered the arm with the bow and held out his other hand to the wolfhound. He murmured soothingly to the dog in his own tongue, and Freki stilled, then took a tentative step toward the red man's outstretched fingers. The two boys, obviously more curious than afraid, watched the man and dog. Then, out of the blue, Eirik stuttered, "Fehki—Fehki, n-nice!"

A queer little feeling feathered through Leif's chest at the sweet sound of his son's voice in obvious imitation of Morgana.

The dog's tail switched once then stilled. He inched closer to Little Thor's hand. The man let the dog sniff his fingers, then slowly reached to scratch Freki behind his ears. The dog was so large, in comparison to even a tall Norseman, that he probably could have leveled the smaller red man with one leap. But his tail began to switch in earnest and he whined.

Little Thor smiled, then turned his attention once more to Eirik. "For . . . you," he said in terrible Norse.

Eirik, evidently somewhat confident because Freki had warmed to the stranger, stepped closer and reached for the bow. The Skraeling's smile widened as he held it just out of the child's reach. *Sly one,* Leif thought with a lift of his eyebrows, *so you'll lure him practically into your lap.*

As Eirik finally took hold of the bow, Leif thought he saw a gleam of moisture in the Skraeling's dark eyes, but couldn't be sure from where he and Gunnar stood.

What did he really know about Little Thor? he thought. The man had told him only that his entire village had been destroyed while he'd been out clearing traps. His wife and children had been butchered.

He thought back to after he'd rescued Little Thor from the sea. He'd demanded the Skraeling tell him why he was so intent upon attaching himself to Leif. Between the red man's smattering of Norse, and the hand signs he'd taught Leif, bits of the story had slowly emerged; but one day Leif would have Little Thor repeat it to him, clarify the things that were still nebulous . . .

Chapter Six

Gunnar's voice reached for Leif's attention. Yet he paused to acknowedge to himself that at least he had the satisfaction of knowing that both Morgana and their son were still alive, which was much more than Little Thor could do now. And if Leif could bear living in Oslof, at least he could see them . . .

A boon, indeed, mocked the part of him that would never settle for less than he'd once had.

". . . also forgetting one important thing, my friend."

Leif raised his red-blond eyebrows quizzically as he accorded Gunnar his full attention.

"Hakon just might go a-viking with the other young men when planting is completed. Especially if 'tis implied that he might be afraid to leave Morgana. Rumors like that might goad him into leaving, if only to show he doesn't really consider you a threat. His concern with his image has grown considerably since Sweyn became jarl."

Leif snorted, the corners of his mouth turning down. "He wouldn't be so foolish, no matter what his pride might require of him. I am not without some influence over Morgana, as you've already pointed out, and I wouldn't hesitate to use every last bit of it." He stroked his newly-shaven chin, suddenly thoughtful. "Yet the less interested in Morgana I can appear—the less opposed to accepting things as they are—the more willing Hakon might be to leave."

Gunnar nodded. "You would have your work cut out for you, though. Morgana bears a deep sense of responsibility toward Eirik. He's known no father but Hakon, and is very attached to him. Your skills of persuasion would be put to the test, even were Hakon to leave for two or three moons."

Leif glanced over at Eirik and Little Thor. When he spoke, it was more to himself than to Gunnar. "Whether he leaves or nay, I *will* get to know my son. Surely if he can overcome his fear of the red man, he can do the same for me."

"Get to know your son, for he's a good-natured, affectionate child and will come to love you. Well-treated children are open and loving, and wish nothing more than to be loved in return."

Leif smiled at his friend's words. "Ah, Gunnar the Wise. I sense that you are telling me that patience and kindness will avail me much more than anger and aggression."

"Aye. But you will need every bit of control you possess, Leif Haraldsson, and that luck for which you are known. You cannot be too obvious . . ."

"And I cannot afford to fail. I walk a thin line, do I not?"

"You do. And you dare not give Sweyn or Hakon a reason to take you before the *thing*, for any judgment by that council will surely be against you if Fairhair has aught to do with it. You might even be outlawed."

Leif's features tightened. If he were outlawed, he'd have no choice but to leave his homeland . . . forever. Or die.

"Tell me, Gunnar," he said in a low voice, "what you know of my father's death."

He began to walk around to the other side of *Wave Rider*, skirting the men preparing to remove it from the water, and pretending great interest in their work.

"The children—" Gunnar began, then fell silent as Leif

put a hand on his arm and inclined his head toward the three youngsters, the Skraeling, and the dog. Little Thor was herding them—Britta included—farther up the beach, away from the water's edge. He'd removed his tunic and was using it to carry, from the looks of it, the precious stones the boys had gathered.

"A strange one, he," Gunnar murmured as he watched his son follow the red man.

"No stranger than most," Leif answered. "Only new to us. I would trust him, I think, with my life." He looked at Gunnar expectantly, then returned his gaze to the ship.

"There is a man—you remember him from last night—Horik Bluetooth, he is called."

Leif nodded. "Kept to himself, I noticed, and observed rather than participated."

"Aye. He can celebrate with the best of us, but he is Fairhair's man. He came to Oslof with his family shortly after you left, and ingratiated himself with your father. At least it appeared that way. Mayhap Harald kept his counsel—or appeared to—only to watch him."

"My father was a fair judge of men, wise enough to avoid risking the wrath of a suspected adversary if he could manage him otherwise."

Gunnar frowned as he watched several logs being rolled into place, as if remembering the accident that had cost him normal use of his right leg. "Horik Bluetooth was among the hunting party." Leif's head swiveled to the side to meet Gunnar's look. "The jarl and Horik were out of sight in a stand of evergreens for several moments. When they caught up with the rest of the party, Harald's face was white as snow. And he seemed dazed. His mount was behaving strangely, as well . . . wild, enraged. Just as it seemed Harald would speak, Geri shied violently enough to unseat the jarl . . . unusual for a horseman such as your father."

"Except that he was dazed. And Geri doesn't spook easily, either. His temperament is stable, courageous."

Gunnar nodded. *"Was.* He's dead."

Leif's fingers fisted at his sides, and he placed tense knuckles on his hips to disguise his reaction.

"The animal overreacted when a hare darted into his path, lost his footing, and threw Harald. Harald died of a broken neck, and Geri suffered a broken leg."

Leif shook his head. "It smells foul. By the gods, it *reeks!*" he exclaimed in a low, agitated voice.

"That is not the worst of it," Gunnar added quietly, his eyes darkening. "Harald sustained a nasty lump on the back of his head—a bump bad enough to daze him. It could have occurred *before* he emerged from the trees with Horik just as easily as it might have during his fall; and after they dispatched Geri, they found a shallow, jagged wound beneath his belly. Horik said the animal might have been grazed by a broken branch protruding from a fallen log on the forest floor. Some went back into the pines and found just such a fallen tree, but there was no blood on any of its protruding limbs. Not everyone was convinced. It could have been a clumsy dagger wound. Yet who could deny aught Horik claimed when Harald, the only witness, was dead?"

In the midst of his outrage, a thought came to Leif. "What of my stallion? What of Hrafn?"

"Morgana rides him occasionally . . . 'twas one of the few things of yours, according to Ingrid, that she wouldn't give up. She'll permit no one else to ride him, and she prefers that Ottar tend to him if she cannot."

A glimmer of hope leapt to life within Leif's breast, but just then Little Thor came striding up to them. He signed to Leif: *Do you have bow and arrow I can use? I have only my knife.*

Leif nodded and translated for Gunnar, then signed back, *Do you wish to show off your skills to the rest of my people?*

91

The red man gave him a ghost of a smile. "Teach Eir-ik
. . . Har-ald," he said in his barely intelligible Norse.

"If you wish. When I return," he answered aloud before
turning to Gunnar. "Come with me to ask Morgana about
Hrafn. If I'm to win her over, I must be more circumspect.
We'll try this your way for a while, eh?"

Gunnar grinned. "It cannot hurt your cause."

Leif singled out Ragnar and spoke briefly to him regarding *Wave Rider*. He swung away then and headed toward
the stable that had once belonged to his father. Before he
and Gunnar had gone ten paces, however, Little Thor had
fallen in behind them. And following him were Eirik,
clutching his new bow, Harald, Britta and—of course—
Freki.

Morgana stared into Leif's somber face. His demeanor
was different, even his voice. "—Hrafn? Gunnar tells me
you've been . . . keeping him," he was saying.

She felt heat suffuse her features at the reminder of the
one possession of Leif's she'd refused to relinquish to another. And, of course, she could not forget what had happened in the bathhouse. "Aye. He's always been yours."
*I couldn't bring myself to give your prized possession to Hakon, not
even in my most bitter moments . . .*

She forced herself to look past him at Gunnar, who was
cuffing Harald playfully, then her gaze came to rest on
Eirik and Britta. And the strange red man standing between them.

Unease filtered through her. "Eirik?" she began, uncertain of her son's safety with the stranger.

"*Já?* Look, Mamma!" he exclaimed and toddled toward
her holding up his bow.

She bent and took him into her arms. As she straightened, she stared over Leif's shoulder at Little Thor, then
felt Leif's steady gaze upon her. Her lashes lowered as she

92

fought to hide her trepidation. " 'Tis—'tis time for his morning nap." She looked at Leif again. "Will you tell him that?"

"Do you think I would subject our son to danger, Morgana?" he asked quietly. "I'd sooner cut out my heart."

She nodded, feeling both ashamed and relieved. "Tell him?" she asked. "I would not offend him if he is your friend."

Leif nodded. "You tell him. He would be honored if you addressed him. No one else seems interested enough to do more than ridicule him."

Morgana was suddenly hard-pressed to pull her eyes from Leif's. Memories of the night before, stirred undoubtedly by the gentleness in his voice—the very sight of him—rose unbidden within her. His beard was gone, and someone had trimmed his hair. Ana? Had the comely slave also combed it out, as a Norsewoman did to her husband every night before retiring?

Jealousy snaked through her.

The roses in her cheeks bloomed further, but she stepped past Leif with Eirik still in her arms and said to the red man, "*Svefn* . . . sleep." She closed her eyes and canted her head until her cheek rested against Eirik's bright curls. "He must sleep now."

Little Thor nodded at her, his dark eyes as fathomless as a forest in the dead of night.

"Can we go to see Hrafn, too, Morgana?" Britta asked, breaking the brief silence.

"Why don't you take Harald home to Ingrid, Britta," Gunnar suggested, "before she begins to worry. Then see if Tyra needs your help since the thralls are all out in the fields. If she doesn't need you, you can meet us at the stable, *já?*"

Britta looked disappointed, but nodded obediently and took Harald's hand. After one last look at Little Thor, she moved off with a reluctant Harald.

93

Morgana moved to turn away, then stilled. "Are you . . . comfortable?" she asked Leif, staring at the hollow where his tunic top met his throat. Her grip on Eirik unconsciously tightened. "I mean . . . at Gunnar and Ingrid's?"

"Aye. Comfortable enough."

"And your wound tended?" The words were a husk of sound as her eyes lowered to the place beneath his tunic where she estimated his laceration to be.

"That wound, aye."

She nodded, trying to ignore the heart-rending implication of those three words, and entered the longhouse . . .

Leaving Leif with only the image in his mind's eye of the shining silver nimbus of her hair.

As he turned toward the stable, he said to Gunnar, his words edged with grim irony, "The time I spent upon that island will be as naught compared to the summer ahead. Even if Hakon goes a-viking . . . even if my self-control holds up . . ."

The stable was cool and dim inside, redolent of leather and hay and animals. Leif stood just inside the great double doors to allow his eyes to adjust, then moved toward the stall that had always belonged to Hrafn. Raven . . . the name he'd chosen after his father had gifted him with the ebony yearling. The horse with whom he'd passed into manhood.

An ox lowed across from him, another horse stomped a restive hoof.

"Hrafn?" he called softly from beside the stallion's closed stall, and was rewarded with a whinny. The animal raised his beautifully shaped head from the feeding trough and presented Leif with his proud profile. "Do you remember me, my Hrafn?"

The stallion whinnied again, his ears pricked forward, and Leif opened the stall gate. He eased in between one wood-slatted partition and the horse, speaking softly, reassuringly to the animal until he felt its velvet-soft muzzle against his palm. "So you *do* remember, sly fellow." He produced a small, dried apple from the pouch at his waist and offered it to the horse. As Hrafn munched it contentedly, Leif leaned his forehead against the stallion's sleek neck and set his mind adrift in memories. His eyes burned with emotion, his throat tightened. If only Morgana had accepted him so willingly, so fully . . .

He straightened after a few moments as the sound of Gunnar's voice came to him. Reaching to loosen Hrafn's lead rope, he felt gratified that evidently Gunnar was attempting to communicate with Little Thor. In the months they'd been on the island, every one of his remaining crew had learned much of the Skraeling's sign language, and in turn, had taught Little Thor some Norse. There was no reason the others in Oslof couldn't do the same.

Leif backed the stallion out into the central aisle, then led him to the open doors and out into the spring sunlight.

"He didn't forget you," Gunnar commented as he watched Leif lead the horse toward them. "He'll let no one near him but Morgana and Ottar."

"And me," Leif added with a grin, feeling suddenly more light of heart than he had since sailing into the fjord the day before.

Hrafn tossed his head and pranced sideways, obviously full of pent-up energy. "Shall we ride, boy?" Leif asked him, patting his withers.

"Good . . . f-fine—?" Little Thor pronounced as he watched Leif and the stallion.

"Horse. Fine horse," Gunnar told him.

"Fine horse . . . for *Kiisku-Liinu,*" he said, and nodded his approval.

"What did he call you?" Gunnar asked, keeping his distance from Hrafn.

Leif hesitated a moment, pretending interest in an imaginary snarl in Hrafn's silken mane. "Sun-Man."

Gunnar folded his arms across his chest in imitation of Little Thor. He pursed his lips thoughtfully and nodded. "Sun-Man? No wonder he's attached himself to you. 'Twould seem he thinks you a god."

Leif dared to look at him then, and noted that Gunnar was struggling to suppress a smile.

"He's better with bow and arrow than any man on my crew. I wouldn't laugh, were I you."

Gunnar shook his head solemnly. "Never."

"Who knows what other skills he possesses."

"Surely. And if he thinks you to be a god, then it must be true."

Leif hid his own grin as he vaulted astride the horse.

"And no saddle," Gunnar continued. "Only a deity would dare ride such an animal without a saddle."

Leif chuckled and nodded, then began to put Hrafn through his paces.

"Just look how he struts! He's haughtier than that damned stallion."

"Hrafn is strutting, Hakon, not Leif."

They were standing just south of the fields, watching Leif canter the horse up and down the beach. Every other pass, man and horse would disappear into the forest, then reemerge, with Hrafn breaking into a magnificent gallop, as if he couldn't stretch his mighty frame far enough during his strides.

Hakon's frown deepened at his father's mild rebuke. "After last night, I'll kill him."

Sweyn's eyes narrowed as he watched the midnight stallion wheel on his hind legs as he turned near one end of the strip of beach. "That you will . . . but not yet."

Hakon fingered the dagger at his waist, oblivious to the cool, light wind off the fjord that lifted strands of his golden hair. "What must he do, Father? Seduce Morgana twice? Thrice?" His fingers spasmed about the dagger hilt.

Sweyn shook his graying head, his thick, wild eyebrows meeting over his eyes speculatively. "Not necessarily. But if it happens again, no one will blame you if you challenge him. The trick will be to kill him rather than getting killed yourself . . ."

At the look that crossed Hakon's features, Sweyn added, "I do not imply that you are inferior; only that no purpose is served in the scheme of things if you die at his hand. Or any other's. If he decides to remain in Oslof, he'll continue to feel out of place. We must be patient, keep our heads, for 'tis doubtful that we could get away with the rigged death of Harald's son as easily as we did that of Harald."

"But Fairhair is behind us!"

"Aye, yet even Fairhair knows when to sit back and wait."

" 'Tisn't his wife who's involved," Hakon said darkly.

"Then get busy and beget me a grandson on her . . . and get her thoughts off Haraldsson. With your attributes you are more than equal to the task."

Suddenly, Sweyn couldn't help himself. As he thought back to last evening and the sight of his stunned and dripping nephew, he broke into laughter. "True, true, my son; 'twasn't Fairhair's wife, but there was something humorous to be found in it, wasn't there?"

Hakon looked at his father as if he had gone mad.

" 'Twas a clever move on your part last night. The look on his face . . ."

Hakon evidently caught the gist of what Sweyn was alluding to . . . evidently remembered Leif Haraldsson's expression in the wake of the frigid deluge Hakon had flung at him and Morgana. His scowl changed into a grin suddenly, then he joined in with his sire's laughter. "Like two curs," he sputtered.

It gladdened Sweyn Estrithsson's heart to see evidence of Hakon's sense of humor. If a man weren't the most intelligent, the ability to laugh served him almost as well in Sweyn's mind. Aside from that all-important entity, luck, of course . . . and both Sweyn and Hakon had had plenty of luck thus far.

Aye, Sweyn thought as he watched his beloved son ease his pain and anger with laughter. They only needed to be patient a little longer. After all, Leif Haraldsson was the one whom fortune was deserting . . .

Ana had returned just at sunrise, in time to quickly comb and braid her hair and change her simple drab gown before taking up her tasks. Gerd had gone to the fields, as had several other slaves. Sweyn and Hakon were supervising and perhaps even pitching in to help those sowing the rye, barley and oats. Of necessity, planting was a cooperative effort.

If Astrid hadn't been present, Morgana would have sent Ana off to the fields as well, just so she wouldn't have had to be constantly reminded of Leif's involvement with her, however fleeting it might have been.

Well, she thought with an inner sigh, after Eirik's nap she would just take him and go to the fields herself, even though she had no right to be affected by Leif's association with a slave. He was no longer her husband and, by her own admission, she had no intention of changing that.

And she certainly hadn't thought of her jealousy and resentment once he'd taken her in his arms in the bathhouse.

Color crept up her face and, in an effort to hide her telltale blush, she ducked into the chamber where Eirik was sleeping. What was she to do? she thought as she stared at her son. Leif's son. Hide from him in the longhouse? Go to the fields and work herself into exhaustion to prove to Hakon that she could be faithful . . . could keep herself from being near Leif? Hope that by the time the fields were planted Leif would go a-viking again? Would the rest of her life be spent gauging just where he would be and making certain she was elsewhere? Or, worse, watching him eventually wed another woman and live in Oslof with the new family he would one day have?

By the gods, *what* had she been thinking when she'd declared herself divorced from him?

You took the chance of creating your own private hell. Was it worth the fleeting satisfaction you felt?

She raised her gaze from her sleeping son to the brightly colored tapestry that hung above the box bed she shared with Hakon. The bed she used to share with Leif. The vivid threads danced before her eyes, merging into formless splashes of color as her eyes filled.

Leif, my love! her heart cried silently. Tears sparkled along her lower lashes and spilled over her cheeks. She swiped at them in irritation. Tears wouldn't help. Nothing could help her now. She still loved Leif Haraldsson. But she couldn't try to correct one mistake by deliberately making another. She owed it to Eirik, who loved Hakon and was too young to understand that the man he called "papa" was not his natural father. She owed it to Hakon, for in his way he loved her and had been good to her . . . at least until Leif had returned. And, in all fairness, Hakon had only briefly vented his anger on her, which he'd had every right to do.

Oh, yes. She was in a coil of her own making . . , a quagmire of contradictions; yet Morgana couldn't see any way out of it that wouldn't cause someone great pain. Remaining Hakon Sweynsson's wife was not only the fairest thing to do—for Eirik and Hakon—but the least humiliating course of action for her pride. Leaving Hakon would be like admitting to everyone that she'd made a monumental mistake.

And if she were brutally honest with herself, she would admit that mistake hadn't really been made for Eirik . . . not to gain the little boy a father. Nor for Hakon. She'd made an unenviable error in judgment two winters ago, and the course of action she'd taken had only been to soothe her wounded pride. A sop to her anger against Leif Haraldsson. If she had at least refrained from wedding Hakon, when and if Leif *did* return, she would have been free—a lone woman with her son, but a landowner. Wealthy enough to need no husband for a time. And, even more importantly, she knew now, she would have been free.

She'd hurt Leif . . . aye, that she'd done. It was what she'd wanted, wasn't it? Just on the off-chance that he was still alive somewhere and would return home? But in the process, she'd also hurt herself more than she had ever dreamed possible. And now she had no real choice, except to live with her decision or never be able to hold up her head again in Oslof.

"Morgana?"

She turned quickly, startled by the soft voice from the doorway. It was Ingrid. Morgana put a finger to her lips, glanced once more at Eirik, and joined her friend. They left the longhouse, and Morgana imagined she could feel Astrid's eyes upon her back, burning two holes through her clothing . . . for Ingrid and Morgana were close friends. And Leif was staying with Ingrid and Gunnar.

"I brought Astrid some of Helga's freshly-made butter," Ingrid said as they walked along, enjoying each other's company and the escape from the dim, smoky hall. It was the first time they were getting a real chance to speak since *Wave Rider*'s return.

Morgana nodded, but said nothing, her gaze on the ground before them. She didn't want Ingrid to see the misery that surely must show in her eyes, nor did she wish her gaze to encounter Leif riding Hrafn nearby, if he'd decided to do so.

What a coward she was!

Aye, taunted a voice. *Where's all that anger and bravado that prompted you to take such an action against the man you loved?*

"How are you, Morgana?" Ingrid asked.

Morgana could see, out of the corner of her eye, Ingrid's right hand resting lightly against her gently swelling abdomen. Morgana could also tell that her friend's gaze was upon her, as questioning and concerned as the tone of her voice.

"I'm . . . well enough."

"Are you really? If so, I'm glad. Come to the byre with me, won't you? One of our sheep dropped a lamb, then died."

Morgana raised distressed eyes to Ingrid's, her own problems pushed aside for the moment, for she had a soft heart and loved animals. Every wounded or orphaned colt or lamb or calf in need of attention was brought to Morgana.

" 'Tis not as serious as that . . . Munin was more of a challenge, I think," Ingrid said with a smile. Munin was a peacock Morgana had saved from death after Ingrid's father, Tostig, had purchased it from a peddler from the East. It had been young and sickly, less able to tolerate the climate than a mature bird; but with patience and care, Morgana had brought it around to good health and Tostig had promptly given it to her as a gift. The old man had died since, and the exotic bird—which was considered a status symbol among Norsemen—was doubly valuable to Morgana now. Munin lived in the longhouse during the winter months, and there was rarely a dull moment with Freki in the same hall.

Morgana caught an unexpected but familiar flash of brilliant blue and, as if conjured up, Munin marched into

101

view and began to follow the two women . . . right into the byre. Ingrid led Morgana to the motherless lamb, and the latter knelt into the straw to examine the tiny animal. Morgana cooed softly to it in Norse as she gently looked it over. " 'Tis a female," she said without raising her eyes from her task. She coaxed the lamb to its wobbly feet, then searched the fragile body with gentle fingers for broken bones or deformities as the newborn began to voice its hunger.

She stood then and looked at Ingrid. "It seems healthy, but if we cannot get another sheep to nurse it, we'll have to use a cloth teat—"

Ingrid put a hand on her arm and stilled her. "Now that we are free of listening ears, I would have you know, Morgana, about what happened between Leif and Ana last eve . . ."

Chapter Seven

Morgana looked straight at Ingrid, now, in spite of her resolve, as the other woman finished her sentence. ". . . naught happened between them last eve."

Relief trickled through Morgana, in spite of her previous denial that she had any right to concern herself with his actions with another woman. But before she could respond, Ingrid added, "They came to the longhouse from Sweyn's hall. Ana slept at one end of the sleeping bench, Leif at the other, near Little Thor."

"You trust that stranger to sleep among your family, Ingrid?" Morgana asked, more from a need to direct the conversation away from Leif and Ana than from any distrust she had for the red man. If Leif trusted him, that was enough for her. It had always been that way.

"He watches over Leif as vigilantly as any parent . . ." She smiled that gentle smile of hers, a smile that made her warm blue eyes glow, even in the dim surroundings. "Being watched can be a deterent to lovemaking."

Morgana was grateful for the deep shadows around them, for she felt her face heat with hectic color at the thought of what had happened later that eve—or, rather, morning. But the vigilant Skraeling hadn't been nearby then . . . or had he?

"His actions cannot concern me now, Ingrid—"

Munin, who had strutted in behind them, let out a squawk, frightening a pathetic bleat from the lamb and causing Morgana to start. She frowned at the peacock, fumbled with one hand in the pouch at her waist, and tossed him a few seeds. "Hissst with you now, silly bird," she warned in a stern undertone. "One more demand like that and you'll end up on a trencher this night!"

As her eyes met Ingrid's, she couldn't help but laugh. Perhaps it was the situation, yet no doubt it was also the relief she felt, no matter how unwarranted she thought it, at Ingrid's news.

"You know very well that Leif's actions *do* concern you, whether you will it or nay. You don't have to hide anything from me." Ingrid paused, watching Munin make short work of Morgana's treat, his irridescent, green-blue neck shimmering even in the shadows as it caught and reflected the light from the open door. "The red man was overcome by ale last night. He was very stoic, I must say, but I'd wager my chatelaine that he suffered an aching head this morn, for he's unused to ale or mead."

Morgana thought of Little Thor dozing in the shadows of the hall the night before. He hadn't left any time soon after Leif . . . proof that he was strongly affected by the ale. "The Skraeling remained for a long time after Leif left—" she began, then could have bitten off her tongue.

"When I returned," Ingrid said, reaching out to stroke the lamb, "Leif was staring into the fire, and Ana was asleep upon the bench. Both were clothed, and Leif's hair had been cut and combed, his beard shaved."

"But you didn't actually *see*—" Morgana cut herself off again.

Ingrid shook her head. "I know what Leif told Gunnar, and I know my own ability to read a situation. Leif wouldn't do such a thing; and if he were driven to it by anger or drink, he certainly wouldn't flaunt his indiscretions in our home."

"What better way to make certain I hear of it!" Morgana snapped, to her irritation with herself, and frowned in self-reproach. She dug out a few more seeds, her eyes downcast in an attempt to avoid Ingrid's perusal.

Ingrid put a hand on her shoulder and gave her a gentle shake. "Morgana, you wouldn't be human if you didn't feel jealousy, whether you're wed to Hakon or not. I know you still love Leif, and you needn't try to hide it from me. I've always been aware of it. And you've always *known* I've known, so what need is there to try to deceive me?"

Morgana raised her eyes to meet her friend's, ashamed of the pity she'd managed to evoke in Ingrid. No doubt she was the object of pity in the eyes of others, as well. "I will tear him from my heart, Ingrid, I swear. Leif Haraldsson made his choice, and I made mine, and I take responsibility for my actions. My life now is with Eirik and Hakon, and it can never be otherwise!"

"And if Hakon were dead?" Ingrid asked in a low, urgent voice, her gaze intent. "You wouldn't be so stubborn then, would you?"

Her question took Morgana completely by surprise. She would never have thought to hear such a query from her friend, a gentle, unassuming but steady soul. "What do you—?"

"I only want you to examine your heart, Morgana. I want you to affirm that you can speak the truth to me. Haven't we always shared everything?" Ingrid sat back on her heels, one hand resting on her abdomen, the other reaching out to Morgana. "I don't want you to feel alone in your regret—"

Morgana opened her mouth to speak, but Ingrid shook her head, one finger to her lips. "I *know* you regret it, there's no use insisting otherwise."

"Then what do you want from me?" Morgana said through stiff lips, staring unseeingly past Ingrid, the lamb and Munin forgotten. "Do you want me to tell you what's in my heart so you can take it back to Leif? So he can continue to anger Hakon and make me miserable? I thought you were my friend." She looked back at Ingrid, accusation in her eyes.

"I'll always be your friend. I only want you to admit to what you really feel—to admit that you might have made an error. Only then, Morgana, will you be able to live your life."

Morgana shook her head stubbornly. "You are worse than my mother."

"Don't you think 'twould be easier if you let everything out to me?" Ingrid pressed, ignoring Morgana's comment. "By all the gods, I love you like a sister . . . know more about what's in your heart than even Tyra, yet you won't trust me . . . confide in me? Declare the choice you have made, even if it pains you, for only then will your heart be lightened, your burden eased."

Morgana shook her head again, but this time her shoulders suddenly slumped in uncharacteristic defeat, her eyes dulling with despair as they clung to Ingrid's in the muted light. The buzz of flies, the soft mewling sounds of the lamb, the bark of a dog from somewhere outside, came to them before she said in a hollow, haunted voice, "My burden can never be eased, Ingrid, as long as I am wed to one man while loving another."

Morgana left Ingrid in the byre with the lamb and went to fetch a scrap of wool and a bowl of milk. As she returned to the sheep shed, she noticed Little Thor following her. It was too late, however, to do anything but continue on her errand. It would also have been rude, she acknowledged, to deliberately avoid the man, even if he unnerved her, yet she didn't want to be alone with him, with only Ingrid there, in the byre . . .

She quickened her steps, and pretended not to notice

him; but the Skraeling's lithe, long strides brought him so close to her that she had no choice but to stop and swing toward him expectantly. Her fingers unconsciously clutched the cloth she held, and some of the milk went sloshing over the rim of the bowl and onto her wrist with her abrupt movement.

Although he was shorter than the average Norseman, the man was still taller than she, and in spite of her apprehension, Morgana found his dark, dark eyes oddly calming and reassuring. And sad, she thought unexpectedly; a hidden pain, the compassionate part of her realized, was there in his black sloe eyes if one cared to notice.

He stared at the curling silver halo of her hair for a moment, then raised one hand as if to touch it. "Fine," he said in a deep, gutteral voice. "Fine hair. Fine *equiwa* . . . woman."

Morgana took a step backward before she realized what she was doing. More milk spilled from the bowl.

Little Thor dropped his hand and gave her what looked like a half-smile. He shook his head, then held up both hands in a conciliatory gesture. Morgana noticed three small arrows in his left hand.

Little Thor's eyes followed her gaze. His smile widened. "Eir-ik," he said.

"For his bow?" she asked, suddenly understanding, and thinking how unfounded were her fears. What had Leif said? *No one seems interested enough to do more than ridicule him.*

He nodded and held them out to her. "Bow. For Eir-ik."

Morgana tucked the wool beneath one arm and, with a tentative smile, reached for the newly-whittled, blunt-nosed arrows, complete with trimmed feathers.

Little Thor's arm froze in midair. He jerked his head aside, his body suddenly tensing, but not in time. A hand came crashing down upon the red man's forearm, sending the arrows scattering at their feet.

Morgana's head whipped around, too, her heart somersaulting in her chest with the unexpected action.

"Don't you ever touch her, *Skraeling*," Hakon snarled, his emphasis of the word weighted with all the derision the term was meant to convey.

Morgana was appalled at both his words and his behavior. "Hakon!" she exclaimed. "He didn't—"

"Haraldsson taught you well," he continued through clenched jaws. He spoke directly to Little Thor, cutting off Morgana's protest. "Neither one of you can keep your hands off my wife!"

Little Thor stood his ground before the angry Norseman, unmoving and, obviously, unintimidated. If he understood Hakon's words, he gave no indication, but merely directed his dark, steady gaze at his antagonist.

"He was only giving me arrows for the bow he'd made for Eirik," Morgana said. "There's no need for affront or insult, Hakon. Can you not be civil?" she asked, glancing at Little Thor, then back at her angry husband.

"Do you, mayhap, fear for my safety, Morgana?" Hakon asked her, his eyes still locked with those of the man before him. "Think you that he might *harm* me?" His voice was suddenly low, taunting.

Morgana stooped to retrieve the arrows. "Don't be absurd. He—"

Little Thor bent to help her, ignoring Hakon. Or so it seemed.

The Norseman went to jam his knee into the Skraeling's chest. He never completed his move. As Sweynsson raised his knee, the red man grabbed it and jerked it toward him so hard that Hakon was pitched forward and over Little Thor's shoulder. He had the presence of mind to duck his head in time to land on his back with a grunt of surprise. The breath knocked from his lungs, he lay there for a moment, stunned.

Morgana, too, was stunned . . . stunned by the unexpectedness of Hakon's action, the speed of Little Thor's reaction. After what seemed like an eternity, she moved toward Hakon.

As she bent toward her prone husband, hoofbeats penetrated her startled senses. Morgana looked up to see Leif approaching on Hrafn, clods of earth flying as the stallion devoured the short distance with his rhythmic canter.

"—kill him!" Hakon muttered, pushing up to his elbows, just as Leif reined in Hrafn and slid from his back. "Damned stinking savage! *You* brought him here," he accused Leif, "brought him here . . . and now he displays his true temperament, that of an ignorant barbarian, with less worth than a lowly thrall! I'll cut out his beating heart for this!"

Ignoring Hakon's ranting, Leif swiftly signed to Little Thor. Morgana caught the words "pale man's temper" in the brief exchange of Norse and hand-signals that passed between them. Evidently the red man understood—and was capable of communicating—more spoken Norse than she had given him credit for.

Hakon got to his knees, then stood and brushed himself off while Morgana remained nearby, uncertain and dreading what could come next.

"I saw what happened, Hakon," Leif said. "No matter what you say, he wouldn't attack you unless provoked into defending himself . . . or someone else."

"So I assaulted him? Or Morgana? Thor's hammer, 'tis his word against mine!"

Leif looked at Morgana. She read several things in his eyes, but first and foremost was trust. Surely he knew she wouldn't lie to defend Hakon if he'd been in the wrong.

"And I was witness, too," she told Hakon, tearing her gaze away from Leif and speaking directly to her husband. It came to her in that moment that Hakon's suddenly obvious shortcomings reflected what some might consider her bad judgment. *Please don't do this,* she silently pleaded with him. *'Tisn't like you.*

Or has he always been that way? With you having chosen only to acknowledge his virtues? a part of her asked.

Hakon opened his mouth to speak, but Leif spoke first, his words taking Morgana by surprise.

"It doesn't have to be this way," he said slowly, firmly. "I can remain here, make a sincere attempt to accept your . . . marriage to Morgana. But I will not abide deliberate provocation by you, Sweynsson . . . or anyone else. This man is my friend . . . and you slander him by calling him a slave. You must take my word that he'd never harm Morgana—if that is what you feared earlier—or anyone else in Oslof, any more willingly than would you."

"There isn't room for both of us in Oslof now, Haraldsson. Nor your *friend*. Why don't you just take him, your horse, your ship, and leave?"

They stared at each other for long moments, the air between them thick enough to scythe. Just then Ingrid emerged from the byre, the lamb in her arms. She paused when she saw the three of them standing unmoving in the quivering quiet.

It was Morgana who finally spoke. "You are a reasonable man, Hakon," she told him, quiet determination infusing her expression. "I know that you are. If Leif speaks the truth, why not give him a chance? We don't need antagonism amongst us here now."

Even as she spoke the words, a sliver of disappointment was working its way through her heart at Leif's apparent willingness to accept her relationship with Hakon.

In the face of that acknowledgment, guilt surfaced within her.

"You *would* believe him, Morgana," Hakon answered her bitterly, "but I don't." He snapped his fingers before her face. "Just like that? Just like that he decides to give you up?"

Morgana shook her head, her chin raising a fraction, her voice steady. "He has no choice . . . I'm not his to 'give up.' I divorced him, and I chose to wed you. Do you hear me, Hakon? I *chose* to wed you." She paused for emphasis. "Show me, husband, that I did the right thing . . . that my faith in you was merited."

Although the declaration stung him, Leif had to concede the wisdom of her strategy. Only an utter fool would do anything but back down before her cleverly-worded request. And, unfortunately, Hakon may have been many things, but he was not quite a fool.

Leif could see the wheels of Hakon's mind working, for he was silent for the space of a few heartbeats, obviously weighing the situation and Morgana's words. And, no doubt, realizing that he would appear churlish and insecure—the lesser of the two men—if he refused to seriously consider Leif's stated intentions. How it must gall him, Leif thought with a glimmer of empathy.

Hakon looked at Little Thor consideringly, his eyes narrowed with dislike, then back at Leif. "I don't believe a word of any of it . . . neither your claim to accept our marriage, nor your reassurances about the Skraeling. But, for Morgana's sake, I'll let his behavior go unanswered . . . for now. And mayhap I'll just wait and see, for a time, if you are as good as your word regarding the other."

He looked at Morgana, a challenge in his eyes. "Are you returning to the longhouse?" It was a statement rather than a question.

Morgana held up the piece of cloth and the half-empty bowl of milk. She nodded toward Ingrid, who was still standing in the doorway of the byre. "I was going to feed the lamb. 'Tis motherless and needs attending."

Hakon stared at her long and hard, as if trying to gauge her sincerity. "Don't be long," he said finally. "I want you to serve me my meal." Without a word or a glance at Leif or Little Thor, he turned on his heel and strode away.

Morgana looked at Leif. "Tell him, won't you, that I regret Hakon's behavior? That we are not all like that?"

The quiet intensity in Leif's eyes reached out to her, tugged at something deep within her. "You may tell him yourself, Morgana. He's not made of stone."

Little Thor had bent to retrieve the scattered arrows as Ingrid came up to them. Morgana reached out to take them, gifting the red man with a beautiful curving of her lips that could leave no doubt as to her good intentions. "I'm sorry for Hakon's behavior."

Little Thor regarded her steadily. "Fine woman. Hakon mistake. Not your." He gestured toward the arrows he'd given her. "For Eir-ik. This one,"—he pointed to himself—"show him. Shoot bow."

"Good." Leif turned to Ingrid, feeling a need to distract his thoughts from Morgana, standing so very close yet, by his own declaration, so far away. "Give the lamb to Little Thor. He has a way with animals. Says his father was *shaman*. A healer . . . a holy man."

Ingrid glanced at Morgana questioningly. Morgana nodded, trusting Leif's judgment. As the Skraeling took the lamb from Ingrid, Morgana noticed the potent look he gave her friend. Then, when Ingrid's eyes met his, the intensity vanished. The corners of his mouth lifted in a rare smile, showing even white teeth and deepening the laughter lines splaying out over his high cheekbones.

Leif said slowly and distinctly to him, "Today is the fifth day of the week. Thor's day. We'll have a celebration again this night, my friend, to honor Thor. You can show your skill with bow and arrow before all . . . perhaps challenge Hakon, *já?*" He signed briefly, as the red man met his look, as if to clarify his spoken words.

Little Thor grinned, and Morgana could have sworn she

saw a gleam of anticipation in his striking dark eyes. "This night. *Já.*"

With the advent of spring, the days were longer, enabling the Norsemen to celebrate outside of the dim and smoke-hazed longhouses after the evening meal. All manner of events could be initiated: swimming, wrestling, racing, contests with weapons, horsefighting.

Gunnar loaned his extra bow to Little Thor in the wake of the red man's challenge to Hakon, and Morgana was pleased that Hakon was gracious enough to accept the challenge with apparent good humor. She had gone out of her way to be solicitous to her husband at the afternoon meal, trying not only to indicate her pleasure with his acceptance of Leif's intentions, but also to reassure him of her affection. Her behavior that afternoon brought out the best in him, and their mutual congeniality was carried on into the evening hours.

Eight men had lined up to challenge Little Thor in an area cleared for the purpose of contests. Hakon would take him on last. "He's very skilled," he said to his father as they watched the red man best the others, one by one.

"Aye. But you and Haraldsson always excelled at archery. You two were the most skilled in the settlement, or have you forgotten?" He tugged at the thick single braid that was his beard. "Leif hasn't challenged him, so we don't know how the Skraeling compares with his mentor . . . or you."

"Oh, I think I know, Father, and mayhap your confidence is merited. 'Tis difficult to think that such a barbarian could be so competent with bow and arrow," Hakon said ungraciously. "I can more easily envision him wielding a crude club."

Sweyn threw back his head and laughed. "*Já.* And so can I."

113

"He also hasn't touched a drop of ale or mead. Of a certainty that accounts for his success."

Sweyn nodded, as unwilling as his son to give credit to Little Thor.

"What kind of man doesn't drink ale or wine? A strange creature, that one, and well deserving of the name "Skraeling." And look at his hair!" Hakon derided.

The colorful, beaded band still encircled his head, but Little Thor had swept the right side of his face free of his long, straight hair and secured it to the other side with a thong. What looked suspiciously like peacock feathers adorned his long, plaited horse's tail.

"Don't let the drink blind you, my son. He's well-made for an inferior being. Height is not necessarily an indication of strength." He looked Hakon meaningfully in the eye. "Nor a strange hair dressing one of weakness."

Much as he loved his son, sometimes Sweyn wanted to shake some wisdom into him . . .

Morgana divided her time between watching Leif talk and jest with his comrades and observing Little Thor's performance. The men from *Wave Rider* seemed to be exceptionally close to the late jarl's son, in spite of everything that had happened. Of course, she reasoned, Leif the Lucky had taken only volunteers—and only two others beside himself had been wed. No man was accepted if he'd shown the slightest reservation. And, despite their misfortune, they'd brought their ship home . . . and a Skraeling in the flesh—something heretofore only heard about—to prove that there indeed existed a land farther to the west than either Iceland or Greenland.

He rarely looked her way, she noticed with unwelcome disappointment, but rather watched Eirik, who was imitating the competing men with his toy bow and arrows, like a hawk. Britta and Sigfred, Morgana's half brother, were trying to teach Freki to retrieve Eirik's arrows rather than chew them to bits. Morgana had to hide a smile at their efforts, for the shaggy wolfhound knew how to retrieve very well, but seemed to delight in stealing the small, blunt-nosed arrows and then loping away with them, always just out of reach, until the children were obviously exasperated. One arrow ended up splintered in half, the chewed feathers dangling forlornly from one end.

Eirik began to cry, and swung one small fist ineffectually at the dog. "Bad!" he accused. "Fehki bad!"

Hakon swept the child off his feet and tossed him into the air. "Here, here," he chided gruffly. "Eirik the Fierce needn't cry over a silly arrow. I'll make you another . . . and then we'll teach that wretched cur some manners, eh?" He kissed the child's forehead, set him down, and looked over at Morgana.

"Your turn to best the Skraeling, Sweynsson," announced Horik Bluetooth, the giant Northman with one great, protruding eye-tooth. "Come and show him how a *man* can shoot." With a grimace of contempt he glanced over at the others who'd attempted and failed and were still speaking of it among themselves with obvious, if reluctant, admiration.

As Leif watched Horik, he felt a powerful urge to charge the man then and there, before witnesses, with his father's murder. He wanted to challenge him, and to the death, for he had no doubt that Gunnar's account of Harald's "accident" was accurate. And who was this man to dare to insult the men of Oslof? Jesting was commonplace—the bawdier and more insulting, the better. But the grimace on Horik's face, the tone of his voice, were no jest.

Before Leif could pursue the urge, Hakon grabbed Morgana around the waist and shouted, "A kiss for good luck, wife! I'll have a bit of honey to sweeten my fortune this eve!" And he kissed her soundly on the mouth, causing

115

irritation to bud and grow within Leif until he was hard-pressed to contain yet another slew of unholy urges.

It was deliberate. One didn't have to be a soothsayer to know that. Perpetrated to reaffirm his claim to Morgana before all of Oslof, and undoubtedly to flaunt it in Leif's face. How was he going to stick to his declared intentions? he wondered bleakly for the hundredth time since the morn . . .

Several of the men cheered, but those who'd returned aboard *Wave Rider* were silent. And, to Leif's added outrage, Morgana appeared disinclined to escape the embrace. She seemed to return the kiss in full measure.

Leif looked away, his eyes meeting Little Thor's. If the Skraeling read the misery Leif tried to suppress, he gave no definitive sign. Except to nod his head ever so slightly, then look away.

What did *that* mean? Leif had the presence of mind to wonder. Was his sorry state so obvious even to a man unfamiliar with their ways? Or had Little Thor picked up enough Norse to understand that Morgana had ended their union while he'd been away and chosen Hakon for a mate? And now Leif was the object of his pity?

Don't let your pride ruin your plans, whispered reason. *What's done is done . . . you can't be overly sensitive when so much rides upon your ultimate success.*

Hakon released a pink-cheeked Morgana at last, and grabbed his bow. He stepped up to Little Thor without so much as a glance at the red man, took up an arrow from a nearby caskful, quickly nocked it, aimed, and took a practice shot. Then three more. He stepped back and motioned for the red man to proceed.

Leif watched through narrowed eyes as Little Thor calmly took his stance and released an arrow. The sudden silence was so piercing that the *whoosh* of the arrow sounded like a winter wind shrieking down from the mountains. It hit the fresh cloth target pinned to the hay bales forty paces off, dead center.

Sweyn folded his arms across his chest and looked at his son expectantly, one bushy brow raised as if in mute challenge. The laughter of several children who were absorbed in their own game of hide-and-seek sounded in the still air, but all else was quiet as Hakon took aim without a word. The arrow whined across the distance and hit the target beside Little Thor's.

It couldn't have been closer, and a cheer went up. Hakon looked at Leif, a smirk smeared across his features. He still refused to acknowledge Little Thor with his eyes.

Leif was inwardly infuriated; not because of Hakon's smug look, but rather because of his blatant dismissal of Little Thor . . . his refusal to acknowledge the man in any way. And Leif knew that it was because the Skraeling had bested him before Morgana earlier.

"Little Thor can do better!" something prompted Leif to call out. His eyes met Little Thor's, but there was no surprise, no recrimination, in the red man's expression; only an impassive calmness.

He stepped forward, nocked another arrow with slow deliberation, and sighted. The wind sighed downward from the mountaintops. The red-gold of the dying sun bled across the scene and limned the Skraeling's proud profile.

Leif held his breath, sensing that if it were within his power, Little Thor wouldn't disappoint him.

The arrow whizzed toward the bale, hit with a solid thunk. As it's quivering stilled, Leif—and everyone else—strained to make out exactly where it had struck.

"By Mjolnir, he's shaved the other two!" Ottar breathed into the singing silence in an awe-tinged voice. "He's smack in between!"

Just then, Munin came onto the scene, picking his way regally toward Little Thor, his long feathers trailing behind him. Little Thor grinned at Leif, then held out one hand to the peacock. It paused directly before him . . . then slowly, majestically, began to parade back and forth. And, wonder of wonders, the proud Munin did something he had rarely done before: he fanned out the beautiful feathers of his train into a spectrum of shimmering blue and green and gold.

In spite of the fact that he was spoiling what felt like an almost sacred atmosphere—for Norsemen were superstitious—Leif had all he could do to hold a straight face. He wanted more than anything to announce that the silly bird was courting Little Thor . . . that the peacock, never having seen one of his own, obviously thought the Skraeling was a peahen, or something close. But he suppressed his merriment, and said solemnly, "My friend's father was a healer, a holy man. 'Twould seem men and animals hasten to do his son's bidding, as well; so beware, people of Oslof, do not slight him in any way, lest he call forth the evil trolls and demons from the forest . . . and visit his black magic upon you all."

Then, unable to resist, he signed to Little Thor: *Next time choose the feathers of a crow, my friend. One peacock is quite enough for Oslof.*

Chapter Eight

No one spoke for a moment as all eyes were riveted to Little Thor and the bird who postured before him with great avian ceremony. Leif's warning words echoed on the wind and then died away, as the great bird gave its shrill lament.

Leif looked toward the forest, unable to meet the Skraeling's regard, for he surmised Little Thor knew the reason for the frustrated bird's actions; and beneath his seeming imperturbability—beneath what could appear to be a fearsome savagery—the red man definitely had a sense of humor.

And Leif wanted to be certain that his words had sunk in, that those who scorned Little Thor would have second thoughts the next time they raised ridiculing fingers at him.

The Skraeling signed to Leif, *Tell them my people raise these creatures and train them to do wondrous deeds. You need not instill such fear into them.*

Norsemen are fearless, my friend. Don't you know that by now? Leif wondered if the intended irony would come through in hand signals.

"What does he say?" Hakon demanded. "Tell him to speak in Norse. I know he can, I've heard him."

"I'll give him that he can shoot a bow, but he's still a

119

barbarian, no matter what else he claims," said Horik as he threw Little Thor a deprecative look.

"All the same," Gunnar countered, "I'd want him on *my* side in a battle. We have only to teach him to use a sword."

"His people are more civilized than we are, Bluetooth," Leif said to the other man, "for they don't kill their own kind." He took the bow from Little Thor with one hand and clapped him on the shoulder with the other.

"And just what do you imply?" Horik demanded, stepping forward and ignoring Munin's great display.

Egil was returning with the arrows Hakon and Little Thor had used, shaking his head. "By the gods, he's a clean shot!" he exclaimed with admiration in his voice, unwittingly speaking into the pulsing pause meant for Leif's answer.

"I don't like what I hear about my father's death. Mayhap your story—or Sweyn's—differs enough to offer a breath of fresh air to what stinks of foul play."

He watched with satisfaction as Horik's face reddened, although whether with anger or guilt he couldn't know for certain. No doubt anger, he guessed, for a man doing Harald Fairhair's dirty work would have no conscience.

"If you wish to prove your manhood, either challenge me, Haraldsson, or take your mewlings to the *thing.*"

Leif openly considered the man before him. He suspected that he could take him on and probably come out alive, for Horik looked at least ten to twelve winters older than him and past his prime. Yet it was doubtful that Harald Fairhair would have chosen anyone but a capable warrior to see to his interests. And then again, Leif wanted to take no chances until he had more proof—if it were ever to be had—before he would risk his future with Morgana and their son. This was a new side to himself that was only just emerging . . . this calm rationality and disinclination to jump into the thick of uncertain situations.

Of course. Now that he realized just how much he stood to lose . . .

Still, Horik Bluetooth was itching for a challenge, that much was obvious. But Leif wouldn't give him the satisfaction. Not yet, anyway. "Rather, I think if my findings are not to my liking, I would be more inclined to settle things in the *holmgänga*, rather than take any grievance to a council controlled by Fairhair."

A ripple of unease moved through the spectators near enough to hear the exchange, and Morgana fought back a gasp, for the *holmgänga* was a duel to the death. It took place in a confined area on one of the many small deserted islands that skirted the western coast of Norvegia. Not only was it legal, but it was almost a magical form of arbitration, based on the assumption that the gods were behind the man in the right.

By the Allfather, what was he about? she thought. He would run a good chance of getting himself killed, for Morgana didn't necessarily believe that Leif the Lucky still had the favor of the gods, whether right or wrong. Too many things had gone against him—her own past actions included. And, even if Horik refused to duel, no one could prove anything, that much had already been established by several of the late jarl's staunch supporters, including Gunnar and Tyra's Ottar. If there were any lurid secrets to be exposed, only Horik Bluetooth and Harold Estrithsson would know for certain.

And, perhaps Sweyn and Hakon . . .

Her mind shied away from this last, damning thought. She couldn't bear the thought of having been so wrong about Hakon Sweynsson; he could never be an accomplice to murder. Nor could Sweyn, especially when it was the murder of his own brother . . .

Why didn't someone step in and avert disaster? she wondered in agitation. Leif was still adjusting to so many

121

changes, and none of them to his liking or advantage. Hadn't he been through enough?

She watched Horik, her breath stuck in her throat, as Leif's mention of the duel to the death appeared to give the older man pause. Her beseeching gaze moved to Hakon, who was watching her, and then moved on to Sweyn. She had always enjoyed a good rapport with Leif's uncle; in fact, Sweyn had been very instrumental in the union of Morgana and his son.

"Enough of this!" Sweyn rumbled. "If you can discover aught of proof positive concerning nefariousness, I would know of it immediately; but I doubt you'll find any stone was left unturned in my inquiry into my brother's death. Now . . ." He took a horn of brew from a thrall and held it up. "Let's see what this Skraeling can do in a physical match with my son . . . or anyone else who'll take him on!"

"If you would have Little Thor take on the entire settlement, then 'tisn't a true test of his strength and skill now, is it?" Gunnar said with a lift of an eyebrow. "Every man has his limits, even the son of a holy man."

Many laughed outright at this, obviously eager to lighten the mood, and quickly Olaf Herjolfsson stepped forward in challenge. "You held the tiller in a storm with the strength of two, my friend," he said to the red man, one side of his mouth curving in a half-smile. "And you bested me on that island with bow and arrow. Let's see just how good you are in a fight man to man, eh?"

Little Thor grinned and nodded, the colorful feathers adorning his club waving with the movement. A fresh patch of the field was cleared; drinks were refilled.

And so, as twilight closed in on the the settlement nestled within the mountains that sheltered the fjord, the mead and ale flowed fast, and the shouts of encouragement and boisterous laughter ricocheted off the sheer and silent rocky cliffs, blending in with the song of the cataract across the fjord.

"You surely have changed, my friend, since you left for shores unknown," Gunnar said to Leif. They watched as Little Thor appeared to be getting the better of Olaf, both their thoughts obviously on other things.

"Think you they'll take advantage of him?" Leif asked suddenly, uncertain of anyone's concern for the Skraeling aside from Gunnar, and aware of the unfairness of half-inebriated Norsemen taking him on one by one until he was utterly exhausted.

Gunnar shook his head. "Not only is he perfectly sober, but if nothing else, the crew of *Wave Rider* will watch out for him. You know he has their respect."

Leif hazarded a glance at Morgana, her shining hair catching his eye in the growing dusk, even among so many fair-haired people. As if in answer, her eyes met his across the small clearing, and a bittersweet yearning seeped through him.

He dragged his gaze away, lest Hakon see him pining over his wife, and Morgana read his mute but firm refusal to ever give her up.

"You've mellowed," Gunnar said in a low voice, for him alone.

"What choice have I with so much at stake?"

"Even before our talk this morn. 'Twas a different Leif Haraldsson who stepped from *Wave Rider*. And 'tis for the better."

Leif folded his arms across his chest and feigned a frown. "You didn't like me before?" He swiveled his head aside, his somber gaze meeting Gunnar's.

"*Nei.*" He watched as Leif's frown faltered. "I never liked you, *vinur mín*. I loved you . . . as a brother. Even

123

before you risked your life to save mine long ago. Ever since I can remember."

Just as Leif's expression subtly changed, just as he threw an arm around Gunnar's shoulders, a roar of approbation rent the air. Olaf had managed to clumsily pin Little Thor to the ground.

"Your Skraeling isn't faring so well against Olaf," Gunnar said with a good-natured grin.

Leif narrowed his eyes at the two men stalemated upon the ground less than a stone's throw away. He released Gunnar and strode forward, parting those who stood between him and the combatants.

"Look at your Skraeling, Haraldsson," someone shouted. "He may be good with a bow, but he's naught man to man. He has whey for muscles!" It was Hakon. He'd been drinking prodigious amounts of mead after being beaten by Little Thor, and even from a short distance, Leif could tell his eyes were bleary, and his tottering stance appeared to be increasingly affected by the whims of the wind.

"*Já,*" added Horik. "*Skraeling* suits him . . . scrawny and ugly!"

"Or mayhap we should call 'im 'Peacock Man,'" Hakon persisted peevishly.

Several others agreed vocally, and a few men and women laughed. It would have been humorous if not for Horik's obvious derision, possibly encouraged by Hakon's comments.

Leif ignored the unflattering remarks, and dropped to a crouch near the two straining men. "Show them, Matiassu," he directed, pronouncing each word slowly and precisely and using the red man's real name. He noticed that Little Thor wasn't panting as heavily as Olaf . . . although it wasn't necessarily a true indication of the red man's degree of fatigue with Olaf's great body pressing down upon his. "Show these Norsemen that you are not *skraeling*. You are a man no less than any man!"

Little Thor rasped a soft, one-word reply, but Leif couldn't make it out. He didn't have time to ponder it, however, as he watched the red man maneuver one bent knee incredibly close to his chest, his left foot suddenly up against Olaf's torso; then, in one swift and powerful movement, he shoved Olaf backward, breaking the Norseman's hold on him.

Cheers went up, and Leif quickly stood and backed away as Little Thor jumped to his feet. The red man launched himself at his opponent, taking advantage of Olaf's momentary surprise, and tackled him around the waist even as the bigger man's arms were still flailing to preserve his balance.

With a loud expulsion of air, Olaf hit the ground, stunned. He was immediately and securely pinned by Little Thor, much to Leif's delight.

When Olaf conceded defeat, Little Thor gave him a hand up. The Norseman shook his shaggy head, and knocked the heel of one hand against his forehead. "I cannot believe it, red man, but my own fellow crew members hail my defeat!"

" 'Tis because we saw which way the wind was blowing, Herjolfsson," Ragnar shouted. "Think you that we are stupid enough to cheer the loser?"

Everyone laughed at that, and a new challenger stepped forward . . . Ottar the smithy. "But *you* were the ones who named him Little Thor, were you not?" he asked those who'd been among *Wave Rider*'s crew. "You'd have been even more foolish if you'd not had confidence in your Skraeling." He looked at Leif, a sparkle in his blue eyes. "Don't worry, Haraldsson, I'll take care of your red man."

"And see that you do, Ottar, or I'll take my business elsewhere . . . to old Orm perhaps, eh?" But Leif knew that Ottar was a good man, and would never take unfair advantage of another. Ottar and Leif had been very close while Leif had been wed to Morgana, the older man's stepdaughter.

More laughter rang through the air, and then, after allowing Little Thor a few moments to catch his breath and take a swallow of water, the contest began.

Leif was suddenly restless; suddenly feeling the strain of being in the middle of a familiar yet alien world . . . a part of it, yet not. He walked toward the stable that housed Hrafn, tempted to ride again. Riding seemed to be the best thing to clear his head . . . to ease his ever-present frustration and tension. He'd always loved being one with Hrafn, feeling the great stallion's power and speed beneath him. Perhaps it was his mixed blood; perhaps it was because Hrafn had been a gift from his father; but Leif secretly believed he loved riding more than any Norseman should have. More than sailing the seas. More than going a-viking.

As he approached the stable, the laughter and cheers fading into the distance, he heard Freki's bark. And what sounded like the footfalls of little feet. He stopped and turned, anticipating the wolfhound's exuberant approach, for the dog seemed to be trying to make up for lost time in his renewed friendship with Leif. Or else he'd been outrageously spoiled by Morgana.

Instead of being attacked by the affectionate canine, however, he saw that he was being followed by—of all people—his own son. Eirik was trying to push Freki away as the hound began to prance about him in a tight circle with short, playful barks.

"Fehki, *nei!*" he cried in his sweet high voice, and swung one short, chubby arm at the dog. "G'way! G'way!" he commanded angrily. His cheeks, already pink from exertion, turned even pinker with anger.

His coloring—his every feature save his mouth, which

126

was turned down by a fierce frown—reminded Leif unexpectedly, poignantly, of Morgana.

Does he have my temper? Leif wondered briefly, with a spurt of fatherly pride . . .

Perhaps the dog only wanted to play, or perhaps he was attempting to keep the child from wandering too far from the others. Whatever the reason, the animal seemed determined to remain between Leif and Eirik.

Leif pointed a finger at the dog. "Sit, Freki. Sit!"

The dog stopped in its tracks and looked at Leif, its tail swishing halfheartedly, as if it were unsure.

"Sit," Leif repeated.

Freki sat, and Leif crouched down, holding one hand toward Eirik. "You can come, now," he said, a smile warming the corners of his mouth. "Freki only protects you, Eirik. He loves you."

And so do I, he added silently before he even realized what he was thinking.

Eirik gave the dog one more frowning look before he toddled toward Leif. "Horse, *já?* 'Afn." He stopped just before Leif and pointed to the stable, a question in his silver-blue eyes as well as his voice. And a sudden excitement. "*Já?*"

Leif studied him as he hadn't before: the fine bone structure of his face; the pale gold eyebrows and long, sandy lashes. The tiny, pert nose. He'd never been quite this close to his son. "Would you like to see Hrafn, Eirik?" he asked quietly, a kind of wonder infusing his words.

The child slipped his thumb into his mouth and nodded, his eyes wide.

"Then come with me." Leif held out his arms. Held his breath, too. Would Eirik come to him?

Perhaps the child had become accustomed to him; perhaps his desire to see Hrafn was greater than his reservations concerning Leif. Whatever the reason, Eirik walked slowly to Leif, pulled his thumb from his mouth, and held out his arms expectantly.

Leif lifted him into his embrace and stood. Warm and wonderful emotions wound through him as he held the son he hadn't known about until yestermorn. Eirik was incredibly light and smelled of fresh air and his own sweet baby scent. Leif put his lips to the child's fine, white-blond hair and felt emotion brimming in his eyes.

It was a unique and moving moment.

" 'Afn."

Eirik's voice brought him back to the matter at hand. "Aye. Let's go see him, eh?" Leif said in a husky voice. He swung back toward the stable and began walking. Freki jumped to his feet and followed in his wake.

Leif wondered where Britta was, for she normally kept an eye on her little cousin. Even Harald Gunnarsson wasn't around, and although Leif knew Morgana would come searching for Eirik soon enough, he was experiencing the most self-serving urge to keep the child with him as long as he could, even in the face of the concern it might cause Morgana. No doubt they were all caught up in the spectacle of Little Thor and his challengers, children included, and Eirik hadn't been missed yet.

Leif entered the shadowy barn, holding his son as if he were a priceless treasure.

He's more valuable than any treasure that could ever exist. He's your son. Yours and Morgana's.

Leif's grip tightened slightly on the boy.

" 'Afn," Eirik repeated, and squirmed within Leif's grasp.

"Nay, Eirik. You must stay in my arms, for Hrafn is big and you're small. He might hurt you."

The child immediately stilled.

As Leif entered the stallion's stall, he spoke soothingly to Hrafn. Leif had given him plenty of exercise and the animal was calmer than he'd been that morning. He looked over his shoulder at Leif and Eirik, shook his head once, and proceeded to munch on his oats.

Eirik, obviously fascinated but unafraid, pointed to the feed trough. "Eat," he pronounced. " 'Afn."

"Aye. He gets hungry just like Eirik does, but his food isn't as tasty as yours." Leif made a face and shook his head. It felt perfectly natural to hold his son, and there were no words to express his quiet contentment to do so. Unthinkingly, in a gesture as natural as drawing breath, Leif kissed his son's temple. He let his eyelids drift shut for long seconds, for surely this was a man's greatest reward in life. and he'd missed the first two winters of it . . . hadn't been there for Morgana when she'd given birth, either.

Disturbing feelings moved through him at the memory of what he considered her betrayal; why couldn't she have waited?

Yet, even stronger, was his own guilt.

In the almost sacred silence in the stable, Leif realized he held half of his world in his arms. The other half seemed lost to him—at least for now. And Hrafn was there, too, in a way representing Harald and his love for Leif.

Freki whined from the center walkway of the stable behind Leif. Eirik peered over his father's shoulder. "Fehki."

"Stay, Freki," Leif bade the dog, then added with a smile, "Freki's jealous, I think. But he can be part of this, too," he added softly. "Would you like to sit on Hrafn's back, Eirik?"

Eirik's blue eyes widened, looking almost crossed, so close were their faces. It was answer enough. Leif carefully raised the child by his armpits onto Hrafn's broad back. The stallion looked around again, but otherwise remained still as Eirik clutched his mane and clamped his short, bent legs against the horse's back.

"So you know what to do, eh?" Leif asked, feeling proud

129

of the toddler who sat so bravely upon Hrafn. "Do you watch your mother ride him?"

Eirik nodded in the dimness. "*Já.* Mamma." His look was most intent for such a youngster, a frown of what appeared to be concentration creasing his brow.

"You understand you must sit very still, don't you? He's a big and strong horse, but one day, when you're grown, you'll be able to ride and control him just like Mamma. In fact," he added, "you'll one day be a hunter and have a horse of your own. Do you understand, my so—?"

He abruptly bit off his word, but not without evincing an unexpected bitterness. Why shouldn't he be able to call Eirik his son? "My son," he whispered, his lips barely moving. Emotion rose within him once again, threatening his composure, as when he'd first held the child.

He determined then and there that he would kill Hakon Sweynsson outright rather than relinquish Eirik and Morgana to him. Even if he had to take on the whole settlement.

You would have your work cut out for you, though . . . Gunnar's words came back to him. *You will need every bit of control you possess, Leif Haraldsson, and that luck for which you are known* . . .

He would also need patience, he realized with a sinking sensation in the pit of his stomach, which didn't normally number among his virtues.

But I've changed . . . even Gunnar noticed. And a man will do anything necessary if something is important enough to him.

"Eirik!"

Leif started and angled his head aside, his eyes never leaving Eirik. "Morgana?" he asked. "Don't startle Hrafn . . . And walk slowly—"

"What are you doing with him?" she interrupted him, an undercurrent of panic in her low-spoken words as she approached more swiftly than Leif would have liked.

He smoothed his hand over the stallion's neck in an

effort to keep him calm, for Morgana's anxious presence might easily exacerbate any strangeness or unease felt by the horse with Eirik on his back. Hrafn had always been intelligent and high-spirited, attributed in part to the exotic blood from the smaller, finer animals bred in the East that ran through his veins. No draft animal, this. Yet Hrafn was extremely partial to careful treatment, could be temperamental, and wouldn't allow just anyone to casually approach him.

"Morgana—"

"He knows me!" she cut him off in a voice shrill with agitation. "But the child! He—"

Hrafn tossed his head, then flattened his ears.

"Stay back!" Leif warned in a low, urgent voice. But it was too late. Hrafn lashed out with his powerful hindquarters. The sound of stomping hooves sounded like thunder in the stable. Morgana stopped in her tracks.

"Mamma!" Eirik cried as he clutched the stallion's mane and sent a wild-eyed look toward Morgana.

Her hand went to her mouth and stifled a scream as she quickly realized her mistake. Eirik was atop the startled animal, and Leif was between the horse and the wooden stall divider . . .

"Sit very still, Eirik, like a brave warrior," Leif told him, even as he sought to calm the skittish stallion. "Easy, big fellow," he soothed the horse, just as Hrafn shifted his weight and swung his rump toward Leif's side of the stall. "Eas—"

The breath was knocked from his lungs as Leif slammed into the wooden planks. The back of his head cracked against a support post in the half-wall, and he saw stars for a moment. He willed his vision to clear, then sucked in a breath as Hrafn straightened and neighed shrilly. He reached for Eirik, who tumbled into his arms in his fright, and quickly handed him over to Morgana.

She hugged the child to her, her eyes on Leif. "Come

131

out, yourself!" she urged in a low, shaking voice. "He'll settle down on his own."

Leif complied without hesitation, his brows meeting over his eyes in a frown. "Is the boy unharmed?" he asked, his eyes settling briefly on Eirik.

"Aye. But what of you?"

The concern in her expression sent his blood surging through him. But he dared not allow it to show, for fear of upsetting his newly-formed strategy.

"Well enough," he said gruffly, "considering how carelessly you came bumbling in here." It pained him to say the words, to affect the harshness, for he thought he could understand her initial reaction. But he was unprepared for her next words.

As old anger and resentment flared unexpectedly within her, her expression hardened. "And what would you know of a parent's fear for her child? Where were you when he was born? For the first two winters of his life?"

Her vitriolic rejoinder took Leif by surprise . . . and brought an acid-honed response to his lips in return. "Certainly not crawling into bed with another."

He spun away, appalled at his own words, his sudden lack of control. *Fool! You'll never convince her of any move toward acceptance of her marriage with such a show of bitterness.*

But rather than swinging back to face her, to retract his accusation, he moved into Hrafn's stall with all the willingness of a man fleeing his executioner. And this time he stood on the opposite side, putting the stallion between him and Morgana.

Morgana's reaction helped soothe his pride. "You prefer the uncertainty of returning to possible danger to remaining face to face with me? To answering honest questions, Leif Haraldsson?"

Aye! he cried silently, *because I love you desperately . . . love our son, and cannot face the two of you without betraying myself and risking losing you both forever . . .*

"I didn't ask you here," he said over his shoulder, revealing none of his inner anguish. "If of a sudden you're so sensitive to my lack of attentions to you, a *married* woman, then have the good sense to leave." He gingerly felt beneath Hrafn's belly, murmuring something under his breath to the horse. "And neither did I lure Eirik in here, if 'tis what you're thinking." His fingers were trembling from more than one emotion, and he was thankful to have something to occupy his hands and his attention.

"I didn't accuse you of any such thing, Leif, but rather wonder at your judgment . . . the wisdom of letting him sit astride Hrafn. Mayhap you seek to win his affections away from Hakon at any price—even risking injury to him? What other reason can you have had for doing such a foolhardy thing?"

It was hurt that made her speak so sharply. Hurt against which she felt powerless. She hugged Eirik to her, then set him down. He immediately pointed to Hrafn, who now seemed calmer, his gaze going to Leif. " 'Afn bad. Hurt." He gestured for Leif to leave the stall.

"He's fine, now, Eirik. See? Your Mamma frightened him and I think . . ." The stallion neighed and tossed his head; he swung his back end toward the same side of the stall again, as if to avoid Leif's questing hands. Eirik tottered backward, bumping into Freki in his haste.

Leif quickly grabbed the horse's halter and stroked his velvet-soft nose. "Easy, boy. Easy."

Morgana grabbed Eirik's hand and pulled him back even farther. "What are you doing to him? He's not normally so skittish . . ."

"He's injured," Leif answered from the other side of the horse. "It feels like someone deliberately wounded him earlier, and from what Gunnar told me, 'tis a similar wound to that found on my father's horse."

Chapter Nine

"Geri?" Morgana asked in disbelief.

"So Gunnar says." Leif straightened and looked at his fingers. There was a trace of drying blood on them.

His gaze met hers over Hrafn's rump, his eyes dark with suspicion and ire.

"Nay," she breathed. "It cannot be. Who would do such a thing? And why? Geri's wound was from a branch . . . an accident—"

"There are others who would disagree with you." He smoothed a reassuring hand over Hrafn's sleek side before stepping out of the stall. "I'll examine it more closely in the bright light of morning when I take him out. But I know for certain that he wasn't hurt while I rode him. It happened between then and now, which would mean—" his eyes narrowed thoughtfully as he watched Eirik and Freki leave the stable, "—that it happened while he was in here."

Morgana took his hand in hers and looked at the dark smear of blood. In spite of the implications of Hrafn's wound, in spite of his growing outrage, desire went humming up Leif's arm in response to her touch. He bit his lip and stared down at their touching hands. *That* would mean," he finished, a catch in his voice, " 'twas no accident."

Her eyes met his. "What a homecoming," she whispered. "Naught but disappointment and loss . . . and now, possibly, treachery."

Here was the sweet and sensitive Morgana he'd loved forever. She knew exactly how he felt, for she was the other half of his spirit.

Moments exquisite with unspoken emotion passed between them in the hush of the stable. Then he spoke, his words a breath of sound: "I can accept anything, I think, Morgana, but your keeping me from my son. I need time to adjust to . . . life without you beside me." He hoped his voice wasn't conveying the profound extent of his misery. "Hakon need not fear my intentions toward you; but let him beware of trying to prevent me from seeing and developing a bond with Eirik."

Morgana nodded, her eyes locked with his, everything within her reaching out to him in mute appeal. "I wouldn't let him keep Eirik from you, as long as the child is allowed to believe Hakon is his father." Her words sounded choked and distant to her own ears, and her world began whirling about her—a sucking vortex of unexpected despair that she'd only felt once before, when she'd realized that Leif Haraldsson was probably dead.

Now a similar despair was upon her once again . . . for all the wrong reasons. Bewildering disappointment tripped through her with frightening pain, for Leif Haraldsson had told her face to face that he would accept the fact that she belonged to another man.

What did you expect? What did you ever expect? Isn't this what you wanted? What you invited when you acted out of childish motives?

Leif turned back toward Hrafn then, obviously eager to get away from her. She couldn't know it was a move purely to avoid disaster—the destruction of his one flimsy and desperate plan to get her back. A destruction that hovered but a hair's breadth away, threatening his control more than at any time within memory.

"Have you any idea who could have done such a thing?"

135

he asked. Morgana shook her head and mumbled "nay," before he added, "Injuring such a fine animal to get at me is the act of a ruthless, completely unprincipled man."

"Or a stupid one."

Leif looked up and studied her briefly. "Aye. 'Twould seem a man with a good plan wouldn't have to resort to such crude methods. But it might also be a warning." As her eyes met his, Leif turned his attention to Hrafn once more. "You'd better leave before Hakon comes looking for you. Providing grist for the gossips wasn't my intent when I allowed Eirik to come in here with me. I merely wanted to get to know my son."

The last two words hovered in the air between them. The only tangible bond they shared. One that time or place or differences could never sunder.

Reluctantly, and with an aching heart, Morgana swung away, conceding to the truth of his words. Hakon would not be pleased to find them alone together . . .

Distant shouts came to her from outside. Leif, too, heard the commotion and moved away from Hrafn to stand beside her. Her first thought was of the children—Eirik— as Morgana hurried through the open stable door and into the dusk with Leif right behind her.

"Where are you going?" Sweyn asked.

"To find my *wife!*"

"Morgana can take care of herself. But what about Eirik? If you were as concerned about your—"

Hakon rounded on his father, his teeth bared in a drunken parody of rage. "That brat is the image of his natural father . . . I see it even more since Haraldsson's return. I care not if he—"

Sweyn's callused hand over his son's mouth stopped Hakon's careless tirade. "Don't even *think* such a thing! What are you about? The boy still has my brother's blood running through him . . . and as long as he knows and loves you as his father, you'll hold Morgana. Don't you understand that?"

Hakon pulled away from his father's restraining grip and strode toward a section of woodland that bordered a cliff overlooking the fjord. "And since when do you hold any love for Harald?" he sneered.

" 'Tisn't love. 'Tis common sense! Harald's grandson is a means of maintaining the loyalty of many of those who followed Harald."

"I thought we were free of most of them." Hakon didn't slow his steps, although he stumbled twice. Nor did he lower his voice. Fortunately, they were by now out of earshot of the group of celebrants behind them.

"Many, but not all . . . Where are you going? No one in his right mind is over in yon trees with darkness approaching. Why—?"

"What better place for a tryst? In the trees . . . in the shadows . . . away from the others. 'Tis not so cozy as the bathhouse, but 'twill serve their disgusting purposes even better. And they're just desperate enough to chance meeting whatever the night holds—"

Hakon trod on a rock and stumbled onto his hands and knees. He shook his head, as if to clear it, then lurched back to his feet.

"And so are you, 'twould seem," Sweyn growled. "Enough of this, I say! You shame me," Sweyn warned his son, but like an irritated, charging bull, the younger man was propelled by angry determination toward his perceived purpose.

"Then go back," Hakon said in a thick voice. "I'll find them myself."

Sweyn was getting winded. He, too, had had plenty of mead. He slowed his steps and considered tackling his son around the ankles to bring him down and knock some sense into him. Or he could go back for help—although they were now too close to the forest and western periphery of Oslof for anyone to arrive in time to prevent Hakon's blundering into the woods . . . or look the fool when he found no one but elves or trolls or spirits, the sight of which would do wonders to sober him.

He stopped suddenly, even though he was loath to let Hakon continue on his foolhardy course. He would either end up breaking a leg in the darkness among the trees, or being confronted by a spirit, or worse.

And, of course, Sweyn thought with a great mental sigh, with absolutely nothing to show for his efforts to expose Morgana and Leif Haraldsson in a clandestine meeting . . . at least this time.

I can remain here, make a sincere attempt to accept your marriage to Morgana.

Lies . . . lies! Hakon thought bitterly. He pushed aside needling memories of Leif's voice and plunged into the forest. None of the night-dwellers of the woodlands held any terror for him now, with anger and drunken outrage shoring him up. He would find them and kill Leif Haraldsson once and for all. Just how stupid did Haraldsson think him? Certainly stupid enough to believe his thinly-veiled lie . . .

Hakon tripped over a branch, but caught himself with the flat of his hands and saved himself from the brunt of a nasty fall. Between the drink and his fury, he didn't even feel the pain of sharp stones and evergreen needles piercing his palms.

Haraldsson may have once been the jarl's son, but Harald Estrithsson was dead—and now so were Leif's chances of becoming jarl in his place. And Morgana was lost to him, as well. She was *his* . . . Hakon's. And so was Eirik.

Eirik. His face rose up in Hakon's mind's eye, only to be superimposed by a young Leif Haraldsson's features just as

Hakon remembered them. How in Odin's name was he supposed to live with a replica of his hated rival beneath his very roof?

His fists clenched as he swung his bent arms for balance, crashing through the trees and undergrowth with a vengeance. "Haraldsson!" he bellowed. His words bounced off the walls of the fjord—which should have warned him that he was heading in the wrong direction. "I know you're here! Come out and show yourself!"

Only the rustling of the wind in the trees and the sound of his own words thrown back at him greeted his ears. He opened his mouth again . . . and then he he heard it: the noise of moving bodies just ahead in the layers of shadows that were settling all around him.

By Thor, he had them now, he thought. He slowed his steps in a belated attempt to muffle his approach. He didn't have the presence of mind to wonder why his shouts hadn't quieted the movements of the lovers. Or why two people would make enough noise to be heard above the rising rush of the night winds.

Or even if those hidden miscreants could be dreaded dwarfs or evil elves.

The trees thinned . . . and disappeared. Moonlight suddenly illuminated a huge form before him, just as he realized it loomed directly before the precipice . . . the precipice toward which he was rushing; the south wall of the fjord. He marshalled every bit of his dwindling reserves of strength and agility in an attempt to swerve to the left—and thus avoid the colossal black shadow just as it let out a blood-chilling roar.

Relief flashed through his swiftly-sobering mind, but it was short-lived. Just as he veered out of the bear's reach, the ground dropped out from beneath him. Arms windmilling, legs reaching for terra firma that was no longer there, he let out a wild wail of denial. *"Neeeiii . . ."*

And then he was free-falling into the Stygian abyss of the fjord.

Half the men in the settlement came running when Sweyn shouted for help, most of them in various stages of inebriation. A Northman's ability to drink himself sense-less—or even to death—was no secret. But surely, Sweyn thought as he began to conjure up all sorts of dire conse-quences of Hakon's rash behavior, only a few relatively sober volunteers were needed.

When a distant but distinct roar cut across the sudden commotion, the situation turned more serious. Everyone recognized the sound. Under different circumstances it would have been an eagerly-sought challenge. But all knew by then that an unarmed man was out in the gathering darkness alone.

Leif emerged from the barn just in time to catch the bear's faint but distinct bellow of rage. "Who's out there?" he called to Gunnar as he caught sight of him.

"Hakon."

Leif's first reaction was relief that it wasn't someone else. Yet he evinced instant self-reproach as he heard Mor-gana's soft cry of denial behind him.

"He's in the west woods—" Sweyn shouted.

Without another moment's hesitation, Leif pivoted on his heel and ran into the barn. In moments, he emerged astride Hrafn, bent low against the stallion's neck to clear the door, and kicked him to a canter with only a halter for control. Someone thrust a spear at him as he passed by. He grabbed it and straightened.

Little Thor suddenly appeared almost directly in his path, one arm held out to Leif.

He leaned over, quickly divining the Skraeling's intent. "So you want to tangle with a bear, do you?" he said into the red man's ear as Little Thor swung up behind him with

140

the litheness of a natural horseman. "Then you'll need more than a dagger, my friend."

Obviously unhampered by the laceration beneath his belly, Hrafn sped off through the night with his double burden, a stream of torch-bearing men loping along in his wake.

It occurred belatedly to Leif that this entire event could be part of some underhanded scheme that had included injuring Hrafn first. If so, he thought grimly, he could be in for the ride of his life . . . literally.

There was no sign of the bear, except perhaps for a trace of his scent lingering in the air—only an underlying smell of blood. In fact, had Leif had more to drink, he would have thought he'd imagined that mighty bellow. He slid from the stallion's back to stand beside Little Thor, who was listening intently to the sounds of the night, head canted, eyes narrowed.

"Hakon!" Leif called into the wind. The rushing sound of the falls across the fjord could still be heard at this end of the settlement, yet he thought he discerned the faint cries of a man in distress.

"From there," Little Thor said, and pointed toward the very edge of the wooded area. "Water."

Leif nodded, lifted his face and cupped his hands about his mouth, then called once more. "Sweynsson! Where are you?"

Little Thor had begun striding north, toward the fjord. Leif followed.

"Hakon!" he called again upon reaching the sheer rock wall above the fjord. His voice reverberated eerily round and round the stone cliffs. Little Thor pointed down into the maw below. "There."

The image of the drop to the fjord at that point flashed through Leif's mind. Although the wall was rocky and barren, the drop wasn't particularly long. The danger of injury to anyone who went over the edge would more than likely be from bouncing off jutting rocks and ledges, rather than from the length of the fall. Or from a bad landing on the narrow, rocky strip of beach. Unless, of course, the victim hit the water and managed to drown. Yet, every Northman learned to swim well before he could even lift a sword . . .

By this time, several others were making their way through the trees toward Leif and the Skraeling, their voices and the wavering light from the torches announcing their arrival.

"Send someone to the bottom of the cliff," Leif called to them, "The bear's gone, but Hakon may be injured. I think he's fallen into the fjord."

And I hope he drowns, added his darker side.

He met Little Thor's look beneath the faint light from the dusk-tinted heavens. With strands of his blue-black hair flying in the breeze, the red man shook his head. *"Nei,"* he said softly, as if reading Leif's thoughts. "Win . . . win woman fair. Not this way."

It was uncanny, Leif thought, how the man read his mind. He certainly possessed a wisdom and insight unknown to many in Oslof . . . including Hakon Sweynsson, son of the jarl.

And Little Thor was right. Any way he could win back Morgana had to be fair—at least in her eyes.

He handed the spear to Little Thor and motioned toward the fjord. "Watch my back. I doubt the bear will return, but . . ." His gaze went to the others who were approaching with torches. "Someone wishes me dead. Hrafn has already been deliberately injured."

The red man nodded, but Leif couldn't make out the expression in his dark and fathomless eyes. His face was cast in angles of faint light and shadow from the half-moon, making his eyes look like two empty sockets.

Leif swung away and lowered himself over the edge of the drop, thinking with a sense of fatalism that although going to Hakon's aid might endear him to Morgana, it would do nothing but increase Sweynsson's hatred and suspicion of him . . .

As he scrabbled down the side of the cliff, Hakon's weak cries came to Leif more clearly. "Help! Thor, help me! I cannot . . ." The rest of his words were swallowed by the wind and the murmur of the water.

Leif half-slid, half-climbed the short descent and landed on his hands and knees. The jagged rocks beneath his palms and thin leather shoes reminded him just how treacherous a fall could be. A man would definitely be better off landing in the water. And not too close to the shoreline . . .

He made his way in the dimness over water-worn boulders and through pockets of standing seawater in sand-scoured holes in the scattered places where coarse sand and pebbles formed a rough beach. Relying mostly on instinct and agility, Leif realized from the distance of Hakon's voice that, fortunately, he'd landed in the water. As he squinted against the darkness, Leif saw the outline of Hakon's head in the moon-dappled water.

"Over here!" Leif called, catching sight of several burning brands bobbing in the darkness as they rounded the corner of the cliff wall to his right. Fortunately not every man had had enough drink to appreciably dull his senses.

"Odin help me . . . Here . . ."

Hakon's voice was fading. Something was wrong . . . he was either caught or injured, or both. Even though inebriated, surely the temperature of the water and the shock of falling would have sobered Hakon enough to enable him to swim back to shore if he hadn't been hurt. He wasn't that far out, just as Leif had surmised.

Leif waded into the icy waters, the first shock of the temperature shooting up his leg like the pain from a wound. He set his teeth against the cold and threw one more appraising look toward Hakon. It was then that he saw several boulders thrusting upward from the floor of the fjord around Sweynsson and looming over him like dark demons.

It was all the answer he needed. In spite of the lingering temptation to allow someone else to effect the rescue—the temptation even to *aid* the sea gods in claiming Hakon's life—Leif plunged into the fjord and swam toward the stranded man.

By the time he'd reached and extricated Hakon from the rocks, several ropes had been tossed their way. Two men even entered the fjord, but Leif ordered them back. There was no reason for all of them to drown, if that was what the gods had willed for him and Hakon.

Of course he was being unnecessarily grim about the situation. Hakon clung to him obediently as Leif tied one of the lines to his waist, more a precautionary measure than anything else. He'd always been a strong swimmer—nothing unusual among those born and raised beside the sea and its deep, narrow fingers, the fjords. As he pulled Hakon along on his back, his left hand gripping the dazed man's chin, Leif suspected that his cousin didn't realize—or probably much care in those moments—who had come to his rescue.

Leif gained the rocky beach quickly, and hands reached out to help him pull the dazed Hakon from the water. "Bear . . . huge bear spirit . . ." he was mumbling.

Leif stepped back then, to let others take over. There was a limit to what he would do for Hakon Sweynsson now, and it began with coddling him like a stray lamb.

He watched silently as one donated tunic replaced

144

Hakon's soaked clothing and several others were used to rub his cold skin vigorously and restore some warmth to his body.

"Good, *Küsku-Liinu,*" called a deep voice from above him.

Leif looked up. Little Thor stood, hands on hips, at the edge of the cliff. Holding a torch high, Gunnar and several others stood with him. "Good, *Küsku-Liinu,*" Gunnar echoed, a grin splitting his face. "Will he live to tell of his narrow escape from the bear?"

"Aye. You certainly made a swift appearance, for a disabled warrior."

Gunnar's grin widened. "I didn't drown myself in mead."

Leif nodded. Then his answering grin faded. "What of Hrafn?"

"He's fine."

"Any sign of the bear?"

"Nay. But from the size of its spoor, 'twas big. And wounded . . . which makes it more dangerous. Little Thor is ready to go after it in the morn."

"No doubt," Leif said wryly. The sight of Gunnar and Little Thor, the sound of their banter, had improved Leif's mood considerably. "Hakon insists 'twas a spirit . . ." He felt incongruous laughter bubble up in his throat.

And then he caught sight of Morgana, the beacon of her hair drawing his gaze as surely as a ray of sunlight breaking through an impenetrable bank of storm clouds. Her features were tense with worry, and he assumed it was for Hakon.

Their eyes met and held, and for a brief moment, Leif fought his angry inclination to allow her to think the worst . . . to wait until someone else told her Hakon was in one piece. Let her suffer one fraction of the pain he carried with him every moment of every waking hour. Wasn't this all her fault?

145

Nei. Not entirely.

"Hakon is well enough," he said at last, impatience and irritation edging his words. Then, dragging his gaze from hers, he called to Gunnar, "I'll meet you around the bend." He inclined his head to the east, in the direction the others had taken along the shoreline, and disappeared into the night.

Morgana watched him walk off, relieved that he was safe. Two men grabbed Hakon under the arms and lifted him to his feet. Anger and disappointment stirred within her. She'd heard part of the exchange between Hakon and Sweyn. It didn't take any deep thought to suspect why Hakon had hied himself off into the dark forest in drunken anger for some imagined offense.

He certainly wasn't making things easier for any of them. In fact, he was adding fuel to the fire; coming dangerously close to insulting Leif. If Leif had told Hakon the same thing he'd told her about accepting their marriage, then Hakon owed him at least a fair chance to prove his sincerity.

If Hakon didn't show some wisdom, disaster would surely ensue.

She hurried back to the longhouse, ignoring, for the most part, what was going on around her. Her thoughts were on Hakon and his exacerbation of the situation. If he didn't get hold of himself, he would surely drive Morgana away from him. Would certainly alienate her and sever the tenuous bonds of affection that bound her to him.

And if he kept up this unworthy behavior, he wouldn't be setting a very good example for Eirik, either . . .

" 'Tis my right!"

In the privacy of their sleeping room, Morgana looked

at Hakon as if he'd suddenly grown two heads. It was indeed his right, but he'd never *demanded* it of her. He'd never had to, for she'd always been willing to oblige him. Sometimes she was even enthusiastic, for she had her own needs.

But not since Leif Haraldsson's return.

"I'm not a thrall," she told him. "Nor do I wish to—"

"*Nei,*" he cut her off, "but 'tis the second time you've refused me since *Wave Rider* sailed into the fjord."

"Lower your voice . . . please, Hakon," she entreated. "Everyone will hear—"

"That you won't oblige your husband? That mayhap you don't want me or my issue now?" His words increased in volume rather than diminished, to Morgana's dismay.

He grabbed her upper arm, his blue eyes dark with frustration. "I won't let this happen. I won't let him come between us. You divorced him and chose to wed me. Do you remember, Morgana?"

"I'm sorry," she answered, his reminder bringing a flood of guilt surging through her. She made a real effort to push Leif Haraldsson from her heart and her mind, frantically seeking to conjure up the physical attraction Hakon had held for her these past two winters—at best, she realized now, a diluted version of what she'd enjoyed with her first love.

But gone was the gentleness, the patience he'd displayed from the beginning, as if he'd always known that he had to slowly erase memories of his rival from her mind. Had it been a facade?

"Sorry isn't enough," he growled, his lips moving over hers.

"Sit," she said firmly, twisting away from him. "You've cuts and bruises to tend, and 'tis difficult for me to think of making love with thoughts of your folly so fresh in my mind."

He glared at her as she moved away. "My folly?"

"Aye. You shamed me . . . and your father, as well." She turned back to him.

"And what of *your* behavior?"

Her eyes met his unwaveringly. " 'Twas abominable, but your actions did nothing to erase mine." She knelt before him. "Such behavior is unworthy of you."

"What did you expect me to think?" he asked through stiff lips. "With the image of the two of you in the bathhouse still branded upon my memory?"

Using a cloth periodically dipped into a soapstone bowl of warm water, Morgana began bathing the blood from the places on his legs where he'd been scraped and cut. The black and blue bruises were ugly, but not disabling. He would be stiff in the morn, but the worst damage was to his pride, now that he was sober.

And for now, at least, his mind was not on lovemaking.

"I'm certain the mead did wonders to revive that very memory." The irony in her voice was meant to reinforce the meaning of her words.

His head jerked up from contemplating her fingers soothing and cleaning his abused flesh; she felt him stiffen, but she wouldn't meet his eyes. "I cannot be expected to put so fresh and potent a memory from my thoughts—" he snapped his fingers, "—just like that!"

"If you cannot forgive me, then you have every right to divorce me for infidelity." Her words were soft, pained.

Eirik was asleep, fortunately, although Morgana feared that their tense exchange would wake him.

"Never!" His dismissal of the suggestion was like an iron shackle closing around Morgana's heart, for there was naught of love in that single word, only obstinancy and pride.

He grabbed her chin with more force than necessary, and jerked her face upward to meet his eyes. She could feel the anger buzzing through him. "I'll see him dead first." His fingers tightened upon her fragile chin.

"You're hurting me, Hakon."

He stared long and hard at her before his hand fell away. "He should be grateful."

Morgana didn't ask why, but continued bathing his legs, afraid the query would only incite his anger.

"You found him a father for his son. He knew I always loved you . . . what did he expect to find when he returned home after so long? When everyone assumed him and his crew dead?"

Morgana's cheeks warmed. "But he doesn't deserve *this!*"

He stood suddenly, upsetting the bowl and its blood-tinged water and startling Morgana. "By the gods, Morgana, *I'm* the one hurting . . . not him!" he shouted. "I could have died in the fjord, and all in the name of preventing you from succumbing to Leif Haraldsson's . . . charms! If 'tis what you want, then *you* divorce *me!* Declare before the entire settlement that I've treated you badly . . . preferred a concubine . . . neglected your son . . ."

"*Our* son."

He began moving about the small room, with only a slight limp hindering him. "How magnanimous of you," he muttered, coming to stand beside the tiny bed where Eirik slept, "now that his natural father is alive and well and here."

Her patience wearing thin, Morgana collected the bowl and cloth and stood. She watched him as he stood over Eirik. "I didn't wait to see if I would become a widow. I—"

"Out of anger!" He spun about to face her, bitterness twisting his features. "And I, like a fool, jumped at the chance to have you for my own. The unattainable was suddenly attainable, and I eagerly helped you wreak your vengeance on Leif Haraldsson."

Morgana's gaze went to the sleeping child, then to Hakon. "Mayhap 'tis something you should think about,

149

Hakon," she said in a low voice. "Did you wed me out of love . . . or your own need for vengeance?"

Before he could reply, she turned from him and left the room.

Chapter Ten

Aside from Morgana and Gunnar, Leif told no one about Hrafn's wound. He knew neither would mention it to anyone else unless he did first, and he thought it wiser to keep the perpetrator wondering.

"I need time to sit back and observe . . . to plan, although extra vigilance is called for in light of what I discovered in the stable," Leif had told Gunnar that night.

Gunnar had agreed. "This new quest to discover the culprits could be a boon."

Leif had thrown him a frowning but quizzical look.

" 'Twill help you keep a cool head where Morgana is concerned."

Leif had laughed softly and without humor. "I wonder if that will be so now that Hakon's pride has taken a drubbing. I should have let him drown."

"That wouldn't have been wise. Help was already nearby when you jumped into the fjord. It would have looked mean-spirited if you hadn't."

"Not to anyone who understands the situation . . . who sees my side of things."

"Now you appear magnanimous," Gunnar continued. "And although you might not have endeared yourself to Hakon, you've probably gained yourself some support, if not among those who are loyal to Sweyn, then certainly

151

among those who had mixed feelings and were secretly sitting on the fence."

Leif opened his mouth to reply, but Gunnar held up his hand. "You can never have too many loyal friends, especially in times such as these, with ruthless men like Harald Fairhair seeking to bring Norvegia under their rule . . ."

And, in the end, Leif knew Gunnar was right. Yet the temptation to think about what Hakon Sweynsson's death would mean was almost too hard to resist . . .

Leif had awakened several times that night and gone to the stable to make certain that Hrafn was undisturbed. In fact, he'd almost spent the night in the stable, fearing for the stallion's life, then decided that it was unlikely the culprit would out and out kill the stallion. The man, whoever he was, obviously wanted Leif dead. Killing Hrafn would avail the miscreant nothing to that end, but would certainly arouse anger and suspicion in many. In fact, it could well lead to an injury to Morgana, for she'd cared for and exercised the horse since Leif had gone a-viking.

That thought, as much as the suspicious circumstances of his father's death, helped stoke the embers of outrage, and not for the first time Leif fought frustration and fury as common sense told him he had to be patient and let his would-be nemesis reveal himself.

Thor's hammer, but he'd returned to a nest of vipers! Some more insidious than others, but vipers all the same.

Some of the men gathered early the next morn to go after the bear. It was rare for bears to come so close to a settlement, unless searching for a lost cub, or wounded and crazed with pain. In the latter case, they were extremely dangerous.

Leif quickly decided to take Little Thor with him. Bear was native to the Skraeling's land, as he'd revealed in one of their many talks during the long moons on the island as each strove to learn about the other.

Something in Gunnar's eyes prompted Leif to include

him as well, in spite of his handicap. Gunnar was still a credible hunter, although some might consider his presence a liability. Leif wasn't necessarily one of those, and couldn't bring himself to further humiliate his friend by leaving him out of the hunting party.

Hadn't he left him behind when *Wave Rider* had left Oslof for its ill-fated voyage?

Of course, Hakon included himself in the hunt. As did Sweyn. And Horik Bluetooth.

Ottar and Ragnar volunteered, as well, and Leif was glad to have more good men at his back. After what had befallen Harald, Leif decided he could be placing himself in graver danger from certain members of the hunting party than from the bear itself.

With a pack of elkhounds, and Freki bounding alongside Leif, they set off. Leif caught sight of Morgana watching them—him, specifically, rather than Hakon. It gave his spirits a lift, that look, yet he didn't hold her gaze. She stood before the longhouse in the pale light of dawn, her hand clutching Eirik's. She looked concerned, he thought, and he longed to reassure her.

But it was not his place now.

Since Leif had been the hero by effecting Hakon's rescue the night before, he was accorded the honor of leading the way, as was customary in Oslof . . . or had been while Harald Estrithsson had been jarl. It was soon apparent, as they left the settlement and moved onto the pine, spruce and oak-shrouded mountainside, that Hakon thought differently.

He caught up with Leif, and for a brief stretch, rode directly beside him on the narrow mountain trail. "This one is mine," he told Leif, his eyes full of challenge.

Leif threw him a glance, then looked away, lest Hakon see the outright hostility that he had difficulty suppressing. Not a word of gratitude. Just, *This one is mine.*

"That may be," Leif said aloud. "But mayhap the bear

thinks the same of you, Sweynsson. After all, he sent you fleeing into the fjord." He heard Hakon's sharp intake of breath. "Or was it unintentional? A loss of balance? A misstep?" He met Hakon's eyes then. "Or the drink? And now you must salve your trampled pride by taking the lead."

He reined Hrafn aside then, without waiting for a response, and fell in behind Hakon. Rather than dwell upon the latter's reaction, Leif breathed in the clean, spicy scent of evergreens, allowing his eyelids to drift closed for a moment as he inhaled deeply of the fresh, pungent smells around him, allowing them to cleanse his mind of sarcasm and anger. It was wise to be prepared for the worst in the chase and battle, but an alert mind also had to be free of unnecessary and distracting emotion.

A low murmur of voices came to him now and then, but otherwise, only the sounds of the forest and the muted clop of the horses disturbed the peaceful silence.

Gunnar, who was immediately behind Leif, leaned forward on his mount and said in a low voice, "I know not what you said, but by the set of his shoulders I would guess he's not pleased."

Leif shrugged and said over his shoulder, "Naught I do seems to please him."

A whispered word from his other side snagged Leif's attention as Gunnar fell back into line. It was Little Thor. *"Mokwaw,"* came the whisper again, as soft as a summer breeze. It was the red man's word for bear.

Leif frowned and canted his head to the left.

Little Thor pulled off to the side.

The five hounds were still ahead of Hakon, obviously on the trail of either the bear in the area, or elk; the hounds could catch an elk's scent from more than two miles away. But Freki had split off to the left just as Little Thor's first softly-spoken word reached Leif. With a low whine, the huge wolfhound silently melted into the dense forest, and

Leif, too, reined in. He motioned the others to continue on after Hakon.

" 'Tis unwise to follow yon hound," Ottar murmured as he passed Leif. "He relies on sight and speed . . . not scent. And he's spoiled for hunting."

Leif nodded in acknowledgment, unwilling to reveal his confidence in Little Thor's intuition. "Keep your ears open, my friend. If you hear the roar of an angry bear, we may need help. Otherwise, we'll catch up."

"Maybe two." Little Thor held up two fingers. "Two bear. One here . . ."—he pointed in the direction Freki had gone—". . . one there." He pointed ahead.

Ottar looked doubtful, but he nodded and followed the others, with Ragnar bringing up the rear.

Leif and Little Thor tied their horses and entered the primeval forest. Leif let the Skraeling lead the way as he sought to adjust his vision to the deeper gloom off the trail. Little Thor seemed to have no problem as he moved forward.

Freki's bark pierced the stillness. Then a screechlike roar sounded. Little Thor glanced back at Leif, his face split in a grin.

"It won't be so amusing if 'tis what I think it is and its mother is the injured one," Leif muttered under his breath. Just as he finished speaking, they emerged into a small area of trampled growth. Freki stood frozen, his coarse gray hairs standing in a ridge of hostility along his neck and upper back.

Less than a stone's throw away stood a bear cub. Judging from its size, it was almost fully grown, last winter's litter. Old enough to take off on its own, yet evidently still preferring to stay close to the sow.

It began growling in earnest as Leif and Little Thor came into view, then swung away toward the trees.

"Take dog . . . go from here," Little Thor said.

"It won't be soon enough for me," Leif answered.

"Freki!" he commanded softly but sternly. "Here." He pointed to the ground at his feet emphatically. "Here, boy. We don't want the cub."

The dog looked back at Leif, then at the young bear as it lunged away, as if in indecision.

"Freki, here!" he repeated, feeling suddenly uneasy. Where was the sow?

Loki, the leader of the pack, swerved off the path to the left. His short, sharp bark jarred Hakon out of his angry thoughts. Elkhounds were quiet hunters, stalking and holding the quarry at bay rather than flushing it with their barking. Loki's signal reminded Hakon that he was hunting a wounded and, therefore, dangerous animal. This was no place for any consideration save the hunt, and he knew it.

Hakon reined in his mount and glanced back just as the others caught up. He gave the signal to follow the dogs, then slid from his horse and plunged into the trees, still seething in spite of his self-admonition.

Gunnar awkwardly dismounted and followed, a frown on his face, the others in his wake.

"Why doesn't he wait," said Ottar in a low voice. " 'Tis foolish to go ahead alone." Sweyn, Ragnar and Horik were right behind him.

"Hurry," Sweyn said, "although Hakon can take care of himself . . ."

Several looks were exchanged, but nothing was said as they followed in Hakon's wake.

"Blood. Old . . . bad blood."

With Little Thor's whispered words echoing through his mind, Leif followed him with caution. The hair on the back of his neck prickled, and his lightweight tunic suddenly felt like a damp second skin. By the gods, how did the Skraeling manage to move so soundlessly? It was uncanny.

A branch slapped him in the face, and he winced, startled. *Stay alert*, he thought. Keep your mind on what you're doing, not on Little Thor. He didn't question the red man's leading him through the thick of the forest instead of back to the trail. He assumed they were going to intercept the others, and hopefully they would all be reunited before confronting the wounded animal.

Unease continued to shadow him, for they were not in the best of positions, having placed themselves between the cub and the sow, if the dogs were on the right scent. The bear's noise hadn't helped either.

Little Thor halted and turned to Leif. He put a finger against his lips and pointed ahead with his bow. Leif nodded. They moved forward again.

Suddenly, the forest was filled with the blood-chilling bellow of what couldn't be mistaken for anything but an enraged brown bear.

The dogs had the sow cornered. Their compact bodies moved in tight circles and quick, darting movements to avoid tooth and claw as she lunged and retreated and lunged again in a desperate, furious rhythm, obviously trying to swipe them aside.

The claws of one great paw connected with the side of Aibe's head, batting it so hard his neck snapped. With a sharp yelp, the dog collapsed in a heap, his open eyes vacant, his head twisted unnaturally.

Hakon nocked an arrow and took steady aim at the bear's heart, his own rapping against his ribs. He would take this bear. It was his, not Leif Haraldsson's, and he was as good a shot as any Skraeling, no matter what had happened in the contest the night before.

He pulled steadily on the bowstring as the sow momentarily rose on her hind legs. It was as if she were striking a victory stance, proclaiming and briefly savoring her triumph over the dead hound. Hakon ignored the stench of old blood and festering flesh, of fear and musky animal, and prepared to release the arrow.

But before it left the bow, a spear whined through the air and pierced the sow's shoulder. She swung sharply aside. Hakon cut his gaze to the owner of the spear. Gunnar the Lame.

Hakon watched another arrow strike the bear as she advanced upon Gunnar. It struck the sow high in the chest, but not hard enough to down her.

With a perverse satisfaction. Hakon allowed his bow to dip toward the ground as he watched Gunnar. Gunnar . . . Leif Haraldsson's best friend. His childhood friend; second only to Leif in all things until his accident.

With remarkable outward calm, Gunnar fitted an arrow to his own bow in the absence of his spear, but the enraged sow seemed propelled by demons. By the time Gunnar took aim, it was too late.

Ragnar's spear whizzed through the air, and caught the sow in the abdomen, but she was already upon Gunnar. The bear bellowed in pain; someone shouted; and, finally, Hakon raised his bow once more . . .

They were suddenly running, heedless of the noise they made. It didn't matter now. All that mattered was that they arrive in time to lend a hand.

Leif stopped dead in his tracks, shoulder to shoulder with Little Thor, at what greeted his eyes. He took in the scene in distinct, if disjointed, spurts: Hakon's bow lowering. . . . The bear charging Gunnar. . . . Ragnar's spear striking the sow, but failing to slow her momentum. . . . A subtle, malicious movement of Hakon's lips as he finally raised his bow again in seeming slow-motion. . . . And

Gunnar going down beneath the raging animal to the horrified shouts of the others . . .

Leif went mad at this last image, leaping toward the bear as it attacked Gunnar. Ducking his head and preparing for the worst, Leif drove his spear through the animal's ribs so savagely, it came out the other side. Blood and bits of bone spewed over the forest floor. Other arrows and spears penetrated the animal's thick coat and hide, but Leif's blow was the one that caused the sow finally to collapse.

Ragnar and Sweyn approached Gunnar, Sweyn throwing the bear a cautious glance, as if he half-expected the behemoth to rise up again—to tower over them and wreak her vengeance. Horik and Ottar then moved in and strained to lift the heavy carcass clear. Hakon joined their efforts.

"Gunnar," Leif whispered, dropping to his knees beside his friend's head and shoulders. Blood spurted from a gaping hole in his neck, spreading in an ever-widening stain over his chest. Leif felt the heaviness of defeat invade his breast. Little Thor motioned for him to help take the wounded man under the arms, and they carefully pulled Gunnar from beneath the sow's great body. No hesitation here, for Leif knew, with a hunter's instinct, that his blow had stopped its beating heart.

Little Thor put his ear to Gunnar's chest, then pulled it away, blood smeared over his ear and cheek, glistening in his dark hair. His eyes met Leif's, a profound sadness entering his own. He shook his head.

Leif looked down at Gunnar, at his blood-soaked neck and tunic, his gore-matted blond hair and beard. His eyes clung to Leif's as they began to glaze over. He moved his mouth, his eyelids trembled, but he made no sound. And as Leif watched, feeling utterly helpless, Gunnar's gaze became unfocused. The spurting jet of lifeblood ebbed . . . until his eyes fixed sightlessly upon the canopy of trees above him and death bore his spirit away.

For a long moment after Gunnar died in his arms, Leif was numb to his surroundings. Then voices rang through his mind with vivid stridency: *What will you tell Ingrid? That 'twas your fault because you asked him to join the hunt? That you were to blame because you allowed yourself to be sidetracked by Little Thor?*

Don't blame the red man. 'Tis your doing. Did you not take on the task of being Gunnar's keeper? From the moment you left him home three winters ago?

Nay! Hakon killed him as surely as if he'd aimed his arrow at Gunnar's heart.

The memory, in blistering detail, returned to him: Hakon standing with bow lowered, satisfaction smeared across his handsome face briefly before he raised his bow and finally loosed his arrow. Allowing just enough time for the sow to reach Gunnar . . .

On the return journey to the settlement, Leif had plenty of time for thought. He'd insisted on bearing Gunnar's body home on Hrafn, leaving Gunnar's horse Sleipnir to bear the sow's carcass. With every movement, the touch of his friend's flaccid and lifeless body served as a grim reminder that Gunnar would never again grace Leif's existence.

He tried to think about Morgana and Eirik, but they, too, were lost to him. As was his father. And now his best friend . . . because of him. Anguish invaded his numbed senses, bringing the piercing pain of reality. Of a bleak, empty future.

And of Ingrid's face. Little Harald's. Of Ingrid's body quickening with Gunnar's next child.

The return to Oslof took an eternity. An eternity in

160

which all the emotions Leif had tried to hold in check beat at his heart and mind like battering rams.

Why couldn't the gods have taken him instead of Gunnar?

And you *made the decision to include him in what you knew would be a dangerous hunt,* reminded his conscience.

He ignored the other voice. The voice that told him Gunnar would have been insulted if Leif hadn't asked him to join them . . . that, in fact, Gunnar needed no invitation to join the chase.

By the time they emerged from the forest, Leif's mood was black and volatile.

At first sight of the returning party, those who weren't in the fields came running. The fact that Gunnar's body was draped across Hrafn's neck was noted almost immediately, for the horn swiftly sounded a mournful call to those who were planting or going about other business.

Morgana reached the group just as Ingrid was leaving the longhouse. "Go to Ingrid," Leif told her in a bleak, harsh voice.

Understanding dawned in her eyes as they moved to Gunnar's body.

"Naught can be done for him now. But Ingrid will need you."

If he'd given her a shove, Morgana couldn't have moved more quickly. She spun and ran toward Ingrid. Leif watched grimly as he slowly rode toward them, painfully aware, with Hrafn's every step, of the body before him. His right hand holding Gunnar in place brought home the fact that his friend was still close by, yet an eternity away.

The deathly silence around them was broken briefly by a cry of denial from Ingrid, but only that. Braced by Morgana's arm around her shoulders, Gunnar's widow stumbled toward Hrafn and his grisly burden, shaking her head, her expression dazed, disbelieving.

Harald emerged from the longhouse behind her at a

161

run, with Eirik close behind. Others from the fields, alerted by the horn, were drawn to the hunting party like magnets, varying degrees of dread and sorrow etched across their faces. The hounds were joined by the village dogs, and began to sniff around the dead bear, causing the horse beneath it to prance and toss his head.

Suddenly, pandemonium ensued.

Hands reached to ease Gunnar's body from Hrafn.

Individual voices rose above the din . . .

"What happened?"

" 'Tis Gunnar the Lame! By Mjolnir, Gunnar . . ."

"They got the bear . . . but what of Gunnar? And Haraldsson . . . ?"

"So much blood . . ."

"Dead."

Dead . . . dead . . . dead . . .

Someone keened loudly, and another took up his cry. Women crowded around Ingrid, offering comfort, until she came to her husband's still and bloodied form lying upon the earth. Someone had laid a dun-colored tunic beneath him. For a moment, her eyes met Leif's. Then she was kneeling beside Gunnar.

Morgana's gaze searched for some sign of injury to Leif, even before she thought to look at Hakon. She read only a dull anguish in his eyes, and instantly she guessed that he blamed himself for Gunnar's death.

Leif pulled his gaze away and dismounted; he went to one knee across from Ingrid. "He died like a warrior, if 'tis any comfort to you," he told her softly. "With weapon in hand, although 'twas too late to save himself . . ."

Through the tumult of his feelings, he heard Morgana soothe little Harald, then Eirik. He felt removed, distanced from the entire scene suddenly. Gunnar was dead. So, it seemed, was his life here.

Morgana was there then, crouching beside Ingrid to hold her friend in her grief. Ingrid reached out to smooth

Gunnar's fair hair from his pale forehead, then gently closed his lids over the lifeless hazel eyes. "He died in your arms," she murmured, glancing at the blood covering Leif. "Then he was content in his last moments, for he missed you these past few winters more than he could ever have said."

Pain twisted within Leif's breast.

"I spared him that danger . . . for *this*." The words fell woodenly from his lips, bitterness tainting the tone of his voice, as he stared at Gunnar's peaceful face.

"He was a man grown," Ingrid said, her tear-filled eyes meeting his. "He made his own decisions."

Morgana reached across Gunnar to touch Leif's arm. "You're not to blame, Leif. Do you hear Ingrid? You're not responsible."

Hakon's shadow fell over Morgana as he emerged from the crowd to stand over the three of them. The unexpected and undiluted malice in his expression left no doubt in her mind that she'd made a grave mistake. She should have gone to him first—made some show of concern.

By the Allfather, what had she been thinking about?

Leif. Of course. First and always, Leif.

"Move aside." It was Sweyn speaking. "Let me through."

But it was too late. "Of course he's to blame, *wife*." The words spilled from Hakon like poison bursting from a putrifying wound. "If he hadn't gone off on a wild-goose chase with your foolish Freki and his *Skraeling* friend, he could have saved Gunnar."

A collective murmur went up. Morgana's startled gaze cut to Hakon. And Leif . . . Leif raised his eyes to Hakon's face, then slowly straightened. "Believe what you will, but I think, rather, the fault lies with you."

"Now just what are you saying?" Sweyn demanded.

Leif spun toward the jarl. "Rather, what is *he* saying,

Uncle? If you, too, are about to accuse me in Gunnar's death, then 'tis only to protect your son."

"I stand by Hakon!" Sweyn said angrily, drawing himself to his full height like a straight and proud—if ancient—oak. "You dare to accuse him of having something to do with Gunnar's death before all of Oslof when you weren't even there?" His braided beard quivered.

"I was there. According to Hakon—unless you're calling him a liar—not only was I there, but I was the one responsible for Gunnar's death. Now who are they—" he inclined his head toward the stunned gathering, "—supposed to believe?"

Sweyn hesitated, then threw a brief, fulminating look at Hakon.

"You were barely there!" Hakon accused Leif. "Your belated burst from the trees was not only too late to save Gunnar, but too ill-timed to allow you to accurately accuse *anyone* of foul play."

"And I saw it all," Horik Bluetooth added with irritating belligerence. "Ragnar's spear caught the sow in the belly, then Hakon's arrow struck her. There is no room to accuse Hakon of aught but trying to save Gunnar's life."

"A hero's burial!" someone shouted, interrupting the angry debate. It was Olaf Herjolfsson.

Morgana couldn't have thought of a better way to redirect attention and diffuse tempers. "Aye," she agreed as she stood. She looked at Sweyn for affirmation. "We should be making burial arrangements, not quarreling."

Tyra spoke then, from beside a grave-faced, white-maned Orm. "My daughter's right. Why do you concern yourselves with such things when one of your own awaits entry into Valhalla?"

Morgana leaned over to take Ingrid's elbow. "Come," she murmured into her friend's ear. "Let the men bear him to the hall. We—"

"A hero's burial?" Hakon asked. He snorted derisively.

"Since when is a cripple a hero?" Horik added. "He was only a liability to everyone . . . even himself."

Morgana suddenly had the sinking feeling that she had, once again, exercised poor judgment. She should have gone to Hakon and soothed his pride, rather than speaking to Sweyn of burial . . . or concerning herself first with Ingrid, in spite of the fact that she and Ingrid were close.

The look in his eyes as she glanced up at him made her regret her lack of foresight. She tried to catch his gaze with hers, but it was not to be. He ignored her, looking directly at Leif now.

"I'll gladly give Gunnar *Wave Rider* to carry his spirit to Valhalla." Leif's voice was soft, laced with menace as his eyes met Hakon's in open challenge.

Obviously bolstered by Horik's caustic comment, Hakon snatched up the gauntlet. His tone of dismissal would have been insult enough had he not even uttered a word. "No hero's burial for Gunnar the Lame."

Morgana felt the world dim suddenly before her eyes. This couldn't be happening . . .

She released Ingrid's arm, collected her scattering wits, and straightened like a plucked bowstring. "Hakon . . ." she began, holding out a hand beseechingly.

" 'Twas Haraldsson who foolishly invited him along," Hakon continued recklessly over Morgana's half-voiced protest, ignoring her gesture.

Something within Leif sundered. The resentment and fury that had been building and simmering just below the surface boiled over with all the destructive potential of raging lava—snuffing out the voice of reason, tossing his good intentions to the wind and, finally, breaking the fragile bond of control.

Utterly incensed, he emitted a cry of outrage and sprang at Hakon.

Chapter Eleven

The burst of pent-up emotion gave Leif the impetus to literally fly at Hakon Sweynsson. Like an arrow toward its target, he slammed into his adversary, knocking them both to the ground.

For the first few moments, others remained rooted in astonishment. Many, no doubt, were keenly aware of the underlying festering issues that produced such murderous intent—thus their initial hesitation before trying to interfere. Then, however, several moved to pull the two men apart.

At first, neither heeded the shouts for restraint, nor the hands reaching toward them. Leif Haraldsson and Hakon Sweynsson were in their own world, bonded inseparably by fierce antagonism.

Morgana looked to Sweyn for help, but Horik Bluetooth was holding the jarl's arm, insisting, "Let them go. 'Twill help ease the bad feeling between them." Then he put his lips to Sweyn's ear and added something for the jarl alone.

Sweyn nodded, though doubt still lingered on his craggy countenance. "Leave them!" he bellowed. " 'Tis a storm that's been abrewing since *Wave Rider* returned."

"*Nei!*" Morgana cried as she saw the men who would have separated them pull back in the wake of the jarl's command. "Stop them!" No good could come from this fight . . . no solution to the problem.

Unless one of them was killed.

Little Thor and Ottar approached, with Olaf close behind.

"Nei!" Sweyn shouted, his hand on the dagger at his waist as he stared through slitted eyes at Little Thor. "As long as the fight stays fair, let them go!" He cast a glance at Horik, as if for support.

Why had she appealed to Sweyn to stop the fight? Morgana wondered as she watched the two men grapple. Not only would the jarl be unwilling for Hakon to look the coward, but also there was Horik Bluetooth encouraging the jarl in that sly, secretive way of his that Morgana had come to detest . . .

Leif had Hakon pinned beneath him, his hands around the latter's throat. He watched with perverse satisfaction as Hakon gasped for air, his face beneath his beard turning bluish.

"I saw your hesitation," Leif panted in a low, venom-laced voice. "You may have fooled the others . . . but not me." He brought his face closer to Hakon's, increasing the pressure on the latter's windpipe. "Do you hear me, Sweynsson?" he hissed. He was oblivious to the noise around him, concentrating only on his adversary. If someone wanted to brain him from behind as he choked the life out of Hakon, then so be it. It would be worth losing his miserable life just to see Hakon's snuffed out.

He suspected, however, that he had enough friends yet to prevent such a craven act.

A metal object caught the gleam of the sun as it skimmed the ground from the crowd toward Hakon's outstretched hand, the elbow of which was pinned beneath Leif's knee. Both men saw it, but Hakon was the first to make a frantic bid for it with his splayed fingers . . . a spastic jerk that allowed him to capture it.

The weapon, however, was useless with his right arm still beneath Leif's knee.

Leif barely had time to wonder what snake in the grass had tossed it from among the onlookers as Hakon, his eyes now bulging, made a desperate move to dislodge him with one leg. He succeeded in knocking Leif backward, but not unseating him completely.

The dagger came up as Leif's knee slid from Hakon's arm. It caught the sun with a flash, and Leif heard a woman—Morgana?—scream. Too late. As he struggled to reestablish his position, he felt the knife slice him across the shoulder blade. Heat zigzagged across his back, but the wound was shallow, the pain muted by the intensity of his concentration . . . his drive to regain a choke hold on Hakon.

Out of the corner of his eye, he saw the blade come at him again, simultaneously felt Hakon's body buck beneath him. This time he had the presence of mind to realize the movement had more force behind it. This time it could deal a lethal blow.

Leif rolled away, dodging the dagger and jumping to his feet.

"Enough!" someone cried.

"*Nei!*" Sweyn answered over another call for a halt as Hakon staggered to his feet.

"*Nei,*" Leif mimicked in a rasping voice. "As long as the fight stays *fair*, eh, Uncle?" He sucked in a shallow breath between his teeth before anyone could answer. "But what you really want is for us to continue now that Hakon has the advantage of a weapon. And won't that accomplish your life's wish? First my father's death, now mine?"

Exclamations sounded. Murmurs rippled through the gathering, peaking and then dying away. Taking advantage of the crowd's full attention, Leif demanded, "What did Fairhair promise you in return for ridding Oslof of those who won't kiss his backside?"

In the next moment, Horik made a low, gutteral sound deep in his throat. Several women began herding their children away. Sweyn's face turned ashen, then livid, his hands clenching at his side.

But Hakon shrieked a battle cry, hurling himself at Leif. Leif attempted to absorb the attack, catching Hakon in his arms, staggering backward with the momentum in a macabre dance. He didn't go down, but neither could he avoid the dagger blade as it buried itself in his right shoulder.

This pain was searing; and Leif knew with a warrior's instinct that this time, if he didn't incapacitate or kill Hakon, he stood a good chance of being killed himself.

" 'Tisn't fair . . ." Leif heard a man shout. It was a dim sound in the chaos of his thoughts, but it reminded him of just how underhanded someone had been in providing Hakon with a weapon. And no one, evidently, was willing to stop him and take it away . . .

Until Little Thor hurled himself at both men, his banshee cry signaling his intent. Hot on his heels was Horik Bluetooth, who tackled the Skraeling behind the knees.

The combined force renewed Leif's trip backward. He slammed to the ground with Hakon on top of him, his teeth snapping together, shoulder throbbing. The sight of Hakon looming over him, gnashing his teeth with determination, his eyes slitted with exertion and hatred, caused a renewed torrent of rage to flood through Leif.

For all the wrongs he'd been done . . . his father had been done . . . Gunnar had been done, Leif Haraldsson sought one thing only in those fleeting moments: vengeance.

Gritting his teeth against the pain in his shoulder, he kneed Hakon in the groin with a belated burst of energy, stunning him momentarily. With his focus on the ultimate revenge, Leif rolled over before Hakon could recover. He felt hands grapple to pull him off . . . and knew he had to do what must be done quickly.

He couldn't live in Oslof with Hakon Sweynsson.

He grabbed the downed Hakon by the throat, as he'd done earlier, but now with the deadly intent of a man needing to kill at any cost. Even if it meant losing his own life.

With one, vicious jerk, he knocked Hakon's head against the ground, intending to stun him and use his own knife, which had dropped to the ground, against him.

The gods evidently wished it otherwise.

Hakon's head cracked against a fist-sized stone half hidden beneath a light dusting of earth. Leif heard his skull split. He stilled, his fingers yet wrapped around Hakon's throat. A deep, contrary satisfaction, rising from his shadowed, primeval side, moved through him as Hakon went limp beneath him, sating every dark desire he'd entertained since returning to Oslof.

He knew Hakon was dead. Now, undoubtedly, he would be put to death as well. But, in those first triumphant moments afterward, he didn't care.

Leif was roughly dragged from Hakon's body as Sweyn sank to his knees beside his son. "Hakon?" the jarl asked softly, and put one palm to Hakon's cheek to cant the dead man's head toward him.

Morgana came forward then, and as she knelt beside Sweyn, for the second time that day the word "dead" echoed softly through the crowd, then faded.

Ottar moved to lift Sweyn from his knees. "Come away, Sweyn. He is beyond our help now."

"Aye," added Horik. "And his murderer still lives!"

Sweyn raised dull eyes to Leif. As they met those of his son's killer, they became animated with hatred. *"Já.* Murderer is what you are, son of my brother. Death is too good for you now."

"A slow and painful death," Horik growled.

Morgana, her eyes haunted, clutched at Sweyn's leg. "Nay, Sweyn. I beg of you . . . don't kill him. 'Twill not bring back Hakon."

Ragnar, the red-haired giant, stepped forward and spoke. "The fight wasn't fair, Sweyn. You cannot sentence Leif to death!"

"Nei!" echoed Olaf and Egil, and Leif knew he still had the support of those with whom he'd shared deprivation and a brush with death. There were some bonds that could withstand even Fairhair's plotting.

Others took up the refrain.

"Let us bury our dead," old Orm said.

"Aye. Before there is any more bloodshed!" Tyra said.

"Finish the matter at hand!" Horik shouted. "Haraldsson must be put to death."

But there was no answering acknowledgment.

Leif turned on his heel and went to help lift Gunnar, but the wound in his shoulder prevented him. Little Thor and Ottar came to his aid, and they began to carry Gunnar to his longhouse. Tostig and Orm went to lift Hakon.

"Wait!" Sweyn cried, his eyes red-rimmed. It wasn't so much a powerful command as a desperate one. "We'll not wait a moment longer to mete out a murderer's punishment." He pointed a trembling finger at Leif and pronounced, "You are outlawed forever from Norvegia. Banished from your home, your loved ones, until your black heart ceases to beat."

Leif turned slowly to face Sweyn. He said nothing at first, for the sentence was just, even if the fight hadn't been. He'd expected death, not banishment.

"You may take your horse, and naught else. Do you hear, Leif Haraldsson? Naught else!"

"And what of my judgment before my peers?"

"You forfeited that when you did murder before all of Oslof."

"And what if Hakon had killed me? An armed man killing a man with no weapon isn't a fair contest."

Sweyn moved closer to Leif and planted a finger forcefully against his blood-soaked tunic, heedless of the bleeding wound. "You are *banished*, Haraldsson," he said through set teeth. "Take your horse and your Skraeling and begone! *Do—you—hear—me?*"

"But he cannot leave here wounded!" Morgana objected. "He'll die."

The look Sweyn turned on her left no doubt in her mind that that was exactly what he wanted. "He'll die if I find him anywhere near Oslof by morn. Take what concessions I grant in the name of my dead son and be satisfied."

He turned away and with stiff steps followed the men bearing Hakon's body to the hall.

"Ingrid bade me offer you Gunnar's horse for Little Thor."

Morgana stood before Hrafn's stall where Leif was struggling to saddle the stallion. He looked over at her. Her face was somber, her manner subdued. Of course, he thought as he let the saddle slip to his feet. She's still dazed. She saw her husband die before her eyes.

"Sleipnir?" Leif pushed aside his thoughts and shook his head. "That is too great a gift." His mouth twisted. "Especially after I failed Gunnar."

Morgana's lips compressed, her eyes narrowing a fraction. "Ingrid sees this as I do . . . as many others do. You couldn't have helped Gunnar. Your crime was deliberately killing Hakon. Now what do you have?"

Her words were bitter, recriminatory.

Leif moved from the stall to stand before her. She was alarmed by the pallor of his face, but the loss of blood hadn't seemed to take away his will to argue with her. "What do I have, Morgana? More than you do! I have my

172

self-respect, for I haven't been living a lie just to avoid admitting I'd made a terrible mistake."

" 'Twas no lie. I needed a husband . . . a father for Eirik. He was a good husband until . . ." Her words died away.

"Until what? Until I returned?"

She looked down. "Aye."

"Then forgive me."

She looked up at him sharply. "For killing Hakon, or for returning?"

"For returning, of course."

He didn't like the glib words that were tumbling from his lips, but he couldn't seem to stop them. Couldn't she see, even now, that Hakon had only wed her because she'd been Leif's wife? That Hakon had not been above deceit to win a wife . . . or cheating to prevail in a fight to the death? The man had no sense of fair play, and he was certainly a stranger to honor.

And he'd never loved her. Not the way Leif had; not the way she deserved to be loved. Hakon loved himself first. He always had. Why couldn't she have seen that? Why couldn't she admit it now?

He wanted to shake some sense into her. Then he wanted to make love to her. More than anything else at that moment. . . . He swayed slightly, gritted his teeth when he realized it, and made a concerted effort to steady himself.

She moved toward him. "You've lost a lot of blood. Let me tend—"

"*Nei.* Little Thor will do it." He knew that if she touched him, what little self-control he still maintained would vanish.

He tried to redirect the bent of his thoughts. "Would you rather Hakon had killed me, then?" he asked her softly. "Would that have restored your life to what it had been? To the way you preferred?"

She stared at him for long moments, but she couldn't, in

173

all honesty, tell him that, indeed, was what she would have wanted.

"You act as if everything were my fault, Leif Haraldsson, but you broke your promise to me. It may sound a paltry excuse in light of everything that's happened, but that promise meant the world to me. Now, 'tis too late."

"And you never gave me the benefit of the doubt, did you?"

She ignored his oft-repeated counter charge and turned away, fighting myriad emotions colliding within her. Much of her bitterness, she acknowledged, wasn't due to Hakon's death but, rather, because Leif had been banished. Any chance for them to put their lives back together as a family with Eirik was gone.

And that, if she were absolutely truthful with herself, was the most telling loss. Yet, there was nothing to be done about it now.

A dull and empty existence, save for the joy of having Eirik, suddenly stretched before her like a yawning chasm with no bottom.

Little Thor entered the stable just then, with strips of clean linen and a soapstone bowl of steaming water. He hesitated just inside the doorway when he saw Morgana.

She motioned to him to continue what he was doing. "Attend his injury," she said, "before he bleeds to death."

Leif watched her walk away, something deep within him shriveling. "You'll have to saddle both horses, friend," he said, his eyes lingering on the doorway after she'd disappeared from sight. "Ingrid has given you Gunnar's horse to ride . . . she said 'twas what he would have wanted." His gaze fell to his own shoulder and limp arm. "I can't saddle one mount, let alone two."

He didn't see the Skraeling's slight hesitation, the arrested look that rose in his eyes, at the mention of Ingrid's name. "In-grid," he whispered, as if uttering something sacred. Then, seeming to recover himself, he pushed Leif

174

gently but firmly onto a bale of hay. "Where will we go?"

Leif shrugged and winced. "Back, mayhap, to your land?"

"Cross Great Water. Need ship, not horse."

Leif set his teeth as the red man slit open his tunic and peeled it away from his shoulder. "Then you'd be willing to return?"

Little Thor shook his head. "Nothing there for me. I go . . . you."

"*With* you," Leif corrected. "If you are to go with me— wherever that might be—you need to speak proper Norse. Learn to be a Norseman."

Little Thor began to cleanse the jagged hole in Leif's shoulder with a piece of cloth dipped in the hot water. "Am Little Thor, *Küsku-Liinu*, not Norseman. Always Little Thor."

Leif nodded, his mood pensive. "*Já*. A man cannot change who he is, no matter how he might wish it. He can change his ways, his beliefs, but not his identity."

Little Thor grunted. "Need rest, not ride," he said, pulling Leif's thoughts back to the immediate situation, more specifically his shoulder wound, and the inadvisability of traveling with such an injury.

"I need mead," Leif muttered. He grimaced as he noticed the ache spreading down his entire right side. "For pain."

"Good wound."

Leif bit down on his lower lip and threw the Skraeling a look askance. "There's no such thing."

Little Thor nodded. "Clean. Through body . . . shoulder. Good wound."

"Aye," Leif answered, feeling more and more light-headed. He was going to faint. By the gods, he was going to faint and Little Thor would have to remove him from Oslof draped like a sack of seed corn over Hrafn's back.

"Get mead," he mumbled to the red man. "From Morgana or Ingrid. Then . . . we'll have to go. We need . . . a good start."

Evidently Little Thor heeded his advice, for when Leif next opened his eyes both the Skraeling and Morgana were before him. Little Thor helped Morgana get some water down his throat.

"Mead!" he insisted.

· "Water first," Morgana said. "For your fever. Drink it all."

He did as she bade him, feeling like a scolded child. When they gave him the mead, it burned all the way down. He knew, however, that it would soon work its potent magic against the pain.

Little Thor pushed him gently but firmly onto his back. "Sleep now," he said.

"How is Ingrid?" Leif asked, his features taut with pain.

"As well as can be expected. She's a strong woman, and understanding. She bears you no grudge," Morgana said. "Sweyn, on the other hand, is ready to slit your throat. You must leave soon. I fear he will go back on his word and—"

"You fear?" Leif asked in a weak but caustic voice. "You fear for your husband's murderer? Now that Hakon is dead, you—"

"Enough! Another killing won't solve anything."

Leif's bloodshot eyes held hers. "You . . . you still won't admit you were—*are*—wrong, will you, Morgana?" His lips twisted, before he said to Little Thor, "Aye, she's right. We must leave." He pushed against the other man's hands, causing himself added agony.

"We stay. No one will hurt you. Little Thor here."

"I'll wake you before sunset," Morgana told him in a calmer voice. "I hope that will give you enough time to—"

"And just leave me here to be stuck with a dagger like Hrafn? I think not!"

"Little Thor stay here," the Skraeling repeated. "Be not afraid."

Against his will, Leif's eyelids drifted shut. "Northmen fear naught, red man ..."

"Northmen stupid then. Only fool or child not fear."

Leif tried to think of an appropriate response, but it was too taxing at that moment. Instead, with an effort, he looked at Morgana once more. "Tell Ingrid—please—I'm so sorry ..."

The last thing he remembered was the profound sadness shading Morgana's beautiful blue eyes.

Leif sat astride Hrafn, still weaponless. Little Thor sat upon Gunnar's horse. The only weapon they had between them was the red man's dagger.

Ragnar walked past Leif, and said in a low voice, "Blood-Drawer is on the north side of the great oak over yon rise." He jerked his chin toward the hillock on the far side of Oslof and continued moving past before Leif could acknowledge him.

Although Little Thor had done a good job of packing Leif's wound, it still leaked a trickle of blood. The short, if fitful, rest had helped revive Leif somewhat, yet even now he fought a new wave of light-headedness as he sat astride Hrafn, feeling an inordinate amount of emotional pain, in addition to the physical, in the wake of this latest turn of events.

Several people had gathered to watch the leavetaking, mostly men, but Morgana had not been among them. He supposed she was helping Ingrid prepare Gunnar for his journey to Valhalla.

Guthrum, Gunnar's grandfather, approached him. "Stay back," Leif warned him. "You'll earn no rewards from your jarl by approaching an outlaw."

Belatedly Leif remembered the grizzled Guthrum was hard of hearing. As the old one stood before him, his thinning white hair blew in the breeze and his faded blue eyes steadily regarded Leif. His quiet manner, his steady gaze, reminded Leif poignantly of Gunnar.

The old man shook his head slightly, revealing by his next words that he'd heard Leif's. "They cannot cause me more anguish than I have suffered with the loss of my eldest son, and now my grandson. But I would have you know, young Leif, that I would never blame you for aught that befell Gunnar. You are a good man and honest, just like your father before you. May the gods guide your steps to a better place than this."

As their eyes momentarily held, Leif knew exactly what Guthrum meant. Knew exactly what Gunnar's grandfather thought of Harald Fairhair and Horik Bluetooth and Sweyn Estrithsson and their ilk.

"My thanks, Guthrum," he murmured, his throat tightening with emotion.

"Hrolf the Walker," the old man whispered, echoing Gunnar's very words. "Find him . . . go to Francia. Hrolf owes me a favor. Tell him I sent you to him." He stepped away.

Leif acknowledged his words with a slight dip of his chin, then looked at Little Thor, suddenly unwilling to draw out the moment any longer. The Skraeling nodded, and, for the last time, Leif glanced about him at the settlement where he'd been born and raised. He felt an increasingly familiar emptiness, distanced somehow from the memories, good and bad. This place held nothing for him now. His father was gone, Gunnar was gone, and Morgana and Eirik were lost to him . . .

And Guthrum had just confirmed what Harald Estrithsson had feared—the total tyrany of a ruthless man who would make himself king at any cost.

And then he saw Eirik peek from the longhouse door. As the child began to totter toward him, Freki nosed his way through the door and followed.

Leif watched his son make his way toward him, trip and

fall with a soft grunt, then get up again, undaunted, and continue his unsteady way toward Leif.

" 'Afn," he called.

Leif's heart turned over in his chest.

Now *what do you have?* Morgana's bitter question flashed through his mind.

As he watched Eirik's progress toward him, suddenly life seemed brighter—even hopeful, as he acknowledged what he had to do . . . what he had every right to do, every other consideration be damned.

"Come," he said softly to Little Thor. He heeled Hrafn's sides, and the stallion leapt forward in a graceful surge. Straight toward Eirik.

The child stopped, his eyes growing wide with sudden uncertainty. And then fear. He stood rooted to the ground in obvious terror.

With every contact of the stallion's hooves, excruciating pain sharded through Leif's shoulder, his arm, his side. But in view of what was at stake in this sudden and audacious move, pain had to be a secondary consideration.

Mogana unexpectedly emerged from the longhouse, one hand shading her eyes from the sun. It took an instant for her to divine Leif's intent. A cry of denial rose to her lips. It emerged as a whisper, for it was too late.

The men standing nearby were in no position to stop either horse or rider. And the dagger Little Thor produced as he followed close upon Hrafn's path was further assurance against interference.

But Morgana was not about to allow Leif Haraldsson to perpetrate this final outrage unchallenged. She flung herself toward Eirik, shouting his name in desperation as he stood frozen, a heartbreakingly short distance away.

Yet just before she reached him, she was forced to watch in helpless horror as Leif, leaning low to the left side of Hrafn's neck, scooped up the child, his gaze locking with hers for an ephemeral eternity—grim triumph and something akin to regret shining in his amber-dark eyes—before he sped away with her whole world in his embrace.

But there had also been something else—indefinable, maddeningly elusive, yet a definite message of some kind . . .

So great was her shock, however, that last thought barely registered before it disappeared in the maze of Morgana's mind. And she never even noticed the huge wolfhound loping alongside the two mounted men and barking frenetically as he followed.

Chapter Twelve

Leif had gambled on a hunch that many of the men would not be so eager to pursue him since he'd taken his rightful son. A few would side, perhaps, with Morgana . . . possibly Ottar, as her stepfather, and others in her family. But, for the most part, even Sweyn couldn't claim Eirik now that Hakon was dead.

Leif and Little Thor crested the rise on the far side of the settlement, and disappeared from view. Once out of sight, Leif handed a bewildered Eirik to the Skraeling and made for the oak to which Ragnar had referred. Blood-Drawer stood propped against the trunk on the north side, exactly as Ragnar had claimed.

As he bent with the last of his strength to grab the sword's pommel, he thought, *Thank you, my friend. You've stood by me through everything.* Gritting his teeth against the pain, Leif led the way west, toward the sea, at a breakneck pace. Most of the journey passed by in a blur, and as the sun slowly sank, the smell of saltwater revived him somewhat, gave him renewed hope that they were far enough away from Oslof—in case any had sought to pursue them—to snatch a few hours of sleep before continuing on their way.

Leif felt hot, the earlier cool clamminess he'd experienced having given way to fever. When they finally stopped, he was vaguely aware of sliding from Hrafn's back, of his knees buckling, and of Eirik's curious blue gaze upon his face just before blackness engulfed him.

Morgana stood, stunned, and stared after them in helpless disbelief.

It didn't last long, however. Her fingers curled like claws, then formed tense fists as outrage washed over.

She was suddenly unaware of the babble of voices around her. Momentarily forgotten were Gunnar's and Hakon's deaths . . . the significance of her widowhood now. She spun about, looking for . . . a horse. She would take Hakon's horse . . .

What can you do against two men? whispered one tiny rational voice from within.

"Think . . ." she commanded herself through clenched teeth. *"Think!"*

Sweyn. That was what she'd do . . . she would go to Sweyn and appeal—

"What happened?" Ingrid inquired from behind her.

Jerked from her frantic, clashing thoughts, Morgana swung to her friend, too distaught at that moment to think of anyone's plight but her own. "He took him! Eirik . . . Leif *took* him!"

Ingrid's face was pale, her eyes red-rimmed, and it was that fact which dimly penetrated Morgana's thoughts. Ingrid was supposed to be preparing her husband's body for burial, and here *she* was, adding to the newly-made widow's burden with her own troubles . . .

Ingrid frowned. It was then that Morgana noticed little Harald clinging to his mother's skirt, his eyes wide with bewilderment.

"Just like that? With Little Thor—" Ingrid began.

In her extreme distress, Morgana interrupted her, attributing Ingrid's seeming slowness in comprehending the situation to her own recent shock. "He took Eirik with him . . . don't you see? Just *stole* him like—"

Ingrid gripped Morgana's arm, her expression losing that faraway look. "A man cannot *steal* something that's already his, Morgana," she said in an undertone, her voice unexpectedly firm and decisive. "Get hold of yourself, for Eirik's sake. Surely the child is in no immediate danger with his father and Little Thor."

Morgana pulled her arm away, her look disbelieving. "Leif is wounded, and the Skraeling . . . by the gods, who knows what he is really like?" She swung away. "I must tell Sweyn. He will send men to—"

"Nei!" Ingrid took Morgana by the arm once more, communicating urgency through her tense grip and the tone of command in her voice.

Morgana looked at her as if she were mad. *"Nei?"* She frowned and shook her head. "Who else, Ingrid? What else can I—"

Ingrid glanced at the dispersing men, as if gauging whether they'd heard Morgana's intent. She drew Morgana toward the longhouse. "Because," she said in a low voice, "it would give Sweyn an excuse to have Leif killed. Eirik might even be killed . . . don't you see?"

"Then . . . Ottar . . . or some of the men who returned with *Wave Rider.*"

"Do you think they would attack the man who led them home? Prevent him from taking his own son? Think, Morgana . . . think!"

Matiassu bent over his friend. He put a hand to Leif's forehead and grunted. Kiisku-Liinu was burning with fever now, the red man's worst fear. He glanced at the child. Eirik was busy exploring the rocks that led to the craggy shoreline. For now, the child seemed content.

Matiassu examined the packing over Leif's shoulder.

The wound was still seeping blood, and that was good, for it was cleansing itself. And the bandage wasn't saturated, which meant that in spite of the jouncing ride on horse-back, it hadn't reopened.

He stood then and thoughtfully surveyed the surrounding area. Pine, spruce and oak trees abounded along the shoreline. But what he needed was the bark of a tree that might be native only to his own land. He didn't know the name in Norse, but there would be no mistaking the tree. Or he could settle for the soft inner bark of the pines that abounded in this land. He had to leave Leif alone for a while to search, and the encroaching darkness told him he didn't have much time. Already the shadows were deceiving.

Matiassu tethered the horses, hiked Eirik to his back, which, from the child's squeal of delight, was obviously fine with him, and set out on his search.

"No fire," Leif mumbled.

"Need small fire—to make drink for pain," Matiassu answered.

"Just give me . . . mead."

"Have only water. Here, drink."

Cool water trickled down Leif's throat. It felt wonderful, even though it wasn't mead.

Leif was half-aware of suddenly being lifted, then lowered into frigid water. The shock to his over-heated body was immediate, and he tensed, then struggled against the red man's hold in protest.

"Be still. Need clean wound again," Little Thor's voice came to him.

As Leif struggled in vain, he never felt the effect of salt-water on his wound, for his entire shoulder throbbed. He finally stilled beneath Little Thor's firm hands, letting the waves wash over him. Then he began to shiver.

"Enough," he muttered, renewing his efforts to free himself from the icy embrace of the sea.

At last he was lifted free of the water and carried somewhere. He tried to open his eyes, but it was dusk, layers of shadows closing in on everything. Little Thor set him down near the tiny fire. He felt a boulder behind him, supporting him. Big blue eyes regarded him solemnly.

"Eirik?" Leif whispered.

A cold nose touched his cheek, then a huge, shaggy dog's face wavered before him.

"Fehki, nice!" the child commanded.

"No fire," Leif said again. " 'Tisn't safe yet. Put it—"

"Be still." Little Thor braced Leif's shoulders with an arm. A cup touched his lips. "Drink. Drink all."

Leif made a face at the bitter taste. He spat out the first mouthful.

"No! Drink!" Little Thor said in a low, threatening voice.

"Are you trying . . . to poison me?" Leif asked darkly. But he drank.

"Must get better," Little Thor told him. "Ride tomorrow." The Skraeling began packing Leif's shoulder with moss, then deftly binding it. The pain seemed to lessen rather than increase with his ministrations.

The brew, Leif thought blearily. Even though it was incredibly bitter, it was evidently helping to soothe the stabbing pain that seemed, at times, to engulf his entire body. It was also making him sleepy. "What . . . did you give me?" he asked, squinting at Little Thor.

"Bark from tree." He said something in his own tongue—probably the name of the tree—which Leif didn't understand.

"That," Leif muttered, too tired to care at that moment, "explains everything." He glanced at Eirik before his eyes began to close. "Must get away. Get Eirik away. Do you understand, my brother?"

Little Thor nodded. "Drink all," he said, pushing the cup back to Leif's mouth. "Then sleep. Leave with sun."

Matiassu stared at Leif as the sun dipped into the Great Salt-Sea. He was still pale, even with the weak rays of the dying sun bathing his face. The boy-child sat beside the dog, chewing contentedly on a piece of fresh fish Matiassu had caught and boned, then cooked over the fire. Now and then the child gave some to the animal patiently watching him.

Matiassu allowed his gaze to roam briefly to the copper-spangled Great Water before him. Across it lay his old home. He pushed the thought away. There was nothing for him there now. Home was with Kiisku-Liinu.

He looked to the mountains that bordered the sea and wended southward. He knew not where they led, primarily because he didn't know where he was, except that it was on the other side of the Great Saltwater. But Kiisku-Liinu knew. He was, among other things, a good navigator; surely he would also know the land around him and where to go.

Matiassu had no doubts. Wishemenetoo had given him Leif Haraldsson, as he was called by his own, and that was enough for Matiassu. The Great One would guide them safely as long as necessary, there was no questioning that. And now, Kiisku-Liinu's son was with them. Surely a favorable sign from Wishemenetoo.

As darkness descended, Matiassu poured the last of his brew into Leif's empty cup, then snuffed out the small fire with several handfuls of sand. He sat back then against a rock, his gaze alternating between Kiisku-Liinu and his son. Sun-Man had called Matiassu "brother." Contentment settled over him like a warm mantle, for Kiisku-Liinu now understood the tie that inextricably bound them, and felt close enough to Matiassu to call him brother.

186

He allowed himself the luxury of drifting back in time . . .

He was dizzy. And faint. He'd been without food or water for four days. Or was it five?

The sun sat low in the western sky, touching his face like the caress of a lover, and tinting the incoming waves from the Great Water with silver. They seemed to dance before his eyes, beckoning him toward them. Toward their deep and mysterious depths.

Not yet, a voice whispered. *Not yet.*

A sacrifice. That was what he needed. A sacrifice to induce the Great One to send him a vision and give purpose to his life. It was the only thing he hadn't done in his quest for a vision. He felt his energy and strength ebbing, knew there wasn't much time before he fell asleep where he sat.

Forever.

With an effort, he pulled his dagger from its sheath and raised his left arm. It felt heavy as stone, and he felt himself tremble. He bit his lip and concentrated on making a small incision with clumsy fingers, midway between wrist and elbow. As blood welled to the surface and threaded across his flesh, as it dripped to the earth, he felt a great satisfaction.

The dagger slipped from his hand to the sand, and he extended his arm in offering toward the westering sun. *Grant me a vision, oh Great Spirit,* he silently exhorted.

His shaking arm fell to his side in spite of his determination to keep it upright. He felt as weak as a newborn.

He closed his eyes, ignoring his burning thirst. He would not eat or drink until his prayers were answered. He would not give up his fast.

He tried to conjure his wife and children in his mind's eye. He tried to envision his village before the enemy tribe had struck without warning, silently and terribly, at dawn's first light. The few survivors had tended their wounds and limped, pitifully empty-handed, toward other friendly villages in the area.

But not Matiassu. He'd been numbed of mind at first, then had decided to take his own life. His despair was so great that he'd had no wish to partake of life any longer. Then, even stronger, came an eerie and unexpected urge to take his skin-covered canoe and venture out alone onto the Great Saltwater. He knew not where he would go, only that he had to move eastward upon the water.

Now, after fasting for four days, after sacrificing some of his own blood, he waited for Wishemenetoo to speak to him, send some sign directing him toward the chosen path . . .

In the midst of his ruminations, he caught the all-but-indiscernable crunch of pebbles against sand. He opened his eyes . . . not so much in alarm as in detached curiosity, even with a glimmer of hope, for perhaps . . .

A figure stood less than a stone's throw away from him, between him and the slowly sinking sun. He was tall, but Matiassu could not discern his features with the sun behind him. Coruscating rays of golden light emanated from around his head, like a brilliant corona.

Matiassu lowered his lashes once more to ease the burning in his eyes and clear his vision. After a moment, he lifted them. Nothing had changed. The beams from the dying sun danced about the unmoving figure like flashes of flame. The ends of his long hair, caught in the sea breeze, appeared the same shade of red-gold as the fireball limning him.

The vision. This was Wishemenetoo's sign. He knew it as surely as he had known anything in his life. He opened his mouth to speak, but only an unintelligible croak emerged. Frustration flared within him.

The figure took two steps toward him, one hand going

to what looked like the long, slender blade of a weapon hanging from his waist. Orange-gold light flashed from the blade, as well, making it look like a living thing to the man sitting facing the sea.

The stranger said something in an utterly foreign tongue. Matiassu couldn't have answered him even if he'd had the strength. He couldn't speak, he couldn't move. He could only stare in awe . . . and burgeoning joy.

With the last of his ebbing energy, he finally managed to lift the arm bloodied by his sacrifice from where it rested against his crossed legs. He tried to hold it out. It was a feeble gesture of welcome, of curiosity, of expectancy.

It was written in the stars, Matiassu knew now. This apparition was his vision. Even as the thought formed, he began to lose consciousness. He swayed forward, fighting his debilitating weakness, and failed. The ground came up to meet him.

Suddenly, strong hands caught his shoulders and helped ease him back upon the sand. He felt water trickle over his dry lips, but barely had the strength to wet his tongue. He lifted his gaze for the last time to look into eyes as golden as the sun.

Here was his purpose for living, he thought, and relinquished himself to a peaceful, welcoming void . . .

Dragging his thoughts back to the present, Matiassu roused himself and looked to the horses. When he turned back to Leif and Eirik, he bent to touch the wounded man's forehead. Warm, but not burning, thanks be to Wishemenetoo. When dawn came, Kiisku-Liinu would be able to travel, although not at the pace Matiassu would have preferred, for they were only two with a sword and dagger between them. Still, it would have to be good enough.

The boy-child lay curled against the dog, taking unconscious advantage of the animal's thick, shaggy hair. Freki's eyes were open, and he watched every move Matiassu made.

" 'Tis good, this watchfulness," Matiassu said in his own tongue. "Both for Kiisku-Liinu and son."

He covered Leif with his overtunic, and settled himself against Gunnar's saddle for the night.

He knew not where Kiisku-Liinu would take him, but it didn't matter. Matiassu would always be there for the man sent to him by the Great One.

Only one person was missing from his life now, but he knew it was futile to even think about . . . her.

Gunnar's body rested on a low table. Morgana watched as Ingrid lovingly dressed him in a bright blue tunic and pale fawn breeches. She girded his waist with a crimson leather belt, and pinned an intricately carved silver brooch at his right shoulder . . . his best and his favorite, Morgana remembered.

Guthrum helped her, his look infinitely sad and far away, as if he were remembering another time. Morgana wondered what he was thinking, for the old man had known much sorrow in his life.

Tyra entered the longhouse, pausing briefly in the doorway to allow her eyes to adjust to the low light. When she saw Ingrid and Guthrum near Gunnar, she stepped toward them. Ingrid caught her eye and shook her head. "Morgana needs you more," she said, in her calm, quiet voice. For once, a warm smile did not soften the lines of her mouth.

Tyra went to Morgana. "Ragnar bade me tell you not to fear for Eirik. Leif would never harm him . . . and the Skraeling is absolutely loyal to Leif. He would give his life for either of them."

Morgana raised anger-darkened eyes.

"Ottar thinks the same," Tyra added.

"That is little consolation when I have lost my son. He may as well be dead—"

Tyra placed a hand across her daughter's lips. "Don't even *think* such a thing! 'Tis the lot of every Norsewoman to see her son or husband come and go with the seasons. Many times they never return, but life must go on."

Morgana turned away and stared at a much-used, beaten shield on the longhouse wall before her. Its boss was dented in many places, its round, wooden surface cracked, the fierce but once-colorful dragon's head faded. "I cannot accept that where my son is concerned! I have nothing now."

Tyra shook her head slowly, thoughtfully. "I love my grandson. I, too, am saddened at what happened. But remember this, Morgana: In a roundabout way, 'tis all your fault. You started the chain of events when your anger and pride prompted you to divorce Leif Haraldsson. You say you have nothing now? How do you think Leif felt upon his return to Oslof?"

Morgana stared hard at her mother, thinking of how she'd changed since Morgana's father, Magnus Longbeard, was cut down in his prime. Tyra loved Ottar, Morgana knew, but he wasn't—could never be—Magnus.

Did her mother really harbor any love for her own grandchild? she wondered. And would she, Morgana, end up as cynical and bitter as Tyra?

"Now, when you should be preparing Hakon for his journey to Valhalla, Sweyn is doing it and won't allow anyone near the body, so distraught is he with grief. Did you ever think of such consequences, daughter?"

Morgana suddenly couldn't answer. She felt bound by such intense emotion she couldn't even open her mouth . . . couldn't think of a single, rational thing to say without dissolving the last remnant of her sorely-tried control.

Gunnar was dead—and her best friend needed her.

191

Hakon was dead as well, and as a dutiful wife, she should have been attending to his body before burial. But life was for the living, and her son had been reft from her right before her eyes. She knew instinctively, in spite of her deepest needs and desperate hopes, that she would never see him again.

And that fact, with all the accompanying bewilderment and frustration and fear, drove all other considerations from her mind. It dominated her thoughts, her feelings. It gripped her soul.

The strongest emotion to emerge from the seething cauldron inside Morgana, however, was rage. Rage at Leif Haraldsson. It was so virulent, and so uncharacteristic of her temperament, that it clouded her thinking. Thoughts and ideas darted through her mind like successive arrows from an expert archer's bow.

She saw Tyra's face before her, saw the older woman's mouth working, but Morgana was in another world, groping furiously for an answer, a solution to her dilemma.

Unexpectedly, out of the shrouded depths of her mind, rose the image of Leif Haraldsson as he returned aboard *Wave Rider* . . .

Wave Rider. Leif's beautiful, graceful ship. The fiery-haired Ragnar . . . her mother had just told her that Ragnar had said to have no fear. That was because Ragnar himself was fearless . . .

Other images drifted across her mind's eye . . . the heavily-muscled Olaf—even the small and nimble-tongued Egil, as she remembered that morn—was it only days ago?

". . . is beyond reason with grief," Tyra repeated, her words finally registering dimly in Morgana's mind.

She didn't respond to Tyra, however, but looked right through her mother as she considered her pitifully few options. If Sweyn was distraught with grief, so much the better, for he would be less inclined to take any action against Morgana's fledgling plan. Surely some of Leif's men would help her . . . not, mayhap, with intent to capture or harm their former comrade and leader, but there *was* another way. An idea was fast forming in her mind even as Morgana swiftly considered and dismissed each objection that reason could fling her way.

Without warning, she pushed past Tyra toward the door of the hall, drawing strength from her knowledge of absolute loyalty among any Northmen who'd challenged and defeated death together; and especially if they'd been well-chosen initially . . .

And her determination to show Leif Haraldsson that although he'd betrayed her trust once before, she'd wouldn't allow him to do it again—and get away with it—as long as she had breath left in her body.

Eirik sat beside Leif, his tear-streaked face pressed against his father's left side. "Mamma," he whimpered softly. "Want Mamma . . . and Papa . . ."

Leif's heart lurched beneath his ribs. He wanted to tell the child that *he* was his father, but it was too soon. Eirik wouldn't comprehend that yet. And as for his mother . . . well, that couldn't be helped now, and Leif deliberately dismissed Morgana from his thoughts. Or tried to.

"Freki's here," he said softly to the child. "And Little Thor, our brave Skraeling warrior. Look, Eirik, how he saddles Hrafn."

Eirik raised his face to look in Little Thor's direction. " 'Afn," he said with a sniff, and pointed to the stallion. Freki's ears perked up and the dog trotted over to them. He put his cool nose against the child's flushed cheek and Eirik broke into a watery smile. "Fehki tickew," he said.

"So he tickles you, does he?" Leif asked, then pressed his cheek to the top of the little one's head. He couldn't seem to get close enough to Eirik—to watch him enough, touch him enough.

Maybe because this was as close as he would ever get to Morgana again.

"Já." Eirik pointed again to Little Thor and the two horses. "Go home?" he asked, and raised his face to meet Leif's regard, his look heartrendingly expectant.

"First we must make a journey, Eirik," Leif told him. "Would you like that? You may ride Hrafn with me, and Little Thor and Freki will follow us."

He released Eirik and rose awkwardly to his feet before the child could answer. It was easy to distract him, yet Leif knew he would have his hands full keeping the boy's thoughts away from all that was familiar.

Anything worth having was worth the effort, however, and the risk. It was just too bad that he hadn't come to that conclusion when first he'd returned to Oslof. He might have had Morgana with him, as well.

Little Thor helped him mount, then handed him Eirik. The red man gave him a probing look as Leif settled himself and the child in the saddle. "We go . . . ?" The red man pointed south.

"Aye . . . south, but east first, to skirt the waterways. 'Twill take us much longer by land, but it cannot be helped. And 'twill be easier to hide from Estrithsson's men if need be."

"Can steal boat, *nei?* Little boat. Better than—" he pointed to the mountains.

"Mountains." Leif couldn't help but smile. "You sly dog! Steal a boat, would you? Mayhap we could, but what of the horses? Gunnar's Sleipnir and my Hrafn—a gift from my father—are too precious to me."

Little Thor shrugged. "Skin more important to Little Thor." He turned away before Leif could answer and vaulted astride the chestnut.

Leif smiled again, ignoring the dull but persistant ache in his shoulder. The Skraeling showed more and more of a sense of humor as time went by. That was good, for Leif would need some levity to make life bearable in the wake of all that had happened . . . and could happen yet. The gods knew what lay before them.

He glanced down at Eirik, then turned Hrafn to face east. Steep, craggy mountains and sheer cliffs bordered the shoreline. It would take many days and nights to cross the mountains. It certainly would have been easier, as Little Thor had indicated, to take to the water rather than travel around the myriad fjords that looped in and out of the heart of Norvegia; but there was no way the two of them could man a ship big enough to carry the horses, let alone obtain one.

He knew where he was going, however. It was crystal clear now. He knew *exactly* where he was going and to whom he would offer his allegiance. He would raise his son in a milder climate than Norvegia; in less hostile surroundings, without the need to seek new lands and riches by plunder.

His shoulder would heal under Little Thor's care, and they would eventually reach their destination. He refused to think otherwise. He would rear Eirik and teach him to work the land; he would reap the benefits of living from the earth and then pass them on to his son.

Mayhap he would have more sons . . .

The renewed ache of lost love, deeper than the hurt in his shoulder, burgeoned within him at the thought of living his life without Morgana.

But you'll do it! whispered a voice. *You'll do what is necessary to live your life for Eirik's sake, if not your own.*

Yet a softer, though nonetheless persistant, voice added, *And you'll hope against hope every day of your wretched existence, Leif Haraldsson, that your incredibly farfetched gamble will one day reap its own reward.*

He urged Hrafn forward, reason telling him he was an utter fool, his heart telling him there was no living without hope.

Chapter Thirteen

St. Clair-sûr-Epte, Francia, Spring—A.D. 911

The warm spring breeze sighed softly through the leaves on the trees and touched the emerald-tinted meadow like a benison in the peaceful morning stillness. White clouds careened across the sky before the same breeze, pristine puffs of purest alabaster against the cerulean sweep of the sky. Dotting the hills on either side of the verdant valley were apple orchards, scenting the somnolent air with their fragrance, their blossoms as snowy white as the clouds above.

Leif Haraldsson sighed into the wind. Surely this place was blessed by the gods, for he'd known no other like it. If only . . .

His lean jaw tightened beneath his beard, and his eyes darkened with the effort to will his thoughts away from where they would roam, training his attention on the scene before him.

At a small table beside the stream called the Epte, not far from where Leif stood with Little Thor, two figures dominated the attention of scores of men standing silently at attention around them. One of the men was impossibly tall . . . a veritable giant. Hrolf the Walker (so called, Leif mused, because he was so big that no horse could hold him, therefore he walked more often than not) had recently taken the Frankish name "Rollo." With a jangle of his golden arm rings, the roistering Northman accepted the quill from the shorter man at his side and bent to put his mark on the parchment spread on the table before them.

The second man, Charles the Simple, new King of Francia, was much smaller and more elegantly clad. Over a linen shirt and simple breeches, his royal blue silk mantle, strewn with its embroidered gold lillies, flowed down his back. It flared slightly with the wind, then stilled as the king waited for Rollo to make his mark.

Leif watched Rollo straighten to his formidable height when he'd finished. An undercurrent of voices rippled through the crowd as a third man, Bishop Francon of Rouen, stepped forward, clad in crimson and sapphire vestments, an elaborate gold and white mitre on his head. He held out a small carved wooden chest, undoubtedly containing a holy relic, upon which Rollo placed his hand as he repeated an oath after the bishop.

Leif knew that part of the agreement was Rollo's baptism and conversion to Christianity. He absently touched the fingertips of one hand to the cross beneath his tunic, feeling the familiar if nebulous bond with his late Christian mother.

The bishop withdrew the reliquary, handed it to a waiting servant, then spoke to both the king and the soon-to-be Count of Rouen. Leif watched Rollo's face unexpectedly redden with obvious anger. The three men looked down at King Charles's feet in unison, and Rollo shook his head emphatically. Leif guessed what was happening.

"I'd wager, as part of the oath of fealty, Rollo must kiss the royal foot," he murmured to Little Thor.

The Skraeling, with his shoulder-length blue-black hair gleaming in the sunlight, looked alien in spite of his tunic, typical breeches, and simple head band. His lips twitched in answer before he shook his head.

Leif found himself suppressing a grin as well . . . something he did rarely these days in spite of the success of their difficult and lengthy journey to the Seine Valley, where they had indeed found Rollo and entered into his service with his army of Danes and fellow Norwegians.

Only the occasional ache in his shoulder remained to stoke scorching memories of Hakon's perfidy. Of Leif's subsequent banishment. And of the gut-wrenching loss of the woman he loved . . .

Rollo shook his head obstinately and folded his arms, directing a marrow-chilling stare at the Frankish officials.

The bishop and the obviously bewildered king put their heads together and exchanged a few words. Francon then spoke to Rollo. The giant started to shake his shaggy head once again, then stilled, his bushy blond eyebrows tenting as if inspiration had struck. With a clinking of several heavy amulets about his neck, he swung aside and allowed his gaze to scan the foremost ranks of his supporters.

His gaze came to rest on one particular man, whom Leif could not immediately single out. A burly, white-blond warrior stepped forward at Rollo's command to stand before Charles and the bishop. Rollo pointed to the ground and spoke in Norse.

The retainer looked at him as if he were mad.

Rollo spoke again, his voice louder this time and weighted with authority. The silence that collected around the gathering of men grew tense, expectant, as everyone waited.

The bishop's expression turned outraged; the king's cha-grined.

The moment stretched taut as wire . . .

Without warning, the summoned retainer bent and seized King Charles's foot. He straightened, wrenching up the king's leg as he did so. As he quickly brought the royal foot to his lips, Charles the Simple's supporting leg was jerked from beneath him. He slammed to the ground on his backside.

Laughter erupted from hundreds of men on this most solemn occasion, reverberating around the meadow, the loudest obviously issuing from the rowdy Northmen whose cohort had performed the deed, rather than the Franks.

Rollo immediately bent and extended a mammoth hand to the unseated king, as if to make up in some small way for his retainer's prank; then, as soon as Charles had regained his feet—if not his dignity—Rollo reached out to the bishop and helped himself to the keys to the city of Rouen.

"Perhaps the newly-made Count of Rouen fears Bishop Francon will change his mind," Leif said to Little Thor, and did nothing to suppress the second smile that softened his mouth.

Little Thor shook his head. "Northman has bad manners."

"Aye," Leif agreed. "He's bold and brazen; but do you see anyone denying him? How do you think he managed to maneuver Charles into ceding these lands to him, eh? Surely not with his good manners."

A corner of the Skraeling's mouth quirked.

"And better to serve a man such as Rollo than one dubbed 'Charles the Simple' by his subjects."

The crowd around them burst into shouts of approval, the noise level rising to echo around the valley as more and more joined in. Leif surmised the most joyful celebrants were Rollo's followers. Few Franks were happy to see the establishment of a colony of Northmen within Frankish boundaries.

Especially Robert of Neustria. Although he might be allied with Charles, it was known that he was unhappy over the loss of part of his duchy, Neustria, to Rollo. He also had designs on Charles's entire kingdom, which consisted of the western rump of the late Charlemagne's divided empire.

As the roar of approbation swelled, then receded, Leif

Haraldsson acknowledged that the Frankish king was in no enviable position; and if an ambitious man were to choose, it would be better to serve the giant Northman than his beleaguered Frankish liege.

Morgana watched the cliff-girt coast of Francia glide past as *Wave Rider* cut through the churning, blue-gray waters of the channel. England was to one side of them, the Frankish empire to the other. The steep cliffs and rocky beaches reminded her poignantly of home.

Your home is where Eirik is.

Tears threatened; but she would not weep. This was neither the time nor the place for that.

Ragnar came up to her. "Look," he said, pointing to the left. "See that bay? Olaf and I agree 'tis the mouth of the Seine, which flows through the heart of Francia."

"Part of Neustria?" she asked, shading her eyes from the sun as her gaze followed his pointing finger.

"According to the stories, it could be part of Hrolf the Walker's grant now." The corners of his mouth turned down, making his red moustaches droop menacingly. "Let us hope so, else we receive an unfriendly reception . . . in spite of our puny precaution." He glanced up at a white square of *wadmal*, a coarse woolen fabric, that flew above *Wave Rider*'s colorful blue and green sail.

Morgana stared at the approaching land sheltered by the bay. Behind her, the wind puffed against the sail with a sound like flapping wings. "We mean no harm," she said.

"Tell that to the Franks," Ragnar said. He pointed to the fearsome dragon's head that graced the prow, its green, gold, and purple hues winking in the bright sunlight; then suddenly the Northman threw back his head and laughed uproariously. Several of the others looked over at him. Olaf at the tiller grinned in response, even though Morgana knew he couldn't have heard Ragnar's comment.

Morgana wouldn't be distracted. "We are looking for a Northman and his small son, most likely in the service of Hrolf the Walker. He travels with a red man called Little Thor." She looked up at Ragnar. "How many red men can there be in Francia? And in the company of a fair-skinned Norseman?"

Ragnar shrugged. "Let's hope not many. We need no added obstacles."

"And what makes you think Leif will give up the boy if and when we find him?" Einar, a somber young man, asked Morgana for the hundredth time. Yet, even though he seemed concerned about their success, he'd not hesitated to offer to help Morgana find Leif and Eirik.

"How quickly you forget, Einar," she said, disliking the waspish tone of her voice. "The agreement was to help me find them. There was no talk of any of you getting involved in my quarrel with Leif."

Einar had the grace to look sheepish, even if he lacked the wisdom to keep silent. "But I still don't like the idea of landing on Frankish soil with only one ship," he added. "A white flag assures us of naught."

Morgana turned her head toward Francia, essaying to ignore the youth's misgivings. He was young and not the most experienced, she told herself. She closed her eyes for a moment against the kiss of the salt spray. *Allfather,* she prayed, *please help us. Guide us to our goal.*

The steel-backboned side of her, however, dragged to the fore by Leif's Haraldsson's actions, prompted her to add in soft but steely tones, "And if you won't, I'll do it alone by sheer dint of will."

". . . headed this way."

Robert, Duke of Neustria, listened to the winded messenger. *"Par Dieu,"* he swore softly, "more Northmen? Is there no end to them?" He ran his fingers through shoulder-length brown hair in agitation, pushing it off his face, as if to better study the problem now before him.

As he stared out over the bay from his retainer's manor house in the coastal village of Harfleur, his face settled into rigid lines of anger. "Before the ink is even dry on the parchment signed by that fool Charles and his misbegotten ally . . . before the ink is even dry, another pirating ship from the north is looking for plunder!"

Eh bien, he'd teach them a lesson! Just how gullible did they think he and his men were? Taken in by a hoisted white flag on a Norse longship sailing straight into their midst . . . ?

It was laughable.

"And how foolish of them to brazenly sail a lone ship into our harbor. Don't you think so, Odo?"

Odo, obviously flattered at being consulted by his duke, responded, "They are connivers, m'lord. 'Twould be more in keepin' with their ways to have another ship hidden out o' sight somewhere, although we saw naught but one, John an' me did."

Robert frowned as he considered this. Then inspiration struck. "Why, I'll beat them at their own game," he said, his frown suddenly transforming into a nasty smile. *"Venez ici, mes fous païens,"* he invited in silken tones, like a spider waiting for an unwitting victim to ram right into its sticky web. "A little farther, my foolish pagans . . ."

He couldn't see the vessel yet, but he summoned a servant who gave both Robert and the messenger much-needed wine. "I'll teach them to underestimate Robert of Neustria," he declared, and raised his cup in salute to the messenger before downing the contents. "No Simple Charles am *I* to take those savages to my bosom."

"Will you call the mercenaries, my lord?" Odo asked, his eyes barely visible through the thick tangle of his sand-colored hair.

Robert set down his cup. His eyes narrowed as he regarded the messenger with a thoughtful look, vaguely remembering that the man's dull exterior hid a sharp mind.

"Think you we should leave them to the tender mercies of their own kind?"

Beneath his mop, the man's homely face lit up with obvious, if fleeting, pleasure. *"Oui,* m'lord."

"Well, Odo, 'tis a fine job you've done in manning the tower on the point. And your thoughts are exactly in keeping with mine, my astute man." He swung toward the waiting servant and motioned for him to refill Odo's cup. "Then fetch Snorri the Black," he ordered. "Quickly!"

He suddenly began to laugh as his gaze moved out to the bay once again. "How eagerly they'll slip right into our embrace when they see one of their own," he said between breaths. "Tricksters outwitted by tricksters!"

And Snorri the Black, he acknowledged silently, was utterly without scruples.

His laughter echoed through the hall: absolutely humorless, darkly premonitory.

Morgana wanted to cheer with triumph, for there, as if anticipating their arrival, came two awesome yet familiar longships, apparently to escort them. The men aboard the two new vessels waved enthusiastically, and the three ships exchanged greetings in Norse.

"I don't like it," Einar muttered. " 'Tis too easy."

Morgana, who was sitting beneath the meager shelter of a small canopy erected for her, caught his words and looked sharply at him.

"We can always fight them," Olaf reminded them.

"The odds are against us," Ragnar said. "We are outnumbered two to one against their swift longships, with Thor knows how many men." He watched the approaching vessels as they split to either side of *Wave Rider.* "And although I wouldn't trade *Wave Rider* for any other vessel were we on an ocean voyage, she's nonetheless a *hafskip* and cannot match a coastal raider in speed and maneuverability. We also have Morgana to think of."

"That shouldn't be a consideration," she said shortly, unwilling to be a burden to the very men who served her cause. "I cannot see why another longship would do us harm . . . especially when we fly the white flag." Yet even as she said the words, she acknowledged that Norseman against Norseman was common—Norwegians against the Danes, Danes against the Swedes, Swedes against the Norwegians. And feuding among their own tribes and families could be fierce, often lasting for generations or until one side or the other was completely wiped out.

"We can offer them gold and silver," Einar suggested, "to better ensure their cooperation. We have some hidden—"

"*Nei!*" Ragnar said. "We know nothing about these men save they appear to be Northmen like ourselves. They could take our offerings and still slay us."

"What matter if they take our ship?" Morgana asked him. "We can always get another. If worse comes to worst, we can offer them *everything* in exchange for safe passage." She couldn't keep the passion from her voice, for she meant every word. Anything could be replaced but their lives.

Ragnar threw her a look that told her exactly what he thought of her suggestion. "There are some things better left to a man's judgment, Morgana Magnussdóttir. We have done things your way, for the most part, until now. We agreed to your terms. But the time has come for you to bow to our wisdom . . . remain where you are and pray to Odin."

Extreme irritation rose within her at the implication that she wasn't as capable of sound reasoning as a man. But she silently acknowledged that the men *were* more experienced, and that experience was the *only* reason it might be wiser to go along with Ragnar.

Before she could answer, he moved to the raised portion of the stern deck. He cupped his hands and bellowed toward the ship between them and the shoreline: "We hail from Norvegia and are seeking one of our own. We believe he is in the service of a man known as Hrolf the Walker. Know you of this Northman?"

The answer came back. Yes, they had heard of him. He was now the Count of Rouen, and they were part of the army who'd helped him wrest a great chunk of land from Charles the Simple, the Frankish king. They were patrolling the bay and, fortunately, the newcomers happened to be smack in the middle of Rollo's newly-ceded lands.

Hope surged through Morgana as she strained to catch the exchange. They would find Leif . . . and Eirik. They were so close now.

What if they perished before they ever reached Francia?

She ignored the voice and its unthinkable implications and concentrated on catching a glimpse of the man speaking to Ragnar across the way. He was dark-haired, although from what Morgana could make out, many among his crew were fair. He was more than likely what they called a black Dane—dark as other Northmen were fair. And no especial friend to the Norwegians.

". . . Snorri the Black," he was saying in a dialect similar to theirs. "What is this man's name? What is he to you?"

Morgana quickly stood and ducked out from under the canopy before anyone could stop her. "Leif . . . Leif Haraldsson," she called out as she joined Ragnar. "He is my husband," she lied without a qualm, "and I wish to find him. And my son."

If looks had been lances, Morgana would have been felled on the spot by the one Ragnar gave her. None of the others looked any too happy, either.

"You put yourself in jeopardy!" Ragnar bit out beneath

his breath. "Or do you like the thought of being raped by Snorri's men and sold as a slave? *If* you're still alive when they finish with you . . ."

The words gave her pause. Her first reaction was to retreat beneath the canopy, as she would have done only one winter ago; yet Morgana was impatient with their exasperating caution, and the woman who'd persuaded Leif's staunchest friends to help her find him—who'd taken outrageous advantage of a grief-stricken Sweyn Esthrithsson and defied him to save Leif's ship from carrying Hakon's spirit to Valhalla—refused to remain hidden and silent beneath a canopy while her future was being decided by men.

Men. The very creatures who'd made the laws in Scandinavia that decreed one of their own could be made an outcast for killing in self-defense—banished by a bitter, hate-filled old jarl who was in league with Harald Fairhair . . .

Men. Those who came and went as they pleased, drinking and brawling and sailing and plundering as they willed, while their women remained home and awaited news of their successes or failures. Waiting. Worried. Frustrated. Powerless. With only a chatelaine at their waists, from which dangled household articles that included scissors, needle cases, purse and, finally, keys, as their only weapons. Keys to the cupboards of stores, symbolizing the female head of the household who wielded her own kind of authority; but nothing when compared to that of a man. Compared to a man's power, which allowed him to tear a young son away from his mother and head for parts unknown . . . forever.

But not this time. Not this woman. And not her son.

"How do we know you speak the truth?" The wind carried Snorri's words to her, breaking into her musings. "Mayhap you have hidden other ships along the coast to attack our count?"

206

"If we were a war party, we would not have a female in our midst. The woman searches for her husband and small son, and the rest of us seek to serve Hrolf the Walker ourselves."

As Morgana looked from Ragnar's angry face to the Dane across the way, it seemed to her that his sleek and swift longship had drawn nearer in the few moments she'd been distracted by the thoughts whirling through her head. The ship that flanked *Wave Rider*'s other side was closing in as well.

"We have no choice," Olaf said. "We can keep our weapons at the ready, but we're badly outnumbered if we need to fight. Perhaps Morgana's right—we might offer them coin in return for safe passage."

"And if they take it and kill us anyway?" Ragnar asked, his mouth twisting beneath his moustache.

" 'Tis well hidden," Morgana threw in. "They would have to tear the ship apart plank by plank to find it, and the very reason we hid it in the first place was for leverage in a situation like this. Yet didn't he say they were Hrolf's men?"

What she hadn't revealed to any of them was the hidden cache of silver and jewel-encrusted treasures—more valuable even than gold—about which Guthrum had told her. It had been hidden in a Frankish graveyard by the old man himself, years ago, after a raid on the monastery of Jumièges. The Frankish retaliation had exacted a heavy toll—the lives of most of Guthrum's fellow raiders—but the plunder was still buried where the Risle branched off from the Seine.

It was obvious that Ragnar's good nature was being sorely tried in those anxious moments. He plainly didn't care to be reminded of the purpose of their original plans as if he were feeble-minded. "The entire concept of leverage vanishes, Morgana, when the ship carrying it sits on the bottom of the sea!"

He swung toward his men. "Weapons at the ready," he ordered, "but not drawn, lest they take it into their heads to slaughter us all out of hand." His eyes met Morgana's. "And *you* remain beneath the canopy until I tell you differently if you would live to find Eirik."

The closer to port they came, the more Morgana's anticipation grew. And her misgivings, as well. The escort seemed well-intentioned enough, but . . .

As they neared the town of Harfleur, a tall, dark-haired man came striding down to the beach. He looked confident and self-assured, and appeared to be a figure of authority from the way the townspeople left their labors to gather nearby and watch him.

"He's no Northman," mumbled Olaf as *Wave Rider* nudged up onto the beach. Several of the men dropped into the shallow surf to pull the vessel farther out of the water. "If this is Hrolf the Walker's domain, what is a Frank doing here as a figure of authority?"

Other Northmen suddenly appeared on foot, and surrounded the men from *Wave Rider* who'd jumped ashore, while the escorting vessels moved close enough for a number of Snorri's men to board her, weapons drawn.

Ragnar, Olaf and several others still on board drew their swords, their expressions taut, suspicious.

"*Nei!*" Morgana emerged into full view. "Let them speak. They are only being cautious. Can you blame them? What do they know of us or our intentions aside from what we chose to tell them?"

"Look at their faces," Egil said. "What more do we need?"

Indeed, Snorri and his men suddenly looked anything but friendly. They moved swiftly to take over *Wave Rider*, their intentions now obvious to anyone but a fool. Snorri himself, Morgana thought, brought to mind a *berserkr*—a

Northman who went wild in battle, baring his teeth, biting the edge of his shield, rolling his eyes, and howling like a wild animal. Such a man usually wore no armor at all or simply animal skins.

And Snorri the Black, with his heavy dark beard and moustache, and the scar that ran from one ear to the corresponding corner of his mouth, thus horribly skewing one side of his face, would have made the perfect, terror-instilling *berserkr*.

His lips drawn back, Ragnar suddenly lunged forward to take a swift swipe at Snorri. A man from behind him used his own blade to knock the red-haired Northman's weapon from his hand. The strident ring of steel meeting steel pierced the air. The sword clattered to the deck, and one of Snorri's men pressed his foot against its hilt to anchor it to the floor.

"Enough!" Robert declared, "Else I have my men slaughter each and every one of you, the wench—comely or nay—included."

No one from Oslof understood his words, but the tone was ominous enough to set Morgana's skin a-crawl.

He strode up a boarding plank that had been hastily set in place, then moved to stand beside Snorri. "Welcome to my duchy," he said in a tone that was anything but friendly. "I am Robert, Duke of Neustria."

Snorri translated.

Morgana returned Robert's stare as his eyes met hers. She opened her mouth to speak, but Ragnar beat her to it. "What of Hrolf the Walker? We were told this was part of his fief, held of Charles of France. That we were among friends." He threw a murderous look at Snorri the Black.

After the translation was done, Robert placed the tip of his sword to the deck and leaned against it. "You, of all people, surely know by now that a Northman's word means naught; that he will resort to any means for gain."

As a tense silence sang around them, Morgana hoped

that Ragnar realized this was not the time to take offense at the insult, but rather to acknowledge, at least, a Norseman's knack for deceit against the enemy.

"Then what do you want of us?" Ragnar demanded of Robert, obviously refusing to look again at his traitorous Norse brother, even though the latter continued to translate for both sides.

Robert smiled nastily. "Why, *pauvre fou*, I want your valuables, of course. And your ship. And Snorri here wants your fair hides to sell on the slave market in Constantinople."

Chapter Fourteen

"Did you have a woman back in Norvegia? A woman with hair as bright as the moon on a clear night?"

Rollo's uncharacteristically lyrical words—to say nothing of the unexpected question itself—caught Leif completely off guard. So completely, in fact, that he couldn't help the brief widening of his eyes, and the startled look that surely had to be written across his face.

"One of my men," Rollo continued, obviously taking Leif's stunned silence for an affirmative answer, "a most trusted retainer, is an informer in Robert of Neustria's employ. He sent a messenger from Harfleur, a small town near the mouth of the Seine . . ."

They were walking through one of several orchards on the fief Leif now held of Rollo. Suddenly Leif was blind to the beauty around him—uncaring about whether the surrounding trees were apple, pear, or peach. His concentration was fully focused on what the huge man beside him was saying.

And the implications, if Leif dared hope that the woman about whom Rollo spoke was—

". . . holding captive a *knarr*, its small crew, and a beautiful silver-haired woman who claims she seeks a man, and his small son, who serves me."

Leif felt the earth drop from beneath him. A roaring

sounded in his ears. And an incongruous mixture of joy and terror spurted through him, sapping his strength for the briefest of moments.

" 'Tisn't worth my while—nor can I spare much man-power—to recapture a lone ship and its crew from Robert of Neustria at the moment," Rollo continued. "He'll smart a long while, I don't doubt, from my having wrested a portion of his duchy from him. If the time for a confrontation must come, 'twill be later rather than sooner, and that will be more to my liking."

Leif looked up at his liege, forcing his mouth to form the words while his thoughts were in utter chaos. "I thought Robert of Neustria was an ally of Charles and, therefore, yours."

Rollo stopped beneath a mature, blossom-laden tree. He lifted his chin and sniffed the fragrant blooms at the tip of a branch in front of his face. "I don't remember so sweet a scent from the few apple trees in Norvegia, do you, Haraldsson?" He slanted Leif a look that Leif missed, so caught up was he in speculation. And emotion. "Then again, mayhap I didn't notice such things back then."

Leif looked at him, trying to focus on what he was saying. He wanted to shout at him, shake him into telling all he knew. But he would not dare to do so now that the outlawed Northman was Count of Rouen and Leif his vassal, according to Frankish custom.

But Rollo evidently wasn't oblivious to Leif's reaction to his revelation. "Robert of Neustria only bides his time. As long as 'tis convenient to ally himself with Charles, he will do so. But he has more ambitious plans, mark me. And he harbors a special hatred for Norsemen, to be sure. I don't envy those unfortunates within his grasp."

"Harfleur?" Leif repeated, his mind suddenly racing with plans as Rollo's last statement reunited him with coherent thought.

"Aye. I can spare you mayhap five or so of my men—

and especially a few like Fingar and Tor, who knew you back in Oslof—if these captives turn out to be friends of yours, and perhaps your woman as well." He gave Leif an assessing look. "If you are interested in a rescue, my friend, you might want to consider this: Robert of Neustria can be utterly merciless when crossed."

"He has *my* wife! *My* crew! *My* ship!"

Little Thor straightened after adding a bundle of faggots to the small fire. "You forget, Kiisku-Liinu, that you have your own life, your son's life. Now a fief, too. No wife. No crew. No ship."

Leif narrowed his eyes at him in annoyance. "You know exactly what I mean."

"Mayhap 'tis Braided-Beard and man with blue tooth. They use the woman to lure you to your death."

Leif glanced over at the door separating Eirik and Hilaire—the Frankish woman who cared for Eirik—from the main hall, and lowered his voice. "By the gods, red man, why would they bother to travel so far just to kill me?" He shook his head and moved to stand directly before Little Thor. "I think somehow they managed to save *Wave Rider*, whatever the reason, and were bringing Morgana to me."

"You think with your pride . . . and heart, not your head. The woman may wish to find Eirik. Kill you herself."

Leif swung away from the red man with impatience. "You don't understand, do you? I'll always love her. Naught she could do can ever change that."

The silence that gathered in the newly-repaired stone and thatch manor hall weighed heavily on Leif in the wake of his words. What did he know of Matiassu's capacity for love? He never spoke of his dead wife and family. He'd once told Leif that his people considered it rude to speak of the dead. But that didn't mean that the red man didn't

213

feel as deeply as any other man . . . hadn't ever loved as deeply as Leif still loved.

"I understand," came the soft reply at last.

Leif's eyes met and held Little Thor's. "Then mayhap you understand that whether or not Morgana wished to lure me to my death, she is a prisoner now. And I will—*must*—go to her aid."

Little Thor looked down for a moment, pensive. "You must determine which men are with her. If they are enemies—Bluetooth or Braided-Beard—you step into another trap . . . even if you fool the Frankish guards." He shook his head. "Very difficult. Dangerous. Maybe impossible."

Leif closed his eyes for a moment, then blew out his breath. His expression was bleak but determined when he looked at his friend again. "I know that. But it makes no difference. You can stay here with Eirik while I—"

Little Thor shook his head. "We must do this at night. I am good at . . ." He considered for a moment, a thoughtful frown creasing his forehead as he obviously searched for the right word. ". . . stealth."

Leif allowed himself a shadow of a smile. "A Northman wouldn't consider that an attribute."

Little Thor's frown deepened.

"A good thing for a man to possess," Leif explained, "this ability to sneak about quietly."

"I thank Wishemenetoo I am not a foolish Northman."

Leif laughed aloud, then quickly sobered. "We'll go to Fécamp for the men Rollo has offered, although I would speak to the messenger from Harfleur first. Surely he can be of help."

Little Thor nodded, and Leif turned toward the partitioned corner where Eirik slept. "We'll leave at dawn," he said softly, then moved away, thinking that he would ask Rollo himself if he would assume responsibility for Eirik in the event of his death.

He didn't want to disturb the child, but in the wake of

the possibility of his death, he had to say goodbye to Eirik in his own mind at least. Much as Leif would have wished it otherwise, he grimly acknowledged the fact that he might not live to see his son again.

Morgana's spirits were lower than they'd been in months—in fact, since Leif had taken Eirik from Oslof. She sat with her back against a crude palisade, contained against her will with the rest of *Wave Rider*'s crew; the very men who had left their homes and relatives, had risked life and limb, to help her find Leif.

They had promised nothing more, since not a man among them would ever have raised a hand to Leif Haraldsson. Most among the half score of men sought new lands and homes, for since their return from across the sea they had known real oppression. Not so much from Sweyn Estrithsson, for he was all but a shell of a man since Hakon's death; useless for much more than grieving and retreating into himself. Rather it was from Horik Bluetooth. The only time Sweyn had shown more than token animation was when anyone questioned Horik's right to assume the jarl's responsibilities as leader: Sweyn would rouse himself enough to turn absolutely savage. Horik's slow, insidious assumption of Sweyn's authority wasn't an outright maneuver, but only a halfwit would have failed to understand what was happening.

Several other Northmen had been sent to Oslof by Harald Fairhair. Morgana and many of the remaining men in the settlement would have wagered anything that those men hadn't just "wandered" into Oslof in search of new lands, as they'd claimed.

If the men who'd manned *Wave Rider* had no wish to harm Leif Haraldsson in any way, it didn't matter to Morgana. All she'd wanted was a means to find Leif; and, therefore, Eirik. She'd channeled her fury into positive forces . . . determination and drive.

Therefore, in the face of this major setback—possibly even an unfortunate end to their quest and their lives—Morgana inwardly railed against the powers that were.

It wasn't fair. Not to her. Not to Eirik. And certainly not to the men who'd taken up her cause.

No one had forced them to go, she reminded herself. If they liked Francia, they would settle here.

Two afternoons had crawled by, both balmy days, the warm sun turning hot as it had passed almost directly overhead. Now it slowly sank into the western sky, bringing twilight, then dusk, and once again, night.

Frustration made her fight the bonds that held her wrists, scraping her skin raw, even as she acknowledged it was futile. The rough wooden stakes behind her were also ineffective in fraying her fetters. With hobbled ankles and gagged mouth, Morgana could do little but lean against the wooden wall, struggling for air, when she'd exhausted herself from her efforts.

The men, she knew, were in even worse straits, for they were tied to iron rings in the stockade and had less mobility than she. She wondered how old Guthrum fared. The frail old man had surprised them all by insisting he go with them.

And so Morgana sat on the earthen floor of the dark, damp compound. She fought for air. Fought the tears that would avail her nothing. Fought the nagging images of Snorri's men as they'd poked and prodded her in private places while dragging her, trussed, into the compound.

"If you don't cooperate," one of the men had rasped in her ear as she'd initially fought like a wild woman for her freedom, "Snorri will allow us to taste your considerable charms—every *one* of us—and you'll surely die before you see another dawn."

It hadn't been the thought of death, or even slavery, that

had frightened Morgana into temporary submission. Rather, the thought of the abuse of her body by the rapacious Norse mercenaries had prompted her to end her resistance.

When Ragnar had thrown himself against his guards, gnashing his teeth in obvious frustration at their rough treatment of Morgana, Snorri the Black himself had threatened, "One more trick like that and I'll carve the blood eagle from your back."

The threat evidently gave Ragnar pause, for although the hatred honing his features didn't diminish, neither did he repeat his foolhardy actions. No man, Morgana thought, could be blamed for preferring to avoid having his rib cage split and his lungs ripped from his back while still alive.

The men were blindfolded, but Morgana had been spared that final humiliation, although what purpose maintaining her sight would serve, she couldn't imagine at the moment. No torches lit the compound. Only those carried by any of their captors who'd entered after darkness had fallen provided some illumination.

It was a dark night, darker than the night before, the inky sky shadowed with even blacker rain clouds—black as Snorri's hair, Morgana thought with bitterness, and his heart; the air was heavy with humidity.

In the midst of her slowly sinking hopes, her growing melancholy, she roused herself to look at the men who'd accompanied her. Even though her eyes had adjusted to the darkness, she couldn't make out much more than outlines against the stockade wall. Their faces were a pale blur, interrupted by the shadowed slash of their blindfolds. If they were all sold as slaves in the East, they would more than likely either perish en route from attempting to escape, or die in captivity. They would never live the new lives most of them were seeking.

" 'Tis all your fault, Leif Haraldsson," she whispered to

the image she conjured up in an effort to stoke the ashes of her anger.

It began to work; she could feel that emotion leap to life within her. It hadn't been far from the surface since the time Leif Haraldsson left to go a-viking—what seemed like a lifetime ago.

"You betrayed my trust. *Just until the birth of our first child.* I asked you, and you agreed. You traitor!"

The night wind soughed through the trees and eddied around the outer shell of the crude compound wall, sounding like a whispered recrimination. It echoed her own softly-spoken words: *Traitor . . . traitor . . . traaaiii-torrr!*

"I want my son back! Eirik . . . Eirik!" she cried to herself, not daring to make a sound through her gag and alert anyone who might be on guard outside their prison. Unwanted, unwelcome tears of anguish spilled over her lower lashes, onto her cheeks.

Before she finally slipped into exhausted slumber in the darkness presaging the dawn, Morgana sat for a long, long time, thinking about her beloved little boy, nursing her grudge against Leif Haraldsson.

In the impenetrable gloom, as the swollen skies threatened to let loose their burden on the earth below, Morgana acknowledged that her profound love for the man who had sired Eirik had finally turned to hatred.

She vowed to every Norse god she knew, that if she lived to see him again, and if Eirik was anything but safe and sound, she would kill Leif herself.

The object of her dire thoughts lay on his belly beside Little Thor, praying for the rain. In the added obscurity of a shower—and preferably a deluge—they hoped to more easily accomplish the taking of the compound guards and the freeing of the prisoners.

With any luck, if the elements cooperated, they could

take the *knarr* as well, leaving most of the men to return to Fécamp with the horses, the others to join the crew in taking *Wave Rider* by sea.

Attempting to avoid thoughts of what failure of their mission would mean, Leif forced himself to mull over what had transpired earlier in Fécamp . . .

Rollo had decided to loan him a score of men rather than only a handful.

"Harfleur is on the northern bank of the Seine . . . territory that I consider within my grant from the king." Rollo's eyes had narrowed as he'd raised his specially carved, oversized cup to his lips. He drank, then added, "Or *will* be part of my domain in the near future."

He'd thrown back his great blond head then and let out a roar of laughter that shook the beams overhead. "I think Robert of Neustria is testing me already over the land around the mouth of the Seine. 'Tis an important area for commerce . . . the gateway to Rouen, and then Paris farther east." His gaze cut to Leif, his eyes probing those of his vassal. "Take a score of men—more, if you think you need them, but do not fail me . . ."

Leif and Little Thor had chosen the messenger from Harfleur, Ulf, who turned out to be an able, strapping man, and nineteen other warriors. With Ulf's knowledge of the number and exact placement of guards, the whereabouts of the prisoners, and the best way to enter the compound, Leif felt his chances of success increase accordingly.

Now, as they lay in wait behind the cover of the riverbank, Leif prayed fervently for rain. Nay, not merely rain, but a heavy rain with, perhaps, the accompaniment of thunder to help conceal any warning cries from the Franks on guard.

If ever he needed a resurgence of the luck that had deserted him in Norvegia, it was in the next hour or so ahead.

He invoked Odin, and Thor . . . and the Christian god, his fingers going to the crucifix against his breast in what had become an unconscious habit since leaving Norvegia.

From his position among his strategically placed men, he strained to catch every detail against the darkness that enshrouded Harfleur. At last, one of the divinities he'd summoned seemed to have heard his plea. The skies were suddenly rent by a jagged seam of lightning, thunder boomed in the distance, and the first raindrops began to pelt the earth.

A rough hand over her throat pulled Morgana from fitful slumber. She was knocked sideways. Her head thumped against the stockade wall behind her, and lights exploded behind her eyes.

As a heavy body positioned itself over hers, her sleep-dazed mind suddenly registered what was happening. The first emotion to hit her was fear—fear of suffocating, for it was difficult enough to breathe through the dry rag stuffed into her mouth, let alone work to suck in additional air as her attacker's weight forced the breath from her lungs.

She tried to scream, knowing even as she made the feeble attempt that it was futile. And even if she could alert the other men with the pitiful whimpers from her throat, she would accomplish nothing except possibly to add to their frustration at their inability to protect her.

"Ah, silver-haired Freya," growled a low voice in her ear. "Don't fret, for I'll be gentle, lest I ruin your considerable market value." He chuckled. "Even among Norse-women, you would stand out."

Morgana strained to make out his features, but she could only discern dark hair framing the lighter shade of his skin. Then, suddenly, lightning sizzled across the sky, backlighting his form.

Snorri the Black.

Rain began to fall. Morgana didn't notice . . . until she realized that if it increased in intensity, there was a slim chance the Dane would give up.

"Lie still and enjoy my attentions," he told her, bursting in upon her brief, desperate thoughts. "'Twill undoubtedly be the last time you're mounted by one of your own kind."

You're not one of my own kind! she screamed silently, attempting without success to bring her knees up and plow them into his belly. He was tall and strongly built, she remembered from what she'd seen of him, and wouldn't budge.

She jerked her head from side to side, trying to evade his mouth, the stink of sour wine and sweat adding to the revulsion that bubbled up in her throat. She heard the bones in her neck creak against the unaccustomed jarring movement, and earned herself a crack across the jaw. The blow threatened to send her spinning into oblivion . . . except that the obscene things he was doing with his hands beneath her skirt, and his mouth, which was moving down her neck, wouldn't allow her even that temporary retreat.

Allfather, help me, she entreated as she fought for air against the choking bile behind the rag in her throat, and attempted to dislodge his crushing weight from her torso. *I don't want to die . . .*

The pouring rain made for treacherous footing, but the crashing thunder was a welcome ally as Leif and his men left their hiding places and put into play their carefully-laid strategy.

As Leif followed Little Thor through the rain, dodging for any cover between their initial position and the stockaded area where prisoners were held, he was relieved to make out a man standing guard in the downpour before the crude gate facing them. He'd been nagged by the fear that they would be too late . . . that Snorri the Black would

221

be eager to have begun the highly profitable, if hazardous, journey to the East with his latest "acquisitions" for the slave trade.

That they would already be gone.

Ulf, Leif had discovered, had accompanied the Dane several times in the past. "He's a wily trader—ill-treats his men and women, then gives them a few days to recover before they reach Constantinople. And he has several men he deals with . . . rich men from the slave trade . . ." He'd shaken his head then. "I pity the woman. She is comely enough to turn even a eunuch's head, and Snorri always samples what he considers his . . . goods."

Leif could only hope that neither Snorri—nor any of his men—had touched Morgana; and every time he thought of anyone touching her, abusing her, his stomach clenched, and helpless frustration fired his fury, for Northmen could be brutal with both men and women.

He used that very anger to drive him through the rain now, imitating Little Thor's every lithe and silent move, discarding what years of experience had taught him—to fearlessly confront the enemy head-on.

Without warning, the man looming over Morgana was jerked away, the fingers of one hand still clinging to the neck of her overgown, causing it to rend as he was dragged from her.

Relief seeped through her, and she pulled her knees to her chest and tried to roll out of the way of the struggling men. Lightning scored the sky and thunder crashed overhead. In the bright flash she caught the image of one man burying a dagger in Snorri's throat. She hardened her heart and ignored the weak protests of her compassionate side. The perverse satisfaction she deliberately nurtured, instead, was contrary to the Morgana of only a few winters ago.

On the heels of relief and hope, however, fear came creeping into her breast. Was she next? She had no way of knowing if it was Robert of Neustria or one his other Franks who had dispatched Snorri. Nor had she any idea why a Frank would come to her rescue if she were destined for the slave market. Unless the other man wanted to have her himself . . .

She tilted back onto her hips to enable her to thrust her bound feet at the newcomer. She could barely make him out, but suddenly he veered away. Another man, smaller in stature than the first, was bending over one of the bound and gagged captives. The barely discernable but welcome sound of a familiar voice came to her above nature's discordant symphony: Ragnar. Then another voice. Then the babble of several.

Lightning flared briefly, enough for Morgana to make out the men from *Wave Rider* pushing themselves to their feet, aided by half a dozen others. One of the latter—she couldn't make out anything more than that he was tall—approached her before she could even think twice about it, and pulled her to her feet by her bound wrists, his apparent urgency communicated to her by his swift and none-too-gentle actions.

Her knees buckled, stiff and sore from sitting for almost two days and nights. In one movement, he hauled her over his shoulder, as if impatient with her temporary disability, and swung toward the gate.

Morgana renewed her efforts to spit out her gag, but in vain. She struggled to raise her head and shoulders enough to squint through the sheeting rain. Were the men from *Wave Rider* coming, as well?

She caught a glimpse of others following close behind. The man beneath her, however, rewarded her efforts with a warning smack on her bottom. Mortified, Morgana stilled, hesitant to earn another humiliating blow in spite of her extreme annoyance.

223

She bounced about uncomfortably on his shoulder as they exited the compound, swallowing her anger as she realized that her cooperation would undoubtedly help ensure their escape. And what did it matter? she asked herself. They were being freed. The method didn't matter, nor, particularly, the identity of their liberators.

Suddenly, Morgana was unceremoniously dropped from the cradle of her rescuer's shoulder. She slipped in the mud and landed on her back. Instantly, he was on top of her.

By the gods! she thought in dismay. Was she to be "rescued" from one attacker only to be set upon by another? She struggled against his weight, and began choking on the saliva gathering behind the gag.

The man put a forearm across her throat in obvious warning, which only made her increase her struggles. His other hand fumbled with the knot beneath her head; then he was pulling the gag free of her mouth.

When she would have spoken, only a hoarse husk of sound emerged, and his free hand replaced the gag. "Be *still*," he hissed into her ear, "else you get us all killed!"

Morgana froze.

It couldn't be . . .

Just then thunder crashed across the roiling heavens, and crackling silver tines pitchforked the sky. Surely Thor himself was riding his rumbling chariot above while Mjolnir spat lightning. It was as if Odin's son had deliberately provided that perfectly-timed, brilliant burst of illumination to enable Morgana to see exactly *who* had rescued her. In spite of his rain-plastered hair, the water runneling down his face . . .

A score of varied emotions tumbled through her, but the most powerful, the one that overrode all others, was rage. Raw, festering, unadulterated rage. Directed at the man she had once loved . . . the father of her child . . . the one who was in the very process of rescuing her.

Morgana did the unthinkable.

With a jerk of her leg—all the force of her long-tamped fury lending her added strength—she kneed him squarely in the groin.

Chapter Fifteen

With a dark sense of satisfaction, Morgana heard his grunt of pain, then received the full brunt of his weight as he collapsed on top of her. She struggled to push him away. Let him lie moaning in the mud until Robert of Neustria or any of Snorri's men found him at first light, she thought spitefully. They'd make short work of him.

Surely you are mad! came an echo of her old self. *He was trying to save your life . . . and those of the other men. And what about Eirik? How will you—*

She didn't complete the thought. Someone else was roughly pulling her up from the ground. Another man bent over Leif. Morgana couldn't make out who jerked her to her feet in the pouring rain, but he was obviously deadly serious about his mission. And none too pleased with what she'd done to Leif.

For the second time that night, she took a glancing blow to the jaw.

"Fool *equiwa!*" grated a voice in her ear, as the storm-ravaged world reeled.

Although she didn't understand what he was saying, the words were ominous-sounding, and Morgana immediately identified him: Little Thor.

He shoved her toward a third man, and bent to join the man crouched over Leif. Between them, they hoisted him to his feet, supporting him beneath his arms. Morgana saw no more, for the man beside her clapped a hand across her mouth and began dragging her away from the manor and compound.

Anger rose within her. Leif had removed her gag, only to have one of his cohorts slap his hand over her mouth. *How can they trust you after what you just did to Leif?* asked a little voice.

Morgana ignored it and silently cursed the physical strength of men, even as, once again, she acknowledged that it was useless to struggle. She couldn't distinguish *Wave Rider*'s crew from their rescuers but, for the moment, as long as they were free, that was all that mattered.

Morgana sensed they were heading toward the ship. She envisioned in her mind's eye the details she'd noticed of the layout of the village and its manor when they'd been herded toward what became their stockaded prison. It seemed to her they were moving toward the beach . . . and *Wave Rider*.

No one appeared to be following them—Leif's party must have dispatched the guards stationed at the compound gate, and the noise of the storm surely covered their activity.

Whatever was happening, wherever they were going, it was well-planned, she concluded. Then she concentrated on keeping her footing in the mud so the man behind her would have no reason to drag and shove her like a recalcitrant donkey.

Without warning, a warrior came at them from the rain-swept darkness—sodden, ferocious-looking, and wielding a battle-ax. It had to be one of Snorri's men, Morgana guessed by the weapon and the stark savagery scrawled across his features. He went for the man holding Morgana.

Without a sound, Little Thor materialized and met the attacking Northman head-on. Morgana didn't see what happened, for her captor didn't let up in his efforts to keep them both moving away; nor did the single man supporting the dazed Leif pause either, she noticed as he caught up with them from out of the curtain of rain. Another man quickly took up Little Thor's burden.

Morgana had no idea if anyone went to the Skraeling's aid, nor did she particularly care. He was little higher in her favor than Leif Haraldsson, and if she'd had the chance, she'd have held a dagger to the red man's throat until she drew blood—or worse—in order to learn exactly where Eirik was.

The mud beneath her feet suddenly turned to wet sand. The going became even more awkward. In the flickering flares of lightning, Morgana caught brief glimpses of scattered men headed toward the bay, and the welcome outline of *Wave Rider* as it rocked invitingly in the shallow breakers.

Morgana huddled within the tent that still stood on the foredeck. She sat directly across from where Leif lay on his side, his eyes closed, his back to her. Little Thor rested on his haunches beside him, his features stern and still as if they were carved from bedrock. He said not a word to Morgana, ignoring her totally.

The storm hadn't abated, and it drowned out most other sounds. The vessel beneath her shifted as *Wave Rider* was nudged from her partially beached position over the sand and backed fully into the water. Morgana knew several men would take up the few oar positions in the bow and stern quarters until they were safely in deeper waters. Dangerous as a storm might have been for the lighter and more flexible *langskip*, the *knarr* was steady as a rock, even in howling winds and towering seas.

"Where is my son?" she demanded finally when she had managed to regain her breath and her composure. Her lips

228

quivered slightly with cold, for her clothing was drenched and clung to her skin like an icy shroud.

Little Thor's dark eyes flicked over her with contempt. Morgana returned his gaze without flinching, totally unconcerned about what he thought of her. Her primary concern was obtaining information from him.

But the red man continued his silence, his attention returning to Leif's face in obvious dismissal of her.

"Is Eirik alive?" she persisted. "Tell me if he is alive, at least!"

In the face of the Skraeling's continued silence, she moved to grab his arm. He jerked it away without so much as a glance.

"Ingrid was so wrong about you," she told him in a voice husky with loathing.

Without warning, his dark gaze knifed into hers, but Morgana was too upset to notice what had snagged his attention.

"She said you were a good man. If she only knew—"

Just then Leif groaned softly, rolling onto his back, his head toward Morgana. She stilled, her gaze going to his face, noting for the first time the beard he'd grown.

And missing the emotion that flared in Little Thor's sloe eyes, the muscle tic in his cheek before he looked away.

Leif's lashes lifted and Morgana met confusion-clouded, topaz eyes. Morgana? he thought, disoriented, and struggling to clear his mind. She was muddy and bedraggled, looking like a drowned muskrat, but never was the sight of anyone more welcome. Relief seeped through him.

He opened his mouth to speak, but she cut him off without ceremony: "Tell me what you've done with my son, you thieving wretch!"

The strident tone of her voice, the outrage darkening her eyes—to say nothing of the words themselves—brought his memory roaring back. And instantly focused his attention on the throbbing ache between his thighs. He hefted himself to his elbows, his brows suddenly flattening into a frown. Nausea spiraled up from the pit of his stomach. The blood receded from his face.

He swallowed once and set his teeth against the pain. " 'Twas *you* . . . you deliberately tried to unman me!" he accused in a hoarse voice. "After I hastened to your rescue and—"

"If I'd known where to find Eirik, I'd not have stopped at castration. Where *is* he?"

Leif eased himself to a sitting position, his initial relief and joy after two endless winters of separation quelled by her greeting. He missed the black look Little Thor directed at Morgana when she'd implied her willingness to kill Leif.

Ragnar ducked under the canopy just then, bringing a shower of water with him. He grinned at Leif through his dripping beard and moustache. "By the gods, Leif Haraldsson, some of that luck of yours rubbed off on us! Here we are, practically on your doorstep, before Loki interferes and delivers us right into the hands of Robert of Neustria and his mercenaries." He glanced at Morgana, who was watching Leif with narrowed eyes. "Thor's hammer, I never expected to have you, of all people, come to our rescue!" He shook his head, then threw it back in sudden laughter. "But then again, who else?"

" 'Tis good to see you—and the others, Ragnar," Leif answered, a smile widening his mouth in spite of the pain in his loins and his anger at Morgana. Then his smile turned to a frown. "Did Sweyn send you?"

"Don't be a fool," Morgana answered as Ragnar shook his head. "*I* persuaded them to search for you . . . for Eirik."

"And many of us wanted to see what better things awaited a man here in Francia, if he was willing to settle down and work the land."

Leif stared at Morgana, remarking how much she seemed to have changed. He'd always suspected she was tough beneath the tender-hearted exterior—tough when she had to be. That suspicion had first been confirmed when he'd returned to Oslof after their unforeseen shipwreck.

Unexpected admiration—and hope—sprang up within him, in spite of her open hostility. "*You* brought them here?"

" 'Twas my idea, but they joined me out of mutual need, the same means to different ends. I needed to find you, and they needed to see if better lives awaited them away from Norvegia and Harald Fairhair."

She leaned forward, her eyes locking with his. "Make no mistake, Haraldsson. I needed to find you because Eirik was with you, and I love my son more than anything! Naught would have stopped me from finding him. Not even your perfidy."

Obviously unwilling to remain in the small enclosure while Leif and Morgana aired their differences, Ragnar said, "Where are we headed? What course shall I set?"

"Ulf will know. He is an informer for Rollo, so tell the others—if they recognize him as one of Snorri's warriors—that he is on our side. He led us right to you, and we are all in his debt. He knows exactly what course to set for Fécamp."

Ragnar's red brows peaked in surprise, before he frowned briefly. "I thought he looked familiar . . . one of the Dane's henchmen." But he merely nodded and backed away, disappearing into the darkness beyond the crude shelter.

Leif looked at Little Thor. "Do you know if we lost any men?"

The red man nodded. "All have returned."

"Good. Will you leave us now, my friend?"

Little Thor straightened, threw Morgana a warning look, then left them alone.

* * *

"We both could have been killed because of your misguided sense of vengeance."

Morgana's look turned to disbelief. "Misguided? I think not! You *stole* my child. You were outlawed . . . banished, and you took a small boy with you—against his and his mother's wishes—into unknown danger!"

"Both Little Thor and I would have defended him with our lives, surely you should have known that. And just how do you know what Eirik wanted?" he asked, acknowledging to himself that it was an idiotic question . . . that he was grasping at straws in an effort to excuse his actions.

"A child who was only two winters old couldn't know what he wanted!"

"You forget, Morgana," Leif charged, fighting the beginnings of another wave of nausea, "that he is my child as well. You cannot steal that which already belongs to you."

A man cannot steal something that's already his, Morgana . . . Ingrid's words returned to echo Leif's.

Morgana dismissed that piece of reasoning from her mind and leaned forward on her knees, her hands braced against them. "Eirik is a person, not a belonging to be hauled about at will. No decent father could ever forget that. How could you be so selfish as to put your own wishes before his welfare?"

His eyes narrowed, but she continued before he could answer.

"The same way you broke your promise and left me before he was born, that's how! I never really knew you, Leif Haraldsson. You're self-centered and arrogant, heedless of the feelings of anyone but yourself."

"I see," he answered, inwardly stunned at her vehement words. His own anger continued to grow apace with hers. "And you could not even try to understand how I felt returning to Oslof—to *nothing*. Learning of my father's very suspicious 'accidental' death . . . seeing my wife wed to another man . . . believing at first that Eirik was yours and Hakon's and not mine—"

"That was your own fault!" she cut across his words. "Because you wouldn't listen to reason!"

He ignored her statement. "When I was banished for defending myself—weaponless, I might add—against Hakon's dagger, I knew you were lost to me, so I took the only thing left. The one thing that was irrefutably mine . . . my son. Not Hakon's son. *My* son."

The volume of his voice had risen, but he wouldn't have cared in those heated moments, even had it been a calm, quiet night.

"He's not a *thing!*" she lashed back, trembling in outrage at his audacious assumption. "In your own selfish, grasping, underhanded way, you aren't any different—not one whit better—than Harald Fairhair or Horik Bluetooth . . . or Snorri the Black! Now, *where is my son?*"

"Safe and sound, Morgana. You'll see him if and when I let you."

"You'll let me see him, all right, and then you'll let me take him home."

"His home is with me. Who's more concerned about his welfare now? You would take him back to Norvegia . . . to Sweyn, who no doubt hates him because he's my son. To Horik Bluetooth? To a Norvegia fast bending beneath the iron fist of Fairhair?" He shook his head. "You may see him, but you'll not take him from my care." Now he leaned forward, their faces less than an arm's length apart. He thrust aside the long-simmering desire that threatened to dilute his anger, the love that refused to wither. "In fact, my unfaithful wife, now you may consider yourself under my care as well . . . as my prisoner . . . my slave . . . mayhap even my whore—"

"Never! I am a free woman!"

"Whatever I deem fit," he continued inexorably, his

features hardening. "We are in Francia now . . . not Oslof."

When he was able to stand without evincing the piercing pain in his groin, Leif moved out onto the open deck with relief. One part of him felt deliriously happy being with Morgana once again—so close to her that he could reach out and touch her.

On the other hand, the tension between them wasn't sexual, as it had been in Oslof two winters before. Rather, it was caused by her hostility and his reciprocal hurt and anger. And the longer he was in such close confines with her, the worse it became.

It greatly disturbed him.

Therefore it was doubly refreshing to feel *Wave Rider* beneath his feet again when at last he stood on deck out in the open—and especially after he'd thought the ship had been sacrificed to bear Hakon to the realm of Asgard.

The oars had been put up, the sail raised, and as they headed northeast, they left the storm behind. The night skies cleared, leaving winking stars overhead and a bright full moon that shone like a shield boss polished to perfection. Leif breathed deeply of the zesty sea air, essaying to sweep Morgana from his mind with the wind.

He embraced Ragnar and Olaf and Egil and the others in his happiness at seeing many of his faithful crew. Rollo's men and those from Oslof soon found much to talk about, especially since a few familiar faces were among Rollo's retainers. It didn't take long for the new Count of Rouen's men to enthrall the crew with their stories of Rollo's largesse; of the verdant, fruitful lands of what some were already calling "Normandy" after the Northmen who held it for King Charles, with its temperate climate that beckoned a man to remain and make it his home.

". . . uncounted orchards with blossoms as far as you can

see," said one, "scented sweeter than aught you've ever known—"

"Save a comely wench's thighs," added one man with a lewd leer, causing the men to break into laughter.

". . . greener than the grass in Norvegia, and warm . . ." continued another when the laughter had died away.

"Imagine the finest summer you can remember from home, but longer and warmer . . ."

"And the winters are naught like home . . . rather like our early spring just before Cuckoo Month they are . . ."

"*Já*. And you don't have to eat seaweed in the winter because times are so bad . . ."

They were like bragging youths, these fierce Norsemen, trying to outdo one another in wondrous revelations, Leif thought with an inner smile.

But in spite of this, as the sun rose higher and they neared Fécamp, a heaviness sat like a stone on his chest. He'd known Morgana would be furious with him for taking Eirik away from her, but he hadn't been prepared for her hatred. He found himself refusing to accept the fact that she obviously felt no love for him . . . or so she had convinced herself.

But if even the most reasonable person considered all that had happened in the last four or five winters—if Leif had put himself in Morgana's place—could anyone have expected differently?

Of course! said his pride.

Mayhap not, countered his more objective side.

They'd both wronged each other, he realized with a jolt. Perhaps, then—as far as Morgana was concerned—it was too late to rekindle what she once felt for him.

Perhaps too much time had passed. Perhaps they had both changed too much.

His mind, heart, and soul shied away from the very thought. He couldn't accept it. *Wouldn't* accept it. Love didn't just vanish! Love lasted forever, didn't it? asked his kinder self—a legacy from the mother he never knew.

After all, he reasoned as he stared unseeingly over *Wave Rider*'s freeboard at the glassy swells of the sea, he still loved Morgana, in spite of what he considered her betrayal.

But then, he remembered, she'd had plenty of time to nurse her disappointment, her anger, her bitterness, in spite of her attempts to portray her marriage to Hakon Sweynsson as happy. A long time for uncertainties to turn to bad feelings. For those feelings, right or wrong, to fester.

And love can turn to hate . . .

Could it? he wondered, suspecting he knew the answer if he cared to give it some thought.

Then and there, Leif Haraldsson vowed to the Christian god he'd recently embraced that he would be patient with her . . . and certainly more gentle. No more rash, irresponsible actions—like the time he'd broken his promise to her. No more hurt or betrayal . . .

He'd learned something of patience during the time spent while *Wave Rider* was being repaired after the ill-fated voyage to the west. And, certainly, living with his small son had taught him patience. Now he had to cultivate it even further—swallow his pride, if necessary. He'd be an absolute fool to discount his phenomenal luck. Morgana had managed to find him. Then he had managed to free her from Robert of Neustria and bring her to Vallée de Vergers. Call it fortune, or the gods, or God—it was nothing short of miraculous.

The least he could do was exercise forbearance and self-control . . .

Morgana finally emerged from the canopied shelter, shielding her eyes against the sun. Leif watched her from where Olaf held the tiller bar, gazing upon her beautiful hair which shone, tangled as it was, beneath the gentle rays of the morning sun. Her profile, as she looked out to sea for long moments, was just as pure as he remembered. Memories of happier times came flooding back, so poignant that he felt a suspicious burning behind his eyes, an unexpectedly powerful and ineffable yearning for what had been.

She looked like Freya, her shimmering hair floating on the sea breeze, her head held high, her shoulders . . .

It suddenly came to him. *That* was what was different about her . . . subtle but definite. Her bearing was more . . . determined. More aggressive, more self-assured. You wouldn't find Morgana quietly submitting to anyone's demands anymore, Leif suspected. The strongest elements of her nature had been dragged to the fore, willing or not, and it was as if Morgana Magnussdóttir had been turned inside out. Her strength and confidence, her resilience, were what characterized her demeanor now, her softer and sweeter side turned inward but, he hoped, still there.

If it weren't, he realized, he might never win her back.

He hadn't exactly attempted to woo her thus far, he thought with heavy irony. Rather, he'd informed her that she was his prisoner . . . his slave. Not exactly the best way to win any woman . . . especially since she seemed to wish him dead.

What a coil! he thought, his gaze still on Morgana. He had her back . . . here, with him. They were a family now, except that Morgana wanted nothing to do with him. She wanted to take their son and leave.

His mouth tightened, his features turning bleak. Never.

In that moment, Morgana, sensing someone was watching her, turned and met his look. It was dark, fiercely determined.

Her own features registered intense dislike as she silently accepted his unspoken challenge.

Wave Rider docked temporarily at Fécamp. Rollo was extremely pleased with Leif's success, and told him so. Morgana and the crew from the *knarr* were all present in the great hall at Fécamp, at Rollo's behest, when he met with Leif to hear what had transpired.

"Right from beneath his nose!" Rollo declared, a crooked grin of satisfaction transforming his huge, fierce face.

Morgana couldn't believe the size of the man. Small wonder the King of Francia chose to deal with him as an ally—albeit in a forced "alliance"—rather than an enemy.

On the way to Fécamp, Egil, as a *skald*, had asked endless questions of the men Rollo had sent with Leif. When Morgana had wondered aloud how Rollo had become a count under the Frankish king, Egil told her, "Charles didn't have much choice, so they say. It seems the giant had already confiscated the lands which Charles formally ceded to him. In exchange for becoming Count of Rouen, Rollo pledged himself to Charles . . . to protect the lands he'd been granted against any foreign incursions—including by other Northmen—and even by some of Charles's mighty subjects who would undermine him from within. Rollo agreed to embrace Christianity and to wed Count Béranger's daughter."

Egil had made a wry face, his dark eyes dancing. " 'Tis, no doubt, evidence of why his subjects call him Charles the Simple."

Morgana had nodded thoughtfully. " 'Twould seem the Frankish king is more unlucky than simple."

Rollo himself broke into Morgana's musings. He stood before her, lifting her chin with his hand, which could have easily engulfed her entire face. Morgana bit back a wince as his fingers encountered the tender spot on her jaw. "A beauty, this one, Leif the Lucky. I see why you were so eager to risk your hide. Your wife?"

"Aye."

"Nei!"

Rollo frowned slightly, then his hand fell away. He threw back his great fair head in laughter that shook the hall. " 'Twould seem that we have a difference of opinion here," he said then, obviously taking into account Morgana's answer as well as the look on her face. He bent until his face was even with hers. "If he wronged you, why did you seek him out, eh?"

A score of answers passed through her head, but before she could speak, Leif interjected softly, "Revenge. She seeks revenge."

Rollo's look changed subtly. Morgana thought she could see new respect in his eyes. "Any Northwoman worthy of her chatelaine would have done the same thing."

"Then tell him exactly what I did, Morgana," Leif encouraged, one of his eyebrows tilted.

A man cannot steal something that's already his . . . Ingrid's words came back to her, for the second time.

She looked at Rollo, then back at Leif, her eyes darkening to the dull blue-gray of an angry, heaving sea. The answer would sound ludicrous, she knew. That was exactly why Leif was encouraging her to give it.

She set her lips in a stubborn line.

Obviously sensing the tension between them, Rollo said with a shrug of his mammoth shoulders, "That is between the two of you. For now, be glad such a woman has braved the perils of travel from the homeland to seek you out, Haraldsson. There must be some reward in that alone." He waggled his eyebrows suggestively, and the men around them laughed bawdily. "Although already 'twould appear she's driven you to violence."

Leif noticed then, for the first time, the darkening bruise along one side of her jawline.

"Snorri the Black struck me," Morgana said quickly, uncertain as to just why she was telling only half of the truth, and therefore shielding Little Thor. Maybe it was because she could understand, even admire, such unquestionable loyalty, she thought with one tiny part of her mind that wasn't tainted by anger and hatred.

239

Rollo nodded. "And he earned himself a dishonorable death—weaponless and having his throat slit like a sheep in Autumn Month—in payment." He looked about him at the other newcomers from Norvegia. "Those who wish to remain here may swear fealty to me, then receive the tenure of a *mannshlutr*—a man's share, and arms and a horse to defend your land and your lord, when called upon. Or you may pledge yourself to Leif Haraldsson, as his retainer in any capacity suitable to both of you . . ."

Morgana turned away and went to sit beside Guthrum on a bench along one wall. She knew it was no use to try and hurry things along. She'd been separated from Eirik for two winters, and now that she knew for certain he was safe, she could discipline herself to wait a while longer.

"What does Hrolf say?" the old one asked her, for he was hard of hearing.

Morgana told him, and he nodded slowly, thoughtfully, his faded blue eyes resting on the man who towered above all others in the hall. Then he looked at Morgana. "I would that Ingrid were here, and little Harald." Sadness entered his eyes, and Morgana knew he was thinking about Gunnar, and Ingrid's subsequent loss of the child she'd been carrying. "They are all I have left, and I would rest easier if they were out of Oslof."

"You fear for their safety?" Morgana asked with a frown.

"Did you not notice Horik's interest in her?" Guthrum asked in answer. "She'll reject him out of hand, and he knows it. Once he tires of trying to insinuate himself into her favor, he'll turn dangerous. He's vicious, that one." Guthrum shook his head, his wispy white hair sliding across his bent shoulders with the movement. His eyes locked with hers. "We all know that, don't we?"

Morgana nodded. It was, in her estimation, a gross understatement. There were things that only Morgana knew . . . that Ingrid had revealed only to her best friend.

"When the time is right, I will talk to young Leif. He must know the truth."

Just then, Leif turned toward them and beckoned the old one to approach Rollo and himself.

Morgana had opened her mouth to question Guthrum, then realized now was not the time. If he wanted her to know, he would eventually tell her of his own volition.

And for now, she cared not one whit about anything Guthrum—or anyone else—had to say to Leif Haraldsson.

Chapter Sixteen

Leif's fief was located midway between Fécamp and Rouen. Leaving *Wave Rider* in Rollo's keeping, and at his disposal should he need the ship, Leif and the men who'd met him with the horses at Fécamp led Morgana and the others a little over a score of miles to Vallée de Vergers.

Morgana rode before Leif on Hrafn. She ignored him—his touch as the cadence of Hrafn's gait forced constant physical contact, his scent, his nearness for the hours it took to reach their destination. She ruthlessly trained her thoughts on her son and the fact that they would soon be reunited.

If she evinced any physical stirrings, Morgana told herself that the body and the mind were two separate entities, and if Leif's touch still stirred her physically, his presence had the opposite effect on her mind. She had once loved him, but he had caused that love to turn to hate, and nothing in this world or the next could ever change it.

She resented her physical response to him, but refused to dwell upon something as insignificant as mindless lust. And that was exactly what it was—she'd expected it, and therefore wasn't surprised when she realized that the response was still there.

"Vallée de Vergers," he whispered in her ear, startling her from her thoughts. "Look."

They were cresting a hillock, and Leif reined in Hrafn at the very top. Below them, spread like a tapestry of blue and green and white, was a lush valley of fields and pastures, orchards pregnant with blossom and scent, and a silver-blue ribbon of a stream bisecting the gently undulating valley almost exactly from north to south. A mill was perched on one bank of the stream, the wooden paddles of the millwheel working constantly with the slow but steady current of the water to create a faint rushing sound.

"The water sings as it goes through the millwheel, Morgana." His lips were at her ear, his breath sighing over her cheek. "Can you not hear it, *ást mín?*"

Even Morgana had to pause in her ruminations to note how reverent were his words, how everything was so green, it almost didn't look real. Except that there were a few men and women working within the ripening fields that basked beneath a benevolent sun.

Yes, it was beautiful, but that gave him no right to use the words of endearment that had just tumbled from his lips. Morgana deliberately ignored the beauty before her and wondered which humble dwelling housed Eirik.

She was dimly aware of the undercurrent of voices as those from Oslof voiced their awe at so beautiful a land. Indeed, in spite of the strange-sounding name of this place, it looked like a paradise.

" 'Tisn't real," Ragnar breathed from behind Leif, "this Val—"

"Vallée de Vergers," Leif supplied. It means Valley of Orchards."

Morgana opened her mouth, about to voice her question regarding Eirik. As if reading her intent, Leif said, "The manor house and the village are beyond yon stand of trees,"—he pointed to what looked like a small forest. "The Frank who held these lands is long since dead, but his tenants are sworn to me now, and I have land aplenty,

243

work aplenty, to offer any of those from Oslof who would remain."

"Where is Eirik?" Morgana asked coldly, as if she hadn't been listening to a word he'd said.

She felt Leif stiffen slightly behind her. She hoped it was with affront, for she wasn't the least bit interested in what he had been doing in Francia, in this place some were calling Normandy. Nor did she care what lands or position he now held. He was a murderer. An outlaw. The lowliest of thieves.

She only wanted her son. Then, she wanted to be gone from this place . . . and Leif Haraldsson.

"You'll see soon enough," he answered in as cold a voice as her own had been. He twisted in his saddle. "Behold what awaits you here, my friends," he said to the newcomers. He allowed himself a grin, for even in the face of Morgana's rejection, he couldn't quite squelch his excitement about and pride in his new acquisition, and his restored status under Rollo, who'd been an outcast from Norvegia himself. He inclined his head toward the valley below, telling himself that he had Morgana here with him and Eirik. He needed nothing else. "Welcome to Vallée de Vergers. Come and see it for yourselves."

The descent was leisurely, and Morgana suspected Leif wasn't only doing it for the benefit of the men from Oslof. He surely wanted to delay the moment when she would see Eirik once more until the anticipation was pure torture. Wouldn't that be just like him?

A small voice from somewhere in the area of her conscience answered, *Nei. Such cruelty was never Leif Haraldsson's way.*

She ignored it.

At last the manor stood before them. It was larger than the largest longhouse in Oslof, and made of the most substantial of building materials: stone. Clustered about it were a number of wood and thatch cottages. And another small stone building that she couldn't immediately identify.

Morgana didn't notice the peasants who ceased their labors to greet their lord. She didn't take the time to notice anything else as she slid off Hrafn's back and began walking, trance-like, toward the half dozen steps leading to the raised first floor.

"Morgana—" Leif called as he dismounted. "Morgana, wait . . ."

She continued walking, disregarding everyone and everything as her steps quickened with her approach . . .

Until a woman appeared in the open door of the hall. A woman with a luxurious fall of dark brown hair that framed a small, piquant face; a face that looked, from where Morgana had halted at the bottom of the stairs, quite comely.

The woman looked beyond Morgana, to Leif and the others. As she did so, a fair-haired child peeked from behind her skirts with inquisitive shyness.

Morgana immediately forgot about the woman in the doorway. She fought to form words, her lips suddenly stiff, her mouth dry. She cleared her throat softly, mobilized her tongue to form the words in Norse. "Eirik . . . is that you? Eirik, 'tis I . . . Mamma, *já?*"

She put her foot on the first step, holding herself back with an effort. Of course he wouldn't remember her—he had only lived two winters when Leif had taken him from home.

The child frowned thoughtfully at her, then looked up at the woman beside him. He asked her something in what had to be Frankish, for Morgana didn't understand it. The woman glanced at Morgana, then answered in a low voice.

What did you expect? Morgana asked herself above the wild thumping of her heart. She knew Eirik was too young to remember her after two winters, yet she'd been hoping against hope that he might dredge up some remnant of memory upon seeing her. Heat seeped into her cheeks—

from frustration, from helplessness, from humiliation. And from anger at Leif.

In the midst of Morgana's agitation, the woman took Eirik's hand and moved out to the top of the steps. At the same time, Morgana felt a presence behind her. Leif.

For a moment she felt utterly alone—deserted, in spite of the men who'd risked their lives to accompany her in search of her son. They couldn't help her now. Nor did the woman standing above her look as if she would be willing to make things any easier. In addition to the slight narrowing of her dark eyes, the set line of her mouth, the rigidity of her posture, a subtle but distinct hostility emanated from her.

And Morgana surely couldn't appeal to Leif for help. Not after she'd told him she hated him . . . had wished him dead. Told him she intended to take Eirik away from him.

Yet help came from the very source she'd spurned. "He doesn't recognize you, Morgana. But be patient," Leif said from beside her. "Eirik!"

The child released the woman's hand and all but tumbled down the steps in his eagerness. "Papa!" he cried, and, after making a wide berth around Morgana, flung himself at Leif.

Leif twirled him around and around, then set him on his feet and watched him dizzily wobble about. Morgana noticed the dark-haired woman had retreated out of sight into the manor.

"Have you missed your Papa?" Leif asked with mock sternness.

Eirik, finally having regained his equilibrium, stopped and faced his father. He stood straddle-stanced in imitation of Leif, and shook his head. An impish smile teased the corners of his sweet, pink mouth.

"*Nei?*" Leif thundered, startling Morgana with the volume and tone of his voice. Before Eirik could answer, Leif swept him off his feet and began whirling him around again. The child's shrieks of delight pierced the quiet day.

The other men had dismounted, and were looking around in wonderment. Little Thor joined Leif and Morgana, and was also the recipient of a hug from Eirik. With uncharacteristic bitterness, Morgana watched how the child welcomed the red man and not his own mother.

Be fair. He doesn't remember you. How could he after so much time? He's little more than a babe!

Little Thor returned the child's hug quickly and turned him toward his father. The red man's dark eyes met Morgana's—although she couldn't read any message in their impenetrable depths—before he swung away toward the men from Oslof.

"Let Morgana and Eirik get reacquainted," Ragnar declared louder than necessary. *"Já."* He nodded vigorously, red mane a-flying, as if his suggestion was the ultimate in wisdom. "You take us around, Skraeling," Ragnar directed, "else we take you back across the Great Water, eh?" He slapped Little Thor on the back and gave him a broad wink. "In a little skin boat, no less!"

The men laughed, but for a brief moment Morgana wondered at Ragnar's judgment. Little Thor, however, seemed to take it in the spirit in which it was given. He grinned and said something in a low voice to the Norseman, and the others roared with a second round of laughter.

Of course. How could she have forgotten that these men had faced death together? There existed a bond among them that would be difficult to sunder.

"Take them into the manor, friend," Leif said over his shoulder to the Skraeling, "and Hilaire can offer them some refreshment after their ride."

Something in the way Leif pronounced "Hilaire" snagged Morgana's attention. Up until now, Leif had spoken mostly in Norse, with a word or two in the Frankish tongue. When he had whispered "Vallée de Vergers" in

247

her ear that first time, the phrase had sounded odd—a bit awkward without the harsher but familiar articulation of Teutonic Norse. When he'd said it aloud to the men, it had a soothing quality to it, she had to admit, a soft, mellifluous sound.

And when he said the name "Hilaire," it rolled off his tongue like the last, savored drop of honey, silky smooth and sweet—the hard-won ambrosia from an angry swarm of bees, every drop precious . . .

Was it the language . . . or the woman?

What do you care? You came here to get your son.

"*Já.* Refreshment first . . . then we can better appreciate our surroundings," Olaf said, and with grins and rowdy comments, the others followed Little Thor into the manor.

Eirik watched the men, Morgana watched Eirik, and Leif watched Morgana. Then Leif caught his son by the arm before the child could scamper up the steps. "I want you to meet someone, Eirik," Leif said in a gentle voice as he smiled into his son's eyes. He spoke in pure Norse, slowly and clearly.

Eirik looked back at him. "*Oui?*" His blond brows drew together as his gaze shifted cautiously to Morgana, who was still watching him, her love shining in her striking silver-blue eyes—gleaming like purest crystal now with the moisture of emotion.

Leif felt an unexpectedly sharp stab of guilt at that un-guarded look. What had he done to her by taking Eirik away?

You took the only thing that was rightfully yours . . . an action no man could dispute.

Leif knelt beside the boy. Morgana noticed that Eirik was about a head taller than when she'd last seen him, his features a little more mature, but he was still a babe to her.

"This is Morgana, my son," Leif said quietly in Norse. "She is your mother." Then he said in the Frankish tongue, "*Mon précieux, c'est ta mère.*"

Morgana stooped to join them, afraid to hold out a hand to her own son for fear of rejection. How silly, she told herself, yet those two words did not move her to any more action than a tremulous smile.

"Já. Eirik, love. I've come a long, long way to see you again."

To take you home with me, where you belong.

Eirik's eyes narrowed a little, a frown of concentration creasing his forehead. Leif smoothed the child's hair back from his brow, and the tender movement unwittingly did something to Morgana deep, deep inside.

"Do you not remember Mamma's beautiful silver hair, Eirik? Surely you've not seen the like here, have you?"

"I don't need your help!" She couldn't stop the harsh, angry words that sprang to her lips.

Eirik, still seriously contemplating Morgana, started, and she instantly realized her mistake. Now was not the time to allow her anger at Leif to interfere with her reunion with her son.

"Have you ever seen such a wonder?" Leif repeated softly, as if Morgana's outburst had never occurred. Eirik, obviously reassured by his father's tone and behavior, slowly shook his head. Morgana felt the stirrings of some unwelcome emotion at the tone of Leif's voice, and the way she felt his gaze resting on her, but she refused to acknowledge it. She hated Leif Haraldsson and would make him suffer the consequences for taking her son away from her.

The little boy took a step closer to his mother and slowly reached one hand toward her hair. Morgana was afraid to move, lest she spoil the moment. "Mamma?" he queried, still uncertain, his frown deepening as he obviously dug deep into the well of his short memory.

Morgana nodded, her breath stuck in her throat.

"Hilaire," he said, uncertainty tingeing his voice. He looked at his father.

Leif shook his head. "Hilaire has never been your

249

mother, Eirik. She takes care of you, loves you, but she is not your mother."

Eirik nodded slightly as he looked back at Morgana. "Mamma," he repeated, the frown disappearing. He reached for her hand.

It was good enough for Morgana. If he wasn't ready for a hug, she would take anything he was willing to give now.

He said something that sounded like *"bienvenue,"* then glanced at Leif. *"Velkominn,"* the child repeated in Norse. And without further ado, he proceeded to pull her up the stairs of the manor.

Morgana deliberately ignored Leif's look, feeling his eyes upon her as she went with Eirik. Leif Haraldsson deserved nothing but her contempt.

He was the one who'd taken Eirik from her in the first place.

"I owe all this—" Leif motioned toward the walls of the manor and beyond, "to Guthrum . . . my best friend's grandfather."

There was a sudden silence among the men from Oslof, and those in Leif's still small retinue, as they sat around a large trestle table in the manor hall. They were near one of the three stone fireplaces—something they'd never seen before—relaxing after their evening meal and discussing the opportunities here in Normandy if a man were ambitious. And, of course, drinking ewers of potent, red Norman wine.

"He holds no grudge for Gunnar's death," Ragnar said into the silence. "Why should he? Every man in that hunting party saw that Leif wasn't at fault." He met Leif's eyes. "And any man who wasn't there—and who knows Leif Haraldsson—would know, as well."

Guthrum himself nodded, then said in his thin, reedy voice, "Hrolf the Walker owed me his life, for I helped him escape from Norvegia when he was little more than a stripling. He was outlawed, and had enemies aplenty tracking him. I helped him escape with his life."

"And I am deeply grateful, Guthrum, for what you've done. You have a home here, if you so wish," Leif said.

The old man's eyes met his. "I only told you what I hoped might help you, young Leif. There were no guarantees. Hrolf could have forgotten, for all I knew . . . or wished to have naught to do with anyone who reminded him of his past. I could only hope."

Leif nodded. "And I owe Ragnar, as well, for hiding Blood-Drawer."

Ragnar waved his hand in dismissal.

"All of you," he added, "for bringing me my ship—" his voice lowered huskily, "and Morgana."

There was a moment of awkward silence, then Olaf said in a low voice, "You'll not find her so easy to win as that first time, Leif the Lucky. She'd just as soon throttle you as look at you." He threw back his head with laughter.

The others joined in, but to a man they avoided looking toward the object of their talk. Yet, as if she read their thoughts, Morgana's head turned their way.

Ragnar's voice boomed in the manor hall, in an obvious bid to throw her off track. "And I say a man should *own* his land, not merely tenant it!"

Einar had no trouble joining the conspiracy. "And a man should not be commanded to forsake his gods and embrace a new religion!" he complained.

"Why not," cut in Father Impirius, the priest who served the needs of the Christians of Vallée de Vergers, "if the religion to be embraced is the *true* religion!" He spoke with fervor, and in Norse. Obviously he wanted to get his point across to the men from Oslof.

". . . nor wed the local women—dark as the Danes, they are . . ." Einar grumbled, completely ignoring Impirius's declaration. He glanced around belatedly, then, as if to gauge the reaction of Leif's three Danish retainers—two of whom were dark, "Or speak the Frankish tongue instead of our own."

Olaf shook his head at the younger man. "Were you listening, Einar, or has the wine already turned your brain to mush?"

Laughter rang out, and Ragnar gave Einar's shoulder a playful shove which nearly set him on his backside on the wooden floor. *"Rollo* agreed to embrace Christianity—to accept baptism. *Rollo* agreed to marry Popa, Count Béranger's daughter. Only *Rollo,"* Olaf reminded him with exaggerated patience.

Impirius glanced at Leif, then said, "'Twill eventually be required of every man under Rollo. Mother Church will not tolerate a horde of pagans in our midst here in Francia."

"It stands to reason, does it not," Leif said smoothly, "that Charles would wish Rollo—whom he obviously considers a pagan—to convert. That would bind him to the church. Marriage to Béranger's daughter would help ensure Rollo's allegiance to Francia, if the count is loyal. Rollo has already proclaimed himself a duke—although supposedly among his own men only—and has already begun expanding the original grant." Leif ignored Father Impirius's exaggerated look of disapproval and took a draught of wine. He shrugged, then said, "To learn the language would be the wisest course, if you think about it. We are vastly outnumbered by the Franks overall . . . what use to continue to use a language that is foreign to them? It confuses issues and could create chaos in instances where it might be avoided with a little simple communication."

"It sounds to me like Rollo wishes Normandy to be integrated—as a Norse duchy, this time—into the whole of Francia," opined Egil.

"Aye. Rollo pats Charles's back, the king pats his in return. And Charles is not so 'simple.' Anything he requires of Rollo, he suspects that Rollo will in turn expect of his followers . . . at least in time. Every step taken at St. Clair-sûr-Epte was designed to bind Rollo to Charles. He needs a good ally—even a Northman—for there are mighty subjects within his own realm ready to swallow him in one greedy bite . . ."

Morgana was listening from the corner. Eirik had sat with her and Freki—at least the dog had remembered her!—until his head finally rested upon the table in sleep. When Hilaire had moved forward from the shadows to take him off to bed, Morgana had shook her head, uncaring as to whether the other woman understood Norse or not. "I'll do it now," she'd told her in a tone that she was certain only a fool could have misunderstood.

Now she sat watching Leif Haraldsson . . . and nursing her grudge against him. She'd accepted the Frankish woman's silent and sullen hospitality, and watched her serve the men. She wondered exactly what part this Hilaire played in Leif's life, then abruptly dismissed the thought.

She spoke softly to Freki when the conversation lowered in volume or bored her; she drank a goodly amount of the wine because it was not only extremely palatable, but because it helped her to relax . . . something she'd been unable to do since leaving for Francia.

She also tried to prevent her mind from returning to the sleeping chamber off to the side of the hall where she'd taken Eirik and placed him in a small bed of his own. A small bed beside a larger one she assumed was Leif's . . .

She would not allow Hilaire to sleep in the same room with Eirik now that she, Morgana, was here. She certainly didn't want the child to think ever again that Leif's paramour—or whatever she was—was the boy's natural mother. If Leif wanted to—

"Ahem . . ."

She looked up into the expressive brown eyes, canine eyes, she thought, of Father Impirius. He looked a rather righteous young man, not much older than herself, and obviously full of his sense of religious importance in the scheme of things at Vallée de Vergers. His healthy girth was further evidence that he led the good life, and he was possessed of a set of jowls that, in addition to his eyes, reminded her of a lop-eared, forlorn-looking hound.

"If you wish to part me from my beliefs, Frank, your efforts will be for naught," she said rudely in Norse, then immediately regretted her words. Why take out her anger on this man?

"Forgive me," she added before he could answer and, quite without warning, tears pressed against the backs of her eyes.

Father Impirius may have been self-righteous, even self-inflated at times, but he was no dullard. Neither was he immune to the distress of a beautiful woman. Any beautiful woman.

"There, there," he told her, and patted her shoulder in a paternal manner. "Now is not the time to discuss such things, child." His Norse was heavily-accented but decipherable. "Although it may interest you to know that your husband has already received baptism. You, therefore, must—"

Morgana's tears instantly disappeared. "He is *not* my husband! He's but a man who took my son from me after he was banished from the homeland by our chieftain."

Impirius's thick, dark brows came together in puzzlement. "But I thought that you were Eirik's mother."

"I am."

"Then you were Leif's, er . . ." he cleared his throat and lowered his voice, "whore?"

"*Nei!*" Hectic color swept across her fine cheekbones. "I was his wife when I bore Eirik, but am no longer. I sund-

254

ered the bonds of marriage when he broke a vow to me."

Impirius's mouth fell open. His frown deepened. "You *divorced* him?" he said in all but a whisper, as if the word were blasphemous.

When Morgana nodded, he crossed himself. "God's blood, but 'tis a heathen custom! The scriptures forbid it." He stared at her as if she had two heads.

"In our culture, it makes perfect sense. What purpose to remain with a man who ill-treats you?" she countered in defense. "And what kind of religion would forbid such a thing?"

Suddenly tired of the conversation and where it was leading, Morgana stood. She had the distinct impression that behind those soulful brown eyes dwelt a sharp and scheming mind. She also thought she was being tested in some way. "You will permit me to retire now? I'm very tired from our travels."

Impirius's hand shot out and latched onto her arm. Firmly, but not ungently. "You cannot sleep in there if . . ." He trailed off. "Well, you are not his wife." He suddenly looked at a loss for words. Morgana pried his fingers loose, one by one.

"And Hilaire is?" The underhandedness of the question was unworthy of her, she realized, but one part of her wanted to know.

"Many would consider her so."

She looked at him sharply, and wondered if he were as proficient at deceit as she suspected. "They can both have the sleeping chamber when I am gone, for I want nothing more than to take Eirik home with me," she told him levelly. "Let them sleep in the hall this night, for I've come a great distance to be with my son, and my place is with him now." She followed his eyes as they found Hilaire, who was watching them from the shadows nearby. "I can take care of myself," she added. "And, if necessary, Hilaire as well."

As he watched her walk with purposeful steps toward the room where Eirik slept, he mumbled, "I do not doubt it for a moment." He glanced at Hilaire, then quickly swung away.

"She awaits you," said Ragnar with a wink, and inclined his head toward the bedchamber door to the side of the hall.

"Like the wolf awaits the rabbit," Little Thor added unexpectedly.

They all laughed.

"We only pledged to deliver her safely to you, Haraldsson," Egil informed him. "We will not help Morgana take Eirik back to Oslof against your wishes, nor will we help you keep her here against hers."

"Aye," Olaf added with a leer, his cheeks ruddy with drink. "Nor will we help you get reacquainted." He wiped his mouth on his tunic sleeve. "Surely you can do that on your own, *já?*"

Leif allowed one corner of his mouth to crescent upward. "No doubt better than you could manage the tiller bar were you at sea this very moment."

When another round of hilarity had subsided, Leif heard Guthrum mumble something from beside him. Leif leaned toward him, content to allow the conversation among the others to drift where it would. "What say you, Guthrum?" he asked in the old man's ear.

"From what I've seen with these old eyes, this would be a fine place for Ingrid and my great grandson." His gaze held a faraway look, as if he were seeing into the past . . . or the future.

"Indeed. And any others of your family—" Leif halted in mid-sentence. He'd failed to inquire about Ingrid in all the excitement. Thor's hammer, what was wrong with him?

For one thing, you would normally have asked that question of Morgana, but you haven't exchanged a civil word yet.

"Harald?" Leif said, breaking off his thoughts. "You're right. Harald and the little one would thrive here. Ingrid would like it, too. What is there to dislike about Normandy?"

Guthrum watched as Bjorn, one of the Danes in Leif's retinue, and Ragnar squared off for an arm wrestling match farther down the table, but his gaze held little interest. "The babe—Gunnar's second child—was born dead." His eyes met Leif's, all the grief he'd suffered over his lifetime seeming to coalesce in that one, potent look. "I've much to tell you when you've made your peace with Morgana, young Leif Haraldsson." He shook his head. "The time is not right yet."

Little Thor stood nearby, far enough away to be unable to hear their conversation, yet close enough for Leif to be aware of his quiet presence. He stood with his arms folded, staring straight ahead, his mind seemingly elsewhere.

Leif looked over at him. "My friend Little Thor is concerned about Ingrid, I think, Guthrum. He's never said as much, but I believe he would take her to wife were she willing and had he the opportunity. I believe also that he would defend her and her son to the death." Guthrum looked at Leif, then slowly turned his gaze to Little Thor. "He is a good man, old one," Leif added quietly. "May I tell him Ingrid is well?"

Guthrum nodded, a thoughtful expression spread across his withered features. "*Já.* As well as can be expected without Gunnar. And after the loss of the babe. . . . You may tell him that you have a common enemy back in Oslof now, and may seek to return there: you to avenge your father's murder, and the red man to avenge the loss of Ingrid's child."

When Leif opened his mouth to speak, his features

rigid with anger, the old warrior warned, "For now, tell him Ingrid is as well as can be expected. As for the rest . . . I'll tell you all you need to know when the time comes."

Chapter Seventeen

Morgana studied the arrangement of the chamber. She could climb into Eirik's bed, but it was very small—just right for a child, possibly even two, but not for an additional full-grown adult.

She hesitated, longing to sleep beside her son. Tenderness flowed through her, and she was hard-pressed to look away from the soundly sleeping child. Now that they'd been reunited, she wanted to be near him every moment she could.

With a soft sigh, she glanced at the other, larger bed, then made her decision. She pulled one of the blankets from it and wrapped it about her. Freki lay beside Eirik's pallet, his head on his paws, his eyes on her. Morgana lowered herself to the hard wooden floor, and curled up beside the wolfhound, taking advantage of his body for warmth, a modicum of comfort . . . and welcome familiarity.

She closed her eyes, certain sleep would be a long time in coming. She knew Leif would eventually retire. And with him, most likely, the Frankish woman Hilaire. Father Impirius's words popped into her mind . . . *many would consider her so* . . . His terse statement plagued her for a while; yet soon she thrust it from her mind and thought about what she would do next. How would she get Leif to let her return to Norvegia with her son now that she'd finally found him?

One step at a time, she told herself over and over again, as mental and physical exhaustion slowly crept over her. Then unexpectedly, all thought, all emotion, dissolved into nothingness as sleep staked its claim.

Leif closed the door softly behind him. The lone candle on the chest beside his bed had burned out, and only a wall torch illuminated the room with its feeble flame. He allowed himself a moment for his eyes to adjust to the darkness after the bright light from the flambeaux in the hall and the glow from the hearths.

He stood motionless for long moments, looking at Morgana. By Odin, he'd thought never to see her again. Had suspected, deep down, that his gamble would never bear fruit.

And here she was, in Normandy, in his bedchamber, beside their son. If she wasn't quite in his bed, where she belonged, she would be. And soon.

All you have to do is make her love you again, whispered a voice.

He tried to ignore it . . . the monumental struggle he would undoubtedly have to convince her to forgive him, to say nothing of renewing her love.

The dull ache in his loins was a sharp reminder of the extent of her anger and, reluctant though he was to acknowledge it, her dislike. But no matter how much they were at odds, no matter how profound his own earlier sense of betrayal and rage—the raw strength of emotions that had driven him to take his son from Morgana—to Leif Haraldsson this woman, more than ever now, was worth any struggle that could ensue.

He moved forward silently, glancing at Eirik, who was sound asleep. Freki was awake, though, his eyes trained upon Leif. He remained unmoving, however, only a flick of the tip of his tail acknowledging Leif's presence.

Morgana lay wrapped in one of the coverlets from Leif's bed. Her bright head was pillowed against Freki's side, her hair spilling over the dog's body like moonfire. Her lips were slightly parted, reminding him of Eirik when he slept.

Leif felt such warm feelings flow through him that he had to restrain himself from reaching out to touch her . . . taking her into his arms and showing her how much he loved her. Had always loved her. Would always love her.

She could never know how profoundly thankful he was for her presence—for her safety; thankful to fate, or Odin, or even the Christian god that his mother had worshipped before him. Surely some divine force had brought her to him for a reason . . .

Then, without warning, her eyes opened. They went directly to him, catching him in his rapt contemplation, his emotions written plainly across his features in the dimness of the room.

She sat up abruptly, her sleep-clouded eyes registering confusion at first. She huddled back against Freki as her expression cleared, as if to get as far away from Leif as possible. Desolation darkened her lovely eyes, replacing the fleeting bewilderment; suspicion narrowed them. She looked like a cornered she-wolf, ready to spring at him in desperation.

"Get away from me!" Her voice was low, but laden with loathing. "I'm not your wife . . . nor your Frankish whore!"

His features hardened. "You are whatever I deem fit, Morgana, or have you forgotten already? And *I* say you are my wife. I am Christian now, and divorce is forbidden."

She tossed her hair from her eyes, moved away from the dog and pushed to her knees. "Then our marriage, according to your new religion, would have been illegal as well. This Christianity means naught to me . . . *you* mean naught to me. You are Eirik's natural father, mayhap, but nothing more—"

Reaching for her, he grabbed her arm and dragged her forward, the brunt of his temper tethered only by a thread of self-control. "I am an outlaw because of you! Everything I am now is because of *you*, so don't tell me I am naught to you, Morgana. Of your own free will you are here with me now, with our son. You will remain with us whether you will it or nay."

Morgana shook her head emphatically, a grim set to her mouth. Even having Eirik back with her couldn't change her feelings toward Leif, she told herself as her naturally compassionate temperament tried to push through her carefully erected layers of resentment and bitterness. She had no liking for the single-minded shrew she'd become, yet something deep within her warned her of the danger of allowing Leif Haraldsson to creep under her guard ever again.

He betrayed you twice. Beware! warned one side—the side that hurt like a gaping wound . . . a wound too great to ever mend itself.

And you betray only yourself by your thoughts, whispered another part of her. *Have you ever truly ceased to love him, rogue that he is? He was your first love . . . father of your only child . . .*

"Oh, but aye, my little she-wolf," Leif was saying in a soft, savage voice. "The only way you can return to Oslof is *alone*—for the men have told me that they will not help you to take Eirik from me against my wishes. But I know you'll never leave without Eirik. And I'll never let him go."

He released her arm and stood over her, a host of feelings threatening to overwhelm him and sever that single thread of control. He spun on his heel then, afraid of waking Eirik . . . or forcing himself on Morgana just to prove to them both that surely there had to be *some* feeling left in her heart beside hate, even if it was only lust. He quickly stripped off his clothing, strode over to extinguish

262

the rushlight, then crawled into bed, thinking he was surely addled to believe he could fall asleep *now* . . .

And that he hadn't had nearly enough wine to drink earlier.

"If you would become his wife, then you must get rid of her, once and for all."

The implication of the priest's words hung in the night air. He secretly hoped that very implication would discourage Hilaire's scheming.

"What about *me*, Impirius," came her bitter words. "Or mayhap you would just as soon not dirty your hands with such a thing?"

Hilaire and Impirius stood in the shadow of the manor hall, outside in the cool night air. The light breeze held a chill, but Impirius was glad for it, for it helped cover the sound of their low voices in the quiet.

He squinted down at Hilaire in the deep shadows of night. She was a comely woman—comelier than most—and could have had just about any man she chose. Impirius's loins tightened at the thought of her compliant body beneath his. She knew how to please a man, as well, while obviously enjoying the physical union herself.

But she had her heart set on the new heathen lord, Haraldsson. The priest guessed it was because of Leif Haraldsson's red-blond hair, his tall frame and very fine form. He also suspected that Hilaire—and every woman who chanced to see Haraldsson smile—found that simple curving of the Northman's lips beguiling beyond measure. Aside from the natural beauty of it, that smile had an appealingly boyish quality about it—a mixture of innocence and deviltry.

Hilaire wasn't above trading her body for a favor—with the right man, of course. But she was shrewd, particular, and very careful with whom she shared herself.

Impirius was vain in his own way, but not vain enough to believe he numbered among the chosen few because of his physical attributes rather than his connection to the king. He was a bastard son of Charles III. He hoped he was on his way to more important things, and Hilaire surely knew this. It wouldn't be the first time anyone had catered to him because of his ties to Charles the Simple. And he understood human nature well enough to know that with both himself and a woman like Hilaire, the forbidden was always more attractive.

He also was not averse to playing both ends against the middle.

"Impirius!"

Her soft but indignant exclamation abruptly brought him back from his musings. He put a cautionary hand over her mouth and pushed her against the stone wall of the manor. "You were made for pleasuring a man," he growled softly, "not scheming your way into a heart that's already taken."

He felt her stiffen. She jerked her mouth free. "I almost had him once," she said, "before *she* came. All I have to do is—"

"You had him *not*, unless you count only the physical. Surely you know that a woman can possess a man fleetingly with her body, but his heart may remain free—or pledged to another."

He watched her frown in the pale light from the heavens, her dark brows drawing together over long-lashed hazel eyes. "But if she were dead, I could claim his heart as well." She drew in a sharp breath. "I thought the North-woman's arrival the worst of luck, but now I see that 'tis a chance to tear her from his heart once and for all. One cannot love a dead woman for very long . . . at least not with one of warm, soft flesh competing for his love."

Impirius sighed and shook his head.

"Can you truly say that I'm not looking out for your

264

father's interests?" she asked him. 'Mingle with and marry them,' he told us. 'Bear their children, teach them our language and religion, and we will absorb them and be stronger for it.' You cannot say I do aught but my duty."

Impirius laughed softly. "So you may say, but I know differently, *ma petite.*" 'Tisn't duty that beckons you to his bed when he has need of you."

Her eyes narrowed at him, but Hilaire was adept at controlling her temper. "Will you help me?"

"Help you do what?"

"Get rid of the pale-haired one," she answered with a touch of impatience.

He shrugged. "You may not need to do aught but wait. I've heard she wants to take the child away from here, back to where she came from."

She stared at him wordlessly for a moment, and he knew hope sprang into her breast. But she was no fool. "Leif will not give up his son."

"And I doubt Morgana will give him up either," he countered, remembering the Northwoman's obvious determination, and the fact that she'd come so far, risked such danger to herself, to find Eirik.

"Then help me! I'll make it well worth your while until . . ." She bit her full lower lip and frowned thoughtfully.

"*Oui,* I'm sure you will, Hilaire," he said softly, suggestively, "but for how long?"

"Until he weds me. But if he discovers our occasional, er, activities beforehand, you will assume the blame . . . you are so good at lying, Impirius. You cannot take offense or deny it."

"Why—"

"Help me, Impirius!" she commanded, allowing one hand to search suggestively among the folds of his dark horse hair robes. "I'll make it worth your while," she repeated. Her hand found what it was seeking, and Impirius groaned softly, in spite of himself. Mayhap he was as bad with Hilaire, at least in the physical sense, as she was with Haraldsson.

He pressed himself against her hand, silently castigating himself. "Have you any ideas, *chère?*" he heard himself whispering heavily into her ear. He sounded more like the demon that possessed him whenever he was in her presence than the priest he was supposed to be.

"What I have in mind will soothe the ruffled feathers of your father's present and unlikely ally, Robert of Neustria. Mayhap 'twould be wise to conduct our business in the name of . . . er, the King of Francia, *n'est-ce pas?*"

Whatever she had in mind, Impirius knew it would be clever as well as self-serving. Yet he had his own purposes—and a secret grudge against Leif Haraldsson. He bitterly resented Rollo and all his thieving hordes. What right had he to any of Francia? And Haraldsson as well?

And what right had a heathen Northman to Hilaire's affections when Impirius wanted them for himself? By the same token, surely Charles would be grateful if Impirius soothed Robert of Neustria's ruffled feathers?

"The orchard . . . meet me in—the usual place, Hilaire," he breathed huskily as she fondled him with the expertise of a natural wanton. There was no question as to her willingness while Leif Haraldsson was occupied with the silver-maned woman called Morgana.

They were too occupied just before they broke apart to see the still, pale form standing not far away. As they moved their separate ways, the figure melted soundlessly into the night-deep shadows that enveloped the manor.

Leif stared at the shadow-shrouded ceiling. He was wide awake, just as he knew he would be. He was half-tempted to collect his clothes and leave, but that would be admitting to Morgana that while she slept, he was too disturbed to do the same.

You could find Hilaire, suggested an imp.

Nei, Hilaire wasn't the answer. She was just a means to satisfy his physical needs when the occasion arose. And although he sensed she had designs on him, she was not the kind of woman with whom he wanted to share the rest of his life. Not the woman to bear any other children he might have . . .

It might make Morgana jealous, pressed the imp.

Nei again, he thought, his mouth turning down at the idea. One thing he didn't need was another mark against him on the tally sheet of injustices in Morgana's mind.

He suddenly sat up in the dark, flinging the covers away. Grabbing breeches and shirt, he strode quickly to the door, then became conscious of the amount of noise he was making, and slowed his movements. By the time he closed the panel softly behind him, he was relatively certain that Morgana must be asleep—or pretending to be.

He moved to the table he and the others had occupied earlier. He reached for a ewer of wine and poured himself a cup, drank it down like a man on the verge of dehydration, then repeated the action. By the time he poured the third cup, Little Thor had soundlessly moved up beside him.

Leif looked up at the red man, his eyes narrowed against the torchlight behind Little Thor. He was beginning to feel very mellow indeed, for the effects of his earlier imbibing, although subtle, hadn't completely worn off yet.

"Wine? Pah! There is only one cure for what ails Kiisku-Liinu."

His low-spoken but emphatic words caused Leif to still in mid-motion, his cup halfway to his lips. He frowned at the red man, then began to down the contents of the cup. Little Thor took hold of his wrist, causing the garnet-red wine to dance in the vessel and slosh over the rim onto Leif's light-colored linen shirt.

267

Their eyes locked. Annoyance darkened Leif's. "Would that it were that simple."

"Not a matter of simple . . . matter of importance."

Leif glanced pointedly at Little Thor's fingers about his wrist, and the red man released him. "Watch," the Skraeling told him, and headed with silent strides toward the door of the sleeping chamber.

Before Leif could say or do anything, the Skraeling had disappeared through the door, then quickly reappeared, a sleeping Eirik in his arms. His dark eyes sent a message to Leif over the small blond head cradled against his shoulder before he swung away and moved to the shadows where he normally slept.

Morgana had finally fallen into a deep sleep. The tension and distraction created by Leif's presence unexpectedly but gradually eased in the wake of her emotional and physical exhaustion.

In the peaceful realm of slumber, she dreamed of Eirik—of chasing him through the fields at home in Norvegia with Freki bounding about them. The fresh breeze off the fjord tickled her nose with the scent of spring; it tousled her hair, and Eirik's too. The sun seemed brighter, warmer. Birdsong filled the air.

Suddenly Eirik stumbled, went down laughing. Freki sniffed his face and barked playfully. The child giggled with glee. "Fehki . . . *nei!*" he cried.

Morgana dropped down beside him, joy sweeping through her as she watched that beloved little face light up with happiness. She pushed the wolfhound aside, planted a soft kiss on Eirik's rosy cheek, and flung herself onto her back beside him. The coarse grass pricked her skin through her gown, but it didn't matter to Morgana as she stared at the craggy mountain peaks poking the cobalt canvas of the sky.

"Look at all the clouds, Eirik," she said, pointing to the pristine puffs overhead as they rode the wind. "Can you count them with Mamma?"

Before the child could answer, a form came between her and the sun, blocking its welcome warmth and glow, and casting her in cool shadow. She closed her eyes for a moment, willing it away.

Suddenly, warm lips touched hers, communicating a mixture of reverence . . . and urgency.

The contact was stirring, riveting her to the spot. Unexpected pleasure rippled through her, making everything else fade for a space of time as she lay there, allowing herself to give in to the languor that quickly invaded her limbs.

"Morgana, my love," the mouth over hers murmured on a breath of sound. "Let me love you, *ást mín* . . ."

Leif. It was Leif. She drifted for a moment on a beguiling swell of bliss, reveling in the feel of him . . .

Until something beneath her shifted and Morgana was rudely pulled from her dream. Her eyelids flew open, and while she could see very little of the face so close to hers, she tasted the sweet residue of wine, the familiar, silken rasp of a tongue playing about the sensitive surfaces of her lips, teeth nipping gently but insistently.

As she struggled to orient herself, Morgana realized who was kissing her so thoroughly. No other man would ever feel the same, taste the same; she'd already acknowledged that. Accepted that. But *this* Leif wasn't the same man anymore.

Reality deluged her.

She moved to shove him away, only causing the warm body beneath her head to shift once again. With a low grunt, it heaved, and Morgana felt Leif raise her head slightly to cradle her face in his hands. While he attempted to spare her from a jarring contact with the floor as Freki lunged to his feet, Morgana thought, *He's going to kiss me*

269

again, and felt panic rise within her as she fought to pull her face free.

She knew that whatever her mind had decided, her senses wouldn't necessarily go along with it. And therein lay her weakness.

Leif pressed his body over hers firmly, but without hurting her. As she opened her mouth to protest, his closed over it. She was literally a prisoner . . . nay, worse that that, for the sweet tortures that he was employing were far more dangerous than ordinary pain.

Evidently Leif knew that as well.

She groaned deep within her throat—a sound of pure frustration—and tried to tear her mouth from his. To no avail. Even if she screamed, she realized as his lips inexorably opened hers and his tongue plied its way between her teeth, no one would come to her aid. Except possibly the men from Oslof. But Leif obviously wasn't going to give her the chance to alert them.

The blanket wrapped about her only hindered her increasingly feeble attempts as he worked his magic over her. As one last sop to her conscience, Morgana tried to lift a knee toward his groin, but Leif only tightened his grip on her, his leg over hers bearing down in a mute but definite message.

Desire drove through her, sending curling heat through her womanhood, liquid fire through her blood. His tongue coaxed hers to touch and retreat, entwine and withdraw, and, finally, to join as one in a love ritual as old as time.

When Morgana was breathless from his kisses, he pulled his lips back a heartbeat from hers. "You are my wife, Morgana," he whispered, their breaths as one, "for now and always. And Eirik is my son. You belong here, with me—nothing will ever induce me to let you go again."

He eased the cover from about her, his lips once again silencing whatever she might have said, and when he began to slide her gown over her head, Morgana felt her recreant body begin to tremble with anticipation. *Allfather help me,* she exhorted, for she hadn't been with a man since Hakon's death.

As he eased his hands beneath her chemise, to her horror she found herself thinking, *What can it hurt? I can use him as he would use me . . . as a man uses a woman's body to ease himself. Why can't two play the game?*

Then his fingers found her nipples, taut and sensitive, tingling with a life of their own . . .

Leif could tell the moment she began to surrender. At least physically. And if he couldn't have her heart right away, he'd wait. He'd win it back if it took him the rest of his life . . . and the physical act of love was as strong a beginning, as firm an anchor, as any.

Exhilaration surged through him, joy swept along his veins. He had his Morgana in his arms, beneath him, heart to heart, ready to love him with her body, if not yet her mind.

He lightly dragged his lips down the delicate stem of her throat, pausing to flick at its base with his tongue, to feel the butterfly-faint flutter of her pulse. He buried his face in the silken flesh of her neck for a moment, unable to move for the ache around his heart. He felt the press of emotion behind his eyes, the tightening of his throat muscles.

If he'd been struck dead in that moment, he would have been content, for he'd faced death several times in his life—but never with this sense of fulfillment, of inexorable destiny.

"Let me go, Leif," Morgana whispered huskily in his ear, rousing him from his brief hesitation.

He raised his head and looked deeply into her eyes. He thought he saw pain in her passion-bright gaze, but her voice was angry. "We'll have only . . . this. Only the physical, naught more, I swear!"

His mouth settled into a determined line. "Then so be it, Morgana. This is better than nothing." He bent to tease her ear with his tongue, then delved into that delicate aperture, knowing how especially sensitive she was there.

Suddenly, like a man flying in the face of destiny, denying the inexorability of impending defeat, he became totally committed in his quest. Surely in finding her again, he would lose himself, but he didn't care. It was worth any price.

She instantly sensed the change in him, the moving urgency that bordered on desperation. And the reverence . . .

In response, she attempted to counter his renewed intensity.

"You'll wake Eirik!" she protested in a breathy rasp. It was one of the last weapons in her dwindling arsenal against him.

"Eirik sleeps with Little Thor this night, love."

Morgana's sigh sounded through the quiet room as Leif's tongue moved from her ear down to her collarbone, setting her flesh aflame as he went.

Her fingers flitted about his shoulders, lightly, hesitantly, then pressed him closer as he suckled the sensitive tip of one breast. When he took it lightly between his teeth, Morgana groaned, then bit her lip.

She tried to picture another—*any* other—more unappealing face above her as a defense, but failed utterly. She tried to picture Eirik present and watching them from across the room. That was equally ineffective. She found her anger, her sense of betrayal, slipping away in the wake of her profound response to him.

Play his game, whispered one remnant of reason before it, too, dissolved into nothingness.

Nei . . . nei! her mind cried silently. *'Tis too dangerous . . .*

And then her fingertips encountered the puckered flesh

of his healed shoulder wound. The wound that Hakon had caused him . . .

Images flashed through her mind: Hakon before a weaponless Leif, a gleaming dagger blade in one hand catching the light . . . striking Leif with that illicitly-gained weapon in the shoulder before anyone could stop him. And later, Leif in the stable, pale, weak, quietly anguished . . . then leaving Oslof, with Eirik, aye, but also badly hurt.

The myriad memories crashed through the last of her meager defenses, appealing to the compassionate and forgiving woman who had loved Leif Haraldsson ever since she could remember. Causing him pain by dealing him a blow in a moment of frustrated retaliation was one thing; the thought of his death at the hand of the man she'd married was completely another.

It was as if, now that her mission to find Eirik was ended, in the heat of those moments of intimacy she realized what Leif's death would have meant to her. That final, irreversible loss . . .

Naught! cried a voice from far away.

Her heart said differently.

Her hips raised automatically as they sought his. Sought his in affirmation of his life and love, even if she chose not to remain with him; for this was not just any man. And certainly not Hakon Sweynsson. *This* was like a bracing plunge into the icy fjord compared to a lukewarm bath.

Her responses suddenly quickened apace with his new intensity. There wasn't a woman alive who could resist this manner of sweet assault; and from a man for whom she had once harbored such depth of feeling. Morgana allowed herself to become caught up in the lightning-strike of carnal need that shook her to the soul, the glory of newly-rekindled, intoxicating desire.

She savored his lips upon her thighs, the teasing tickle of the ends of his fire-kissed hair as his head moved over her lower body. His callus-rough fingers invaded the swollen, silken depths of her until she writhed against him, swept up in a riptide of emotion that made her cry aloud.

Then his lips were capturing the sounds of her abandon as he positioned his hips above hers. With a graceful turn and thrust, he impaled her, promising with his body that which she wouldn't believe from his lips.

And if she'd met his potent gaze in the moment they reached the pinnacle of physical fulfillment, Morgana would have seen what she refused to accept: the solemn pledge of everything he was, in that moment, and would ever be; and an end to betrayal.

But afterwards . . . after he'd carried her to his bed . . . after he'd anchored her to his side with an arm across her waist, she'd turned away from him. After a long silence, she felt the even cadence of his breathing in repose, and allowed her guilt and regret to torture her far into the night.

And in the tumult of her thoughts, couldn't decide who she detested more . . . herself or Leif Haraldsson.

Chapter Eighteen

Morgana watched Eirik splash among the stones in the shallow stream bed. The sun was warm on her bare legs as she sat on a moss-covered log, her gown hiked up over her knees and her feet dangling in the water. Freki was off in the trees somewhere, chasing rabbits no doubt, she thought with a faint smile. But he would be back soon, for he couldn't seem to stay away from them for very long, despite the temptations elsewhere.

They were alone together, for the first time in two winters, and Morgana was determined to enjoy her time with her son. Too much time had gone by, been wasted, for her to miss any further opportunities.

As she watched Eirik frolic, Morgana couldn't help but wonder if she would have been better off if she'd had a child with Hakon. A child to have kept her occupied in and tethered to Oslof. Although she suspected that one child could never replace another, perhaps she wouldn't have been quite so devastated . . . would have had enough to keep her thoughts and intentions more . . .

More what?

Would she have left Oslof on a risky search for Eirik if she'd had another son or a daughter?

A hand on her arm startled her. She swung her head in

surprise to meet Little Thor's dark gaze. By Odin, the man moved as silently as a shadow!

Eirik looked up, waved at the red man, then renewed his play as Freki joined him, bounding out of nowhere and charging into the water with such abandon that he sent a crystalline sheet of water geysering into the air. Water droplets sprayed Morgana's warm skin like a gentle spring shower.

Her expression, however, immediately turned cool, wary. Little Thor looked typically unperturbed; yet there was a subtle softening of his stern features, a sincerity shining in the dark depths of his eyes.

"This one—*I*—am sorry . . . I struck you, woman of Kiisku-Liinu."

Surprise sprouted within her at his unexpected words. "I'm not his woman," she answered in a quiet but firm voice, "and my name is Morgana. But I accept your apology. I—understand that your loyalty is to him."

What else could she have said? True, the red man had accompanied Leif when the latter had abducted Eirik; but Morgana knew, too, that Little Thor had been responsible for treating Leif's knife wound, and helping both Leif and Eirik during what must have been an endless and arduous journey by land to Francia. He had doubtless saved Leif's life, and in the process helped ensure Eirik's safety.

Morgana was not vindictive by nature. The only person against whom she'd ever held a grudge was Leif Haraldsson, and she felt she'd had more than enough reason.

"Even if he did kill a man in cold blood," something prompted her to add under her breath as she frowned down at her feet dangling in the water. Perhaps, one part of her thought, it was some deep-seated need to force the red man, who was as close to Leif as a brother, to defend him. The gods knew, she hadn't had many positive thoughts about him, nor feelings toward him since shortly after their marriage.

"You do not know Kiisku-Liinu if you believe this. You say so only out of . . . bitterness."

Her eyes, narrowed slightly in challenge, met his. "What are you saying?"

"Kiisku-Liinu did not tell you," he answered. "Hakon killed Gunnar."

Morgana's eyes widened. "But I thought . . ." Her look turned to frowning disbelief. "You saw him raise a weapon to Gunnar?"

"I saw him . . ."—he frowned in concentration as he seemed to search for the word—"hesitate. He did not raise his bow in time to *save* Gunnar as he could have; then he blamed Kiisku-Liinu."

Morgana was silent a moment, trying to absorb this, for if it was true, then rather than convince her of what kind of man Hakon really was, Leif had wanted to protect her from the knowledge of Hakon's perfidy. He'd avenged Gunnar's death, while looking like Hakon's murderer to those who didn't see what the latter had done. Or—if Little Thor were to be believed—not done.

And what kind of man was Hakon really?

She tried to ignore the implications of *that,* as she'd managed to do up until now. For it meant her judgment of men was poor . . . that—the gods forgive her—she'd made a major error in a moment of hurt and anger . . .

She dragged her runaway thoughts back to the business at hand. And Little Thor's words. How had Leif answered Hakon's accusation? She closed her eyes for a moment, conjuring up his words to Hakon . . . *I think, rather, the fault lies with you.* An accusation, to be sure, but with no attempt to explain or clarify it after that.

Little Thor's revelation was unsettling, to say the least, and Morgana didn't want to allow its implications to influence her in any way. After all, it was too late. Much too late.

"Why are you telling me this? 'Twill change nothing. If

277

he were the noblest man alive, it wouldn't change the fact that he took Eirik from me."

The red man shrugged, a vaguely contemplative gleam in his loam-dark eyes as he studied her. "Your doing. Your fault."

Morgana's chin jerked up. Her mouth tightened with anger. Staunch loyalty toward one man was one thing. Outrageous distortion of the truth in the name of that same loyalty was completely another.

"He had nothing left except his son," Little Thor said with simple forthrightness. "You made a mistake when you . . . deserted him. When you took Hakon to your bed."

"What do you know of these things?" she asked, flushing. "What do you know of his oath to me? His—"

Little Thor swiftly struck his chest with his fist. "This feeling . . . feeling in the heart, forgives all."

He turned his gaze abruptly to Eirik, presenting her with his proud profile as he watched the boy. It was an obvious signal to end the discussion.

Morgana struggled with her irritation with him for a moment, and to absorb the new knowledge of the extent of his intelligence, the depth of his perception and feelings. Now that he obviously had a better command of the Norse language, knew Leif and Eirik much better than when he'd first come to Oslof, he obviously wasn't afraid to reveal his opinions.

And Morgana suspected that when Little Thor chose to speak, the listener had no choice but to hear him out.

When she'd regained her composure, she said of Eirik, "He has grown." She was relieved to change the subject, even though she had more to say in her own defense. It was obvious that nothing she could ever say would change his opinion of her . . . or of Leif Haraldsson. "He is healthy—"

"And happy," Little Thor added. "The boy thrives."

Morgana threw him a sharp look, the corners of her mouth turning down at the inference of his words.

"He obviously doesn't need his mother then, is that what you imply?"

The Skraeling shook his head slowly, and was silent for a moment, as if searching for the right words. "The boy is most important, is he not? Why not stay here, for his . . . sake?" He gestured toward the lands around them. " 'Tis good for Eirik here."

Morgana's frown deepened. Surely he was attempting to make her feel selfish, something she hadn't been able to acknowledge to herself.

"Norvegia is his home," she said quickly, a stubborn set to her mouth.

Little Thor turned his head to meet her look. The breeze ruffled his straight, deep black hair, blowing a few strands across the regal cut of his cheekbone. He remained unmoving, his regard never wavering, and she inwardly braced herself for disagreement.

Instead, he asked, "How is Ingrid?"

"Ingrid?" she asked in surprise. "Why, Ingrid is . . . well." She wondered why he would ask about her close friend, then decided it was because both Gunnar and Ingrid had accepted the Skraeling unquestioningly. And Ingrid had also given Gunnar's horse to Little Thor to accompany Leif. No mean gesture, that.

Something prompted her to add, "Though she . . . lost the last child she carried."

The lift of his eyebrows and the fleeting frown that followed was unexpected, for his expression was usually impassive, hiding his thoughts and feelings well. "How?"

This question was more unexpected than the first. She averted her gaze, staring out over to the other bank. Little Thor's hand on her arm, his softly spoken, *"Equiwa? . . .* Mor-gana?" arrested her.

She looked him straight in the eye. "Many think 'twas because of Horik Bluetooth. He pushed himself on her relentlessly—there was even an attempted rape, although

279

Ingrid told no one but me. She wanted no more trouble, even though she'd begun bleeding, and feared she was losing the child . . ."

His grip on her arm tightened before his hand fell away. He suddenly turned his head aside and canted it slightly as something else caught his attention. Leif broke through the trees, leading Hrafn behind him. He spotted them, dropped the stallion's reins over a low branch, and strode in their direction.

" 'Tis too late, anyway," Morgana heard herself explain in a low voice, referring back to Little Thor's words about Eirik and Normandy. "Leif has changed . . . I have changed." Her eyes narrowed as she watched him move toward them, deliberately hardening her heart against the images of what had happened the night before. "Naught is the same, nor can it be again."

Little Thor glanced at her. "You must forgive. Start here—" he touched his breast over his heart again, softly, thoughtfully, this time. "You are young. Kiisku-Liinu is young. New land . . . new beginning." His eyes went to Leif, who was almost upon them now. "I . . . know of these things, Mor-gana."

He nodded at Leif, then swung away toward the stream where Eirik and the wolfhound were still playing.

Morgana deliberately turned her back to Leif. In spite of her resolve to be cold to him, however, she couldn't stop the slow rise of heat in her cheeks.

You merely satisfied your physical needs, as he did, she reminded herself.

Is that all? The taunting query danced around in her head maddeningly.

"So there you are," Leif said from behind her. "I—"

"Aye, here I am!" she snapped before he could finish his next sentence. "But not for long, you can be sure." She threw him a withering glance over one shoulder. "I was enjoying my time alone with my son. Now it appears half the hall is here." An exaggeration, obviously, but Morgana couldn't seem to stem the rise of sarcastic words. "This place is more crowded than Oslof."

She meant to hurt him with words, for it was the only way she *could* hurt him. She was his prisoner in every way. He definitely had the advantage, but her pride wouldn't allow her to acknowledge his victory.

He opened his mouth to speak, then closed it. She threw him a glance from beneath her lashes, caught the puzzlement in his eyes before he drew in a breath and slowly blew it out.

Morgana turned on him, still smarting from Little Thor's words, and vivid memories of her wanton capitulation the night before. "Did you think to have recaptured my heart because my body surrendered to yours last night?" The question affected her in a way she hadn't foreseen . . . so much so, that her next statement came softly and with a catch in her throat, reminiscent of an earlier Morgana. "Some wounds don't heal with time."

His lashes lifted; their gazes met and held. There was a suspended look in his eyes. His lips parted, as if he would speak, but she cut him off, knowing that the best defense was offense.

"Naught has changed, renegade," she continued coldly in an attempt to seal the crack in her composure by sheer dint of will. "Remember, you were the one who came crawling to me . . . not I to you! I merely enjoyed your body as you did mine." To her mortification, however, perversity pushed to the fore and prompted her to add, "As you would that of any female, including . . . *Hilaire.*"

'Tis jealousy, not perversity, sneered a nasty voice.

And you sound like a perfect harpy! accused another. *What man could ever abide such a sharp-tongued shrew?*

281

His gaze narrowed slightly. "I came not a-crawling, as I remember," he said quietly.

"Oh, aye . . . the conquering Northman, wielding your staff with the best of them!" She tried to laugh but, to her added humiliation, a half-sob emerged instead. "I hate you more than ever," she whispered, a soft but savage edge to her words, as she slid from the log.

She landed between two fist-sized rocks, her foot forcing them apart. Her ankle twisted beneath her, and she reached out automatically for balance. There was only Leif to grab onto, and self-preservation prevailed over pride. They clasped each other at the same time, then Morgana pushed away and gingerly began to limp out of the water.

"Can you walk?" he asked, his hands falling to his sides. He was torn between wanting to take her in his arms and kiss some sense into her . . . and shaking her. Prudence, however, won out.

"Mamma!" Eirik cried before she could answer Leif, looking up from his play and obviously noticing her unsteady gait. He moved clumsily through the water toward her, concern etching his small brow. *"Qu'as tu?* Hurt?" He gazed up at her, grabbing her hand. His blue eyes, so like her own, mirrored his distress.

She smiled and shook her head at him in reassurance; but before she could speak, the child glanced up at Leif. "Papa?" He looked down at Morgana's foot.

The look of expectation, of simple adoration, on his features as he obviously looked to his father to correct the situation, grabbed at Morgana's heart in a way that Leif's words had so far failed to do. How could she, in good conscience, tear this child away from the father that he obviously worshipped?

The boy is most important, is he not?

By the gods, she thought, even the Skraeling had managed to challenge her motives! Was it selfish of her to want to take Eirik away from Leif?

No more so than Leif tearing Eirik away from you!

She bent down beside Eirik, ignoring the twinge immediately above her foot and thinking of the adage that two wrongs didn't make a right. Putting one arm about the child she pulled him to her, her breath disturbing the silky golden hair over his ear. "I'm unharmed, sweet," she murmured. "Let me see your smile, *já?* I think 'tis hiding from me."

She held him at arm's length then, a bright smile curving her own mouth as she looked into his eyes. It pleased her enormously that he made an effort to speak to her in Norse.

He giggled. *"Pas . . .* not now, Mamma. Look . . ." And he gave her an answering expression of happiness that, obviously, he thought would prove his smile had returned.

Over Morgana's shoulder, Little Thor caught Eirik's attention. The boy's smile brightened even further as he pointed to the Skraeling. *"Regard*—Look," he told her. "Look," he repeated to his father.

The red man was standing with a small, wriggling yellow perch in his bare hand, a triumphant grin spread across his dripping wet face.

"You earned a bath, as well," Leif added, grinning back at his friend. "When you can catch one without getting soaked, you can teach me too."

Little Thor moved through the shallow water toward Eirik and Morgana, holding out the fish to the boy. "Kiisku-Liinu is too clumsy," he stated as he flung the hair from his eyes.

The red man's grin widened briefly before he suddenly swerved away from Eirik as Freki came flying through the air, directly toward the squirming fish. The wolfhound's teeth missed Little Thor's prize by a whisper as the Skraeling reacted with uncanny swiftness.

"Freki, no!" Leif reprimanded the dog, and gestured toward the bank. As the dog slunk away, Little Thor bent to offer the fish to Eirik, whose eyes were wide with wonder.

"Poisson! Quel beau poisson . . ." the child said in an awe-struck voice as he reached for the perch.

"Aye," Leif said softly, looking at Morgana over Eirik's head for a moment, then giving his attention to his son. " 'Tis a handsome fish, even if a bit . . ."—he looked at Little Thor meaningfully—". . . scrawny."

" 'Tis golden, like the sun," Morgana said to Eirik. "But 'tis too small to eat. What will you do with it?"

Eirik looked up at her, then at Leif, delight flashing in his eyes as an idea dawned. "Keep him, *oui, Papa?*"

Suddenly Morgana felt like her defenses were being stripped away as, for the second time in only moments, she acknowledged the adoration in her son's eyes when he looked at his father. How could she ever separate them?

Doubt burgeoned within her. And hard on its heels, annoyance.

"Let the fish go free," Little Thor said, breaking into her thoughts.

"Aye, Eirik. Wild things don't thrive in captivity." At Eirik's frown, Leif clarified, "Wild creatures get sick . . . they die if you take them from their natural homes . . ."

"And from others of their own kind," the Skraeling added.

Morgana felt a tearing urge to silence them both, even as she realized their words weren't necessarily meant for her—didn't necessarily pertain to her and her determination to take Eirik back home. Guilt made her read much more into their meaning, made her defensive. Leave it to Leif Haraldsson, she thought darkly, to compare removing an insignificant fish from a stream to her taking Eirik back to Norvegia. And the red man, with his unexpected bursts of sagacious eloquence. Why, it was enough to—

Eirik was bending down and releasing the fish. Morgana

watched it flash in the sun and surge downstream to freedom, her throat tightening inexplicably.

She turned away and limped up the grassy bank, then automatically toward Hrafn, glad suddenly to have something at which to direct her attention. The stallion's ears pricked at her approach. He neighed softly in obvious recognition, and dipped his beautiful head as if in greeting. She reached out to smooth her palm over his neck and shoulders, allowing her eyelids to close for a moment as she tried to collect her wits.

She let her fingers drift down to his satin-soft nose. The animal nibbled at her empty hand. "I'm sorry," she whispered to him. I have naught to gi—"

The sound of someone behind her stopped her mid-word. It could only be Leif, and she wasn't ready to face him in those quiet moments of wit-summoning . . .

"Morgana," he said in a low voice. "Morgana, there's no need for you to leave us. If you want to spend time alone with Eirik—"

"Just let me be!" she said over her shoulder. "I don't need your permission for anything." She gave him her profile. "I'll have all the time in the world alone with my son . . . when we return home."

She gave Hrafn a parting pat and moved away, in the direction of the manor . . . and thought how childish she sounded, how silly were her words in the wake of the wearing down of her will.

He took her arm and she stilled. "Naught has changed," she said in a brittle voice, her eyes moving to the offending hand. She swung toward him, lowering her voice. "Because I let you . . . because we . . . coupled last night doesn't mean that anything is different." Once again, her cheeks stained a brilliant hue. "A woman has needs just like a man, and I enjoyed the physical joining for what it was."

" 'Twas more than that," he insisted softly, the look in

his eyes suggesting the unthinkable to Morgana: certainty . . . and pity.

"Don't try to speak for me!" She shook his hand from her arm. "What happened last night came about because *I* wished it as well as you." She jabbed a finger at her chest as if he were incapable of understanding anything but hand signs. "But you can appeal to my carnal appetites until the breath leaves your body, and 'twill change nothing! There is naught left for you in my heart but contempt. You destroyed any feelings I still harbored back in Oslof when you took Eirik, and I came here not for you, but for him." She drew in a shaking breath to finish. "I *will* leave this place one day soon with my son, whether you wish it or nay."

Patience, a voice warned Leif as their eyes locked. *Patience, or you'll never win her back.*

He nodded, although his eyes told her he didn't agree. He stepped away to allow her room to move past him and toward the stream where Little Thor was pointing to something in the water and speaking to Eirik in low tones. "'Twill be as you wish," he said, sending hope skittering madly through her for an all-too-ephemeral moment. Then he clarified, "We'll leave you alone with Eirik. You need time together."

Of course, Morgana thought as bitterness replaced her foolish hope. What had she expected? Certainly not, "You may take Eirik back to Oslof with you."

"I do find it revealing, however," he added in a low, flat voice, "that you wouldn't allow anyone to separate or alienate Eirik from Hakon, yet you're most eager to reft him from me." His eyes bored into hers. " 'Tis obvious you don't love me now, Morgana, but I wonder if you *ever* did." He immediately motioned to Little Thor, giving her no chance to respond, and the Skraeling left the water with long strides to join him.

As Morgana walked toward Eirik, refusing even to think

about the man standing behind her, emotion blurred her vision as she tried to make out the child. Leif's words had hit home, like a spear to her soul, stopping the very breath in her throat. Of course she had loved Leif! *Too* much, she acknowledged with asperity. He was just unfairly appealing to her softer side . . .

Yet his words had struck at something vital, their echoes reawakening the strains of deeply-buried guilt that she'd refused to allow herself to examine. Especially since Leif had taken Eirik from her.

The child was bent over the shallow water as it splashed over the stones around his feet, evidently intent upon catching his own fish bare-handed in imitation of Little Thor. Part of his small frame was cast in shadow by Freki's looming form, and he seemed totally absorbed, as if oblivious to or having forgotten the tension between his parents only moments earlier, and his father's departure.

Morgana slowly sat down where she'd been perched before, a thoughtful frown on her face. It was no use trying to pretend otherwise. The events of the previous night had diluted some of her anger at Leif, and most definitely had lessened what she'd considered acute dislike.

Of course. How could you share yourself so intimately with a man and actually hate him at the same time?

The answer was simple. You couldn't. At least *she* couldn't. She'd have to be an absolute wanton to do such a thing, or a contemptible fool.

Her damaged pride made Morgana decide in that moment that she would do anything—including gain Leif Haraldsson's trust—to lull him into complacency. Then, she hoped, it would be easier to whisk Eirik away—with the cooperation of the men from Oslof, or without.

Common sense warned her that she was clinging to false hope, but she obstinately refused to examine her decision any further.

She hadn't thought much beyond retrieving Eirik—that

goal in and of itself had seemed almost insurmountable; yet determination and obstinancy had sustained her through the long weeks and months. The present situation, however, was untenable to her. She felt more miserable and confused than she had in a long, long time.

Now that she'd accomplished her objective, in spite of her bold words to Leif, what was she really to do? What if the men from Oslof chose not to return? At least not enough of them to make sailing *Wave Rider* a viable option?

Then you're on your own. You'll go by land . . . or in a smaller vessel.

"*Já!*" she exclaimed under her breath. Even if she and Eirik had to live in a cave somewhere in Francia, she would take him away. *Anything* to be free of Leif Haraldsson and his utterly unwelcome hold on her.

Chapter Nineteen

Morgana would have given much to have had Ingrid there to talk to in those lonely moments. Ingrid was calm, as Morgana had always sought to be, certainly not whimsical and then shrewish in later years, as Tyra had been. Nay, rather serene and unflappable as Ingrid . . . *that* was what Morgana wanted. Cool-headedness and tranquility were qualities that had attracted Morgana to her when they were barely old enough to toddle about Oslof.

Few would have guessed it, for Morgana had been more admired, her bright beauty attracting far more attention than Ingrid's simpler comeliness. Although Ingrid had always seemed content with herself, content to walk in Morgana's shadow, Morgana had always envied Ingrid her serenity. Through the years of their friendship, she'd sought to be more like Ingrid than her natural disposition would have permitted, and she'd thought she'd succeeded . . .

Until Leif Haraldsson had gone sailing off to the west one sunny spring .morn and sent Magnus Longbeard's legacy boiling through her blood. A legacy that had included a temper, however rare its appearances and short-lived its durations.

A shadowed side to a warm, loving nature . . .

Morgana pulled her thoughts from herself.

Ingrid. How was she faring? Was she happy? *Nei . . .* Morgana shook her head. How could she be with Gunnar gone and his second child dead as well? With old Guthrum, to whom she'd been closer than anyone else in Gunnar's family, having chosen to leave Oslof? With Leif having been banished from Norvegia, and Morgana having hied herself off to find him?

And with Horik Bluetooth dogging her every step, more and more boldly with each passing day?

It came to Morgana in those reflective moments that Ingrid's burden was much greater than her own. She remembered the wistful look in Ingrid's eyes after they'd embraced, before Morgana had swung away toward *Wave Rider.*

By the gods, she thought suddenly. Why hadn't she offered to take Ingrid with them?

Because she wouldn't have left little Harald. Nor would she have wished to venture forth on a mission that could have ended in his death. Or her own.

But deep down, Morgana knew better than that.

"Any Norsewoman worth her chatelaine would have been willing to risk the unknown," Morgana whispered. "And especially Ingrid. With Gunnar dead, and his best friend outlawed . . . with the jarl bereaved to the point of madness and under the influence of one such as Bluetooth, what was left for her in Oslof?"

Many of the young men had left after Harald Estrithsson's death—or murder—before Leif and his crew had ever returned. Even some of Ingrid's own relatives . . .

How is Ingrid?

Little Thor's words returned suddenly. And the memory of the steely grip on her arm for a brief space of time as she'd revealed what Horik Bluetooth had attempted to do.

Equiwa? Morgana . . . ? The query crept softly through her memory.

"I never really asked her if she wanted to go with us,"

Morgana whispered again. It now seemed to her that Little Thor was concerned about Gunnar's widow. Was it possible that he really cared for her? Was in love with her?

And Ingrid had given Gunnar's Sleipnir to Leif for Little Thor—a revealing gesture, especially in the midst of her grief. That showed, at least, her genuine regard for the red man . . . her concern for his well-being. And, ultimately, how much she respected him.

Or had it been merely the mindless gesture of a bereaved woman? Ingrid hadn't mentioned Little Thor in the months before *Wave Rider* had left Oslof this last time . . .

Eirik's laughter momentarily drew Morgana from her musings. She watched him thrust his tiny hands into the gurgling water . . . and come up empty for at least the second or third time. Freki barked, which, Morgana decided, didn't help Eirik's cause. The child unexpectedly looked up at her, a smile of pure happiness transforming his features.

As tender affection for her son sifted through her, Morgana felt her throat tighten with love. And regret. Regret that she would have to tear Eirik away from the security he evidently felt in Vallée de Vergers with his father. And regret that she'd been so wrapped up in her own misery, she'd done nothing to help alleviate Ingrid's.

In retrospect, it seemed, the possibility of doing just that had existed . . . and she'd completely overlooked it.

Eirik grabbed her knee with his dripping hand, speaking to her earnestly. ". . . help me, Mamma? Catch a fish . . . *já?*"

She smiled and pushed his wet hair off his forehead. "Aye, love. We'll catch a fish or two." She stood, the pain in her ankle suddenly subsiding before the bright expectation of his smile.

For him she would do anything . . . and she would begin by helping him catch a fish bare-handed.

"But you must tell me Little Thor's secret, Eirik," she said after pursing her lips thoughtfully. A conspiratorial look entered her eyes. "Show me what he showed you, my love . . ."

Impirius stared at Snorri the Black.

"You thought I was in Valhalla!" the Northman exclaimed in a raspy voice. An ugly, puckered scar ran alongside his jaw from his ear to his throat, another trophy in the collection of disfigurements that made up his face.

"Rather Hell, I should think," Robert of Neustria added with a humorless twitch of his lips.

Impirius inwardly braced for the Dane's affront, but Snorri threw back his massive dark head and laughed uproariously. Of course, the priest mused, the reference to Hell would have insulted a Christian, but meant nothing to a heathen.

"As you can see," Robert added, "he still numbers among us. 'Twould take more than a mere dagger wound to send off Snorri's soul."

If he has one, Impirius thought.

As if reading the cleric's uncomplimentary thought, Snorri stilled his laughter as suddenly as he'd begun it. His face, being already skewed on one side, gave him a fearsome look. He frowned.

"We don't take lightly to being attacked," Robert said to Impirius. "Snorri and his men could easily be induced to march to Vallée de Vergers and raze it."

Impirius evinced a fleeting glimpse of mortality in the wake of Robert's words. He was about to say, " 'Twould anger Rollo," then thought better of it . . . even though it was surely that fact that had held Robert back from his hunger for retaliation.

". . . but mayhap you've come here with an offer for us that would be equally, er, satisfying?"

Impirius nodded. "In the name of my father, who values his closest and much-respected ally, I have come to offer you a means of revenge against Haraldsson."

"You have his head on a spear?" Snorri snarled.

Impirius shook his head. "But I can offer you his woman and boy-child. You couldn't hurt him as much if you took his very life, however slowly and painfully."

Robert of Neustria nodded. "I see. *Eh bien,* let's hear of this plan . . ."

"Plan?" Snorri snorted derisively. "And from a priest?" He shook his head. "I'll not settle for aught less than Leif Haraldsson himself. I want not his woman and child!"

Robert threw the Northman a piercing look. "That wound must have affected more than your voice, Northman. Have you forgotten already the silver-haired woman? The *pleasure*"—his voice turned silkily suggestive—"you would derive from her before selling her? And think of the price any issue of hers and Haraldsson's would bring in Constantinople's slave market."

The Dane grunted, and appeared to mull over Robert's words.

"And Morgana's willingness would simplify matters for you," Impirius told Robert. "She has agreed to go with you—thinking, of course, that you will help her and the child leave Francia." Put into words before these men, the plan sounded more like something Snorri would dream up, not Impirius.

What was he about? he wondered with a belated burst of conscience.

"She has agreed to return with *us?*" Snorri asked in disbelief.

Impirius shook his head. "She has not been told exactly *who* you are."

"And even if she knew," Robert of Neustria said, "mayhap she would rather return to us than remain with Haraldsson." He smiled nastily. "What a beautiful retribution

293

. . . to take his woman and child from beneath his nose after he risked himself and his men—a few of Rollo's, no doubt, as well—to rescue her."

Robert motioned to a table set with red wine, fruit and cheese. "We can listen to what you have to say over good wine. I would also like to know just how Haraldsson got word of the arrival of his woman." At Impirius's look of bemusement, he said, "Come, come, good father, surely—"

"What do I know of Rollo's spies? If there were any at Vallée de Vergers, that might be different. But I only know of what goes on in Haraldsson's fief."

Impirius got the distinct impression, however, especially as the evening shadows lengthened and candles were lighted to banish them, that Robert of Neustria was only using him and his "plan." That he, Impirius, had quite possibly made a mistake in coming to the dangerous Robert of Neustria for *anything*, let alone revenge against the new lord of Vallée de Vergers. The new lord who'd not only outsmarted Robert and his Norse mercenaries, but now held a valuable part of what had once been Robert's holdings.

Was it worth the fickle Hilaire and her promise of sexual pleasure? Was it worth the risk to his ambition—mayhap his very life—it suddenly appeared to be?

"The exact time and place," Robert of Neustria said much later, effectively taking all control from Impirius, "must be entirely up to us. I can assure you 'twill be sooner than later, but that is all. We need the element of surprise should the lady decide to change her mind between now and then . . ."

As time passed the summer turned sweeter, and even Morgana couldn't help but notice. She gave it little thought, however, concentrating rather on establishing a tentative truce with Leif without ending up in his bed. And without revealing her real intent.

She took Eirik for long walks, the sun on her skin, the wind in her hair, and the benevolence of the land unexpectedly beguiling. She was weakening and she knew it. The longer she stayed, the stronger became Leif's hold over her; and that of this lovely land some were already calling "Normandy" after the Northmen who were settling it.

One morning after the fast had been broken, Impirius approached Morgana. "May I take our Eirik with me this morn? He might help me with some small tasks in preparation for the mass on Sunday."

Morgana pushed aside the thought of the clergyman instructing Eirik in his strange religion. If Leif had already converted, no doubt the same was planned for Eirik and for the moment there was nothing she could do. She hoped the priest wouldn't keep the boy long, either, for she was at loose ends. The manor house wasn't hers to manage—nor did she wish to give the impression that she desired to do so.

She savored every moment with Eirik.

She watched Impirius walk toward the door with the boy, her heart suddenly weighing upon her ribs like a stone.

Freki's cool nose touched her hand, claiming her attention. She stooped to hug him, then grabbed his ears with gentle playfulness and put her nose to his. Her eyes crossed until the dog was a blur. "Outside, Freki? Walk?"

The wolfhound pulled back his head and bounded about her in answer. He gave one short bark, then trotted jauntily toward the door. Morgana obliged him and followed them out into the sun-splashed day.

Impirius and Eirik were walking toward the small stone church across the way, one tall and clothed in dark robes, the other a third again smaller than the priest, mop of golden hair blazing beneath the sun and short legs working to keep up. However, it was Leif astride Hrafn as they emerged from behind the church and into view that unexpectedly captured Morgana's attention. It was too late to retreat into the manor, for she would look the coward if anyone were to see.

Why do you care what they think?

She told herself she didn't, really, but Morgana also didn't want Leif to suspect the true motivation behind her attempt at a truce. Maybe he still loved her enough to believe what he wanted to believe . . . that she was succumbing to the charm of Vallée de Vergers. And, even more, the lure of his love, the magnetism of the man himself—a subtle quality that drew decent men and women to him as surely as the darkening of sunstone upon being pointed toward an oft-obliterated sun.

Her mouth twisted scornfully, but her heart jarred just a little within her breast.

Freki caught sight of Leif and bounded forward toward his master; but Morgana froze on the second step from the bottom, torn between avoiding Leif and appearing either rude . . . or reticent for any reason.

"He is like a king in his own right, *n'est-ce pas?*" came a voice from beside her.

Morgana stiffened at the sound of that voice, for it was unwelcomely familiar to her now. She looked into Hilaire's hazel eyes, detecting deep and mysterious currents behind them. And a challenge.

A light frisson passed through her, then was quickly gone as first suspicion, and then irritation, took hold of her.

Hilaire gave Morgana her proud profile, but not before Morgana had noted full, rosy lips made fuller and rosier by kisses, and the remnants of dreamy somnolence in the Frankish woman's eyes. Hectic color dotted her cheekbones, as well.

Morgana glanced at Leif across the way. Who had been

Hilaire's partner in what surely must have been stolen moments of pleasure?

What do you care?

That annoying voice again . . .

"Some might say that." Morgana's voice was deliberately flat as she answered finally, tamping her more feline urges and making no attempt to communicate in the smattering of the Frankish tongue she couldn't have helped but pick up. Her eyes met Hilaire's again. "But of a certainty, not me."

Hilaire said nothing, her gaze returning to Leif, who reined in the stallion and frowned at Freki as the dog approached. Morgana wasn't sure the woman had understood her, but neither did she particularly care. Impirius and Eirik had disappeared through the church door : . .

"You wish to leave here?" Hilaire asked in a soft, cunning voice.

Alain, one of Leif's Frankish retainers, caught Hrafn's reins just as the animal began to raise up on its hind legs, and shooed the wolfhound away with a single word and a sharp gesture of his free hand. He barked something in Frankish to Hrafn, and the agitated stallion dropped onto all fours.

Hilaire's words echoed through Morgana's mind, in spite of the minor commotion occurring across the yard. Morgana looked askance at her. "Not without my son."

Hilaire nodded again. "Then if it can be . . . arranged, you will be *agréable?*" You will be ready when you are told the . . . time is at hand?"

Morgana was about to agree when a sudden thought struck her. What if this was merely a trick? What if Leif was testing her loyalty through Hilaire? Testing the sincerity of the motives for their tentative truce by placing temptation before her like a glittering cache of jewels?

"Who is behind this?"

Hilaire smoothed her dark hair back from her face. "Not

Leif, you can be sure. But I am not . . . alone." Her eyes clashed with Morgana's, all dreaminess dispersed now. Only cold determination, animosity, remained. And the slightest puffiness to her lips—a damning reminder that she was Leif's concubine. *"Un mot seulement . . .* but one word from you, and 'twill be arranged," she added. "I can say no more." She swung away to mount the stone steps, one hand lifting the hem of her ankle-length green bliaut out of the way.

Morgana's fingers gripping her arm checked her in mid-motion. "Out of Francia? And Eirik unharmed . . . can you swear it?"

"Je vous jure!" the other woman said in a low, fierce voice, obviously annoyed at Morgana's demand for assurances. She shook free of the latter's grasp and ascended the stairs.

"Mamma!" Eirik was calling her, claiming her attention. "Look at Papa!" he shouted as he scampered out of the church door and toward his father. Impirius came running behind him, robes riffling with his movements.

Just in time the priest caught up with the boy and lifted him into the air, making a game of it. "Oh no you don't," Impirius said with a laugh.

It couldn't have been more perfectly timed, Morgana thought with one part of her mind, if Eirik had wanted to interrupt her thoughts and divert her attention before she could think about Hilaire's proposition too carefully.

Or if Impirius had planned it.

"But I am not . . . alone."

Could Impirius be in collusion with Hilaire? Or was Hilaire bluffing to gain Morgana's confidence in the proposed plan?

As she reluctantly moved forward, girding herself to face Leif for Eirik's sake, she determined to press Hilaire for further details. As her lips curved softly in a loving smile for her son, Morgana's mind raced. It was Thor's day, which

298

meant there would be feasting and celebrating that eve in spite of the adoption of Christianity by many.

Surely she could corner Hilaire later. Demand more information of her during the thick of the festivities . . .

Be ready . . .
When?
Soon. You will know . . .

Morgana allowed the swell of noise around her to blend into a dull roar as Hilaire's earlier words drifted through her mind. She held a sleepy Eirik in her arms now, her head bowed over her precious burden, her tresses a platinum tapestry between them and the boisterous crowd. She wished she could just put him to bed and retire as well, but it wouldn't have been seemly. Nor did she want to arouse Leif's suspicions in any way.

She stood, glanced about her, and found her gaze caught by Little Thor. The Skraeling stood slightly apart from the milling men, a faint frown marring his high forehead directly beneath his headband.

The sound of a man's shout of challenge distracted her, and Morgana looked away. Alain and Einar were boistrously debating the role of horses in battle. The men immediately around them loosely formed two groups—those from Oslof, who agreed with Einar; and several Franks and the Norsemen who'd been in Francia with Rollo before the treaty at St. Clair-sûr-Epte, who sided with Alain.

Hilaire appeared and took the sleeping child from Morgana. She allowed this, for once, wondering with rue if Hilaire was attempting to garner the smallest bit of her favor, but intrigued in spite of herself by the argument.

"Rollo needed not horses to do battle and win these new lands!" said the young but serious Einar. "Horses are for hunting . . . ask any Northman!"

Tall and husky Alain, unruly dark hair gleaming in the torchlight, asked with open disdain, "Heard you not of Rollo's defeat before the walls of Chartres, Northman? The King didn't grant him holdings because of any battle victory—"

As if he suddenly realized his position—vassal of a Northman who served Rollo, newly-made count—and therefore was speaking treason, he stilled suddenly, his mouth closing slowly.

Unexpectedly into the sudden, tense pool of stillness, Leif's voice said with an underlying firmness, "Although, Alain of Francia, I would never speak of such a thing again were I you . . . I find myself agreeing with the advantage of a destrier—a horse trained for battle in the Frankish tradition."

Ragnar, who'd been drinking heavily, raised his over-flowing horn in challenge, foamy ale splashing down his heavily-muscled bare arm. "Then let's *see* who's better," he shouted, "mounted or—"

" 'Tis dark now, fool," said Egil sourly. He, clearly, was feeling his ale, for few dared to call Ragnar the Red "fool," whether sober or otherwise. "You cannot challenge in the middle of the night."

Morgana, glimpsing an unexpected opportunity to speak again to Hilaire—perhaps get her to be more specific—turned away from the men and toward the door to the sleeping room.

Little Thor loomed before her, an ominous shadow breaking from the layers of darkness around the edges of the hall. She should have known, for his own unique scent—clean but subtly different from her fair-skinned countrymen—had come to her a split second before he materialized before her.

Morgana looked up into his dark eyes, bottomless black holes in the shaded hollows of his lean face. He put a hand on her shoulder. "Trust no one but Kiisku-Liinu," he said softly, "or you will bring about his . . . destruction."

Returning his steady regard, Morgana answered, "I trust no one but myself, red man." Nonetheless, a nebulous fear like the tickle of frigid water skittered down the length of her spine; this man, she was learning, never spoke lightly. He had an uncanny way of divining things others didn't see; an aura of ancient wisdom about him that belied his years. And a wraithlike quality in his movements and gestures, which only added to the impression of an almost mystical omnipotence.

His grip tightened before his hand fell away, his voice now a husk of sound. "Especially, Mor-gana, trust not the woman called Hilaire, for I am to protect the one who commands my loyalty. Against even you . . ."

Her eyes widened, and Morgana wondered briefly if he were trying to frighten her. Certainly he was capable of that . . . dark and alien deity that he seemed. Utterly steadfast in his purpose, silent, and lethal.

He's only a man—like any other . . .

They stood for a long moment, gazes fused, before a clatter at the door of the manor broke their soundless stalemate.

Morgana swung away as Little Thor retreated into the shadows . . . and watched, her mouth opening slightly in awe, as Hrafn gained the top of the stone steps, head and satiny neck bursting into view. The stallion paused infinitesimally at the threshold of the hall door; then with an eerie equine shriek and a gathering of powerful muscle and sinew, leapt into the hall like a great, dark phantom out of the even darker night.

Torchlight flashed across his gleaming hide, and the soft *swoosh* of his magnificent passage touched every man and woman in the hall like a sigh from the gods.

Odin upon Sleipnir, moving as one . . .

The thought flickered through Morgana's mind, as she

301

watched Leif, hunched low over Hrafn's neck, guide the stallion right into the hall. At his urging the animal gathered himself once again and, as if he had invisible wings, effortlessly vaulted over the nearest trestle table. As men scrambled from his path, Morgana noted the marked contrast between their clumsy, panicked movements and Hrafn's graceful flight.

The clatter of the horse's hooves against the wooden floor bounced off the walls and the ceiling, creating a dull roar like thunder. Hrafn whinnied loudly, the shriek adding to the sudden sense of unreality, of confusion. Some of the men were too well into their cups, nonetheless, to do more than stare slack-jawed at the spectacle.

"Tell me what an unmounted man can do that we can not?" Leif challenged as Hrafn rose up on his hind legs, forelegs slashing the empty air before him. Leif's torso was almost parallel to the stallion's back before Hrafn whinnied again, then dropped to all fours.

"You've improved since this afternoon," Alain said with irony.

Scraps of laughter sounded here and there.

Leif grinned, as well, but his eyes went to Morgana. "I can learn swiftly when 'tis required," he said, his voice lowering with meaning.

Morgana didn't hear the comment; she was looking about her, a frown between her eyes, and noting what she feared most in spite of herself: disdain dawning upon the faces of the Franks who served Leif. Surely they considered themselves infinitely more civilized than a barbaric Northman who'd brought a stallion crashing into the middle of the manor hall. The Franks—many of them who regarded the Northmen with contempt—also expected them to adopt their religion, speak their language . . . even wed their women. No doubt, Morgana thought grimly as she noted the expressions on many faces, they sought to teach

302

these newcomers their customs and code of behavior as well.

In spite of her grudge against Leif, the thought of any of the men present disapproving of his actions—even if he *had* overimbibed—pricked her Norse pride. More, she thought, than it should have.

Perhaps it was because he was Eirik's father; perhaps because he, like Morgana and the men from Oslof, was Norse. She stepped forward, refusing to think further about the implications of her actions. No one moved to stop her, and she silently invoked the Allfather that Hrafn wouldn't lash out at her as he'd been taught to do. For, after all was said and done, she was not the real enemy.

"Leif," she said quietly as he stroked Hrafn and murmured to the animal in soothing tones at her approach.

"*Já?*" he answered in a low, expectant voice as he straightened and looked over at her . . . answered in endearing Norse, not in the Frankish tongue.

She put a tentative hand on his thigh.

His eyes darkened almost imperceptibly.

"You do yourself a disservice before these Franks." Her voice dropped to a murmur. "Where is your pride?"

He stiffened; she could feel it in the muscles beneath her fingers. "I seek not to criticize, but rather to remind you . . . that you are the son of the great Harald Estrithsson, grandson of the lauded Estrith the Stern." Her voice lowered even further. "Do not give these men aught to laugh at behind your back! To find you wanting when they compare you to their Frankish lords."

If Leif had been the least in his cups, his eyes seemed to clear in those moments as she appealed to him, her hand touching his leg of her own volition. "What would you have me do, Morgana?" he asked, although he knew the answer.

"Dismount and let a Frank—Alain—lead the stallion

from the hall in affirmation of your position as lord. And do not ever do such a thing again."

He appeared to ponder this for the briefest time, with no sign of ire. Then his look turned very somber. "Will you sit beside me at the head table then?"

Lull him—disarm him, whispered a voice. *Agree to anything* . . .

But her answer came as naturally to her lips as life-sustaining breath. *"Já."*

One side of his mouth lifted in a disarming smile. "Alain!" he called, as he lifted one leg over Hrafn's neck and slid to the floor.

"Oui?"

"Take Hrafn back to the stables, won't you? I think we can pick up where we left off . . . in the morn, and outside the manor." He held out a hand, and Morgana took it. As Alain led Hrafn from the hall, Leif led Morgana to the head table, and the revelry recommenced.

" 'Twas a noble thing you did earlier this eve," Leif told her much later, after the hall had cleared and she'd retired to the sleeping chamber.

To her dismay, he'd followed her.

"You wouldn't have done that for just . . . anyone."

"You are not *anyone.*" She looked up at him, tall and proud in the dimness of the bower, yet also somehow humble in her presence now, and thought of the reasons why she had fallen in love with him long ago.

Without warning, for some unknown—or unacknowledged—reason, the alarm she'd felt melted away. She couldn't see the expression in his eyes, only the fall of hair about his face, the pale and elusive kiss of candlelight as it subtly played about his features. She still felt the rich wine she'd drunk; it heightened her sense of touch, of smell. Everything about Leif Haraldsson came to her magnified,

304

or so it seemed, by the wine. His scent filled her nostrils, the sensation of his muscled thigh beneath her hand lingered to tease her memory.

Or was it just that magic that had always been between them? That magic that had been denied, but never quite extinguished.

When he spoke she could tell by the sound of his voice that he was smiling. Then, too, did she detect a wistfulness? "Do I dare believe there is hope for me? That I can win you over and—"

She swung away, moved toward the sleeping Eirik. "I never said that I could be *won over* like some lovesick young girl."

"Morgana . . ." His voice caressed her ear, his fingers touched her shoulder lightly through her linen overgown, but with all the effect of flesh upon flesh.

"I need time," she insisted softly, caught between her own desire and the guilty knowledge of what she was planning to do. She could feel his restraint, and secretly marveled at his newfound patience.

Until his tongue touched her ear . . .

Chapter Twenty

The flesh on her neck prickled. Pleasure rippled down her spine. His touch, his breath sighing across her cheek, were as lulling as warm water lapping gently over her body.

A warning went off in some dim recess of her mind, but Morgana's willpower was fast-dissolving . . .

"Trust me, *ást mín* . . . I'll never hurt you again," he vowed to her, an underlying fervency in his voice lending credence to his words. His lips glided from her ear down the velvet-soft flesh of her neck, to the hollow where it joined her shoulder.

Morgana whimpered softly, her head dropping back as his mouth nestled in that sensitive curve. His tongue skimmed her flesh, sending more tremors streaking through her. Languor spilled through her limbs, stoking a pulsing heat within the lower, feminine reaches of her body as his arm slid about her waist and pulled her up against him until they were nearly one.

Leif rested his head on her shoulder briefly, savoring the feel of her willingly in his arms. This was all of heaven—if not according to Christianity, then by his own vision of it—his wife and their child in a new land of promise, the future spreading before them like a vast, unexplored sea.

He bent and lifted her into his arms, then bore her to his bed like a treasured thing . . . a priceless part of his life he'd

306

almost lost forever. Morgana allowed him to do so without a word or gesture of protest.

He couldn't believe it wasn't a dream: first her actions in the hall, now this. He couldn't quite believe that it wouldn't shatter into a thousand shards of deepest disappointment, myriad broken images of what could never be again.

Leif Haraldsson didn't know if he could endure that now without going mad.

He showed the woman beside him just how profound his love still was, through the slow and tender undressing, his raging need and desire held rigidly in check, and through the tantalizingly deliberate worship of her body. With callused but ever-so-gentle fingers and questing mouth he followed every sweet contour he'd dreamed about, savored every exposed plane and shadowed hollow with a patience and appreciation even he didn't know he possessed.

His message was as clear as if he had spoken to her. Clearer, even. And he felt her capitulation, her slow-building eagerness, until words and deeds held no meaning in that dim bower. Morgana's answer was all that he'd ever dared hope for as she lifted her hips in invitation to the ultimate intimacy—the sharing of her very essence with the man above her.

The father of her child. The man who, her body acknowledged if her mind and spirit would not, still held her heart in the palm of his strong but tender swordsman's hand.

Ulf knew what he had to do. He also knew it could very well cost him his life. But he was staunchly loyal to Rollo—hence the reason he'd been assigned so dangerous but important a role.

He frowned as he slipped away from Harfleur well past midnight, hoping no one would miss him before dawn, and knowing that whether they missed him sooner or missed him later, his observations of Robert of Neustria's activities were, of a certainty, at an end.

But, he hoped, so would be the nefarious dealings of one Impirius of Vallée de Vergers. If Haraldsson survived, he was the type of man who would see justice done. If Impirius succeeded in bringing about the Northman's demise—for surely Robert of Neustria would prefer to capture Haraldsson himself, even if the priest had offered only the woman and child—Rollo would make sure he was taken care of, churchman or nay.

Bastard issue of King Charles or nay.

Ulf raced his mount into the night, having risked taking his own fleet-footed and trustworthy mare, Valkyrie, rather than another horse, and therefore being identified almost immediately when the animal was declared missing. The risk was worth the advantage, he'd decided with his typical quick-thinking cool-headedness.

Heading almost directly east toward Vallée de Vergers, he heard a tiny voice say, *You could always change sides—go back to Harfleur and Robert's cutthroat mercenaries . . .*

Ulf dismissed the half-formed thought with a snort of derision. Snorri and his band reminded him too much of the murderous jarl back "home" who'd usurped power at the price of many good men, including Ulf's father and two brothers, in the name of Harald Fairhair half a score of winters past. Ulf had barely escaped with his hide.

Then there was the rape and murder of his wife and his unborn child . . .

He diverted his thoughts abruptly, the hurt still greater than any physical wound he'd suffered yet. Rather give his life for Leif Haraldsson, he thought as he willed the cloud cover to hold for a while longer, a man who'd won Rollo's trust and esteem. And Ulf knew that it would take men like Haraldsson to build and convert the new Norse acquisition in Francia into a powerful and independent entity.

The wind whipped his hair, the humidity from the coast penetrated his clothing, but it was summer and dampness was better than chill. As he moved farther and farther from Harfleur, his confidence began to build. His decision to save time and go directly to Vallée de Vergers began to sit better with him. It had been the wisest thing to do under the circumstances. There was so little time to warn . . .

The whine of a flying missile came to him then, bursting into his thoughts. Immediately following, he felt the piercing jab of an arrow in his left thigh. He couldn't stop to remove it now, no matter how it pained him.

Whoever his attacker was, he was a poor shot, for not only had the man failed to hit a vital spot for the kill, but the arrow head protruded from the flesh on the outside of his thigh. It was a flesh wound, the arrow having missed the bone. Blood darkened his breeches.

Ulf urged Valkyrie on, using his heels and causing his wounded thigh to throb with the movement. He bit his lip and leaned forward over the mare's neck.

This time he didn't hear the whine of the arrow, for the wind in his ears was louder. It struck him between his shoulders. Although he thought it was a shallow wound, fire spread to every muscle in his back.

And the shock of the unexpected pain, like yet a second blow, made him lurch sideways and tumble toward the ground. But not before he noted with dim contempt that his enemy was sorely in need of practice with bow and arrow.

As the new day lengthened, Morgana found herself consumed with guilt. And following the guilt, anger directed at Leif, then at herself.

When it came to Leif Haraldsson, she thought in extreme irritation, she hadn't the backbone of a worm. Only weeks after her arrival, she was allowing herself to put aside her own wishes . . . and Eirik's best interests.

This was exactly what she had tried to prevent by wedding Hakon Sweynsson—Leif's insidious influence upon her heart. She was being soft now . . . a sentimental fool over her first love, just like Tyra.

Blame Tyra now . . . and Magnus, why don't you? 'Tis easier than confronting your own weaknesses.

What had happened to her anger? Her righteous outrage? What she had thought was her *hatred* for him? She wouldn't let him have his way again—not after one betrayal on top of another.

And isn't this what you wanted? To throw him off his guard so you could somehow get away?

Of course it was! Had been since she'd found her son alive. If she could get safely away with Eirik, the score would be settled. She would never have to deal with Leif Haraldsson again. She would go far, far away—it didn't matter where.

It does matter where! And what of a plan?

She ignored that. No one would be harmed, she told herself. Hilaire had sworn as much.

Can you trust a woman like Hilaire? A foreigner? A woman eager to get rid of you? She cannot even tell you when it will happen.

"I have no choice," she snapped with annoyance, then cast a furtive glance about the half-empty hall, lest anyone wonder why she was talking to herself as she fed an extra portion of leftover scraps to Freki. Guilt made her uneasy and suspicious, yet, as she had done once before, Morgana stubbornly pushed aside every emotion but her outrage. Leif Haraldsson had stolen her son. Now she would take him back, and anyone—Northman or Frank—who tried to stop her be damned! Including Leif.

That was all there was to it. She would keep busy to prevent herself from thinking too much about it. Surely it would happen soon—she just had to string Leif along. He certainly looked like a man happy with his lot after last night.

Hectic color lit her cheeks at the thought.

You enjoyed it well enough, too.

She closed her eyes briefly. Once she was free of Leif Haraldsson, she could think clearly. Her life would be unencumbered by the unwelcome emotions he stirred within her. Everything would be simpler.

Eirik came into the hall from outside. "Mamma . . . come and see! Come and see the peddlar!" He beckoned excitedly and left the hall as quickly as he'd appeared.

As Morgana straightened and smoothed her gown, Hilaire came from the kitchen area and headed toward the door. She paused as she passed Morgana, looked about her, then said in an undertone, "The time approaches— soon you and Eirik will be free, *n'est-ce pas?* Are you ready?"

Morgana ran the tip of her tongue over her top lip. Was she ready? Did she really want to go through with it after last night? What if Eirik was hurt? Or Leif?

He played you false twice, and you're concerned about his safety? Soft-hearted fool!

"*Eh bien,* are you prepared? Or will you throw away your only chance?" An urgent note entered Hilaire's voice with the last two words.

Freki finished the scraps and nudged Hilaire's hand, obviously looking for another handout. One of the elk-hounds approached them, sniffing the air. Hilaire threw some tidbits to the dogs, pretending great absorption in their actions. "Be on your guard—they'll be here soon."

"Who?" Morgana asked in a whisper, keeping her eyes on the dogs as she spoke.

Hilaire brushed off her hands and swung toward the great wooden door, which stood open to the summer sunshine and fresh air. "You will see." She stepped away then, and Morgana wanted to grab her and shake her. Prudence, however, kept her still. And only when Hilaire had disappeared after Eirik did Morgana will herself to move outside, an uneasy feeling tightening her chest.

Indeed there was a small peddlar's train before the manor: eight sway-backed mules and three olive-skinned men. The leader was a short, wiry man of indeterminate age. He was appealing to those around him in an incongruously deep voice, speaking heavily-accented Norse and then translating immediately into Frankish. "We come from *far* away," he told them, his glittering dark eyes widening with emphasis. "From Novgorod to Kiev . . . from Hedeby to the City of Constantine we've traveled!" He motioned the nearest bystanders closer. "Come and feast your eyes on the treasures we—"

He saw Morgana and trailed off.

"I have just the perfect complement for so bright a star," he said after a moment, straightening to his full but unimpressive height. Even so there was something commanding about his bearing, a shrewdness about his even features, and definitely an appealing quality to his speech. "Theo!" he said over his shoulder to his closest man. "The cage . . ."

" 'Twould seem you haven't enough pack animals to bear goods from such widespread travels," Leif said to the man, walking up to him, his right hand unobtrusively positioned near the dagger that was always at his waist. "What do they call you?"

The trader's mouth tightened, his dark eyes narrowed slightly. "I am Noor. And we were attacked as we entered Francia—lost half a score of our animals and most of the goods they carried."

Leif nodded, his gaze assessing each mule, and each of the other two men. "I'm sorry."

"Not as sorry as I," Noor said with a shake of his dark head. "I lost four good men. But I thank you, ah . . . ?"

"Leif Haraldsson, and if you are an honest man, you are welcome to show your wares." He looked over at Morgana

312

just as Eirik dared to venture from behind him, blue eyes wide with wonder.

"Your lady is very beautiful," the small, dark man said under his breath for Leif's hearing only.

Allowing Noor to assume what he would, Leif flashed a smile. "She is that, Noor." He reached down and lifted Eirik, who was obviously bursting with curiosity, into his arms.

"Watch him . . . he's a trickster," Alain said from behind Leif. Then he moved forward and slapped Noor on the back in a hearty welcome. "I see you've lived another few winters to return and swindle the residents of Vallée de Vergers."

Noor's chin lifted at the insult. His eyes flashed. "I have never cheated anyone—least of all those I've dealt with over the years."

Alain grinned broadly. *"Oui.* I'll say that much for you, Turk."

"And you have the memory of a snail, Frank," Noor corrected, obviously unintimidated by the bigger man. "I've told you before that I am not a Turk," he said, his gaze briefly seeking the sky. "I am from Macedonia—like the Emperor Leo . . . and Basil before him."

Leif raised one red-blond eyebrow. "I suspect Alain remembers very well, friend. He but seeks to tweak your nose in his normal, irritating way." He put a hand on Noor's shoulder. "But he is a Frank, *já?* He knows no better."

Alain opened his mouth to retort, then evidently realized Leif was giving him some of his own medicine.

And Morgana couldn't help but appreciate Leif's remark, even if diluted by a jesting tone, after what she considered his foolhardy stunt the night before.

"Have you aught among your goods worthy of so lovely a lady as Morgana?" Leif asked.

Noor returned the smile and nodded. "Indeed, Leif Haraldsson." He turned to Theo, who had untied a bulky rectangular package from one of the mules and placed it carefully on the ground near Noor. "Behold!" And with a flourish, the trader lifted a worn brocade cover from what was revealed to be a wooden cage. From within its confines a bedraggled bird regarded Noor, Leif and Eirik with surprisingly bright, beady eyes.

"He's worse for wear, I fear," apologized Noor, "but—"

"Munin!" Morgana exclaimed, moving forward until she was beside the cage. "He looks just like Munin when he first came to Oslof." Memories washed over her, and unexpected emotion momentarily blurred her vision. She knelt before the cage and stared at the peacock, everything else forgotten.

Leif looked down at her, tenderness moving through him. "But mayhap 'tis ailing," he said softly, wanting to give her anything that was within his power to give, but not something that was unhealthy.

"Merely unhappy," Noor said with a shrug. He produced a few seeds from a small pouch attached to his belt and squatted to join Morgana. "Watch." He held the seeds on two fingers and poked them through the bars. The bird did nothing until Morgana made a soft, chirruping sound. It straightened and strutted forward, obviously curious now. Ignoring, at first, the seeds on Noor's fingers, the peacock came to stand before Morgana. He returned her stare.

"Ah!" said Noor. "The bird is mesmerized by the lady. He seems to have found a home."

"Ugly bird," Einar commented to no one in particular. ". . . filthy and scrawny. Mayhap it should be put out of its misery."

Morgana looked up sharply at Einar. Then at Leif. "He is alert and seems spry enough." As if in affirmation of her words, the bird suddenly pecked the seeds from Noor's hand, his sorry crown quivering. "He's not sickly—just lonely." She reached for the wooden peg that held the cage closed, then remembered herself and stilled. This creature didn't belong to her. It wasn't Munin . . .

"Go ahead, take him out," Leif said. "I'll pay whatever price he asks." He threw a measuring glance at the trader, however, as Morgana removed the peg. He wouldn't take kindly to being tricked into buying a peacock that wouldn't last a sennight.

Noor helped settle the bird within Morgana's embrace. As they straightened, he said to Leif, "I feed and care for my animals—they are part of my livelihood. Fortune has been unkind to us of late." There was a touch of affront in his deep voice. "The bird will thrive with care—'tis full grown and hardier than a young one. In fact,"—a sly gleam entered his eyes—"the lady can have him in exchange for a good meal and a place to spend the night."

"Fair enough," Leif said as Eirik reached out tentatively to touch the peacock's train. The bird seemed content in Morgana's arms.

"What would anyone do with such a creature?" Hilaire asked with obvious distaste. "It has no use."

Noor looked at her as if he were about to answer, but it was Alain who spoke. "Rollo keeps such a bird. 'Tis a status symbol among the Northmen."

"Bel oiseau," Eirik said as one small finger touched the bird's colorful trailing feathers. The creature turned its head toward the child with a jerk, but it didn't move otherwise.

" 'Tis a peacock, Eirik. Watch," Morgana said, and set it on the ground at her feet.

Just then, Little Thor stepped forward. His eyes met Leif's, a trace of good humor in them, as he hunkered down before the bird and held out one hand. He made soft, cooing sounds to the creature, and murmurs sounded here and there as some of the men from Oslof obviously remembered Munin's initial reaction to the red man.

"You push your luck, my friend," Leif said with soft irony. One side of his mouth curved upward as he watched Morgana set the peacock on its feet.

Little Thor didn't answer as the bird hesitantly approached him.

"His father was a healer, didn't you tell us?" Ragnar asked, arms akimbo and gaze fastened with great interest on the Skraeling and the bird. "Does that mean he can work magic? Or—"

Eirik was moving slowly to the red man's side, his bottom lip between his teeth. Without warning, the peacock gave a shriek that startled the boy—and cut off Ragnar's words—then slowly and ceremoniously fanned out the feathers of his train; some of them were soiled, some of them broken, but it was an impressive display to a child of four nonetheless.

"I'd watch that bird were I you, Morgana. Little Thor may be tempted to go back to wearing feathers in his hair with so bright and bountiful a supply close at hand."

Little Thor was watching the peacock strut about him as the others laughed at Egil's remark, Leif most heartily. Even Morgana had to smile. Her eyes met Leif's, shared memories and merriment between them.

Noor had been closely watching Little Thor. Although the Skraeling was dressed like a Northman, he was obviously different not only from them, but from the Franks, as well. Nor did his skin have the little man's olive tint.

"And where are you from?" he asked.

Little Thor turned his attention from the peacock to the trader. "Across the Great Salt Sea."

Noor nodded as he continued to regard Little Thor with interest. He scratched his dark-bearded chin. "Ah. A red man from across the ocean. I could use a man like you—if you were interested in traveling with me."

The red man narrowed his eyes a fraction. "I have no wish to leave Kiisku-Liinu." He looked at Leif as he said the name, then turned his attention back to Eirik and the bird.

"Show us what else you have, trader, before we find some cold meat and ale for you and your men. You may share the evening meal with us later."

The words were no sooner out of Leif's mouth when the faint sound of a horse's hooves against the ground made them look toward the west. Father Impirius was riding toward the manor house on his small mount. As he drew nearer, it was apparent he was tired . . . and he looked like he had been unseated a time or two in the course of his travels.

"Father Impirius!" Noor exclaimed. "Another familiar face!"

Leif turned, his eyes going to the priest. He surely looked exhausted from what he'd said was to be a visit to several surrounding farms . . .

. . . *only be gone a few days*, he'd told Leif. Then why did he look bone weary? As if he'd been traveling hard for days?

Leif caught Little Thor's eye. Suspicion flashed in the red man's look, echoing Leif's sentiments exactly.

Ulf became dimly aware that it was daylight. And he was still alive.

From his uncomfortable position among the tangle of weeds and saplings at the edge of the woods, he could discern birdsong and wing-flapping, crickets chirping, and the faint gurgle of water, an inviting sound to his dry lips and throat, his stiff and sore body.

He raised his head slowly, and was rewarded with a slicing pain that corkscrewed from ear to ear. He must have hit his head in his fall from Valkyrie's back. The mare . . . he wondered briefly where she was.

He licked his parched lips and tried to whistle. The

sound that emerged in no way resembled what he sought. He struggled to gather saliva in his mouth for what seemed a wasted eternity, and was finally rewarded with a decent, if pathetically short-lived whistle.

Nothing.

He tried again, wondering whether he would be alerting his attacker if the man was still in the vicinity. Nay, the man was a poor shot—either he was a coward, to shoot another in the back twice rather than confront him face to face, or he wished to remain unidentified—which wasn't any better in Ulf's opinion. Aye, he would have wagered his dagger that the culprit was gone—hadn't even ascertained that Ulf was dead. Or, further proof of his ineptitude, had thought Ulf *was* dead.

Impirius? he thought as he took hold of a slender sappling trunk with his right hand and dragged himself upright, allowing his good right leg to take his weight. Most likely, fool priest . . .

He eyed the arrow still protruding from his now swollen leg, then moved his left hand to take hold of the shaft. Just touching it in its bed of tightly drawn flesh made his eyes water. Better leave it be for now . . .

He heard a whinny, and squinted through the haze of his pain toward the sound. *By Thor's mighty hammer, let it be Valkyrie,* he silently exhorted, for he couldn't wet the inside of his mouth enough for even one more whistle.

The mare appeared through a copse of trees across the path, reins dragging, bridle askew. Ulf felt hope surge through him, for he knew that in and of themselves his wounds weren't mortal. If he could get back on Valkyrie and continue steadily on to Vallée de Vergers . . .

With great effort, Ulf hobbled toward her, his swollen thigh hurting more than the wound in his back, or his aching head. "Valkyrie," he rasped. "Easy . . . lit-tle one."

The mare's ears pricked, she raised her head alertly,

obviously spotted Ulf as he croaked her name once again, and moved daintily toward him.

Beneath the warm afternoon sun, Noor displayed his goods on colorful blankets for everyone to see. For the women he produced several bolts of crimson, aquamarine, and jonquil silk, perfumes, two small ornamental braziers, combs, scissors of varying sizes, and a large glass ball which, when heated, was used for smoothing pleats and seams on linen garments. "My beautiful silver spoons and glassware—all stolen or shattered," he lamented, "but not before I slit the throat of their leader's horse, and then the man himself!"

For the men he had a small assortment of hats, belts, and beautifully-grooved oriental daggers (which, he'd told Leif, had been well-hidden beneath the leather pannier of the smallest mule and, therefore, overlooked by the miscreants before they were driven off).

"Now, look," he said after setting out a few dolls, tiny swords, daggers and helmets for the children, "at one of my greatest treasures." He proceeded to remove from beneath various articles of clothing on his spare body, and those of his two companions, small jade chessmen so exquisitely carved that everyone soon crowded around him to admire them. "There are sixteen pieces, my friends," Noor reminded them. "I either leave with the set intact, or someone here will line my purse well for the lot of them." He winked at Morgana, who was closest to him. "And I'll throw in the hand-decorated board for nothing. Do we understand?"

"We are not thieves here," Father Impirius said indignantly, his cheeks still flushed from his unaccustomed exertions astride a horse.

The diminutive Byzantine looked at him for a long moment. "I know that. Otherwise you would never have

319

seen my jade treasures. 'Tis just a precaution . . . you cannot blame a man who's been robbed for being cautious." He looked at Leif, as if for affirmation.

Leif shook his head slowly, studying the piece in his hand. "Nay. No one can fault you. I will accept personal responsibility for any of your goods while you are in Vallée de Vergers. Fair enough?"

Noor nodded. He pushed up his baggy silk sleeves and dropped to his knees on the blanket closest to him. One by one, those who had been holding the chess pieces placed them on the delicately carved chessboard before the Turk. As Leif bent to replace his piece, the filigreed gold cross suspended from its chain about his neck slipped through the V in his bright green tunic. It scintillated in the sunlight like a living thing . . . and caught Noor's eye.

"Where did you get that?" he asked slowly, his look suddenly intense as he stared at the cross. A frown darkened his brow.

Leif looked up from the chessboard, his eyes locking with the Byzantine's. " 'Twas my mother's," he said softly.

Chapter Twenty-One

"Intriguing . . ." Later, within the shelter of the hall, Leif looked at the Byzantine trader in the wake of Noor's remark as the man studied again the cross that rested against Leif's breastbone. He resisted a childish urge to snatch the filigreed symbol and drop it between his chest and shirt.

Everyone around them appeared to be caught up in the antics of Theo and Bardas, Noor's men, who were juggling knives. The steel blades flashed in the torchlight as the men juggled singly, then exchanged daggers from ten paces apart.

As the sounds of approval grew, the two men increased the distance between them.

"What is so intriguing about a symbol of Christianity? In Constantinople they must be all too common."

Noor shook his head and helped himself to a lush-looking pear from a soapstone bowl of fruit. "Not that particular design." He bit into the pear and grunted in appreciation. Clear juice dribbled down one side of his chin. He immediately wiped it with his well-used, silken sleeve.

Morgana, who had been watching Eirik's fascination with Theo and Bardas, glanced over at Leif and the trader. Out of the corner of her eye, she saw Freki approach Hugin—as they'd named the peacock, after Odin's second raven.

Fearing the worst, Morgana turned her head toward the potential trouble in time to witness the awkward flapping of Hugin's wings as he scuttled away from the frisky wolfhound. Freki cocked his head, evidently puzzled, for the original Munin was more tolerant of the dog. Morgana suspected Freki remembered enough to associate a different reaction with the bird before him.

As if for good measure, Hugin let out a scream of protest. To Morgana's horror, the sound promptly startled Bardas into sending one of the flying knives spinning over Theo's head. Morgana's hand flew to her mouth as Theo ducked dramatically, then straightened, grinning at his astonished audience.

Noor leaned around Leif. "Fear not, lovely one. They but play, for those two could continue to juggle unperturbed through a howling thunderstorm . . . even a pitched battle. They merely take advantage of any unexpected noise for effect."

Theo leapt into the air and swiftly pulled the dagger from one of the low overhead beams before he landed lightly on his feet again. He grinned at Morgana, then the others at the tables, and sketched a brief bow before sending the blades in quick succession toward Bardas.

In spite of herself, Morgana couldn't curb her curiosity regarding Leif's amulet. For once—however briefly—something overshadowed the guilty feelings she felt whenever Leif turned his golden gaze to her. She was seriously considering telling Hilaire that she'd changed her mind about leaving with Eirik, yet maintained serious misgivings about remaining in Normandy with Leif.

"What is so significant about Leif's necklet?" she asked Noor in an attempt to direct her thoughts away from her dilemma.

He lifted a horn of wine, washed down his mouthful of pear, then answered her. "That particular filigree design is worn only by the royal family—the Macedonian dynasty established by the late Emperor Basil."

Morgana was silent a moment, absorbing this. But Leif's gaze moved slowly from the two men juggling among the tables to the Byzantine's face. He shook his head. "You are mistaken. My mother was a slave . . . purchased by my father for his pleasure."

Noor reached out and caught the golden symbol in his hand. "If I may?" he asked after the fact. He ran the pad of his thumb over it, his eyes narrowing thoughtfully. "I am not mistaken. I was once apprenticed to the royal gold-smith—there is no mistaking the intricate design. 'Tis unique."

Leif smiled suddenly, attempting to make light of the little man's unbelievable assertions. "There's a simple enough explanation. 'Twas stolen, no doubt. By my mother—although I am loath to believe she was a thief— or by someone else, who gave it to her." The smile slid from his face as he gave Noor his profile, hoping to indicate his reluctance to give the Byzantine's theory any credence. "I have no connection to any Byzantine nobility. My father was once jarl of Oslof. He, and his father before him, were wise and courageous and respected. That kind of nobility is natural to certain men, no matter their origins. And that is what is important to me."

He looked at Morgana, a slow, deliberate smile soften-ing his lips. His eyes moved down to her mouth, lingered a moment, then returned to her eyes. Even Eirik could have read his message, so clear was it.

Neither one of them noticed Hilaire staring at them with ill-concealed anger. Nor Father Imperious watching Hi-laire, a frown forming beneath his tonsure.

"And I tell you, Leif Haraldsson, there is a whole new world open to you in the East if your mother was who I think she was."

"My world is here . . . with my son and his mother," Leif

answered, dragging his gaze from Morgana's countenance to meet Noor's regard head-on. "I was outlawed from my own land . . . lost nearly everything. Now I serve Rollo, and have recovered that which I most value. Naught, Byzantine, could ever drag me away from the sweet temperament of this land, the bounty and opportunity available here if a man is willing to work. Not even—"

"Not even if I told you that your mother was the Princess Alexandra? Only niece of the late Emperor Basil? Abducted from Constantinople on her wedding day, never to be seen again?"

In spite of his surprise, Leif was firm. First he tried diplomacy. "I appreciate your intentions, and I respect your feelings. I don't want to seem ungrateful or unfeeling, but I am not interested."

The Byzantine leaned toward Leif. "Not even if I told you that certain factions would support you as a possible heir to throne? When the Emperor Leo dies, his reprobate brother Alexander will succeed him. But he'll not last. Then there is only a young son whose legitimacy is refuted by many—including the patriarch. On the other hand, Basil's blood runs through your veins . . ."

Would the man never quit? Leif thought in growing irritation. Were it not for the fragile state of affairs between Morgana and him, he could have laughed with genuine humor, dismissed Noor's tale with a shrug. But he believed he was close to winning Morgana back—so very near to getting all he wanted from life, which wasn't any more than living peacefully, ordinarily, with his wife and son and building something worthwhile to pass on to Eirik and Eirik's children.

By Mjolnir! he swore to himself—forgetting in his agitation that he'd been baptized Christian—they'd been through enough!

He threw Morgana a look askance and saw her eyes

widen; he hoped it was only surprise, for *he* wasn't impressed. Even if by some quirk of fate it were true.

"My mother's name was not Alexandra."

"What was it?"

"Ana."

"That is Norse!" Noor said with a trace of exasperation. "What was her *real* name?"

Leif shook his head. "My father mentioned no other."

"She may have chosen not to reveal her name, but that doesn't mean she wasn't Alexandra! I saw the princess twice, a lovely girl with auburn hair and golden eyes—most rare. Golden eyes have been known to appear in the Macedonian dynasty. Gem-gold eyes, just like yours."

"Enough!" Leif said with finality, then softened his tone. "I mean you no offense, trader, but all of that means nothing to me. There is no proof of aught. Even if there were, I was born a Northman, and I will die one, here in Normandy, where I now belong. And so, let us speak of things more relevant."

It was an order, not a request. With a sigh and a shake of his head, Noor let the golden charm drop against Leif's chest, glanced at Morgana, then with obvious reluctance turned his gaze thoughtfully to the two men now entertaining the small gathering with acrobatics.

"Hilaire!" Impirius said in a low, insistent voice. "Cease your staring!"

She looked over at him, and he wondered peripherally why he had never noticed how unshapely her lips were. Full and pouting when she wanted, but otherwise shapeless. Morgana, he suddenly remembered, had a beautifully-molded mouth.

As Hilaire poured more wine into his half-empty tankard, she bent her head toward him. For once her nearness, the scent of her hair, failed to distract him.

"I risked much for you," he muttered, his head bowed. "And all you can do is stare at Haraldsson like a lovestruck fool!"

He knew he sounded peevish, and he hated it. But he was weary—ready to sleep for the next two days or so—and irritable. Jealous, too, he realized, and, naturally, worried. The Byzantine's preoccupation with Leif's crucifix had brought to mind Impirius's own. Or rather its absence. He'd lost it when he'd thrown away Robert of Neustria's borrowed bow. He acknowledged he was no man of weapons . . . especially an archer! He'd had no need for the bow, he'd told Robert, but quite unexpectedly he'd come across the man called Ulf as the latter was racing toward what Impirius suspected was Vallée de Vergers. The priest hadn't known for certain, but if this Ulf had been riding to warn Haraldsson, Impirius was finished.

The bow had caught on the long silver chain about his neck as he'd flung it away with the passionate energy of fear: fear brought on by the newly-realized horror of damnation for having taken a man's life.

Like a sign from God, the chain had broken, and the cross had gone spinning off into the trees. And Impirius hadn't dared stop and search for it . . .

"And how much of it was for your own advancement?" Hilaire murmured, her sweeping, dark lashes demurely downcast for the benefit of those around them. "Keeping your sire's ally happy? And what did Robert promise you in return, Impirius?" Her eyes met his briefly before she set down the ewer of wine. "You're tired of your position as a lowly priest with an obscure Northman for a lord." She smoothed the sleeve of her undergown and plucked a piece of lint from it. "If you were less than satisfied with the outcome of your meeting, do not blame it on me!"

She cast a look at the others remaining at their table before returning her attention to the jugglers in haughty dismissal.

"And what of your eagerness to get rid of your rival?" he asked nastily, for he wasn't about to be dismissed so carelessly.

He was rewarded with her attention once more. " 'Tis settled then?" she murmured, her eyes carefully on the half-empty board before them.

"Come to me later, and show me just how much you want to know!"

His gaze brushed Leif and Morgana before Impirius turned his outward attention to the entertainment. Hilaire be damned! he thought, and was relieved his choler had gone apparently unnoticed by Leif, especially in the wake of Hilaire's flippant words. In spite of himself, he began to seethe inwardly. How fickle she was! But hadn't he always known that? They were merely using each other . . . but later he would show her. He would make her beg for what he had to tell her—and make him forget his sins for a few passionate hours . . .

The hair on his neck suddenly raised. He looked across the room.

Little Thor stood near Eirik as the child stroked Freki's head, his attention riveted on Theo and Bardas. The red man, however, directed his shadowed and unwavering gaze at Impirius and Hilaire. As their eyes met, the unease that prickled the churchman's neck moved down his shoulders and then touched his back, turning into an involuntary shudder.

The red man seemed to be looking into the priest's very soul.

Blasphemy, Impirius thought, and looked away.

Noor joined his men and the three performed remarkable acrobatic feats, cartwheeling and somersaulting, balancing with practiced precision. Then they were ready to form human pyramids, for which they lured others to form

327

the foundations. This delighted not only those participating, but also the remaining onlookers, both Norse and Frankish.

"Will you go to the East to see if the Byzantine's story is true?"

Leif looked down at Morgana. "Nay, *ást mín*. I have no wish to go anywhere beyond my new home. I would devote my life to you and Eirik. Every word I said to Noor is true."

He caressed her face with his gaze, emotion darkening the green-flecked gold irises of his eyes. His hand covered hers, and she stared down at it with its sprinkling of sandy hairs on his knuckles. Desire wended through her, warming her in places better tended to in the privacy of a sleeping chamber.

"I haven't said Eirik and I wish to remain," she said so softly he had to bend his head to catch her words.

"Oh, but you have, Morgana," he said against the fragrant hair covering her ear, his wine-sweet breath feathering over her cheek. "You told me last night."

With a burst of willpower, she pulled her head away and met his eyes, trying to conjure up annoyance at his bold assertion.

"Papa?" Eirik's voice broke into the building tension between them. He was looking up at Leif, his eyes wide and sparkling with excitement. "Papa, come and help us, *oui?*" He shook Leif's arm with childish insistence. "Please?"

Leif looked down at his son, and Morgana was once again reminded of the love between them. She couldn't tear them apart now. Could she?

And could she separate *herself* from Leif now?

You're weakening, allowing him to get his way, as always.

But that wasn't really true—for first he'd lost eight crewmen, his wife, his father, his best friend, then his home . . .

'Twas his own fault.

Leif rose to join the men forming a pyramid, his look to

328

Morgana apologetic as he allowed the child to lead him away from the board. Pulled by powerful and conflicting urges, Morgana stood abruptly. She noticed Impirius had left the board and drawn Noor aside from the group. Hilaire had risen and was taking an empty ewer to the vat of wine. The rich, ruby-red liquid stained the side of the container like a streak of fresh blood, unexpectedly reminding Morgana of the hazardous nature of the life of the Norsemen in their homeland when the younger men went a-viking in search of either riches and adventure, or new lands to settle.

What had Leif said? *My world is here . . . naught could ever drag me away . . . from the bounty and opportunity available here if a man is willing to work.* It sounded like a pledge to her that he would never repeat what he'd done before Eirik was born. That he would work the land and build their future here in Normandy.

Hilaire was staring openly at Leif as he lithely climbed atop the second row of men, her ewer suspended over the wine cask.

"Come, Skraeling!" he shouted to Little Thor with a challenge shining in his eyes and the beautiful, good-natured grin that made Morgana's heart flip over within her breast. "Show them your talents."

Few men could resist him, she thought, or women . . .

"M-m-my lady?" stuttered a masculine voice, breaking into her thoughts. She looked up into the flushed face of young John, the late miller's son. He looked little more than a youth, but Morgana knew that he was good at what he did, for his father had taught him everything he'd known about producing fine flour. Yet the lad, who was suffering from a persistent rash of bright pink blemishes, seemed unsure of himself before both Leif and Morgana. Morgana also thought he harbored an affection for Hilaire, which served to increase the hue of his already hectic complexion whenever the woman was in sight.

Wishing to put him at his ease, even though she was uncomfortable being addressed as the lady of the manor, Morgana bit back her correction and gifted him with an engaging smile. *"Já?"*

His face turned redder. He licked his lips, looking awkward as he stood, stick thin and gangly, before her. *"Eh bien . . .* er, I w-w-wondered if you and Hilaire m-m-might come to the mill on the morrow. I would have you try some of the f-flour ground by the new millstone."

"Surely, John," she said, disliking the idea of being in Hilaire's company, but seeing his request as the perfect opportunity to tell the woman once and for all that she had changed her mind about leaving.

"Ou peut-être—perhaps—I should bring it myself—"

Morgana put a hand on his arm, her lips curving again. His face turned scarlet. "We'll come to the mill about mid-morn, so you don't have to interrupt your work."

He nodded, his eyes lighting. *"M-m-merci, madame,"* he stuttered as he backed away. Morgana thought it a pity for such a good lad to waste his wishes on one such as Hilaire.

She turned her attention to the object of her thoughts, who was still staring boldly at one among all the others participating in the pyramid building. Suddenly, as if remembering herself, Hilaire dipped and filled the ewer until it was overflowing, then swung away and moved toward the board. And Morgana.

Morgana held out her cup deliberately, even though it was still almost full. As Hilaire leaned to pour, she said in a low, urgent voice, "Hilaire, I cannot go—"

Without warning, the ewer slipped from Hilaire's hand, dropping to the board with a dull thunk. Droplets of wine spewed into the air like so many glittering rubies before they landed to stain the tablecloth. Blood-red fingers splayed across the linen from the overturned vessel.

"Mon Dieu!" Hilaire exclaimed in what appeared to be startled embarrassment. *"Je me regrette . . ."* she apologized as Morgana stood and stepped away from the bench, effectively cut off.

Morgana was suddenly not surprised. She surmised Hilaire had known exactly what she was doing . . . preventing Morgana from speaking. Evidently the Frankish woman guessed what she was about to say and didn't want to hear.

She was now in the unenviable position of having to pin down Hilaire and tell her in no uncertain terms that she wanted no part in the supposed plan to leave Vallée de Vergers.

Or she could go to Leif . . . no. That was inconceivable with the tenuous state of affairs between them. There was no telling what his reaction would be, and if Morgana could put a halt to her departure without his knowing she had ever agreed to such a thing, so much the better for everyone involved.

But what if, when she finally cornered Hilaire, she discovered that it was too late to call it off?

She left the noisy merriment of the hall to collect her composure in the cool night air outside. And her wits.

Leif rubbed his sore side. "Sweet Christ, man," he swore like a proper Christian, "you've a mean kick when you climb!"

Little Thor grinned up at him from where he sat cross-legged on the floor before the warmth of the stone hearth. "You are a good . . . con—con—" His brows drew briefly together as he obviously struggled to think of the word.

"Convert."

"Já. Convert."

"You must learn to use the Frankish, Skraeling, if you want to be a proper Norman." Leif returned the smile from the stool where he sat nearby. "And of course I'm a

331

good convert. I'm a Norseman. I am good at all things."

"Save humility."

Leif stroked Freki's shaggy head when the wolfhound put his muzzle in his master's lap, and gave no reply, allowing his friend to have the last word.

"And I have no wish to become a Norman," Little Thor added. "I am who I am."

Leif blew out his breath with affected resignation. "I suppose 'tis better this way . . . Ingrid would not understand you if you spoke the Frankish tongue."

Little Thor's gaze met Leif's. The latter nodded his head. "Aye. How would you like to go back to Oslof?"

The red man looked away, into the softly hissing fire. "A bad place, Oslof. Bad men would rule. Bad things happen."

"You like it here better?"

Little Thor nodded but didn't meet Leif's look.

"But what if we just raided the settlement—just went in to kill Horik Bluetooth? He murdered my father, after all." Leif's voice lowered with emotion at the memory. "Old Guthrum hinted as much . . . and he's not the first. I think Bluetooth was also somehow responsible for the loss of Gunnar and Ingrid's second babe." He paused. "Surely you can be persuaded to avenge the wrong done Ingrid?"

Little Thor's head swiveled aside, his eyes meeting Leif's. "If 'tis true, I need no persuasion. But what right have I to do so?" One fist tightened on his bent knee. He looked down at his clenched hand in silence, a hank of his gleaming black hair shielding the lower portion of his profile.

"The right of one man to avenge the abuse suffered by a friend's family." Leif's voice became a murmur. "Gunnar was my friend. And he was fast becoming yours." Their eyes met again, before Leif added, "Then, too, you have the unequivocal right of a man to avenge the woman he loves."

332

Leif could have sworn that a flush tinted the red man's high cheekbones, but Little Thor turned the tables and took the initiative. "Kiisku-Liinu must take care of things here first. Look past the starlight in Morgana's hair, Northman, and see what is before you."

Leif's eyebrows tented, his chin dipped fractionally. "Ah, I see, our Skraeling *skald*." His expression swiftly sobered, however, in spite of the light tone of his words. "Let me guess. You distrust the priest . . . you noticed his crucifix was mysteriously missing upon his return." He leaned forward slightly. "And you, too, never thought Impirius capable of any action strenuous enough to part him from his crucifix."

Little Thor nodded. "He is sly. More greedy for power than any holy man ought to be. But more than that. The Frankish *equiwa* hates Morgana. I think she plans evil against your woman and your son."

Leif's eyes narrowed, and his look turned harsh. "There is hostility between them, aye . . . 'tis natural. But plotting evil against Morgana and Eirik?" he asked softly. "Surely you exaggerate."

Little Thor shook his head. "Morgana plans with Hilaire. To leave here. She knows nothing of the woman's evil intent. I feel it here," he touched his heart. "And I have seen them speak in such a way—furtively."

Something deep within Leif twisted painfully at the implication of this. If Hilaire had promised to help Morgana leave Vallée de Vergers, that was a blade to his heart; for Morgana had done a credible job of lulling him into believing all could be well again between them.

But of more immediate importance was the possibility of Hilaire tricking Morgana. He looked at Little Thor, his thoughts awhirl. The red man sensed danger. What if someone was helping Hilaire trick Morgana? Someone who hated him—had a grudge against him?

His mood began to turn as dark as his countenance, for

over time he'd learned to trust the Skraeling's instincts. And his own were suddenly screaming in warning.

Yet he hoped his friend was wrong this time.

"Even if 'tis true, what has this to do with Impirius?"

"The Frankish woman shares his pallet. This I know."

Leif couldn't have cared less what Hilaire did with Impirius . . . or any one else for that matter. If she'd offered herself to every man in Vallée de Vergers it would have made no difference to him.

But if what Little Thor said was true, that put an entirely different light on things. The question then became, just how far would Impirius go to please her?

And where exactly had Impirius gone on what he had claimed were his "rounds" for Mother Church?

In a tiny room at the back of the church, soft sounds of pleasure came from the pallet against one wall, on which hung a crucifix—the only adornment in the spartan cell.

"You've had a change of heart?" Impirius murmured against Hilaire's dark hair. "Have I convinced you of the success of my mission?"

He wanted to throttle her, as he so often did, yet her hold over him was strong. Strong enough to overcome much of his annoyance with her. They were both caught up in a powerful physical attraction, although it held nothing of deeper feelings for Hilaire. And Impirius had not yet acknowledged the intensity of his affection.

A purr of contentment came in answer to his query.

"Hilaire, you must remember one thing." The thought of their discovery was sobering enough to suddenly dampen his passion.

"Ummm?"

"Hilaire!" He grabbed her by the shoulders, for her mouth was a breath away from his manhood. To allow her to continue would put an end to all coherent thought.

She raised her face to meet his eyes, lips swollen, large hazel eyes glowing with lust, dark hair in disarray about her face like a wild thing.

"If we are confronted by anyone, deny *everything*. Do you understand? Swear on your very soul, or 'twill mean your death."

His last words did much to clear her expression. She shifted upward, sliding provocatively over his naked flesh. "You wouldn't let me die, would you Impirius?"

He grabbed her hair and lifted her mouth to his. A fierce kiss followed. "Nay, *chère,*" he answered when he pulled away at last.

Her fingers traced his mouth. "Tell me 'twill be soon, for I fear she will tell Leif."

"I know not if 'twill be tomorrow or in a sennight. But I can give you sound advice, Hilaire. *Ecoute bien, petite* . . . listen well. If she changes her mind, go along with it. There is naught to be done now, and you can be sure that Robert and his mercenaries won't be stopped now that the seed has been planted." Thinking back to his meeting in Harfleur, he added grimly, "Somehow, some way, 'twill be done."

Hilaire was obviously relieved, for she renewed her assault on his flesh, her tongue flicking around his paps, then tracing the hollow between them down to his rounded belly and lower to his navel.

He groaned softly, his grip on her shoulders tightening reflexively before he released them.

Without warning, the door to the room burst open, banging against the wooden wall, the noise echoing through the small church behind, and shattering the somnolent, sensual mood like a rock slamming against a smooth sheet of ice.

Leif stood before them, tall and regal, his expression stern, implacable, like one of the avenging pagan gods his father's people had worshipped for centuries.

The cool air from the stone church wafted over the two figures on the bed with a premonitory chill, in spite of the crude iron brazier that radiated heat from the center of the room. Hilaire sat up, boldly allowing the cover she had momentarily clutched to her breasts to slip to her waist before the man for whom she was willing to do murder to possess.

Impirius, sitting up almost as quickly, had the presence of mind to lift the loose blanket from about her waist and push it against her breastbone.

"Forgive me for not knocking, but the urgency of the situation made me forget . . . protocol." The last word was weighted with sarcasm.

Impirius found his voice. "What situation?" he asked, his indignation growing by the minute.

Leif's eyes bored into Hilaire's for an assessing moment as he stepped farther into the room, deliberately neglecting to close the door behind him. He raised one foot to the wooden handle of the brazier, and leaned his arm across his bent knee. With an insulting lack of interest in his expression, he looked away from Hilaire in dismissal and moved his stern gaze to Impirius.

His eyes narrowed. "Where exactly did you go on your *rounds*, holy man?"

Impirius cleared his throat. "Why, I went to the settlements I normally visit—those around the periphery of Vallée—"

"You didn't by any chance," Leif interrupted with quiet menace, "go to the coast, did you? Say, to Harfleur?"

Impirius felt his stomach drop to his toes. Hilaire's fingers tightened within the shielding blanket. "Harfleur?" the cleric bluffed. "Of course not! To what purpose? 'Tis far beyond my jurisdiction."

Leif stepped away from the brazier and came to stand before the two people on the pallet. He hunkered down before them, his eyes level with theirs. "I am very glad,

Impirius," he said softly. "For had you had any dealings with Robert of Neustria regarding my wife and son, I would have had to kill you."

Impirius held his gaze, Hilaire temporarily forgotten. His mouth went dry, his bowels churned, but he managed to say firmly enough, "I know not what you imply, but I swear on my immortal soul that you seek some nefarious dealings here that do not exist."

"For your sake, priest, I pray—to your God—not." He glanced up at the cross above the pallet, then stared pointedly for a long moment at the cleric's naked chest, where the missing chain and crucifix should have been, even in his state of undress. His gaze clashed with Impirius's. "Do you understand? *Both* of you?"

Hilaire moved to touch Leif's hand imploringly with shaking fingers. He glanced at her, down at her offending hand, then slowly wiped his own on the knee of his breeches.

Impirius felt Hilaire stiffen at the blatant insult. He sent up a silent prayer that she would not show her affront—at least until Haraldsson was gone.

Leif stood. "Remember what I've said, both of you." He glanced at the crucifix again, then down at Impirius. "But especially you, holy man, else you will burn in your Christian Hell for more than breaking your sacred vows. After you deal with *me.*"

Chapter Twenty-Two

Noor and his men left shortly after sunrise. The Byzantine told Leif and Morgana that he would head west, toward the coast, then follow it north and east to Hedeby, the great Norse trading center.

Before the little train had departed, Leif privately told the man from Constantinople, "I will grant you and your men food and shelter anytime you are near Vallée de Vergers, for as long as you choose to continue to come our way and ply your trade . . ."

At Noor's raised eyebrows, he'd added, "All I ask is that you keep your ears open in Harfleur. Robert of Neustria bears me a grudge . . ." He trailed off and shrugged. "It could be something, it could be nothing. But if you hear aught, send me word . . ."

He'd had no doubt that Noor was capable of playing both ends against the middle when necessary, yet he also felt he had made a friend of the Byzantine . . . and the man was obviously impressed by his own belief that Leif was related to the late Basil of Macedonia. It wouldn't hurt, at any rate, even if Noor told Robert of his offer, to let them know in Harfleur that he was prepared for any of their tricks.

But are you? How can you be prepared when the betrayal might come from within your own ranks? From Morgana herself?

He'd glanced at Morgana as they'd watched Noor depart, reliving the night before, his expression thoughtful. He'd been distraught enough to avoid his own bed. It wasn't the wisest move, he acknowledged, yet he couldn't bring himself to sleep beside Morgana in light of Little Thor's suspicions.

Patience was one thing, making love to a woman who was possibly plotting behind your back was another. He didn't want to believe it; yet once in a while, Morgana had acted unpredictably. And Leif Haraldsson was no fool.

What made him all the more more uneasy was the fact that she hadn't appeared to register any puzzlement while they'd broken the fast together earlier . . .

Was it because she was too proud?

Or was it because he was completely wrong about her slowly coming around to his way of thinking? Because she had every intention of leaving with Eirik . . . and she hadn't really wavered in that respect from the moment she'd arrived in Vallée de Vergers?

Even though Leif made Noor promise to return as soon as his travels permitted, the manor suddenly seemed empty and dull to Morgana after he'd gone.

"We have Hugin, Mamma," Eirik told her, in an obvious and endearing effort to cheer her. He put one small hand on her hip. "We c'n care for him and make him more beautiful, like Munin, *oui?*"

Morgana gazed down into her son's face, then at the scraggly peacock strutting around the manor yard now as if he owned it. She laughed, in spite of herself, and ruffled Eirik's hair. "I think we'd better, love, else someone mistakes him for a pheasant and kills him for dinner."

At his look of dismay, she hugged him briefly to her. "Hugin will lose his old feathers within the next winter or so and grow new and beautiful ones."

"Truly?" he asked, his look brightening.

"Truly."

Later that morning, Morgana, Eirik and Hilaire went to the mill to honor Morgana's promise to John. Somehow, Hilaire had been so occupied with Eirik and Freki that Morgana hadn't found the appropriate opening to approach her. It also made it even more difficult with Bjorn and Torvald, two of of Leif's Norse retainers, accompanying them.

Leif had given no explanation, except that he couldn't accompany them himself. Why would he need to? she wondered.

The day was sun-gilt and balmy. It was mid-morning when Morgana, Eirik and Hilaire walked away from the mill, the two women each carrying a small sack of freshly milled flour John had given them. Eirik, who was barefooted, chased Freki through the shallow water at the fjord, shrieking in delight as the great dog shook his coat and showered the child with the cool stream water.

Morgana looked askance at the two retainers, Bjorn up ahead, and Torvald casually bringing up the rear. She drew in a breath and said in a low, firm voice, "I've changed my mind, Hilaire. Call it off."

As she waited for Hilaire's reaction, she thought wryly that at least the woman hadn't a ewer of wine in her hands this time to cause a diversion. Although she could always drop the flour . . .

Hilaire glanced at her from beneath her lashes and said simply, "As you wish."

Morgana was taken aback. " 'Tis that simple? It can be arranged before—"

"*Nous ne sommes pas foux* . . . we are not fools!" Hilaire cut her off, a sour note in her voice. "We took certain . . . precautions, for we suspected you would not go through with it. Leif can be very . . . persuasive."

As I'm sure you can attest, Morgana thought with an undeniable stab of jealousy. How good it would have felt to dump her bag of flour over the Frankish woman's head. And how childish.

Think about it all you want, Morgana, Ingrid's voice, laced with laughter, unexpectedly came to her, *for thoughts can hurt no one, and mayhap will salve the wound. Just don't do the deed!*

Ingrid. Dear friend and confidante, forever out of her life . . .

Abruptly her thoughts changed. She suddenly wondered why Leif hadn't come to her last night.

Mayhap I should have gone through with the plan, she thought spitefully as the image of Leif and Hilaire together popped into her mind's eye. *That* would have shown him how persuasive he was! *And I could have gone back to be with Ingrid . . .*

They left the stream behind them and moved through the mill orchard, as it was known, bordered on the north and west by forest. As her thoughts turned melancholy, the sun didn't seem as warm—surely not any warmer than during the summers in Norvegia. And there were orchards back home, as well, although nothing like this, she had to admit as they walked through the myriad rows of apple trees.

Hilaire moved ahead of her, as if dismissing their conversation and the change of plans. The Frankish woman laughed aloud at Eirik and Freki, and the child reacted with more antics. It was obvious he was attached to Hilaire, although it was also obvious that Hilaire had been willing enough to allow him to leave Vallée de Vergers with Morgana, possibly endangering his young life.

His affection was misplaced in his childish innocence, she thought, and renewed jealousy snaked through her, unwelcome and unfamiliar.

Now you have some idea of how Leif felt while you were wed to Hakon. Indeed, she thought as she half-heartedly kicked at a stone, it was a maddening, unproductive emotion. Enough to drive one to desperate measures . . .

She looked at Hilaire's back, envisioning Theo and Bardas' daggers protruding from it like so many silver spines. It wouldn't have surprised her to learn that Hilaire had made up the entire affair, just to make her look the fool. Or had run to Leif and told him—last night perhaps?—while neglecting to mention that *she* herself had initiated the plan . . .

Morgana was rudely jolted from her maudlin musings as Freki, who'd been bounding along beside Eirik, let out a high-pitched yelp. He twisted unnaturally in midair, then came down on his side with a sickening thud.

Bjorn, who was off to the side of Hilaire and Eirik, turned to them and motioned them frantically to the ground. As he crouched and spun toward the direction from which the arrow had come, he himself was hit by a second.

He collapsed soundlessly. Morgana ran with wordless horror toward a bewildered Eirik. Passing Bjorn, she glimpsed the shaft of an arrow jutting from his neck.

A chilling cry sounded from Torvald behind her . . .

"Someone has been here."

Little Thor's low-spoken words echoed Leif's very thoughts as he crouched to study the trampled foliage just off the path that ran east and west through the forest.

"Why not any of our men?" Alain asked.

"To a good tracker 'tis as blatant an indication of strangers as the presence of the culprits themselves," Leif told him, his eyes following the red man's over the crushed undergrowth and hoof-marked soil.

Alain looked dubiously at Little Thor.

The Skraeling straightened. "Careless men who cannot cover their tracks."

"Or mayhap did not wish to," Leif answered, studying the ground a few moments longer before he stood. "About eight or ten I would guess."

The Skraeling nodded.

"Then they passed through last night, for there are no strangers about Vallée de Vergers," Alain said.

Leif thought of their festivities in the hall the night before, while in their midst had walked a silent enemy. "Not that we *know* of." And he thought immediately of his new enemy in Harfleur, Robert of Neustria.

"Back to the manor," he said, "and quickly. Alain—"

The sound of a plodding hoofbeat along the path came to them from the west. A horse snorted.

Leif swiftly withdrew an arrow from his quiver and nocked it. Little Thor followed suit, the blade of his dagger already gripped between his teeth. Alain unsheathed his sword and the three spread out at the very edge of the trees, out of sight.

And waited.

A horse came into view, walking wearily in the direction of the manor. Its reins were slack, hanging almost to the ground, and a man was slumped over the animal's neck, his long brown hair shielding his face. Aside from rocking with the gait of the horse, the body was still.

Leif carefully moved out onto the path, motioning the others to remain where they were. With part of the reins the rider's hands were clumsily bound together beneath the mare's neck. Blood stained the back of his tunic, and the entire right leg of his breeches was dark with blood as well. An arrow was lodged in one swollen thigh.

Leif took the mare's reins. She came to a stop with a snuffle. He carefully pushed aside the man's hair and frowned, essaying to place the vaguely familiar features. He glanced back in the direction from which horse and rider had come. All was still, save for the normal sounds of

343

the woods. He motioned with his chin over one shoulder for Little Thor and Alain to join him.

Leif cut the man's bonds, wondering why his assailant hadn't just killed him instead of tying him to his horse—unless it was a grisly message from someone . . .

Ulf, he thought suddenly as recognition dawned. The man was one of Rollo's informers—the one who had told Rollo about Morgana and the men from Oslof. The one who had guided them to Harfleur.

The one who was directly responsible for saving Morgana and the men with her.

If his true purpose had been discovered, that would possibly explain why he was wounded. But—

They eased Ulf from the horse, onto the ground. His body radiated feverish heat, and Leif's concern increased, for he owed this man much.

A shiny object caught the glitter of sunlight that streamed unevenly through the tree branches above, then it dropped to the forest floor beneath the mare with a soft clink, unnoticed . . .

Little Thor cut away what remained of the right leg of Ulf's breeches and examined the wound with exploring fingers. "His wound festers—he is burning up." He dug one hand beneath the detritus on the ground and placed some cool loam against the wounded man's forehead.

"Mayhap 'tis Robert of Neustria's retribution," Leif said with a grim set to his mouth. "To wound the informer, then send him as an example."

Alain asked, "Then why didn't Robert send this man to Fécamp . . . to Rollo?"

"Rollo wasn't on the raid. *I* led it." Leif had been reluctant to reveal all the details to Alain, a Frank, when he wasn't certain of the man's loyalty.

"He needs water," Little Thor said.

Leif nodded, but before he could speak, Ulf's eyelids

trembled, seemed to struggle to open. He groaned softly, then shivered.

"Ulf?" Leif asked, supporting the man's head and shoulders. "Ulf, what happened? Who did this to you?"

He opened his eyes then. His gaze was murky, disoriented, his features contorting when Little Thor gently touched the arrow lodged in his thigh.

"Easy," Leif said. He motioned with his chin to Alain. The Frank stood and began to search the trees around them with narrowed eyes.

Ulf focused his eyes on Leif. "Haraldsson?" he rasped, his voice a raw husk of sound.

"Aye."

"Bad shot . . . lost the cross. Clumsy. Robert sent him—to stop me. From warning . . . you," he huffed, and broke off with a grimace.

"We'll get you back to the manor—there's water there—"

Ulf grabbed Leif's arm and squeezed. "Nay! The cross . . . where is it? Priest . . . a coward! Bad shot. Look . . . the saddle pouch . . ." He stilled and closed his eyes.

Leif looked at Little Thor. "Search the saddle—the ground around the mare."

The red man rose to do his bidding.

"Your wounds aren't mortal," Leif said to him gently. "We'll take you back to the manor house and tend them—"

Ulf's eyes opened. "Nay . . . hurry! Before they take—the woman and child."

"Who?" Leif asked, feeling his skin crawl at what he began to suspect.

"Robert and—the Black Dane . . ."

"Snorri's dead."

"Nay, he lives . . . he's *here!* Vallée de . . . Vergers . . . hurry . . ."

He slipped into unconsciousness, and a feeling of doom

began to creep over Leif. Surely someone under Robert of Neustria's direction was either on their way to Vallée de Vergers—or was here already. For a malign purpose.

He felt as if he were in the grip of a nightmare, his mind and body suddenly paralyzed. In painfully slow motion, an image of the two people he loved most filled his mind . . .

Little Thor suddenly stood before him, dispelling the mental picture. Neither man said a word as Leif's gaze moved to the red man's hand. And everything began to fall into place.

For spilling from his fingers, winking at Leif in the muted beams of sunlight, was a silver chain . . . and crucifix.

Morgana dropped the sack of flour and scooped Eirik into her arms, searching wildly for a place to take shelter. Suddenly the peaceful orchard with all its beautiful trees was a deadly cover for an unseen enemy. The child began to cry, calling Freki's name softly.

She ran, trying to crouch, toward the other end of the orchard and the ruins of an old Roman wall—which now looked disconcertingly distant. She stumbled along in her semi-stooped position, expecting the bite of an arrow in her back at any moment.

They were well out of sight of the mill—no help from there. And they were too far yet from the manor for anyone to hear a cry for help . . .

It flashed into her mind: *They've come! 'Tis too late . . . and they will kill us, not help us!* She wanted to scream at Hilaire—to turn around and vent her fury on the Frankish woman, but she did not dare. She had to get Eirik out of their range and sight.

She heard a blood-curdling battle cry, and chanced a quick look over her shoulder. Torvald, a big and burly man, was wrestling on the ground with another man, whose wild dark hair rang a bell in Morgana's mind. He dispatched Torvald with the aid of another who approached from behind, then straightened and impaled Morgana with his piercing stare.

She swiveled her head around and kept running, a score of thoughts shrieking through her head in silent chaos. Who was he?

Snorri the Black, her memory whispered. The mercenary who had tried to rape her in Harfleur. Terror shuddered through her, fueled a spurt of energy.

Ahead of her the thunder of fast-moving horses helped dispel the shock of recognition. Odin help her, they were coming at her from the other side of the orchard, too! How could that be?

She could veer left or right, acknowledging in despair that the ancient wall would offer no protection now, but rather trap her.

Allfather, help me! she prayed fervently as she clung to her son and awkwardly swerved to the left, toward more rows of apple trees.

As if in answer to her prayer, two riders appeared through a break in the wall. Friends, not foes! she thought, for the first was Leif, the ebony stallion beneath him bursting through the gap in the wall. Half a length behind came Little Thor on Sleipnir. Leif rode low over Hrafn's neck, and came straight at Morgana, while the red man nocked an arrow and let it fly toward the attackers.

"Hurry!" she whispered. "Please hurry!"

As Leif came closer, Morgana realized what he was about to do, and she swung toward the swiftly approaching horse and rider. Leif leaned even lower and to one side. Morgana clutched Eirik with her left arm, reached to accept Leif's help with her right, and swung clumsily up onto the stallion behind him, almost unbalancing them both.

She was dimly aware of a woman's screams nearby . . .

347

With a tremendous jolt, clods of dirt and grass spewing into the air, Hrafn skidded to a stop. Leif spun him back in the other direction toward the wall, and gave him his head. Morgana held tight, her cheek pressed against Leif's back, Eirik pinned tightly between them. She saw Little Thor loosing several more arrows before wheeling around and, lowering his torso until he was almost one with Sleipnir, following right behind them toward the largest opening in the wall.

The stone ruins came into clear view and Morgana dared to hope they could escape with their lives; for beyond the wall was an open field, another smaller orchard, and then the manor. And safety.

The shrill scream of a horse shattered her hopes. She dared to glance back in Little Thor's direction . . . only to see Sleipnir rear up in reaction as an arrow pierced his flank. Little Thor fought to swing him back in the direction of the wall, but the horse shrieked angrily and slashed the air with his hooves. He pivoted slightly toward the attackers. A second arrow took him directly in the chest, then a third, while he was momentarily an easy target. Blood darkened his chestnut hide.

He dropped to all fours, whirled away from the miscreants at Little Thor's urging. With one last burst of energy, the powerful stallion rose and hurtled toward Hrafn and his burden, away from the attackers, who were coming out from hiding behind the trees and the woods beyond . . .

Just before the wall, Sleipnir slowed, then stumbled to his knees. He started to roll to his side, and Little Thor leapt from his back.

"Here!" Leif cried as he caught sight of his friend turning and dropping to one knee, his bow poised to shoot. "Here, Thor!" And he slid from Hrafn's back so suddenly that Eirik went right with him. He caught the child against his chest.

348

"Take them!" he directed the red man. *"Take them!"*

Little Thor spun and ran toward them, a question in his expression. "Mount!" Leif ordered as he cradled his softly weeping son to his chest. "I'll hold them here . . . you get help."

The red man shook his head.

Leif's expression turned ferocious. "Aye! You are lighter than I—Hrafn can carry the three of you. Get help . . . *Mount!*"

Morgana watched as several fleeting expressions crossed Little Thor's face—saw his obvious struggle between saving the man to whom he had willingly bound himself, and obeying Leif's trenchant command to desert him.

"Give your loyalty to Eirik now, Matiassu! *My son."* The look on Leif's face was frightening as he fought for Eirik's safety.

An arrow zipped by, ruffling the hairs in Hrafn's mane. Another clattered against the stone wall and fell harmlessly to the earth.

Little Thor vaulted astride Hrafn. Before he could move or speak, Leif shoved Eirik at him. "Take my *son* now, red man! My woman and my son!" He slapped Hrafn hard on the flank, and the stallion started forward. Little Thor gave him his heels then, and the animal leapt forward and through the closest gap in the crumbling stone.

A silent scream of protest shrieked through Morgana's mind. She felt tears fill her eyes as she looked back one last time. Hilaire lay sprawled face down on the ground a stone's throw from Leif, flour powdering the air and whitening the ground about her, an arrow between her shoulders.

And Leif. The image burned into her memory forever: Leif stationed against the wall, his single bow aimed at the riders hurtling toward him . . .

* * *

Before Alain could even get Ulf to the manor, Little Thor had delivered Morgana and Eirik safely to the hall and summoned what remained of Leif's men. They immediately rode off to his aid.

Alain arrived soon afterwards, gave Ulf into the care of his wife, Genna, and spoke briefly to Morgana.

"They killed Bjorn . . ." she told him, distress darkening her eyes, "and Torvald, I think. They were hidden in the mill orchard, near the west woods . . ."

"How many?"

"I know not. Half a score . . . mayhap more." She rocked Eirik in her arms as she sat on a bench, his soft sobs breaking her heart, as did his mumbled "Papa" and "Freki." "Leif surely couldn't have sur—" She broke off, suddenly aware of what she was saying with Eirik in her embrace.

"Impirius. Where is he?"

"Why . . . wouldn't he be off with the others? To help Leif?"

Alain frowned. "I don't know." He turned and strode toward the door, then halted and turned back to them. He motioned toward the wounded man. "His name is Ulf—he works for Rollo—an informer in Harfleur. He came from Harfleur to save you and Eirik from Impirius's treachery. Although," he added bleakly, "it may be too late now for Leif. He instructed me to give the man the best of care, for he guided Leif to you when you were held captive."

"Have a care," Genna called to Alain anxiously as he exited the hall. She looked at Morgana, her expression grave. "Hilaire?"

Inwardly sick with worry, Morgana knew she could do nothing more for the moment than wait for the men to return. She kissed Eirik's forehead, and stood, still holding him close. Genna's words registered then. She shook her head silently, not ready to reveal to Eirik that Hilaire was dead.

But she approached you. No doubt she knew of their intent—not to help you escape, but rather to kill or capture you.

It appeared that Hilaire had schemed with the wrong people, and had paid for her treachery with her life.

And Impirius . . . he apparently was in league with Hilaire. A holy man? she thought bitterly. If what Alain had told her was true, the churchman wasn't any better than the meanest, most conscienceless barbarian. And he was trying to win the Norsemen over to Christianity?

Genna looked genuinely distressed, for she was a sweet and compassionate young woman, even if Hilaire hadn't been any kind of friend to her.

"Eirik?" Morgana said into his hair. He raised his tear-swollen countenance to hers. A soft hiccup escaped his lips. "Look—there's Hugin! He looks for you, love."

She set the child down on the ground. He stared at the bird for a long moment, one finger in his mouth, the tear tracks drying on his face. One of the elkhounds immediately approached Eirik and licked his flushed cheek before the boy could push it away, eliciting the beginning of a watery smile. Hugin issued an eerie, humanlike screech. The hound turned toward the peacock, a ridge of hair raising along his neck and back.

"There . . . you see? You must teach them to be friends while I help Genna for a few moments, *já?*" Morgana gently guided him toward the dog, then turned to help Genna and the wounded Ulf.

Old Guthrum emerged from the shadows, and shuffled toward them. He squatted before Ulf and silently watched as the women bathed him with cloths dipped in a bucket of cool stream water, then carefully turned him to his side to tend the less serious wound between his shoulders.

"The arrow must come out," Guthrum said finally.

"Aye. And so it must," Morgana said, glad to have something to occupy her hands and mind in the face of her fears.

351

"Before he awakens," the old man added. "We'll hold him, Morgana. You pull it out, *já?*"

Morgana felt the blood recede from her face. Evidently Guthrum saw it too. "You must!" he insisted. "You owe him your life. We from Oslof *all* do."

She nodded, feeling the numbness of terror for Leif begin to creep through her. And an excruciating guilt she felt for her collusion with Hilaire. She took hold of the arrow. Just touching it made Ulf groan, but Morgana held firm. If this man had risked his life for her twice, the least she could do was help pull an arrow from the festering wound in his thigh.

When it was done, Genna brought a fresh pail of hot water from the edge of the kitchen fire, and cleansed the wound. Ulf regained consciousness briefly. "Water . . ." he croaked. "Please . . . water."

Morgana held a cup of cool water to his lips as Genna and Guthrum carefully supported his head and shoulders. No one spoke as he drank. Then Morgana took the cup from his lips. "Only a little now. Later, a little more."

He sighed and allowed them to ease him back down. Morgana brewed a tea for him with willow bark for pain, her thoughts a mad jumble. Eirik joined her near the cooking fire. "Papa?" he whispered, his earnest eyes meeting hers. "Hilaire?"

"We must wait until the men return, love," she said, trying to conjure up some kind of smile. As she stooped before the small fire and began to prepare the tea, he leaned his head against her shoulder and was silent.

Finally, after what seemed like a lifetime, hoofbeats sounded outside.

Chapter Twenty-Three

It was with great difficulty that Morgana resisted the urge to run to the door and out into the bright and beautiful afternoon. An afternoon that had suddenly turned tragic . . . could very well turn even more catastrophic.

She closed her eyes briefly, silently thanking the gods that, exhausted from his ordeal, Eirik was napping.

She straightened slowly and turned toward the door, her heart in her throat, her breath trapped in her lungs. She forced herself to walk forward, dreading to hear what had befallen Leif, yet acknowledging a glimmer of irrepressible hope that flickered deep within her.

It came to her in those agonizing moments, that life would be utterly empty without Leif Haraldsson. In spite of past misunderstandings, in spite of the emotional pain and anger they'd caused each other, she had never really stopped loving him. And now that they were together with their son—

She felt old Guthrum's hand on her shoulder, and drew some strength from his touch.

Alain came through the door, his face grim. Little Thor followed. His expression, as usual, revealed nothing. Axel and young John carried in Bjorn's body . . .

"Leif?" she whispered, her face ashen.

. . . and placed it on one trestle table.

"Gone. We found only his bow and quiver," Alain told her. He held them up, and Morgana felt an invisible blade shear through her breast. She looked at Little Thor, an appeal in her fine blue eyes.

"Kiisku-Liinu is not dead," he said as he neared her then stopped, his eyes hard. "Yet." He looked older, suddenly, by years.

She touched her fingertips to her mouth, his face blurring before her as emotion gathered in her eyes. "How—how do you . . . ?"

"If they'd wanted him dead, they would have killed him then and there in the orchard," Alain said. A wave of relief washed through her, threatening her with giddiness. At least she knew he lived. For now.

Alain threw a fulminating look toward the door as a subdued and pale Impirius walked into the hall, his hands bound before him, his eyes red. Olaf entered behind him with, a small miracle, Freki limping in his wake. The great dog moved slowly, drunkenly, toward Morgana with a weak wave of his tail, then collapsed with a soft whimper at her feet, one side of his body blood-spattered.

Morgana bent beside him and scratched him behind the ears, joyful that he'd survived, yet wishing that it had been Leif instead.

Little Thor said, "The dog's wound needs to be tended, but he will live to see his little master again." He took something from a small skin pouch at his waist and held it up before Morgana, taking her attention from the dog. It looked exactly like Impirius's missing crucifix. "The holy man lost his magic," he told her, "when he tried to kill the man called Ulf. The Great Spirit will not protect an evil one."

Morgana frowned and slowly straightened.

"Eh bien, it seems," Alain said as two men carried in Torvald's body and laid it on another table, "that instead of visiting far-flung villeins, Impirius went to Robert of

Neustria and offered him a way to retaliate against Leif for freeing you." He inclined his head toward the wounded man. "According to Ulf, Impirius attempted to kill him to prevent him from warning Leif that Snorri the Black and some of his cohorts were on their way to abduct you and Eirik. Or Leif, if they could lure him to your defense without alerting all of Vallée des Vergers."

"Kiisku-Liinu will die," said Little Thor. *Because of you.*

Morgana held his gaze, her chin lifting a fraction at the accusatory look in the dark and menacing depths of his eyes. He surely couldn't know of her part in the plan unless Impirius had told him. Neither could the others. And if no one else knew, why should she acknowledge her part in this whole affair? They might have believed she only wanted to take Eirik and leave, but why risk directing their anger at her? Especially since she'd changed her mind?

By all the gods, she had never expected this!

She glanced at the cleric. He looked absolutely miserable, and almost immediately she guessed the other reason why: two more men were entering the hall, bearing Hilaire. Much of her body was filmed with flour, an incongruous reminder of their innocent errand earlier.

So Impirius was the other person involved? Morgana thought. A religious man? She stared at him, unable to conceal her dismay. He had made a serious mistake in attempting to deal with Robert of Neustria and his mercenaries. He'd bitten off more than he could chew, and now it seemed that he'd lost the woman he evidently loved.

"Hilaire had naught to do with my—my sins," he said in a strained voice. He looked at them all, acknowledged guilt in his eyes, yet also a glimmer of defiance in obvious defense of his illicit love. "So you need not tarnish her memory—"

"Her name was blighted when she plotted with you to rid Vallée de Vergers of Eirik and Morgana," Alain said in terse dismissal. "Will you try to hide behind Charles's robes now, priest?"

Impirius's cheeks flamed, but he said nothing. He moved toward the table where Hilaire's body rested.

"We must go to Leif's rescue!" Egil the Tall exclaimed. Other men voiced their agreement.

"Aye," Ragnar added. "No Norseman worth his place in Valhalla would allow a black Dane—a mercenary against his own kind—to get away with this!"

"First carve the blood eagle from the priest's back!" snarled Olaf.

Impirius's bowed head came up, but he merely looked straight ahead over Hilaire's body, unseeing and silent.

Alain shook his head. " 'Tis a barbaric custom—forbidden by God."

"Yours mayhap, but not Odin . . . not Thor!" Ragnar growled.

Obviously wishing to avoid more trouble than they already had, Alain held up one hand for silence. "Let the women prepare the dead for burial. Then I will go to Rollo . . ."

The same underlying strength of character, the often impulsive motivation to act against all odds and opposition that had led Morgana to divorce Leif in anger, had sent her from her homeland in search of her child, now charged through her once again.

"Aye, we'll go to Rollo," she broke in urgently, "and tell him that I will pay the death price—whatever it may be—for Leif. But I need him to intercede with Robert."

She looked at Guthrum for affirmation. He nodded. Not long ago he'd revealed to her where there was enough treasure for a hundred death prices. Buried right there in Francia . . . under Robert of Neustria's nose. And there was also silver and gold hidden aboard *Wave Rider*.

"King Charles might intercede, as well."

Morgana looked at Impirius who, in spite of the words

he'd just uttered, was still staring into the middle distance across the room. She frowned uncomprehendingly.

"Father Impirius here is the king's natural son," Alain said. "Mayhap 'tis why he allowed himself to become embroiled in underhanded affairs. He thinks that he is above reproach—protected by God and the king."

Impirius turned to him, his features bleak. "I but seek to do what I can to right a terrible wrong. The messenger didn't die—thank God! But Hilaire did, and I cannot bring her back. Nor the two retainers who lost their lives. But mayhap I can help save Haraldsson."

Several men growled their obvious disapproval, their renewed distrust.

"Ask him," said Little Thor, and jerked his chin toward Ulf, who was conscious once again.

Alain moved toward Ulf, to whom Genna was giving water. "Ulf, think you that there is a chance Duke Robert will accept silver in exchange for Haraldsson's life?"

"The duke, mayhap, but . . . not Snorri. You must get to Robert . . . before he lets the Dane have his way."

"Haraldsson slit Snorri's throat, but didn't quite kill him," Impirius said. "The Dane will take nothing less than his life."

"Time passes." Little Thor's words fell ominously into the sudden silence.

"I—I'll send a message to the king," Impirius offered, turning away from the table. "Now. Just unbind my hands so I can write . . ."

"*Non*," said Alain. "Send a message by word of mouth immediately. Waste no time writing! And some of us will go to Rollo at Fécamp . . . at once."

He looked around the hall, obviously deciding who would go and who would stay.

* * *

Leif drifted upward toward the bright light of consciousness. His eyes opened, but darkness still surrounded him. He blinked once, twice, then realized it was night.

He was unbound, lying curled on his side upon an extremely uncomfortable surface. The sea breeze whispered in his ear, murmured through the leaves on the surrounding trees. Ocean waves heaved and retreated in the distance, their rhythmic susurration reminding him of *Wave Rider*.

He licked dry lips and tasted salt. He was on the coast somewhere, that much was clear to him. He moved to sit up . . .

. . . and felt as if hundreds of needles were piercing his flesh. His raw wrists and ankles burned from being bound—that much he remembered. His ribs and belly were tender and his back muscles stiff. His entire head hurt and he couldn't seem to clear the cobwebs from his brain—especially when it hurt so to move.

Images of the ground passing beneath him, then rough masculine voices in the background, came to him suddenly. He'd been trussed and roughly slung over a horse, then carried for hours at a bone-jarring trot before his captors took a short rest. He, however, was not given any respite from his awkward and uncomfortable position or offered any water. All too soon his torture was resumed, and then he must have passed out for he remembered nothing after that.

No wonder he felt half dead.

He looked about him with narrowed eyes, straining against the cloud-covered night sky to see exactly where he was. The moon briefly broke through the curtain of clouds and he saw crude bars . . . four walls of bars, bars overhead, bars beneath him.

He was in a cage. Taken captive where he'd knelt at the wall—evidently struck from behind. He gingerly felt the back of his head, and encountered an egg-sized lump. He winced, then ascertained that he hadn't any other wounds.

He was lucky. *Aye*, he thought grimly, *Leif the Lucky*. Here he sat, in Harfleur he was certain, prisoner of Robert of Neustria and Snorri the Black. The man he hadn't killed after all. Ulf had been right, and Leif had heard the Dane's name called several times on the journey to Harfleur. And the horrible rasp that answered—a ghastly reminder that Leif's dagger hadn't gone deep enough to kill, only to maim. Or that the man was invincible . . .

He pushed his back up against the bars, trying to get comfortable—an impossibility, considering the abuse his body had taken and the cruel confines of his crude prison. There was nothing else in the cage—no food, no water, nothing with which to protect himself from the night chill besides a brief loincloth. They had left him clad only in his breeches, and he thought ruefully that his summer-weight mantle would have been welcome now.

What did you expect, Haraldsson?

Well, at least he knew that Eirik and Morgana were safe. Yet he couldn't help but wonder if Morgana had had any part in what had happened. Was Little Thor right? Apparently his suspicions about Impirius and Hilaire had been justified, but what about Morgana?

In an attempt to put aside his disturbing thoughts—and temporarily forget his thirst and hunger—Leif began to run his fingers along the bars closest to him, feeling for weak spots. When he encountered none within reach, he got to his knees and reached forward, testing the cage floor, then the opposite wall of bars. The entire structure was too small for him to stand or to stretch out fully while lying down.

Out of nowhere a figure appeared and slammed a staff against the bars . . . and his searching fingers. Pain splintered through his hand and into his wrist.

"Unhappy with yer quarters?" taunted a voice. "We gave ye the best we had . . . and strongest, for Snorri'll take

359

no chances with ye." He chuckled. "He's got a score to settle."

"*Já*," added another, and then viciously poked something through the bars and into Leif's already tender ribs. The blow took his breath away. And there was nowhere for him to move to avoid such punishment.

"Don't kill him, fool," the first man growled, knocking the second man's staff aside with his own. "Snorri wants him to die slowly, not before the second day, and not of inflicted wounds."

"A few blows'll just soften him up," the second man defended his action in a surly voice. He grinned suddenly, his teeth a white blur beneath his moustache and beard. "But Snorri's way'll be sweeter torture—drawn out . . ."

"Don't even think about escape," the first man warned Leif, his leering face carelessly close to the cage.

Leif's good fist shot out and smashed into his nose. The guard dropped his staff, and doubled over as he steepled his hands over his injured nose, howling with pain. Blood began to trickle through his fingers.

"Now we're even," Leif said in a flat voice, his features stony.

"Why you—" the second man gritted, his lips flat against his teeth in fury. He shoved his staff through the bars again. Leif threw himself aside, but there was nowhere to pull out of reach completely. A second blow grazed his side, dangerously close to where the first one had struck. He gasped in pain, his stomach suddenly nauseous with it.

"What's going on here?" Through waves of agony, Leif recognized that horrible parody of a male voice. Snorri moved closer to the cage—but not too close. "What have you done to Argus here?" he demanded of Leif, sounding more like a dreaded forest troll than a man.

Leif returned his stare. And kept his silence. The Dane looked like a nightmare, his features even more disfigured with the angry-pink slash Leif's dagger had carved across his throat and jaw.

"He hit 'im in the face with his fist," the first man said.

Snorri looked at Argus. "Serves you right, fool, for getting close enough to allow it.

"At dawn we'll enclose the cage in a larger one, for the protection of any other fools in my service who might make the same mistake. 'Twill also ensure that Haraldsson remains where he is."

He looked at Leif, his face even more hideous in the play of moonlight and shadow. "Are you thirsty?" he asked slyly.

"Only for the chance to finish what I started."

Snorri picked up a pail of water sitting at his feet and flung its cold contents over Leif. He laughed aloud. "Have a drink, Haraldsson . . . on Snorri the Black."

In a room deep within the keep behind the great walls that protected the city of Paris, Charles III bade the kneeling messenger from Vallée de Vergers rise. He listened in disbelief to what the man had to say. Impirius and his ill-conceived plot threatened the tentative peace in the region the king had granted to Rollo. And his own intervention on behalf of the Norseman Haraldsson would anger Charles's tentative ally, Robert of Neustria. This he had tried hard to avoid, for he knew full well that the duke would jump at the chance to become king of Francia if anything should happen to Charles.

And he also suspected that the Duke of Neustria had kidnapped Haraldsson's wife and men to stir up trouble in the first place. He obviously desired to keep things in a turmoil, in spite of St. Clair-sûr-Epte, in order to camouflage his ambitious and furtive maneuverings. Sweet Jesu, the duke was a fool to anger the fierce and fearless Rollo!

"The lady Morgana will pay Haraldsson's death price a

hundred times over, she vows, if Robert can be persuaded to release him. Alain and several others are more than likely at Fécamp by now to request Rollo's intervention."

Charles, whose demeaning sobriquet was more a result of being unlucky than simple, was afraid to ask where this Morgana would get enough silver to buy Haraldsson's release. No doubt from some Frankish monastery or church pillaged by her fellow Northmen. "If Snorri the Black wants him dead, and Robert allowed the Dane to raid Vallée de Vergers, I would wager 'tis Snorri's decision, not Robert's . . . especially if Snorri has a debt to settle with Haraldsson." He pursed his lips, his expression more than a little concerned. "And the Dane will not listen to Rollo, either. He detests him, by all accounts; if he didn't, he surely wouldn't have abducted one of Rollo's vassals."

Richard, the Frankish messenger sent by Impirius, accepted a mug of cool cider from a servant. He was of middle age, Charles guessed, medium height and solid build, with long sandy hair and beard, and even features. His expression bespoke fatigue, his clothing covered with the grime of hard travel. Yet he looked capable and level-headed to Charles. Surely Impirius wouldn't make a second foolish mistake by sending an untried youth, a dolt or a hothead to plead his case. Charles decided to trust his judgment.

"Haraldsson is favored by Rollo, is he not?"

"*Oui*, my lord king. 'Tis believed both are from Norvegia . . . both outlawed from there, although at different times and by different leaders."

There was no one else but a servant or two in the room. Charles slowly rose from his carved oaken chair and moved to a large, crude map of his domain on a table close by. He was bareheaded, a man of medium stature and not particularly regal-looking, despite his bright blue silken robes, which rustled softly with his movements. Yet he moved with an easy grace, as befitted his station, in spite of his disappointment and chagrin. In spite of his urge to throttle his overambitious and meddling bastard son.

He put a beringed finger to pursed lips as he studied the map. "Haraldsson was taken yestermorn?"

"*Oui.*"

The king nodded. From Paris, Fécamp was a good ten hour ride at a slow gallop, to get the most from the horses, and with perhaps two brief rests. And no sleep, he thought with a sigh. Yet he must keep peace between the discontented Duke of Neustria and the Northman Rollo at all costs or Francia would disintegrate into a dozen warring factions. Charlemagne's kingdom would revert to less than it had been before his consolidation.

For more than one reason, Charles III, great-great-grandson of Charlemagne, could not let that happen. *Would* not let it happen.

With another inward sigh—and a few choice but silent oaths for the brazen Robert of Neustria—the king looked at Richard. "Very well. I'll ride posthaste to Harfleur, but I know not if we will be in time to intercept Rollo . . . or to negotiate for Haraldsson's life."

Early morning brought Noor and his small train filing into Harfleur. They moved directly toward the manor hall, as Noor was familiar with Mauger of Harfleur, petty lord of the area, and his family. As they made their way through the village, children came out and regarded the mules and three men with typical curiosity. A few of the older ones moved closer and called out in greeting, for Noor the Byzantine was a fairly regular visitor to Harfleur.

Dogs barked and hens scattered before the newcomers. One foolish cur nipped at the heels of one of the pack animals and was rewarded with a kick in the head that sent him scuttling away with a sharp yelp.

Theo moved toward the children and began to hand out

sweetened almonds, a strange and wonderful treat. This obviously did much to banish their shyness.

"Master Byzantine," said one boy of about ten, "where are the rest of your mules?"

Noor smiled and waved. "We lost them, boy." His smile faded. "We were ambushed near the eastern border."

"Master Byzantine," called out another boy of about the same age. "We've got a man in a cage yonder—" he pointed off past the center of the village. "What'll you offer for 'im?"

"Deux cages!" offered a dirty little urchin of indistinguishable gender with a stranglehold on the puppy in its embrace. "Two!" The tiny creature slid to the child's feet and landed with a soft plop in the dust as the little one eagerly reached out for almonds.

A raven-haired little girl elbowed the older boy in the ribs. *"Que tu es bête!* Snorri won't give 'im to *anyone.* Don't you listen? They're going to *starve* 'im."

Noor smiled without humor. It sounded like something Snorri the Black would do if angered enough. He was a devil—without conscience, without scruples. It paid to stay on the Dane's good side—this, Noor had known since he'd first met the mercenary in Constantinople.

He wondered what poor unfortunate Snorri had caged. Evidently he wasn't even destined for the slave market if what the little girl said was true. He shivered involuntarily, then dismissed his musings with a mental shrug. It was Snorri's business, not his. He never dealt in slaves.

The urchin began skipping alongside Noor at the head of the train, the puppy evidently forgotten. The Byzantine suspected that she was hoping for another helping of almonds. He produced several from a pouch among the folds of his baggy breeches. "Is Lord Mauger here?" he asked.

"Oui. Et le Duc, aussi."

As she skipped ahead, Noor decided that a little excitement here in Harfleur was just what he needed after the troubles he'd had recently . . .

"You're an utter fool, Dane," Noor said to Snorri, hoping the element of surprise would spare him a blow from the savage-tempered mercenary.

It was dusk, and the two men stood near the outer cage that held Leif Haraldsson. The lord of Vallée de Vergers ignored them both after a glance through his lashes as they'd approached, and the astute Noor decided Haraldsson would not reveal any kind of friendship that might have sprung up between them.

The look Snorri gave the Byzantine in the wake of his insult sent alarm buzzing along his veins. Noor tensed, but continued. "I was at Vallée de Vergers briefly, and discovered something very interesting about our prisoner here," he said with a deliberately sly note in his lowered voice.

"Whatever it was, it had better be worth calling me a fool, Byzantine, else you'll *join* him."

Noor swallowed, and dared to ask, "Why have you consigned him to a slow death?"

Snorri regarded the smaller man through slitted eyes, then suddenly jerked his chin to the side, exposing his newest—and most disfiguring—scar. "He tried to kill me for his woman and the men we'd taken captive. Now he pays for leaving the job half-done."

Robert of Neustria bears me a grudge . . . Evidently Haraldsson hadn't known the black Dane was still alive.

Noor stroked his bearded chin in affected thoughtfulness, although his thoughts would of a certainty have caused Snorri to make good his threat. "A good reason to seek revenge," he agreed. "But you cannot fault a man for coming to the aid of his own." He was hoping for further revelations from the Dane, but Snorri obviously wanted to hear why Noor had dared to call him a fool.

365

He stared at the trader with such ferocity that Noor thought it time to try his strategy. "This man is worth more silver than you've ever collected. On *any* past business in Constantinople."

Doubt crept into the Dane's eyes, then outright suspicion. "What tricks are you up to now, Byzantine?" he rasped, his fists clenching at his sides as he looked over at Leif, then back to Noor. "He's worth no more than any other Northman—possibly a small ransom from Rollo, but naught more." He leaned toward Noor. "And 'twould take a hefty amount of coin to replace the satisfaction of watching him die slowly."

Noor nodded, thinking of the good treatment he'd received at Vallée de Vergers—of his host's words about having lost nearly everything after being outlawed . . . *My world is here . . . with my son and his mother* . . . Noor himself had a wife and two grown sons back in Byzantium . . .

And there the Northman sat, like an animal on display in a menagerie . . . worse, for he had no food or water or even the meanest comforts. Aye, there he sat, looking death in the face. And why? Because he'd dared to rescue the woman he loved, the beautiful and kind Morgana, from this barbarian Dane with the skewed face to match his twisted mind.

It didn't matter how or why Snorri the Black had captured her in the first place, nor even if Robert of Neustria had been behind it. If the Dane had tried to interfere with the rescue, he'd deserved a dagger in his throat.

". . . suspected you were soft-hearted, Byzantine, by your refusal to deal in slaves," Snorri was saying. He grabbed the neck of Noor's silk tunic, lifted him from the ground, and drew him nose to nose. "Or have you *really* something important to spill from that sly tongue of yours, eh?"

Taking his cue from Leif Haraldsson, who sat unmoving

within the double cage across the way, Noor didn't allow his fear to show—nor his misgivings about the wisdom of what he was about to say. If he didn't do something to buy Leif Haraldsson some time, he would surely die. A slow, agonizing death, with Snorri the Black and God knew how many others to witness it . . .

"The cross he wore beneath his tunic . . . I would know it *anywhere*," the little man said. " 'Tis worn only by a few in the City of Constantine." He dared to peel Snorri's fingers from their grip on him, seeing that he'd snared the man's interest. "When I was a young man, I was apprenticed to the royal goldsmith. The filigree design on the cross that was around your prisoner's neck is worn only by the royal family in Constantinople."

Snorri frowned, his wild black hair fluttering in the evening breeze. Noor hoped he never chanced to meet the man in a darkened alleyway—for he looked the stuff of bad dreams. "So? It could have been stolen . . . probably was." Snorri pulled apart the V in the neck of his own tunic to reveal Leif's crucifix and chain. He grabbed the cross and pulled it out, fingering it as he leered at the Byzantine. "He'll have no need for it now anyway, will he?"

Noor looked over at Leif, sitting unmoving within his prison, staring into the distance . . . east. Was he lost in thoughts of his wife and son in Vallée de Vergers?

"He says his mother was a Byzantine slave girl who died after giving birth."

"So?" growled the Dane.

He could tell that Snorri was getting impatient. No use to stretch things out any more than necessary. "The Princess Alexandra was abducted on her wedding day and never seen again. She would have had a cross like the one you're wearing.

"I would wager everything I have that Haraldsson is

Alexandra's son . . . of royal blood. Descended from Emperor Basil of Macedonia, and worth an emperor's ransom to Leo. Therefore to let him die would be a grave mistake, to say the least."

Chapter Twenty-Four

The giant Rollo stared long and hard at Morgana, as if he would reach into her mind and examine it minutely. She returned his look unwaveringly in the hall at Fécamp. She, Alain, Little Thor, Guthrum, Ragnar, and two other men from Vallée de Vergers had traveled there posthaste.

"I understand my man Ulf will recover, thanks in part to your efforts."

"And those of Alain's wife and Little Thor."

"Ah, yes. The Skraeling." He glanced at Little Thor, who stood silently nearby. "He's not a talker, that one, but that isn't important in a warrior. And Leif sets great store by him . . . considers him a brother."

"There is none better," Morgana said without thinking. And realized she meant it—had grudgingly acknowledged it long ago.

"What makes you think you can obtain Leif's release merely by paying his death price? Mayhap there isn't enough silver in Francia to convince Snorri the Black to let him go."

"Every man has his price," Morgana answered in a hard voice. "One only has to find out what it is. But I need your help . . . your influence."

Rollo shook his head, and for the first time since hearing of Leif's captivity, Morgana felt despair threaten her. "As much as I would like to free Haraldsson, there is little guarantee that Robert of Neustria would even allow me near Harfleur. He regards me, at the very least, as an interloper."

"But we must make an attempt," urged Alain. "The cache of jewels and precious objects is buried where the Risle intersects the Seine—about ten miles from Harfleur—"

Rollo leaned forward in his great carved chair, his gaze on Guthrum. "Could that treasure have been taken from Jumièges, you wily old warrior?"

Morgana spoke for him. "Guthrum was there himself, helped take it, helped bury it, and planned someday to return."

"And he saved my life long ago," Rollo said softly, his eyes still on the old man. He stroked his blond beard thoughtfully, barely suppressing a grin. "What irony! Yet mayhap if we offered Robert of Neustria the means to restore the monastery—which was stripped and is now deserted—'twould induce him to convince Snorri to release Leif."

Alain shook his head. "What of Snorri's revenge? We must compensate *him* and compensate him well, or all is for naught."

"I know where there is even more silver and gold," Morgana said. "If we need it, I will produce it. But I need your help to dig up Guthrum's cache—to ensure the safety of the men and the treasure when 'tis so near Harfleur." She added bleakly, "Else we from Vallée de Vergers end up captured, and the treasure in Robert of Neustria's hands."

"Where he would say it belongs," Rollo said with a grin. "But we'll not return one item unless he cooperates." His grin quickly disappeared. "Let us make ready. If we leave shortly, we can reach the place where the treasure is buried by dawn." He glanced at Guthrum. "If no one else has been there before us, that is. And 'twill be easier to find it in daylight, although mayhap more risky. If we have enough hours of light left, we can go on to Harfleur and bargain. If not, we can rest until first light."

"But—" Morgana began.

"I would not bargain with Robert of Neustria *or* Snorri at night—even in the most brightly lit hall. Outside in the open in broad daylight it must be done, where there can be no tricks or ambush.

"If I know Snorri, Haraldsson's death will be neither swift nor easy. I would wager aught that the Dane will prolong it as long as possible. 'Tis almost two days since he was taken, am I right?"

Morgana nodded, disappointed in spite of herself. Was Leif still alive? Or was he dead even as they formulated their plan?

She wouldn't accept that he was dead. She would know it if he were.

"Impirius has made an attempt to atone for his sins," Alain told Rollo. "He's sent a messenger to the king, hoping Charles will intercede for Leif."

Rollo threw back his great blond head and roared with laughter. "Oh, indeed! I wonder what Charles the Simple can do that we cannot?" He shook his head. "But we'll soon see, won't we? We'll soon see!"

Tall pitch torches encircled the outer cage, hissing and popping as their flames danced in the breeze. The air was heavy with their acrid odor.

Even at night, Leif mused, he was visible to any who would see him. He had no privacy for his needs, his body was stiff and ached all over, and his thirst, after being all day in the summer sun, was burning.

He was covered with bruises, for whenever he tried to sleep, because they couldn't approach him close enough to

371

poke him with staffs or sticks, the guards would fling rocks at him until they found their mark. Even the noise from those that missed was startling enough to keep him from doing little more than dozing fitfully.

He allowed his thoughts to take him elsewhere. Somewhere where he could forget his deprivation and humiliation. His coming death. He pictured Eirik's beloved little face; but Morgana's perfidy intruded. It seemed, he mused with despair, that their love had been doomed from the beginning. And, he acknowledged bitterly, by their own actions.

Mayhap he'd pushed her too hard recently . . . hadn't been patient enough with her. Or mayhap *he* hadn't had enough time.

She'd gone to Hilaire . . . or had been approached by the woman and agreed to her plans. Had she plotted his capture as well as her own escape? He wanted to believe she was innocent of collusion against him, yet he'd not proven a good judge of her. Except when he had gambled on her coming after him when he took Eirik away. And he'd been right on the mark . . .

This time, however, it appeared that he was wrong, and he wondered if he could ever trust her again.

He closed his eyes in defeat, his spirits at a dangerously low ebb. Would it never end? He'd broken a promise to her, and she'd retaliated by divorcing him and wedding Hakon. He had hurt her by snatching Eirik; she'd found him, and now, it seemed, was getting her retribution. And, if he was brutally honest with himself, he'd been the one who had touched off the chain of events, albeit unwittingly. His pride and the hot-headedness of youth had prevented him from admitting it, even to himself, until now.

Yet hope, springing eternal, whispered, *Mayhap Little Thor was wrong. Mayhap Morgana knew nothing of this.*

It began to rain. He leaned his head back and opened his mouth to receive a sprinkle of water. It was infinitely welcome, if hardly satisfying. How long would it take to get a decent swallow? he wondered wryly. But with the rain came cooler winds from the sea, and soon he was chilled to the bone. He tried to control his shivering and continued his patient quest for a drink, the will to survive stronger still than the acceptance of death . . .

. . . until pain exploded through his jaw, blurring his vision for a moment, searing the entire right side of his face. The rock bounced off his cheek, clattered against the bar floor beside him, then fell to the ground before he could marshal his wits and grab it. He would have dearly loved to fling it back. He looked over at the guard who threw it.

It was Argus, with his ludicrously swollen nose. He grinned malevolently at Leif, then cut it short, obviously because it hurt to move his mouth. He raised his fist at his prisoner, hawked and spat on the ground and turned away.

Just after dawn, Robert of Neustria came to see Leif. Noor and Snorri the Black accompanied him. He ignored all three, even though by now his situation—along with his physical and mental injuries—was exacerbated by his absolute inability to do anything. He felt like screaming at them, bursting through the bars and pouncing on them—on anyone within his reach—in one last, desperate act of defiance before his ebbing energy disappeared altogether.

He retreated inward, taking some satisfaction from envisioning what he would have done if he could . . .

Until he heard the name Morgana. ". . . planned to escape . . ." The voice shattered his self-imposed mental isolation. ". . . hoped you could be taken, as well, and dispatched." Robert of Neustria was speaking to him.

"Aye," Snorri added in his eerie rasp. "Was she worth rescuing, Haraldsson, when she would so eagerly turn on you? Was she worth earning my emnity?"

Leif slowly turned his head until his eyes met the Dane's. In a voice hoarse from disuse, he spoke. *"Your* enmity? You surely strike terror in my heart, Dane. I tremble before you." And in spite of his better judgment, in spite of the fact that he would probably pay dearly for his insolence, he contorted his features with an exaggerated expression of fear—causing pain to skitter through his jaw—and raised his arms as if to ward off a blow.

He slowly lowered his arms then, looked straight at the Dane, and spat.

Snorri launched himself against the bars in fury, and Leif gave him a slow, taunting grin as the Dane clung to the wall of the outer cage and rattled the framework. Robert put a hand on his sleeve. "Be not a fool, Dane. Calm yourself and enjoy your revenge."

With a bellow of frustration, Snorri jumped down. "I want him dead *now*," he snarled. "Let him loose so I can silence him forever!"

"What?" Robert said, an eyebrow quirking. "Put a *sword* in his hand so he can go to your Valhalla?"

Leif, listening to their talk with half an ear, wondered how big a part the Duke of Neustria had played in his capture. He suspected that Robert had encouraged Snorri to go along with Impirius's plan purely out of deviousness. He no doubt enjoyed stirring up trouble between Rollo and the king, despising them both—one for taking part of his duchy, the other for bargaining it away—in spite of his supposed alliance with Charles.

"It wouldn't matter to Haraldsson, for he has converted," Noor said. "But have you forgotten—" he began, glancing at Snorri. Then, at the look of purest savagery the Dane cast him, he fell silent.

" 'Tis a preposterous story, Byzantine. Even were it true, I care not! But I'll not put a sword in his hand—'tis too good for him." He paused a moment, seeming to will himself to a less agitated state. "I've something much better in mind. But first, we must assemble all the villagers for the entertainment."

Robert of Neustria said, "Very well, he's yours to do with as you will, Snorri, but if you're going to dispatch him, do it quickly and get on to other things . . . like preparing to defend Harfleur from Rollo's wrath." His last words were heavy with irony.

It was obvious to Leif that as long as he was alive, Robert had no real fears regarding Rollo. Of course, the duke could have used his prisoner as a bargaining tool, no matter what the Danish mercenary wanted. But with Leif dead, Robert's bargaining power was drastically diminished. The game of cat and mouse would be over, with the powerful and angered cat in a position to inflict much damage if it came down to that.

It also meant that death was near, and although Leif didn't fear death, neither was he particularly eager to leave behind his son and a future that had already shown such promise. That is, until Morgana had turned on him once again . . .

He watched as they dismantled the outer cage . . . and happened to catch Noor's eye as the Byzantine remained on the perimeter of the activity, Theo and Bardas with him. His expression was genuinely distressed, and Leif took some small amount of comfort from the fact that he'd made a real friend.

He ignored the persistent imp that tried to persuade him Noor was unhappy because of the missed opportunity for any reward he might have collected for his part in having discovered Alexandra's son—if that highly unlikely story proved to be anywhere near the truth. After all, what did he *really* know about the character of Noor the Byzantine?

Two men approached the cage, opened it and pulled him out. He allowed them to do so without resistance because he was so stiff and cramped that he would surely have looked the trembling coward if he put up an ineffective struggle and then collapsed. Indeed, his knees buckled when his feet touched the ground, but his guards dragged him forward, toward four wooden stakes that had been driven into the earth.

Leif fought to walk on his own, but he wasn't given enough time or distance to adjust after being confined for two days and two nights. His tangled auburn hair blew about his face, for they'd stripped away his headband when they'd taken his clothing. Yet he didn't need to see clearly to guess his fate. The stakes sent a mute message.

Men, women, and children, mostly Frankish, had gathered around to watch. Leif caught expressions of distress on some of their faces, and suspected that they were there on Snorri's orders, not of their own volition. He withdrew from all of it once again, from the humiliation as they knocked him to the ground and made him lay on his belly; from the pain as several rocks pelted him while they tied his wrists and ankles to the stakes.

"Enough, fools, lest you hit us!" growled one of the men securing Leif's ankles.

"Then have the sense to duck!" called out one of the culprits, and several of Snorri's men laughed. The ripple of laughter dimly penetrated Leif's concentration.

"And *you* have the sense to aim at *him* and not us," the man retorted before he gave one last jerk on the rope around Leif's ankle. He stood and moved away. The man who tied Leif's badly abraded wrists pulled the bonds so tightly the circulation was impeded. Then Argus stepped forward and deliberately stepped on the fingers of Leif's injured hand. The hiss of sharply indrawn breath was his only reward.

Argus lifted his foot in preparation for a kick, but Snorri said sharply, "Enough! I want him fully conscious when I split him open."

Leif kept his forehead to the ground. And prayed. To every god he knew—to the Christian God, to Odin and Thor. It couldn't hurt to invoke them all. Little Thor had often said there was only one Great Spirit who went by many names.

He prayed for the strength to remain silent—to keep from crying out in anguish when they slit his ribs from the back and tore out his lungs as they flapped like wings with his dying breaths. Beads of sweat sheathed his forehead, and he bit down hard on his bottom lip in preparation, splitting the fragile flesh and drawing blood. It threaded down his chin, onto the earth beneath his face. He didn't notice.

Snorri bent low over him, razor-honed dagger poised. A hush descended over the crowd. Something sharp sheared lightly down the length of Leif's back, like a cold caress. A mere tickle of pain, and a hint of what was coming . . .

" 'Tis the practice stroke," Snorri said in his awful voice. "No quick death for you."

"You'll burn in hell for allowing this, Robert of Neustria!" Noor called out suddenly. " 'Tis barbaric . . . no good Christian would permit this to happen!"

All eyes went to him. "You'll all burn!" he cried to the crowd of villagers, many of the children already hiding their faces in their mothers' skirts. "Each and every one of you for watching and taking pleasure from the sight . . . even your children!"

Robert threw Noor a chilling look that warned him to cease.

And in that screaming pause, the sound of fast and furious hoofbeats came to them. One of the duke's retainers came racing into the village. "The king!" he cried. "And Rollo! They come with scores of men . . ." He tumbled from his horse in his haste, his face white. "All heavily armed and riding straight for Harfleur! Their archers shot the horses out from under Will and Reynaud, but I was closer to the village . . ."

"All the more reason to finish what I started," Snorri cried. "I'll not let *this* one get away with—"

"Nay!" commanded Robert. "If they come to intervene, mayhap 'twould be to our benefit to show them Harald-sson lives—at least for now."

Snorri straightened, his legs still straddling Leif's torso. He glared at the duke. "You gave him to *me*. You will go back on your word now?"

The muffled thunder of many horses came closer, louder, turning more ominous with their swift approach.

"Snorri, I command you stay your hand!" Robert barked with stern authority. "You still work for me. *I* pay your wages, and better compensation you will not find!"

Still, the Dane kept his position, obviously vascillating between relenting and the tantalizing prospect of bloody, retaliatory sport.

"Lower your dagger, lest I turn your own men on you."

Snorri looked up in surprise, the hand that held the dagger lowering slowly to his side. "They obey *me*, and not you, Frank. They've *always* done my bidding, whether I followed your orders or nay."

His body taut as a bowstring from clenched fists down to rock-hard calves, Leif wondered if Robert of Neustria had enough courage to turn his Frankish retainers on Snorri and his mercenaries. How appropriate—the merce-nary warriors turning on their employer. Woe to the man who hired the unscrupulous.

"And you wouldn't dare harm me before my men, or you're the *dead* Duke of Neustria!" With a bellow of rage, Snorri jerked up his arm once again, adding his other hand to the dagger's hilt in the process. He brought it slashing down toward Leif's spine . . .

. . . and froze in mid-motion as an arrow struck him in the back with such force that it skewered his heart before the wicked head came to rest, jutting from the left side of his chest wall. He spun slowly toward the ground in a grotesque death spiral, the weapon still clutched in his right hand. And landed on Leif with one final, gasping exhalation.

A single horseman came charging, bareback, onto the scene ahead of the others, his long, ebony hair flying, skin shining bronze in the sun. Snorri's men drew their swords.

"I wouldn't if I were you," Robert warned as his Frankish warriors drew their own swords in answer.

The dark-haired warrior who'd killed Snorri the Black slid from his horse and bent to roll the Dane's body away from Leif. He swiftly took the dagger he held in his teeth and cut Leif's bonds, then carefully turned him over.

"You always *were* the best archer, my friend," Leif muttered. "Why do you think I rescued you in the first place?" He gave the red man a weak grin.

"Kiisku-Liinu," Little Thor said softly as he helped him sit up, "you look bad."

As Leif looked into the red man's eyes, his own were warm with gratitude and affection. In spite of everything, life had never seemed sweeter. "And 'tis about time you developed a sense of humor, Skraeling."

His husky words were lost in the cacophonic commotion of an army of men, some Frankish, some Norse, as they swiftly maneuvered to surround everyone from Harfleur, warriors and citizens alike.

"Make way for the king," someone called out, and Charles III rode through a pathway that opened before him like magic. Rollo, on what had to be the largest horse in the realm, followed, flanked by Alain and Morgana. Behind them came four packhorses, each laden with a carefully covered and secured burden.

Charles, looking the worse for wear, nodded at Robert of Neustria, then looked over at Leif, who was being helped to his feet by Little Thor. "I dislike having to hie myself off in the middle of the night, Robert, to keep your mercenaries out of mischief."

To Leif, it sounded like a light slap on the wrist rather

than a royal reprimand, as the king avoided implicating Robert of Neustria directly. Yet surely Charles the Simple had to tread carefully. It was not in his best interests—nor those of Francia—to alienate a Frankish ally. Nor, moreover, could the king afford to anger Rollo, whose newly granted holdings were to act as a buffer between Francia and other raiding Norsemen.

The Duke stepped forward. "You seem to have taken care of *that*, my lord king. Yet this man Haraldsson took *our* prisoners—more Norsemen in search of plunder—from beneath our noses, and thus owed us reparation."

"And what of Snorri?" snarled one of the mercenaries. "The Skraeling murdered him!"

"What of him?" Charles asked. "You work for the duke, do you not?"

"We took orders from *Snorri*," growled another man.

"Who took orders from me," Robert said, "and therefore you indirectly worked for me. But if you like, Nils, you may go elsewhere. Unfortunately," he added with a frown, "death is one of the hazards of the job of mercenary. Snorri knew that—although he appeared to think himself invincible. He was killed in the act of defying me, and rightly so, even if he would have you believe that he obeyed me at his own whim. He also threatened my life, and it matters not *who* killed him."

During this brief interchange, Morgana's eyes kept going to Leif, who was speaking to Little Thor in low tones as the red man looked over his injuries. She had to quell the urge to go to him and tend him herself . . . and a host of other urges, as well.

Evidently the king noticed where her true interests lay. "The lady would speak to you," Charles said to Robert as he looked over at Morgana. She tore her eyes from Leif, who had given her a single, unreadable glance before looking away.

She couldn't let that interfere with what she had to do

now. "We did *not* seek plunder, my lord duke," she said firmly, "but flew the white flag. Every man among you knows that. Yet in the interest of peace between Robert of Neustria and the lord of Vallée de Vergers, I offer you Leif Haraldsson's death price—one hundredfold." She motioned toward the packhorses.

Robert didn't move, but her words caught Leif's attention. He pushed away from Little Thor's supporting arm and straightened slowly to his full height. "What have you taken from another to save my hide?" he asked in a rough, halting voice, for his jaw felt ten times its normal size. Suspicion was apparent on his face and in his tone.

"Only what was stolen by Norsemen in the past," Morgana answered. "I will give you everything we've brought with us, my lord duke," she said to Robert. "All I ask is Leif's return, and a truce between you and him."

Leif limped toward her, his bruised face lending him a fierce look as his eyes met hers and held. "What is this belated attack of conscience, Morgana?" he asked. "And whose help did you enlist to make up for your meddling? Guthrum's?" He added in a voice meant for her ears only, "Now you seek to run my fief? If so, you should have let me die!"

He hadn't meant to sound so bitter—even to say those precise words, but he couldn't help but *be* bitter. Morgana's actions—her very presence—were proof of her intentions where he was concerned, confirming what Robert of Neustria had told him. She could have left the dealing to the king and Rollo, but her direct involvement indicated to Leif that she sought to make up for her collusion against him. At least he knew her that well.

Evidently escaping Vallée de Vergers with Eirik wouldn't have been enough for her.

"I am not the same woman you left behind in Oslof," she said in a low, fierce voice. "But, with typical male pride, you continue to refuse to see that."

Charles, who had dismounted, interrupted their quiet but tense disagreement. "We can better sort out these things later. For now, may we show Robert what recompense we bear him?"

Leif looked at the king, remaining stubbornly silent. Morgana, however, nodded. "Of course, sire."

At a nod from Charles, Alain and Little Thor moved to uncover the panniers that straddled the three packhorses' backs. Guthrum slid from his horse and moved stiffly to join them. "Do not take Morgana to task, young Haraldsson," he said to Leif. "I had offered her these valuables aboard *Wave Rider* before we ever touched Francia's shores."

"And what if I want no part of this truce you seek to arrange?" Leif asked, his eyes flashing bright with anger. "I trust not this man—nor will I ever!"

Robert of Neustria's eyes met his, an answering anger in their depths. "Nor do I trust any Norseman among you! Tricksters all, taking pleasure from placing informers in our midst!"

Rollo, having dismounted, strode toward Leif and the king. "And this entire affair is exactly the reason for informers," he said in his deep, booming voice. "I am afraid I would have had to attack you with vigor, Frank, had you dispatched my faithful and valuable vassal here." He towered over everyone else, powerful, fierce, and implaccable. "Now, I advise you both to accept this truce, in the interests of everyone." He glanced at Charles, then directed the brunt of his unnerving gaze at the Duke of Neustria. "Else we take Haraldsson *and* our offer back to where we came from, and you be damned!"

Robert opened his mouth to speak, but Charles raised his hand. "See what they offer you, Robert." He lowered his voice. "It may very well help soothe your irritation with them."

Leif threw a look at Morgana, then moved toward Alain

and Little Thor. Rollo intercepted him and draped one huge arm carefully across his shoulders. "You are all fools," Leif said in an undertone. He grimaced slightly, and the giant eased his arm back until only his hand remained on Leif's shoulder. "You owe him no death price!"

Rollo shrugged. "The King is assuaging his conscience, for he knows Impirius was behind this. Let him make amends, at least in his own mind, eh?"

"But I'd heard stories back in Oslof when I was a youth . . . of a fabulous amount of stolen wealth from the monastery of Jumièges. What if 'tis true, and Robert demands another reward . . . since we might return that which belonged to them originally?"

"He wouldn't dare," Rollo said, his eyes lighting up as Alain produced a large silver chalice from one of the panniers. It was tarnished from age and neglect, but impressive nonetheless. Murmurs and exclamations sounded from the crowd at the sight, some in awe, some in outrage.

"What a loss!" Leif said with a grimace as Alain handed the chalice to a waiting retainer and produced a golden crucifix half the size of a longbow. "You could have used them to restore a monastery—even build one—within your own domain."

Rollo chuckled and squeezed Leif's shoulder. "What a fine convert you're becoming, to be so concerned about restoring Christian monasteries." His grin widened as one of Robert's men came forward and handed Leif his tunic and breeches. He leaned his head down to whisper into Leif's ear, "But Jumièges and all the riches in these saddle pouches will one day be part of Normandy, and I want you alive to see it!"

Chapter Twenty-Five

"*Eh bien*," Charles said to Robert when the last religious artifact was safely repacked in the panniers and taken to the manor by several of Robert's men, "as your king, I would request a good meal, a feast to celebrate this . . . understanding. And to show good faith, a night's lodging for us all."

Rollo's men immediately began to boisterously voice their agreement. Robert was silent a moment, as if caught off guard. There was no such accord among his Frankish retainers or the mercenaries. The Franks obviously wanted none of Rollo and his men among them, and the mercenaries still held a grudge against Frank and Norseman alike over Snorri's death.

Robert turned to his vassal, Mauger, lord of Harfleur and the surrounding fief. "Can you accommodate them all?" he asked, obviously putting the burden on his man rather than accepting it himself.

Mauger, a tall, sandy-haired Frank with a mild demeanor, cast a dubious glance at the small army around them. Then he looked at Charles. He clearly had no choice. It was his obligation, as it was any vassal's—including Robert—to host his king and his retinue at his own expense, whenever and for however long it was required.

He nodded, looking as happy as if he'd just granted

permission for a horde of locusts to devour all his crops and pick clean the bones of every deer and boar for miles around.

"I'll give you permission to hunt in the forest, and I can send a few huntsmen to help your men," Charles graciously added, obviously guessing Mauger's concerns.

"And I'll sleep under the stars," Rollo said with a sardonic twist of his lips. "An entire hall of Franks makes me uneasy, especially when I am expected to sleep." He looked at the king, his expression hardly apologetic. "I mean you no offense, sire," he added to Charles. "If any of my men wish to remain the night in the manor—and can be accommodated—they are free to do so."

Leif threw him a wry look, turned away from the assemblage, and limped toward the sea. Out of the corner of her eye Morgana saw Little Thor move to join him, but as she hurried after Leif herself, the red man was left behind.

"Leif . . . where are you going?" she called. "Let me—"

"Water," he said shortly.

"You cannot drink seawater!"

He spun around, his expression hostile. "Don't be absurd, Morgana," he rasped through his swollen jaw. "I know that! I'd like to tell you that I'm going to *drown* myself in the sea so you can go on your way. That I'm going to finish the job for Snorri the Black, so you can be free." He swung away. Morgana grabbed his arm and he stilled. "That Guthrum's treasure will be wasted then, in your eyes, because it will be returned to Jumièges." He shrugged. "But I cannot, in truth, tell you such things, because I have a son to live for." He looked down at her hand, fighting his feelings for her that decreed he would always love her . . . fool that he was. "And now, if you would allow me to bathe in the sea—I am not only hurting, but I stink as well."

"But you can bathe in the manor and I—"

"In spite of the king's wishes, I will accept *naught* from

385

Robert of Neustria, be it a bath or a roof over my head for the night."

"What of water to drink?" asked Noor, who had come up behind them. "From *me*." In his hands he held a ewer and a cup. Morgana watched the contradictory emotions that crossed Leif's face before he finally held out his left hand for the cup.

"I thank you, Byzantine. And for what you tried to do last eve." He allowed the man to fill his cup then downed it so quickly that much of it ran down the sides of his mouth.

Morgana touched his arm. "Easy, else you toss it back up."

"Most of it's on the ground," he growled as he held out the cup for more. "My lips are swollen and 'tis hard to swallow.

"You told no one else, I hope?" Leif said to the Byzantine.

Noor shook his head.

"Good . . . lest I have others like Robert of Neustria forever plotting to ransom me in Constantinople."

Noor took a small bundle of clean cloths from beneath one arm and gave them to Morgana. "To bathe his hurts," he said simply, then turned and left them.

Leif swung toward the sea again, clutching the ewer and mug, his tunic and breeches still draped over one shoulder. He was thinner, of course, from the leanness of his face to the long, well-formed length of his legs; and as he moved, his natural grace was hampered by hours of confinement and weakness from lack of food. There were ugly, purplish bruises all over his body, and a thin, barely-clotted laceration that ran along his spine from between his shoulders almost to his waist.

She wanted to hold him to her heart in exquisite relief, in celebration of life. She wanted to minister to him, soothe his pain, tell him of her regrets. And her love. Instead, however, in an attempt to draw him out she asked, "What did the Byzantine try to do?" She was afraid to offer him an apology yet, or to give her explanation that she had had no wish to have him harmed or captured. He was hurting and in a bitter mood—who could blame him? He'd been cruelly abused and had escaped death by a heartbeat. And all because of her.

She felt as uncertain as if she were walking on eggshells.

"Told Snorri that silly tale about my mother—in an attempt to convince the Dane that I was worth more alive in Constantinople."

"He's a good man," she said, hurrying to keep up with Leif's lengthening strides as some of his stiffness receded.

"He's more than likely hungry for riches himself," he said shortly.

He reached the beach and sat down on a smooth boulder, around which water swirled and eddied with the rhythm of the waves. He closed his eyes and sighed, refusing to look at Morgana.

She dipped one clean cloth into the water and moved closer. "This will sting," she warned, her hand trembling as she went to touch it to his back. His only reaction was to stiffen as the salt water touched his wounded flesh. She didn't see his grimace, but knew it was there.

"How is Eirik?" he asked through set teeth.

"Eirik is well. He was badly frightened, but much of that fear was eased when he was told you were alive."

"Bjorn and Torvald?"

"Dead."

He was silent for a moment, and Morgana knew he was mourning the loss of two good men.

"What of Impirius? And Hilaire?" he asked at last.

"Hilaire was killed by an arrow. Impirius was very moved by her death—and also remorseful about what he'd done. You know of his part in the . . . plan?"

Leif nodded.

"He appealed directly to the king to intervene on your behalf. I think things got out of hand—that he hadn't expected to have to attempt murder. Nor did he anticipate an ensuing bloodbath . . ."

"He's a fool," Leif growled through stiff lips.

Morgana nodded, then moved from behind him. She gently turned his face toward her. Their eyes met, hers luminous with emotion . . . his shadowed with suspicion. "Who struck you?" she whispered, an ache centering deep within her at the abuse of his masculinely beautiful—and beloved—visage.

Just when she thought he would not answer, he said, "Does it really matter? Does anything really matter except that everyone in Francia now knows what a complete dupe I am?" Even though it hurt to speak, he managed to inject his words with heavy self-loathing. "I am as big a fool as Impirius, for he loved the treacherous Hilaire, and I loved you. In truth, Morgana, you are no better than she—both schemers, both willing to emasculate any man mad enough to care. And both utterly without conscience."

Ire rose within her, but she tamped it down. He had every right to be angry. "I agreed to Hilaire's plan—to leave Vallée de Vergers with Eirik. Nothing more. There was no talk of anyone being hurt or killed. Do you really think me capable of plotting anyone's death?"

"And after what had happened to you, did you expect fair play from someone like Snorri the Black? Or Robert of Neustria?"

Morgana took his injured hand in hers, gently sliding the pads of her thumb and forefinger along the length of each of his fingers, searching the bruised and swollen bones for breaks. She felt him stiffen when she encountered a bruised knuckle. "I knew not with whom I was dealing." Did it sound as idiotic to him as it suddenly did to her? "I was desperate . . ."

"Desperate." The word was quiet, almost a whisper. "It

seems you are forever desperate, Morgana, when dealing with me."

She looked up at him suddenly, and caught the unguarded look in his eyes. Anguish, pure and simple. He stared blindly out to sea, his lower lashes glistening.

Something within her sundered; real, physical pain rampaged through her breast. "I—but I—" she began huskily against the blockage in her throat, then trailed off in silent misery. How could she make him believe that she'd changed her mind? Changed her mind about leaving Vallée de Vergers? And would it matter to him now?

He suddenly met her look, his golden eyes dulled by defeat. "This time, however, you involved Eirik—risked his *life* on a whim."

Guilt surged through her, and the blood rose in her cheeks in mute but irrefutable admission, for he spoke the truth. She had no words to defend herself against his accusation.

It was the first time she had allowed herself to contemplate the fact that Eirik could have been harmed, and it was frightening to think how easily his innocent and precious life could have been ended.

". . . you were right." Leif's words came to her from far away.

She frowned uncomprehendingly, blinking away the answering emotion that blurred her vision.

"To want to leave."

Leave? The thought burst through her growing numbness like a bolt of lightning. *Leave?*

Suddenly she didn't want to hear what she feared he was going to say.

She snatched at the first thing that came to mind, a mad, panicky babble of words: "But—but Ingrid told me once that you—that you *loved* me! So much—you loved me so much that you took Eirik . . . took Eirik in the desperate

389

hope of luring me to follow you! That you loved me so much you risked my hatred—"

"Of course I love you," he said quietly, tiredly, his eyes still locked with hers. "More than my life. I have *always* loved you, Morgana. *Will* always love you . . . until they send me to Valhalla—or Heaven or Hell. Until my name isn't even a memory . . . until the ashes that once were my bones are scattered to the four winds, my spirit will carry that love beyond the boundaries of time and place, this world and the next . . ."

"Then," she broke in wildly, "why do you want me to leave?"

"I had actually begun to trust you. But not now, not ever again. No matter what you ever say or do, that trust has been destroyed."

"*Nei!* It can be—"

"*Já.* Distance cannot destroy love, Morgana. But if you remained, you would destroy me physically when you felt . . . *desperate* again. You would deny me the chance to raise my son at the slightest provocation . . . the chance to see him take over all that I would build for him, bequeath to him.

"You must return to Norvegia . . . with Eirik." Her mouth dropped open, though for a completely different reason than he would have guessed. "In fact, I'll take you myself." Her breath stopped momentarily. "Take our son back with you, for that has been your heart's desire; but I warn you, I'll return for him when he is ready for manhood. I will come for him when he has seen twelve winters, and no force on earth will keep me from him then."

She felt as if the earth were moving . . . as if the coarse sand beneath her knees was shifting . . . receding into nothingness—

She plunged the rag she still held into the brisk water at her knees, then mindlessly pressed the dripping cloth to a particularly nasty bruise on his shin. It worked. The cold seawater around her wrists and hands worked to stem the darkness that reached for her, that had begun to shade the edges of her consciousness.

". . . find a simple woman who requires no more than a warm body beside her at night," he was saying. "A woman who cannot have my love, but won't know any better—who won't expect any better. Who'll be content with the physical side of my affection, naught more."

Morgana blindly dipped the cloth into the small pool again, willing herself not to weep. He couldn't mean what he was saying! He was hurt and angry. He was trying to hurt her back . . .

He watched her then, feeling utterly empty inside. He was giving her her wish—he was commanding her to leave and take Eirik with her. Why did she look so miserable? It had to be shock. She was stunned by his about-face. That was it.

He bent to take the cloth from her, pressed it against his throbbing jaw and cracked lips, then over his burning eyes. He eased his tunic over his head and shoulders, then stood and held out his good hand to her.

"Your breeches," she mumbled irrelevantly, grasping at something to say, to do.

"It matters not," he said on a sigh, but she was already moving to help him put them on. He couldn't walk back to Robert of Neustria half naked.

He held out his hand again. She accepted it only because she didn't trust her legs to support her. And he was leaving her . . .

Leif didn't want to be alone with her now, he acknowledged, for as uncomfortable as he was, he didn't trust himself not to pull her into his arms . . . never let her go. Not even when the tide came in, then washed them both out to sea. Forever . . .

No. He needed comfort, love and security, just like anyone else, but he couldn't accept it from her. Not now. Not ever.

"I need more than water to ease my hurts," he said. *And numb my foolish and breaking heart,* he added silently. "It looks as if I have no choice but to partake of Robert's hospitality . . . at least a bite of food. And some wine. A lot of wine."

Morgana followed numbly one step behind, clinging to his hand as if it were a lifeline.

"Papa!"

Eirik flung himself into Leif's arms and clung. Leif closed his eyes for a moment, wishing he could absorb his son's body into his own so they could never be separated. He wondered how he would be able to live without him for eight winters; how he would explain his decision to Eirik.

By God it was good to be home . . . *his* home now. Vallée de Vergers. He was welcomed by those who had remained behind, retainers, villeins, and peasants alike. And Freki. He felt a simple joy at the sight of the wolfhound. The dog moved more stiffly than did Leif, but the vigorous movements of his tail and his whimpers of delight were undimmed by his injury. The animal was indefatigable, Leif thought wryly.

Genna, with her glossy chestnut hair and spritely step, welcomed Alain, then turned shyly to Leif. "Welcome home, my lord," she greeted him. "Look . . ." She turned and pointed to the manor door. Ulf stood there, leaning on a T-shaped crutch. He looked pale and less than robust, but obviously glad to be alive, for he smiled broadly at Leif.

Leif gave the man what he hoped was an answering smile around his battered jaw. "Your valiant efforts weren't in vain, my friend," he called. "Thank you for my life, and that of my son and my . . . and Morgana."

" 'Twas really the red man who saved them," Ulf replied. "And that high-spirited stallion of yours."

"Rollo sends you his good wishes for a speedy recovery. He awaits your return to a more ordinary job, like settling down with a good woman . . ."

Guthrum descended the steps, regarding Leif through eyes narrowed against the bright day. And as if he couldn't believe what he saw. "The gods be praised!" he said as he reached the bottom. His eyes were suspiciously moist. "You are whole." He put an arm around Leif and Eirik, who was still in his father's embrace. "You are a second grandson to me. Gunnar was with you, surely, young Haraldsson. I prayed it would be so."

Leif nodded. "And so he was, *Afi.*"

The old one's faded blue eyes lit at the title "grandfather."

"Where's Impirius?" Leif asked Ragnar.

"On his knees before his God," the red-haired Northman answered. "He helped prepare and bury the dead, helped tend Ulf . . . even the wolfhound, and has been in his temple across the way ever since." He spat on the ground. "He claims to have answered a calling to the Christian God? Norse gods are surely more worthy of a man's faith."

"There are good and bad men—wise and unwise—in any religion," Leif told him. "And there are those who will always use another man's faith—or his own position—to his advantage."

"Well, no matter whose servant he thinks himself, he's human just like the rest of us," said Olaf with a grimace. "He'll show his face when his belly's empty."

Guthrum shook his white head. "He'll not come out until he feels forgiven. He drowns in the blood of two fine men and a woman. He has much praying to do."

"I say string him up by his fat neck!" cried Einar. "Death to the traitor!"

"*Non!*" Alain said emphatically, then reddened as if realizing all eyes turned to him. "God is merciful. Impirius is miserably guilty—he seeks to atone for his sins. Punish him, *oui*, but don't kill him. It won't bring back anyone."

Leif nodded thoughtfully, thinking back to the religious instruction given him by Impirius himself. There would be time enough to deal with Impirius. The priest had to learn to live with not only his own guilt, but also the responsibility of Hilaire's death. And, after all, the cleric had summoned King Charles to Leif's rescue. There was something to be said for that.

He handed Eirik over to Morgana. "Greet your mother, Eirik," he bade the child softly. "She's missed you." But his glance only touched Morgana before he turned again to Guthrum. "And to you, *Afi*, I owe much. How can I ever repay your generosity?"

" 'Tis easy to give up riches, young Leif, when you acknowledge that a life is of infinitely more value. And stolen riches are even easier to give away."

"God will bless you, old one, for returning the treasures of Jumièges to their rightful place," Alain said.

Guthrum nodded. "I will need the blessing of *every* god, Frank, for I would ask of Leif a great favor in return."

"Now you'll pay, Haraldsson!" cried Ragnar, immediately lightening the mood.

Leif looked at Ragnar, who laughed aloud. One corner of his mouth lifted in answer before he turned to speak to Guthrum, the half-smile still lingering. "Anything within my power to give."

The ancient one put a hand on Leif's arm, his expression very somber. "Then I ask you as one Norseman to another . . . will you take *Wave Rider* back to Norvegia? And deliver to me my grandson's wife and only child?"

"Listen to your heart instead of your head."

"And I ought to put you in a skin boat and send you back where you came from!"

Twilight was settling over the land. The air was still,

birdsong clear and sweet as it bade the day farewell. Hrafn snorted softly, stomped a hoof, then stilled.

Leif and Little Thor stood in the mill orchard, where the attack had taken place, a stone's throw from the old Roman wall. The three victims had been buried in the small cemetery behind the church, but Leif had wished to visit the orchard once again. He somehow felt the essence of the two dead men here, where they had been cut down in the flower of manhood.

He thought briefly of Hilaire, but evinced no satisfaction, even though she'd unwittingly become a victim of her own machinations.

In the surrounding silence, as the shadows lengthened and the dying sun bloodied the western sky, he thought about Little Thor's words. Staring at the trampled grass beneath the apple trees, he thought how his heart had betrayed him. Better to heed the dictates of his mind, for emotions were not involved then.

As usual, Little Thor seemed unperturbed by his friend's irritation with him. When the Skraeling didn't dignify the half-hearted threat with an answer, Leif asked in a milder tone, "And what has listening to my heart earned me thus far? Naught but pain and sorrow."

"Life, Kiisku-Liinu, is full of these things, pain and sorrow. There is no . . . guarantee against such hurts." He reached to stroke the muzzle of the horse he rode now, his eyes on the animal's head. Even through his own bitter disappointment, Leif heard the red man's pain.

Leif stared hard at his friend. "Could *you* live with a woman who had planned to have you killed?"

"She admitted to plotting your death?" Little Thor asked, his eyes still on the young chestnut gelding given him by none other than Rollo.

Leif shook his head. "But she didn't make a point of denying it. She said only that she planned to leave Vallée de Vergers with Eirik."

"There." Little Thor looked at Leif.

"That means naught. She was putting her life—and that of Eirik—into the hands of men like Snorri the Black!"

"Did she know this?" the red man asked quietly.

The muted chorus of myriad frogs along the stream began to herald the approaching night. The caroling of the birds began to die away. Shadows deepened as the scarlet sunset turned a livid purple, then toned down to mauve and dusky rose striations that layered the horizon.

Leif lifted his gaze from the blood-soaked grass to the crumbling ruins of the wall close by. "She would be an utter fool to admit such a thing."

"You did not answer my question, Kiisku-Liinu."

Leif remained stubbornly silent.

"Then ask the holy man. He has nothing to lose by lying now."

Leif walked over to Hrafn and said over his shoulder, "Ah, yes. Ask Impirius, a snake in the grass if ever there was one. What makes you think," he asked as he swung up into the saddle, "that Impirius would be any more truthful than Morgana?"

Little Thor led the gelding toward Leif and stopped to look up at him. "He has nothing more to lose," he answered simply. "Go and see for yourself."

Leif quietly entered the dim stone church, and allowed his eyes to adjust to the low level of light. Candles lined the two longer side walls, and lit the simple, cloth-draped altar at the far end. His steps echoed softly against the rough flagstones as he moved forward.

He felt suddenly more at peace than he had since encountering Ulf in the west woods. It was as if a mantle of calm was settling over him, benevolent, comforting. Even if the man who betrayed him was kneeling before the altar only a few paces ahead . . .

Leif continued toward the front of the church, then stopped just behind Impirius. The priest was a pathetic-looking mound of horsehair robes and cowl; head bowed, back hunched, and unidentifiable save for the fact that he was the only religious man within Vallée de Vergers and its environs.

"Impirius," Leif said finally, softly. "How long do you mean to remain here?"

The priest's cowl-covered head slowly rose. When he turned his face to Leif, the latter was astonished by the sunken and bruise-ringed eyes, the hollow cheeks and pale flesh. "Until God grants me my wish and stills my heart forever."

Leif wasn't convinced. "Self-pity, Impirius? Mayhap you are deserving of as much pity as you can get—your own included—for surely you'll rot in your Christian Hell for what you did."

The priest canted his face slightly toward the altar, throwing much of it in shadow. "His will be done."

Leif sighed inwardly. Had it not been for his remorse-ravaged features, Leif would have wondered at his sincerity. Yet obviously the man had loved Hilaire. As Leif knew only too well, such a loss—no matter how undeserving the woman—would be nearly unbearable. And for the attempted murder of Ulf by his own hand . . . for the senseless deaths of two other good men who had never harmed Impirius . . .

Leif did not envy the priest, in spite of his own troubles.

"I am ready to accept my punishment."

Leif shook his head, studying the altar before them. His hand automatically sought his mother's crucifix where it rested against his breast as he stared at the simple, unadorned cross above the altar. "I haven't decided what to do with you, holy man. Rather, I am come to ask a question of you . . . in the hope that you will give me an honest answer."

Impirius bowed his head again.

"Are you prepared to do so?"

"At the least."

"Good. Tell me, then, if Morgana . . ."—his next words caught in his throat for an instant before he forced them out—". . . plotted my death."

Impirius slowly raised his right hand, which had been hidden among the folds of his robe. In it he clutched his silver crucifix, his fingers as bloodless as his face. "I am not worthy to wear this," he said in a low but firm voice. " 'Tis why God took it from me after I attempted murder. Yet as I seek to strengthen myself against the Devil's influence, I am done with dishonesty. I kneel here before my God, confessing to him my vile sins and seeking forgiveness, and swear to you that Morgana agreed only to escape from Vallée de Vergers with your son. She said naught about harming anyone."

Leif was silent a while, allowing a breath of relief to move through him. It did not absolve her of violating his trust. It did not hurt him any less, although it explained her actions. And it did not absolve her of seeking to take Eirik away from him, of exposing the boy to mortal danger, however unintentionally.

Leif made his decision then. "I ask that you leave Vallée de Vergers, Impirius. I think, in the way you once taught me, I can forgive you. But I cannot ever forget what you did. And I doubt if you could earn my trust again."

"Oui," the priest muttered, his voice sounding broken. He remained huddled where he knelt, returning the badge of his office to the folds of his robe, bowing his head once again and withdrawing into himself to wrestle with his own personal demons.

Leif opened his mouth to thank the man for his revelation regarding Morgana, then decided against it. As he retreated from the church, he acknowledged that giving him a truthful answer to his question was the least the clergyman could do after all the havoc he'd wrought.

Chapter Twenty-Six

With Alain in temporary charge of Vallée de Vergers, they sailed from Fécamp a fortnight later. Every man from Oslof—including Guthrum—was on board, as were Leif, Little Thor, Morgana and Eirik.

The ancient one stood beside Morgana and Eirik as they watched the shores of Francia recede. Eirik was excited beyond words to be aboard his father's *hafskip*. Guthrum, frail as he was, had insisted on joining them on the voyage that he'd instigated. And like a true Norseman, he seemed to draw strength from the sun and the sea. Even as evening drew near, the old man was disinclined to retreat into the coarse wool awning set up for Morgana, Eirik, and himself.

At Leif's insistence, however, with the dependable Olaf at the tiller, a meeting of sorts took place beneath the protective awning as night fell. Leif summoned Little Thor, and they joined Morgana and Guthrum after Eirik was safely asleep in a small skin sleeping sack.

A single oil lamp lit the interior, its flame bravely resisting the sea breeze that slipped beneath the makeshift shelter.

"I think 'tis time, Guthrum," Leif said to the old man, "that you reveal exactly what you know about Horik Bluetooth. I want to know exactly what he *did*."

Guthrum nodded, remaining silent for a moment. He

looked at Little Thor, then at Leif. "Your life is in jeopardy if you set foot anywhere near Oslof. You surely know that?"

Leif nodded. "I was outlawed. Anyone can kill me without fear of reprisal."

"Then send the red man and Ragnar—or Olaf—to fetch Ingrid and Harald. No one needs to know you are even on the—"

"I'll not hide," Leif interrupted him. "Especially when I was unfairly outlawed. We'll get Ingrid and the boy first. I'll have loyal men at my side to ensure her and Harald's safety. Then we will take Morgana and Eirik to Tyra and Ottar."

Guthrum nodded. "They are safe enough in Reyk to the north, a settlement still uninfluenced by Fairhair and his minions, at least for now. Ottar swore to leave Norvegia forever if his children couldn't live free of Fairhair's iron fist."

"Good. I would know that my son is safe until I return for him." Leif's eyes narrowed slightly, his mouth tightened. "Now, Guthrum, tell me what you know."

The old man sighed, his eyes moving to the opposite wall of the tent, as if seeing into the past. "I overheard them speaking—Horik Bluetooth and Sweyn Estrithsson, brother of your father. It matters not how 'twas done—for naught can change the fact. But 'twas Horik and Sweyn who plotted to murder Harald, and carried it out while you were at sea." He looked at Leif, who was watching and listening intently, his features carefully expressionless. "He is a beast—a brutal, evil man, much like Snorri the Black, only more underhanded in his methods. After you were banished, he began to look upon Ingrid with lust, then pressed his attentions upon her. She would have naught to do with him, and he made her pay."

Morgana realized that she wasn't the only person in

Oslof who knew about the attempted rape. Evidently Guthrum knew as well. Knew that and more.

"Horik tried to rape her—while she was with child. He struck her several times when she wouldn't submit, and she sustained scratches and bruises for her resistance. The child was born early . . . and dead."

Little Thor drew in his breath with a hiss. Leif's fists clenched. "Why didn't she tell anyone of it?" Leif asked, outraged.

"She told all of us that she had lost her footing along the cliffs of the fjord while searching for Harald one morn. She blamed the babe's death on the fall. Only when I was about to leave Oslof did she reveal to me what had happened." He leaned forward toward Leif, his thready voice suddenly stronger, his rheumy eyes catching the flickering light from the flame and turning opaque. "She lost the child almost immediately after the attack. Horik had carried her back into Oslof—appearing her savior when, in truth, he'd been responsible for her injuries. And he told her that if she ever revealed what had really happened, if she ever tried to leave Oslof, he would kill Harald."

Morgana suddenly felt sick inside, yet she also felt somewhat vindicated in not having asked Ingrid to join them on the voyage to Francia. Her friend wouldn't have risked Harald's life. So why would Ingrid willingly expose the boy to harm now by trying to leave Oslof with *Wave Rider?*

"But now, when she sees you at the helm," Guthrum said to Leif, as if reading her very thoughts, "and these good men at your side, she will put the child's life in your hands."

"No harm shall come to the boy while I live," Little Thor said unexpectedly, his voice soft but steely.

"You can believe him," Leif told Guthrum. "He is a man of his word—a man of honor and loyalty. A man to match *any* man . . . even a Northman. He's worth a score of Horik Bluetooths."

"I only hope he hasn't forced her to become his concubine," Morgana said, voicing her thoughts.

Leif looked at her askance. "Surely things haven't deteriorated that much? Enough of her family is still in Oslof to ensure against that?"

The look on her face, however, aroused a real concern in him.

"Things have changed since you left."

"*Já.* And so they have." He looked toward where Eirik was sleeping, a small mound in one corner. "Given what you have told me, I am bound to kill Bluetooth. I will avenge my father, and free Ingrid."

"You dare not!" Guthrum warned. "You cannot just walk into Oslof as an outlaw and then challenge one of Fairhair's men! A favorite of the jarl! And as the original families leave, there appear ever more of Fairhair's supporters to take their place, who—"

Morgana watched the flame play over Leif's auburn hair, bringing out the red within the gold. She wanted to reach out and touch it, smooth it back, press her lips to his forehead. It was a powerful urge to resist, yet the idea of appearing the fool—the spurned woman—held her back with a threadlike tether.

"I have no intention of challenging him, *Afi.* A man such as he deserves to die in the same manner that he has chosen to live."

Now what did he mean by that? she wondered, frowning and unconsciously worrying her lower lip.

"Mayhap he has gone a-viking with the younger men," Morgana said, hoping secretly it was so. Even though revenge for the outright murder of a family member was an important part of a Northman's honor, she was afraid for Leif. After seeing how close he'd come to dying—how Little Thor's skill and quick thinking had saved his life at the last possible moment—Morgana acknowledged that Leif Haraldsson was more precious to her than ever. He was all too human, in spite of his strengths. Therefore, if fewer men were present in Oslof, so much the better. And if Horik was gone, Leif couldn't come to blows with him.

Leif shook his head. "If he knows Ingrid at all, he wouldn't chance it. She could leave Norvegia well before he returned to make good his threats against little Harald." He gave her a lingering look before he added, an infinite sadness in his eyes, "And 'tis Corn-Cutting Month—the men may have returned already."

He was not about to be diverted from his purpose, that much was evident. Morgana, unable to sit and listen to their plans—which would mean Ingrid's rescue, but possibly also Leif's death—ducked out under the awning.

The sky was clear and ink-black, stars winking down at her from an eternity away. The moon was almost full, beautifully bright, a scintillant silver coin set against the Stygian backdrop, waiting to be plucked from the sky by any man who dared.

There was no one manning the few oars, for the *knarr* depended upon the wind in its huge sail more so than the fighting longship. Olaf was at the tiller, but everyone else was asleep in their sleeping sacks.

Morgana stood there for a long time, allowing the soft lap of the waves as they rocked the ship gently against the ocean's bosom, and the lullaby of the wind as it blew across the oak-planked hull and played about the sail, to soothe her, to calm her erratic thoughts and racing heart.

She had no wish to be parted from Leif Haraldsson now. No wish at all. Nor did she wish to part him from his son for another eight winters.

By the Allfather, how could she persuade him to trust her again? At least give her a chance to try to prove herself?

There was no answer in the chanting of the breeze, the song of the ocean.

* * *

In the gauzy morning mist, they sailed up the smaller, parallel finger of water just south of Oslofjord. Morgana guessed that they were going to beach the ship and cross overland to approach the settlement from behind.

Of course, she thought, as she watched the rocky beach approach. Underhanded . . . just like Horik Bluetooth. Leif was probably right—some of the younger men had more than likely returned for harvesting. If many of them were strangers, or men who backed Harald Fairhair in his bid to be king of all Norvegia, it would have been foolish to sail smack into Oslofjord and announce their intentions.

Eirik, who'd turned subdued with the approach of land—for Leif had told him that he was to remain in Norvegia with his mother until he had seen twelve winters—stood beside Morgana, sucking his thumb, something he did now only when he was anxious or frightened. Morgana rested her hand on one small shoulder and squeezed gently, trying to impart reassurance when she felt none at all herself. She lifted him in her arms then, and held him close as they silently waited for *Wave Rider* to touch land.

Morgana's melancholy had begun to turn to a simmering anger at Eirik's growing silence, his listlessness after Leif had told him of their plans. How could he do this to the child? He'd surely been adversely affected in his head while in that cage, to think of insisting that Eirik be separated from him after so long. What kind of father was he?

One who loves you so very much that he would not part you from the child until manhood. He doesn't trust you, yet his love remains steadfast. He told you so, and his sacrifice is proof of that love.

"Morgana?"

She turned to him. The strong wind ruffled the sun-lightened auburn hair held down around his forehead by a red head band. Its sting caused him to narrow his bleak but determined topaz eyes as he held out the filigreed cross and chain that had belonged to his mother. "I would have

Eirik wear this, as I have since childhood." He reached to place it over the child's head to hang near his heart. "To remind him that he is my son—and anyone else who needs reminding . . . perhaps another husband of yours." The barest hint of sarcasm had entered his voice. "Also, to remind everyone that he has been baptized Christian. I would not have him worship pagan gods."

Morgana's lips thinned with extreme annoyance. "He will wear it, but I know naught about your new religion, and can only allow him to believe as he will in your absence."

Leif nodded. "The necklet is also valuable, should you ever need coin. Or, if you should need my help, send it to me at Vallée de Vergers and I will come immediately."

She tossed back her moon-bright mane of hair in irritation. "Aye, you'll come flying to Eirik's aid from distant Francia. How generous of you to make such a flimsy promise!"

His eyes darkened, and a muscle jumped along one side of his newly-healed jaw. "For now I can give him nothing more than the cross and my pledge."

Wave Rider nudged the shore; men jumped into thigh-high water with heavy ropes to haul the prow end up onto the beach to secure it.

"You will remain here with several of the men and Eirik. There are provisions if we should be delayed—"

"I will not! You may have decided to banish me to Reyk, but you'll not keep me from helping Ingrid and Harald."

"Be reasonable!" he said through set teeth, and Eirik, obviously sensing the tension between his parents, began to cry. Morgana rocked him from side to side, and lowered her voice to a fierce whisper as she held his cheek to her heart.

"Why? You're not my husband. Nor, obviously, do you wish to be. Therefore I'll do as I like. Eirik will be just as safe here without me as with me, for I am no warrior."

"Exactly. And only skilled warriors can accomplish what we've come to do."

"Then you'll have to tie me to the mast to keep me here!"

He swung from her angrily and moved away. The mists were clearing, the sun trying to burn through as Leif consulted briefly with Little Thor, Ragnar, Einar, and Egil. Olaf and the other seven men were to be left behind.

"And what of me, young Leif?" asked Guthrum. "I am not too old to help—especially when Ingrid and Harald are involved."

Leif decided to be brutally honest. "Can you say, old one, that you wouldn't hinder our progress? That you could keep up with us?"

Guthrum nodded, knocked one gnarled fist against his breastbone. "I am not useless just yet. And I can still shoot a bow with accuracy, even if my sword arm isn't as strong as it once was."

Leif stared at the old man, obviously debating, then said, "So be it, Guthrum. But you might jeopardize all of us if you impede our escape."

Morgana felt a twinge of guilt at his words, but refused to compare her strength and agility to that of a man of Guthrum's age.

Guthrum straightened and said to Leif, "I will not fail you."

They left within the hour, armed with bows, daggers and battle-axes. Leif had decided that swords were too heavy for climbing the low mountains that ridged the strip of land between the two fjords. The going was steep at first, but Morgana kept reminding herself that the distance wasn't more than three hours or so on foot. She was more concerned about Guthrum than herself.

It was cooler higher up, and they would have encountered snow had it not been the end of summer. Morgana was glad that Leif had insisted each of them bring along a mantle for warmth. A few times, Morgana aided Guthrum along some of the more difficult parts of the trail, determined that none of the warriors would be held up by helping them.

During those times, she would feel Leif's eyes on them, but she refused to meet his gaze and determinedly did what was required to make certain neither she nor Guthrum became a handicap.

No one spoke, for talking wasted precious energy and could alert anyone else who might happen to be about. Besides, they had already made their plans while aboard the *knarr*.

They stopped twice for brief rests. These were, Morgana suspected, out of consideration for her and Guthrum rather than the needs of the other men.

Shortly before the sun was at its highest point, they entered the woods that separated the mountains from the fields, with Leif and Little Thor leading. Since it was late summer, the debris that covered the forest floor wasn't primarily dry, dead leaves and vines, and Morgana was glad. Not even Leif could match the red man's silent way of walking through the woods.

Behind the camouflage of tall pines, beech, ash, birch and shorter but nonetheless thick and concealing foliage that edged the forest, they studied the small meadow below them and the adjoining west field. A few men were cutting wheat with sickles, some were heading away from the field, but most had evidently already returned to Oslof for the midday meal.

The faint drift of laughter caught Leif's attention, and he looked more closely from his position behind a tall spruce. Settled within the fresh green of the meadow grass were a woman and a boy. They sat upon what looked like a mantle, and were evidently sharing a simple meal. The boy pointed up at a circling raven and the woman's head tilted upward in response.

Their voices were indistinguishable, their faces almost a blur, but Leif knew them. Ingrid and Harald. What impossibly good luck . . .

He glanced over at Little Thor. The red man was stone-still, his eyes on Ingrid and her son, so near and yet so far.

It was impossible to tell if all the men had returned from their summer sojourns, for often more than one ship sailed off, and then returned separately. There weren't enough men remaining in the west field to determine how many had returned so far.

The muffled sound of the horn came to Leif. It either signaled time for the noon meal or the return of a ship. At this distance, among the sound-absorbing trees, it was difficult to determine which signal it was.

It could also have been a hunting horn, and thus infinitely more unwelcome.

Ingrid, who looked thinner to Leif even from this distance, froze and slowly turned her head toward the settlement. The child put his hand on her arm, as if in reassurance, but Ingrid remained unmoving for long moments.

One of the men who'd been working in the field moved toward Ingrid and Harald. He spoke and gestured toward Oslof. Another woman joined him, sickle at her side. It appeared they were trying to convince Ingrid to return to Oslof with them. She shook her head and gestured for them to leave.

Leif looked at Little Thor again, then moved to stand beside him. "We must somehow get her attention without alarming her."

The red man nodded. "But wait until they are alone." Even as he said the words the man and woman, whom Leif did not recognize, were moving away from Ingrid and Harald and toward Oslof.

Ragnar said softly to Leif, "Bluetooth never goes a-viking, too much could happen in his absence. And he shadows Ingrid's every move. 'Tis unusual to see her alone with Harald, and I would wager it won't be for long. We must make a move."

Leif looked at Little Thor, who was watching the woman and child across the way. He was disappointed that Bluetooth wasn't to be seen, for it would have been his opportunity to kill the man and avenge his father's death, no matter the circumstances; Horik Bluetooth deserved no better than he had meted out to Harald Esthrithsson. Yet Leif evinced a powerful sense of obligation toward the Skraeling whom, he felt, deserved a chance with the woman he obviously loved. And at last Gunnar's widow and child would be in good hands once again.

As Gunnar's best friend, Leif could do no less than assure the safety and well-being of Ingrid and Harald, if he had even the remotest chance to do so.

Little Thor cupped his hands about his mouth, and imitated the distinctive shriek of a peacock.

Astonished, Morgana looked at him, as did the others.

The red man stepped out from where he had been concealed, and stood, unmoving, in plain sight of Ingrid, if she cared enough to study the wooded edge of the meadow. Her head lifted, her gaze immediately moving toward the source of the sound.

Little Thor repeated the call, this time making it sound as if the peacock were wounded or suffering. Ragnar broke into a broad grin, looked at Leif, and then had to cover his mouth to contain his laughter.

Of course, Leif thought. Ingrid and her concern for animals. She couldn't pass up a creature in distress, be it an orphaned lamb or a bear cub. Leif didn't know if Munin was still alive, but surely Ingrid would understand the significance in the call of a suffering peacock from the forest.

He glanced at Morgana. She was watching her friend

with hope lighting her features, expectation in her eyes. The sun dappled her silver-blond hair beneath the sketchy awning of the woods. She reminded him of a younger Morgana, who had followed him as a youth into every conceivable sort of mischief—thus winning not only his friendship, but his admiration, and finally, love . . .

Harald jumped to his feet at Little Thor's second call, but Ingrid stood slowly, looking toward where they stood. The boy suddenly pointed toward the Skraeling—although it was hard to tell if they had spotted the unmoving red man.

Ingrid bent and said something into Harald's ear, then put a hand on his shoulder. She stared in the direction of Little Thor, but they couldn't be certain she saw him, standing quietly and unobtrusively before a trio of towering pines.

Taking Harald's hand, Ingrid began to walk toward the western edge of the meadow. Morgana dared hope . . .

Leif dared hope . . .

Harald suddenly pointed directly at Little Thor. Ingrid gave him what looked like a soft but sharp command, and his arm fell to his side. Her steps quickened.

Little Thor remained unmoving, blending in with the forest behind him except for his bright headband. Leif marveled at the red man's patience, yet knew all could be lost, their very lives jeopardized, should someone unexpectedly appear and divine what was happening.

Guthrum stepped forward until he was beside Little Thor, his white hair a sharp contrast to the red man's black mane.

It was obvious by now that Ingrid was trying not to run, and Leif suddenly felt the chill of premonition. The muffled sound of horses came to him. Little Thor canted his head, obviously listening, his eyes still riveted to Ingrid and Harald . . .

. . . who stopped suddenly in their tracks. The boy

looked up at his mother, near enough now for Leif to see the questioning look on his face. She quickly turned him around, and they started back toward their half-finished meal spread out on the mantle . . . just as a group of six men thundered into the meadow from the forest to the south. Their leader, Leif could tell even at this distance, was Horik Bluetooth. He would have known the man anywhere. The others, he didn't recognize.

Little Thor took Guthrum's arm and they stepped back into the shelter of the trees. Morgana clamped one hand over her mouth in dismay, and the remnants of levity on Ragnar Thorrson's face turned quickly to a black frown.

Automatically, Egil and Einar pulled in protectively about Morgana, who'd retreated a few paces from the edge of the forest. They were immediately joined by the other four men.

"What now?" Egil asked with a frown.

"Wait . . . watch," Little Thor said before Leif could answer. He moved back to his original vantage point, hidden, but with an unobstructed view of Ingrid and Harald.

Leif glanced at him, then nodded. "There's naught else to do but wait and see what Bluetooth does first."

Little Thor watched as Bluetooth alone dismounted and approached Ingrid. The woman lifted her chin to meet the big man's eyes. She looked thinner to the red man, but not intimidated. Was she unhappy? How could she feel anything but unhappiness with a man like Horik Bluetooth aggressively dogging her every move with unwanted, unwelcome attentions?

Little Thor wanted to kill the Norseman. With his bare hands. His fingers curled at his sides in unconscious reaction; he closed his mind to the soft murmurs of the others nearby and concentrated solely on Ingrid and the boy. If

411

thoughts could have killed, Horik Bluetooth would have been dead a hundred times over.

But Little Thor would give that chance, if it came, to Kiisku-Liinu.

Even as he watched, Horik took hold of Ingrid's arm and pulled her closer. She appeared to stiffen, but did not resist. Harald put one hand on his mother's other arm and said something to Horik, but Little Thor couldn't make out the boy's expression.

Suddenly, Horik forced his mouth down over Ingrid's, one huge arm encircling her shoulders and breaking Harald's light hold on his mother. She attempted to pull away, and it was all the red man could do to remain where he was. He could have put an arrow to his bow for Bluetooth's black heart, but at this distance, he wasn't certain it would have enough power behind it to kill the man.

Harald launched himself at Horik, and the laughter of the other men came to Little Thor on the breeze. With a sweep of his free arm, Horik knocked the boy away. Harald stumbled backward and landed on the ground. He appeared to be dazed, but not for long. He scrambled back to his feet, but it was too late. Without warning Horik released Ingrid, turned his back to her, and remounted behind a deer carcass secured to his saddle.

Mother and son stood glaring up at the Norseman as the others swung toward Oslof with their prizes and began to move away. After a few words to Ingrid and a gesture that was obviously threatening, Horik followed the others as they skirted the half-harvested field that bordered the meadow and rode off toward the settlement.

Little Thor watched as Ingrid hugged Harald, then motioned for him to sit down. They both recommenced eating their meal, but Ingrid kept raising her head, evidently listening for the sound of Bluetooth's return. She would glance furtively toward the forest, then back in the direction the men had gone.

After what seemed a long enough time to Little Thor, he stepped before the same group of pines as he had earlier. He repeated his call. Both Ingrid and Harald looked over in his direction. He raised one hand, and signaled for them to come toward the woods.

Ingrid rose, looked toward Oslof one more time, then grabbed Harald's hand and snatched up the mantle. She began moving quickly toward Little Thor, leaving behind the scattered remnants of their repast.

Come, my golden one, he willed her silently, *and you'll never have to suffer the Norseman's attentions again.*

As they neared the forest, Ingrid began to run.

Chapter Twenty-Seven

Morgana held her breath, praying that they would make the trees without being seen . . . before anyone could return to the fields. Before Horik Bluetooth could change his mind and come back for Ingrid.

Within moments, Little Thor had them within his grasp, Harald clinging to his arm, Ingrid pink-cheeked and breathless and looking at him with a fragile hopefulness . . . and obvious relief.

Morgana watched as Little Thor led them to the others. Ingrid cried her friend's name softly and threw herself into Morgana's arms. Harald hugged his great-grandfather, murmuring, "You came back! You came back . . ."

Leif said, "We have no time to spare. *Wave Rider* waits on the other side of the mountain." He hesitated. "Are you willing to leave Oslof, Ingrid? Norvegia?"

She looked at him, her eyes bright with unshed tears, and moved to hug him. An emotional silence gathered before Ingrid said, "This is not our home anymore. Everything has changed." She shook her head, and looked from one to the other. "I cannot believe you risked your lives for us."

"You cannot?" Leif asked in feigned astonishment. "For shame, Ingrid. We may be many things, but never cowards! No true Norsemen would have missed this for aught.

We have tweaked Bluetooth's nose . . ." His expression turned grim, "Although anyone among us would gladly have killed him."

"Thank you, young Leif," Guthrum said, still holding Harald close.

"You owe me no thanks, Guthrum," Leif answered.

Little Thor was watching Ingrid. Suddenly, he turned toward the meadow, listening. "We must go," he said, urgency underlying his words.

Leif moved quickly to the tree line. No one appeared, but it wouldn't be long, he knew. He turned to Little Thor. "I'll wait for Horik's return. I owe it to my father." He gestured toward the others. "You take them back to the ship. I'll join you as soon as I'm finished here."

His expression was determined; his tone brooked no argument.

"But—" Morgana began, suddenly frightened for him.

Ingrid's happy expression vanished.

"I'll catch up with you later, or meet you at the ship. But not yet," he said to Little Thor.

"But you'll surely be outnumbered!" Morgana exclaimed.

"Bluetooth will come alone first—I'm counting on it. If not . . ." He shrugged. "I'll deal with it as it happens."

"But—"

Leif's look turned fierce. "Don't question me, Morgana! Go . . . *now!*"

Little Thor looked at him long and hard, as if debating whether to remain or go.

" 'Tis my decision, red man," he said emphatically. "And my *command.*"

Finally, Little Thor nodded. "We will wait for you on the far side of the forest," he said. "If you do not join us before the sun begins to sink in the west, I will return for you." He swung abruptly away before Leif could reply, signaled the others to follow, and moved off deeper into the forest.

Leif watched them slip through the trees until he could no longer make out Morgana's bright hair. As good as he felt for having successfully taken Ingrid and Harald, a concurrent, empty feeling was centered deep within him . . . a sense of impending loss.

'Tis your own doing.

No. This particular feeling came from a sudden uncertainty as to his ability to challenge Horik Bluetooth and survive the struggle. Leif the Lucky he had been called since he was a youth, but luck had deserted him ever since the last time he'd gone a-viking. Would he ever see Morgana or Eirik again?

He turned abruptly to take his mind off such thoughts and also to observe the bright meadow before him. He had to plan his strategy, and thoughts about ill luck would serve no good purpose.

Besides, he thought in an effort to disperse his doubts, Christianity supposedly didn't embrace superstition.

He moved to a good vantage point and narrowed his eyes against the bright day to watch for his enemy. It was a typically delightful Scandinavian summer day. The sun was a golden sphere against a cobalt sky, the meadow grass beautifully green as it rippled before the breeze.

But the air was warmer in Normandy, the sun brighter, or so it seemed, the scented breeze sweeter. Even the grass was a deeper, lusher green . . .

Enough of such thoughts. He had things to do while he waited.

Leif had just enough time to set several carefully hidden traps to hinder anyone who entered the trees directly around him from the meadow, in the manner Little Thor had taught him.

Men and women began returning to their tasks in the field almost immediately after he'd finished, but there was no sign of Horik Bluetooth. Hopefully, the Norseman would believe Ingrid had gone back to work in the field—what would have made this day different from any other?—and he was meanwhile involved in supervising the skinning of the hides and preparation of the meat. He certainly couldn't know that Leif and his men had returned to the area.

Several hours passed before the fields cleared in the face of imminent dusk, which came quickly in Norvegia, especially near the end of Corn-Cutting Month. Still Leif waited, willing Horik Bluetooth to appear and meet him face to face . . .

A hand on his shoulder caused him to jump, his own hand homing to his dagger hilt, even though he knew it was too late . . .

He looked into the shadowed features of Little Thor. Relief flowed through him. "What do you here?" he demanded, trying to hide his dismay at being such an easy target for the Skraeling had he been an enemy.

Little Thor grinned. "You have the ears of an old man, Kiisku-Liinu, when I can come up behind you so easily. You could have been food for the ravens."

Leif had to shake his head with rue. "I am not a red man—I was not raised in the forest, although I've learned much from you." He frowned again. "Where are the others? Why are you not with them?"

" 'When the sun begins to sink in the west,' I told you. Is your memory as poor as your hearing? The others are safely hidden. They will await us until the moon is highest. Then Ragnar will lead them over the mountain, with or without us."

Leif nodded. "I intend to be aboard *Wave Rider* when it sails."

"Have you set traps?"

"Aye."

"Then we wait."

"Remember, red man, whatever else happens, Horik Bluetooth is *mine*."

Little Thor nodded.

"And let's hope he doesn't bring many of his cohorts to help him search. We are only two."

Shadows deepened, birds began to quiet, and the subtle forest noises grew more distinct before Leif made out the sound of approaching horses. Horik and three others came cantering along the northern edge of the fields, then cut diagonally across the meadow to the place where Ingrid and Harald had been earlier.

The huge Norseman dismounted. The others remained astride their horses as he hunkered down and examined the crushed grass, the scraps of their meal, as if in search of clues to their whereabouts.

Leif watched him, remembering all that he had been told regarding the suspect circumstances of his father's death. He allowed Guthrum's revelation to thread through his thoughts, rousing further his long-buried anger. Bluetooth's contemptuous treatment of Gunnar and Little Thor. His threats against little Harald. His abuse of Ingrid, which had resulted in the loss of her child. Gunnar's child.

Since when is a cripple a hero? Those distant but derisive words came back to Leif with punishing clarity . . . as if it had been only yesterday.

Horik stood suddenly and looked toward the forest with an angry jerk of his head. Leif couldn't make out his expression, but Bluetooth slammed an object to the ground with such force that Leif knew exactly what the Northman

418

was feeling. The violence in that motion only served to inflame the growing rage that Leif was carefully, steadfastly stoking. The following bellow of rage reverberated through the meadow before it dissipated.

Leif only wished that he'd had Hrafn with him. He was certain that he could have openly challenged Bluetooth right there in the open meadow with the stallion beneath him, trained in the Frankish manner, and come out the victor. Although the other three men would definitely have been a hindrance, Hrafn's training would have drastically reduced the odds. As would Little Thor's presence.

There was little hope now that any of them would allow him to openly challenge Bluetooth one on one, for Leif was an outcast. A renegade. His life was worth less than nothing in Norvegia. Anyone could kill him without fear of retribution. Therefore, he couldn't just reveal himself and challenge Horik, even had the Northman's companions been honorable men instead of, undoubtedly, more of Harald Fairhair's cutthroats.

So now it seemed he would have to use cunning against an adversary who was well-practiced in the same. Yet even though there were four against two, Leif was heartened by Little Thor's presence. The Skraeling was worth several good men, and in spite of his earlier show of anger, Leif was grateful his friend had returned to help him in the face of the odds.

He glanced at Little Thor, suddenly wanting to tell him that he loved him as much as any brother. Horik Bluetooth's second shout of rage swerved him from his purpose, however. He looked back at the Northman.

Bluetooth was bending to pick up something else . . . a sickle. Ingrid's discarded sickle. The Northman brandished it in the gloaming, and it caught the dying rays of the sun like blood on the blade. He vaulted astride his horse, sickle still in hand, a long, fierce battle cry spewing from his lungs. Birds flapped their wings noisily as they scattered through the darkening canopy above, fleeing the prolonged and threatening sound.

"Is he planning to cut Ingrid down?" Leif muttered, "or does he suspect an enemy hides nearby and he prefers a sickle to a sword?"

Little Thor didn't answer, but motioned him to retreat. The two of them withdrew quickly and quietly into the swiftly deepening dusk of the forest.

The four men cantered toward the trees, then slowed. Leif watched from his concealed position in a heavily-branched beech. He and Little Thor, who was hidden in another tree nearby, could have immediately taken two of them with an arrow each, but that would have revealed their presence. Also, Leif wanted to confront Horik Bluetooth directly, not kill him with an unexpected arrow through the heart.

Leif watched, his heart thumping against his sternum as Horik and his men trotted steadily toward the first of the trees. They made the foolish mistake of underestimating their enemy, thinking, no doubt, that it was only a runaway woman and child they sought. With a deplorable lack of caution, in the growing dimness two of them blundered into Leif's traps and were unseated by a vine strung among several trees.

One man was caught across the neck. With a cry of surprise, he was knocked backward and tumbled to the ground. The horse of the second man caught another vine across its forehead, over its eyes. It instantly threw itself up onto its hind legs with a shrill whinny, then plunged to all fours with a violent shake of its head. It broke through the entanglement, and its rider was pitched sideways. He landed hard on the forest floor and remained there, unmoving.

"Bertil!" Horik roared, reining in his skittish horse. Bertil, the first to be unseated, was shaking his head as if to clear it. Then, in a lower voice, Horik demanded, "What happened?" He moved his mount cautiously toward Bertil, past the unmoving body of the second man.

"Some—something caught me across the throat," Bertil answered in a shaky voice. "And Greger, too, looks like."

The fourth man dismounted and approached Greger. He glanced around him, upwards too, before crouching to put one hand to the downed man's neck. "Dead," he pronounced after a moment. He shook his head and tried to approach Greger's horse. The animal danced away, then turned suddenly and dashed off into the shadows.

"Let him go, Reidmar," Horik said. "We must find the wench afore 'tis too dark to see aught."

"She'll come back," Reidmar grumbled as he re-mounted, "if she has any—"

An arrow streaked through the air from above, striking the top of Reidmar's shoulder beside his neck and plunging downward toward his heart. He let loose a gasp before he slid back to the ground, one foot still lodged in the stirrup. His horse pranced uneasily, partially anchored by the weight of Reidmar's caught ankle.

Before Horik could move, another arrow struck Bertil where he sat. With deadly force, it bolted through his midsection, knocking him backward and pinning him to the ground. Blood ran from his nose and mouth. He tried to speak, but no sound came from his lips. Then he was still.

Horik, obviously at a loss to explain the unexpected and swift attack, wheeled his mount in confusion, then shouted in desperate anger, "Who's *there?*"

The shrill, almost human cry of a peacock came in answer, seeming to mock him. He froze, his eyes rapidly scanning the darkening forest around him. "Munin?" he mumbled, then shook his head. "Spirits!" he exclaimed under his breath, and jerked his mount's head toward the edge of the woods.

"Help . . . me, Horik . . ."

The plea seemed to come from Reidmar. Horik swung back, nudging his horse cautiously forward. "Reidmar?" he asked in a tentative voice, a frown darkening his features.

And then suddenly, as if understanding dawned, he slowly raised his eyes to the branches above.

But it was too late. A body came hurtling downward from the umber shadows, and an arm around his neck pulled him inexorably from his saddle toward the ground. At the same time a voice rasped in his ear, " 'Tis no spirit, murderer. 'Tis Haraldsson . . . come to avenge my father's death."

They rolled over once, then Leif jumped to his feet and backed away, giving Bluetooth the opportunity to stand and face him.

He derived a certain amount of pleasure from watching Horik's face, for the man looked like he was, indeed, seeing a spirit. But he recovered quickly. *"You!"*

"Já."

"You dare to show your face after you've been banished?"

"Only to you, Bluetooth. And you know why."

Horik's eyes narrowed, his jutting eyetooth menacing in the growing gloom. "You can prove nothing."

Those very words were an admission to Leif.

"I don't need to. However you accomplished it from the cover of that stand of evergreens, murder is murder. You'll die before the day does, and rightly so."

Horik drew his sword in answer.

Leif had only his battle-ax and dagger. He pulled the ax from his belt.

Horik lunged with surprising speed for a big man and thrust his sword tip toward Leif's belly. Leif had barely enough time to position himself for the engagement and was forced to spin blindly away from the bite of the blade. It struck the tree immediately behind where he'd been standing with enough force that Horik had to use two hands to pry it free.

Bluetooth spun around, his features tense in the wake of his brief vulnerability.

"I wouldn't hack a man while his back was turned, Bluetooth. I rather thought that was *your* wont."

With a snarl, Horik once again lunged at Leif. Sword blade met ax blade with a resounding clang, and Leif had to jump back immediately. Weapons-wise they were unevenly matched, with Leif at a definite disadvantage. As he retreated, however, Horik's blade zipped down his tunic front, rending it and the shirt beneath, and drawing blood in a long, thin line.

With only weeks between him and his ordeal at Harfleur, Leif knew that, short of direct divine intervention, the contest had to be brief if he wanted to win it. He also knew that he couldn't afford to lose any appreciable amount of blood, for that would further sap what he'd regained of his strength and stamina.

As Horik sprang forward again, Leif successfully parried the thrust with his ax, knocking the sword to the side. He took swift advantage and with two hands brought the ax arcing horizontally toward his adversary, intending to cut him in two. With the instincts of a warrior, Bluetooth ducked the wicked blade, dropped to the ground, and rolled away. It passed over him with a deadly whistle.

Leif saw Bluetooth's hand go for the discarded sickle, which lay nearby where Horik had dropped it. Leif's heart tripped within his chest, for the contest would be even more unfair with Bluetooth in possession of two long-bladed weapons. Yet even as he thought of launching himself recklessly at Horik before the latter could gain his feet, a projectile whizzed through the air with a deadly whine and the big Norseman let out a howl of pain.

A dagger pinned his outstretched left hand to the ground beneath it.

Little Thor. Leif didn't know whether to thank or curse the Skraeling.

Horik released his sword, all but foaming at the mouth in fury, and jerked the dagger from his hand with a growl of pain. Leif was quick to take advantage. He dropped his ax and threw himself on top of Horik. The bigger man pitched backward, releasing the dagger. He wrapped his legs about Leif's in reaction, but Leif went for his neck, fingers desperately digging into flesh and tendon, elbows spread to block Horik's hands.

"You'll die without your sword in hand," Leif panted, "just like you deserve."

Horik's large hands, one slippery with blood, went to Leif's neck in answer, as he'd anticipated. Bluetooth squeezed until his features danced before Leif's eyes, his eyetooth seeming to grow and protrude like the wicked fang of an enraged lynx. Leif's arm muscles began to burn, and he felt his strength suddenly start to ebb.

He had to do something quickly. Or die.

He had the advantage of being on top. As close to dark as it was, his eyes had adjusted to the half-light, and through his peripheral vision he caught the dull gleam of the dagger blade that Little Thor had used on Horik's hand. It was more immediately accessible than the knife within its sheath at his waist, but it wouldn't be easy to grab by any means.

In fact, even attempting to reach it could be fatal.

As stars exploded before his eyes, Leif grunted with exertion and heaved Horik's head up from the ground. He slammed it against the forest floor, hoping to stun the bigger man. Horik gasped, and Leif tried it again. Horik's fingers loosened their hold upon Leif's neck fractionally . . . and Leif took a gamble. He loosed his right hand from Bluetooth's throat and reached for the dagger.

He succeeded only in pushing it farther away.

Horik seemed to recover, and, enraged, strengthened his stranglehold in spite of his injured hand.

Would the man never give up?

With one last summoning of strength, Leif brought up one knee between Horik's great thighs. There was not enough power behind the blow to cause even temporary paralysis, for even though Horik's legs had loosened their hold on Leif, they were still a hindering entanglement. But the move took the big Norseman by surprise. It also knocked the breath from his lungs, and in those fleeting seconds Leif grabbed desperately for the dagger.

His fingers closed around the hilt, and before Horik could respond, he plunged the blade into the man's throat up to the hilt . . . and held it there with every bit of his dwindling strength, as he should have done with Snorri the Black. There would be no half measures this time, he thought as he watched with savage satisfaction while the life drained from his adversary's eyes, listened until his death gurgles ceased.

Leif rolled off Bluetooth's body, feeling drained and strangely hollow inside. He'd never particularly derived satisfaction from killing—perhaps it was his mother's legacy, for it certainly wasn't in keeping with a Norseman's zest for physical conquest.

Little Thor dropped lightly to the ground close by, and approached him. "Another's death is a hollow victory," the red man said quietly, "but he will cause no more of it."

Leif sat up, still breathing hard. He looked at Little Thor. "You wouldn't have let him kill me."

The red man shrugged. He examined the shallow laceration across Leif's chest. Then he finally answered. "You killed him. That is what you wanted." He held out his hand to Leif and drew him to his feet.

"But you saved my life. You crippled his hand and prevented him from using that sickle."

"Who can say? I only know that 'twas written in the stars, this bond between us."

Their eyes met, held. *"Bróir mín,"* Leif said gruffly as he hugged the red man to him, his heart bursting with emotion. "We are even now, and I thank you, my brother."

Leif released him after several expressive moments, and the red man moved to retrieve Leif's bow and quiver from where they'd dropped when he'd left the shelter of the tree. As he handed them to Leif, one corner of his mouth quirked. "You would like to believe so, Kiisku-Liinu. But I do not. You were my vision from Wishemenetoo. We can talk later. Now we must leave here, quickly."

"Já. Before half of Oslof comes a-searching for them." He glanced at the dead men around them, then swung toward the mountain and began moving swiftly through the darkened woods.

Morgana felt weak with relief when Leif and Little Thor appeared out of the darkness before the shelter the other three men had hastily set up. It consisted of a huge fallen birch, the base of which provided a natural windbreak. With additional pine bows as a camouflage from any who might chance upon them, it was almost as secure as a cave. Before he'd left them, Little Thor had shown Ragnar how to make a small fire of dry wood, should the women and child need it, which would produce little smoke.

In the faint light from the flames, Morgana anxiously took in Leif's condition—bruises on his neck, a bloodied chest. He was dirty and disheveled from head to toe. But he was alive. She wanted to throw herself into his arms, but her fear of rejection held her as securely as an iron fetter.

"Did you get Bluetooth?" Ragnar asked.

Leif nodded grimly. "And three others. We must get back to *Wave Rider* before their bodies are discovered."

"Or their horses return without them," Little Thor said.

They scattered the remnants of the fire and dismantled their temporary shelter, taking care to erase all evidence of it, even though it would have been hard to make out in the darkness.

Little Thor took the sleepy Harald in his capable arms. "Let him sleep," he told Ingrid in a low voice, a smile softening his handsome mouth. "He is but a small burden."

Morgana watched her return his smile, and from the depths of her own despair, she felt immeasurably happy for her friend. She was sure Guthrum would tell her of Little Thor's interest—although she suspected that Ingrid would discover his affection quickly enough on her own. Morgana would encourage Ingrid to eat once they returned to Vallée de Vergers, certain her friend would blossom in the warm affection of the red man, heal and thrive beneath the warm sun of Normandy . . . aye, when they returned—

You aren't returning.

She stumbled as they began their climb, then quickly regained her balance before anyone noticed. The worst was ahead of them, and here she was already stumbling about like an uncertain toddler.

Leif was beside her in an instant. "Are you all right?" he asked, his hand beneath her elbow.

She wanted to touch his fingers on her arm. Her cheeks suddenly flamed as the urge to make physical contact became almost an uncontrollable need. She drew a deep breath and stilled her trembling, traitorous hand. *"Já,"* she managed to say, glad for the darkness that kept him from seeing her flush. *Except that I am to be banished from you until Eirik is on the verge of manhood. Then you will take him away, and . . .*

The thought was so unbearable that she felt her anger and frustration suddenly building at an alarming rate. Words rose to her lips, in spite of her intentions to keep silent.

"Except . . . that you are punishing me for daring to think for myself—to plan my future and course of actions like a man rather than a meek and dependent woman!" She lowered her voice even more, so he had to bend his head to hear her. She had the mad urge to pull his head even closer and press her lips to his, to cradle his head to her breast, to cleanse the bitterness from his heart. And her own. "You once said that you wondered if I ever really loved you; but *I* wonder if you ever really *knew* me. If you ever really understood me—or cared to."

His fingers tightened on her elbow as he guided her forward in the meager light. The moon peeked through the thinning trees as they began to climb the slanted slopes, and she shivered in the chill mountain breeze.

"Are you cold?" he asked softly.

"Inside, *já.*"

"Morgana," he said. "This is not the place to—"

" 'Tis the *only* place," she countered sharply. "For within hours *Wave Rider* will set sail for Reyk. The place to where I will be banished . . . Eirik will be banished." She glanced up at him, caught only his profile as the moonlight limned its chisled lines. "Surely you of all people can understand *that.*"

He met her gaze. Her eyes were wide and dark, beckoning pools well-remembered by his body as well as his heart. Her mouth was soft and full, still tempting. But it was her spirit, the essence of her, he realized, that he would miss the most. For she was unpredictable at the most unexpected—and often inopportune—times. That was what had intrigued him when they'd been children. She could be as docile and malleable as any of the girls, but behind those lovely crystal-blue eyes dwelt an intelligence and, aye, a rare courage and mettle. He'd recognized those half-hidden traits of hers, secretly admired them, and loved her for them, even if he sometimes chose not to acknowledge them.

By the gods, hadn't he even gambled on her pursuing him if he took her son from her? And it had worked. Beyond his wildest hopes, his actions had brought not only Morgana to him, but his precious ship and dependable, loyal men from Oslof.

Yet he was punishing her for doing the things that made her Morgana Magnussdóttir, for exhibiting the traits that had attracted him and, later, anchored him to her in love. For doing exactly as he'd hoped. Then, when she'd continued to be outraged, planned to escape, he'd decided to send her away from him.

With these dark, confusing thoughts churning through his mind, he moved ahead of her and fell into place behind Ragnar, allowing the red-haired Northman to guide them back toward the ship.

And acutely aware of the woman behind him, who would have been beside him as an equal partner if he had but allowed it.

Chapter Twenty-Eight

I was wrong. I admit it. I was wrong to ever have divorced you . . .

The words of her dream jolted Morgana awake.

It was near dawn, still dark. The darkest time of the night. *Wave Rider* gently rode the ocean swells, their soft susurration disquieting to Morgana, for she was being taken farther north than she had ever been, to Reyk.

Leif hadn't wanted to anchor after they'd left the vicinity of Oslof. Obviously, he couldn't wait to get rid of her, she thought darkly, although common sense tried to tell her that he sought to outrun any pursuers.

Ingrid and Harald were asleep. But Morgana, although by no means rested, could not do the same. Especially with those words ringing in her ears, disquieting thoughts whirling through her brain.

She quietly slipped from her sleeping sack and left the shelter of the awning. She leaned against the high free-board of the *knarr*, huddled in her mantle. It was still cold, in spite of the wrap. She shivered, but the coldness came from within, too. That coldness could not be banished by heavier garments or a crackling fire.

Mayhap she would never be warm inside again.

She was glad to have Eirik with her. Glad she was going to see Tyra and Ottar, Britta and Sigfred. Yet miserable that she was being separated from Leif . . . that she had to tear Eirik from his father.

You don't have to do any such thing.

She thought of her dream. She thought of Little Thor's words to her at the stream that ran through Vallée de Vergers: *The boy is most important, is he not?*

The red man had more sense than she. Of course Eirik was the most important one. Her needs, Leif's needs, were secondary. Would always be secondary, until Eirik became a man and went his own way, raised his own family.

What a good father Little Thor will be to Harald, she thought. Wise and compassionate. Loyal and kind. In love with Ingrid. Willing to accept Gunnar's son as his own . . .

To her dismay, a tear slid down her cheek, but the sea wind almost immediately blew it away. The woolen sail flapped overhead with the brisk breeze, but other than that and the waves nudging *Wave Rider*'s flanks in passage, an absolute stillness prevailed.

I have always loved you, Morgana. Will always love you . . . until they send me to Valhalla—or Heaven or Hell. Until my name isn't even a memory . . .

Another tear tipped her lower lashes and was whisked away. At least it was warm, she thought, as she tried to put Leif's words from her mind. It was the only warm thing in a suddenly cold, cold world.

The sun peeked over the horizon, rose slowly higher and began to take some of the chill from the air. A flap on either side of the awning had been thrown wide for light. Little Thor came to take Harald out into the fresh sea air. He looked at Ingrid, his dark eyes warm. "Will you come, too?" he asked her.

She returned his smile shyly. "*Já*. But first I must speak to Morgana."

He nodded, looked at Morgana, who was sitting beside one of the open flaps and staring out at the cloud-dotted sky, and withdrew with the boy.

"Why are we going north?" Ingrid asked, putting one hand on Morgana's shoulder. "Has it something to do with your unhappiness?"

Morgana looked at her friend, noting how blue her eyes looked above the sapphire blue of her gown. Or was it a new happiness? For surely, from Ingrid's thinness, the hollows beneath her cheekbones, she'd been unhappy in Oslof—no doubt from the strain of constantly standing up to Horik Bluetooth. "We go to Reyk, to Tyra and Ottar. Eirik and I will live with them until Eirik is twelve winters. Then Leif will return for him." The words were stilted, without emotion.

Ingrid frowned, her fingers tightening on Morgana's shoulder. "You want this?"

Morgana turned her misery-darkened eyes toward the light. "Isn't it obvious? Of course I don't want it, but he's made his decision. He feels I betrayed him—again." She told Ingrid about her desire to escape Vallée de Vergers, her plans with Hilaire, and the disastrous result of those plans. "But I didn't know who was behind it . . . didn't know 'twould be Robert of Neustria and Snorri the Black! And I had changed my mind . . . I told Hilaire that I'd changed my mind, but it was too late . . ."

Suddenly, Ingrid's arms were around her, pulling her close. The tears began to flow as the dam of sorrow finally burst. This was the first opportunity they'd had to talk, but Morgana could do nothing for long moments but weep.

Ingrid put her cheek to Morgana's hair. "Hush now, things can't be that bad. Good and loyal men were killed, *já*, but surely Leif can forgive you. He knows you better than anyone else . . . except Tyra," she added with a note of wryness. "And possibly me. You wouldn't be Morgana

432

if you hadn't attempted to leave, and especially after you declared your intentions right from the beginning."

Morgana raised her tear-tracked face to her friend's. "He said he's always l-loved me. Always would love m-me. But he can never trust me again—I destroyed his trust, put Eirik's life in danger . . . on a *whim*, he said." She felt the rise of more tears, and was ashamed to weep so in the arms of her dear friend. Ingrid, who'd lost Gunnar, then a babe, then had been forced to battle an adversary mentally as well as physically or lose her other child.

"He's only hurt . . . and angry. He won't let you go *anywhere*." Ingrid stroked Morgana's hair, then wiped a finger gently across her cheeks, sweeping away tumbling tears. "Trust me, Morgana. I know him almost as well as you. He'll change his mind—"

"*Nei!* I don't want his pity! I don't want him to ask me to go back to Vallée de Vergers because he feels sorry for me. Or guilty. I was . . . I was *wrong* to divorce him, Ingrid. But I could never tell him that. Instead, I'll . . ." She hesitated, fighting her emotions. Why was she suddenly so *weepy?* she wondered with one part of her mind. "I'll tell him Eirik can stay with him. I cannot tear the boy away from Leif now. They've grown so close . . . the love between them runs deep. I've seen it firsthand. How could I ever, in good conscience, separate them now? When Eirik is old enough to be badly affected by such a thing?"

Ingrid took her by the shoulders, gave her a light shake. "You'll go to Reyk alone? Without your man? Without your son? After you went all the way to Francia to find them?" Her look of shocked disbelief made Morgana feel suddenly, briefly, foolish.

Her gaze fell. "I went to find my son, not Leif Haraldsson. And I'll be with Tyra and Ottar . . . with Sigfred and Britta. There are others in Reyk . . . others who aren't influenced by Fairhair."

"Aye. And you'll be miserable for the rest of your life."

433

Morgana drew in a deep, bracing breath of sea air. "Mayhap." Her voice dropped. "But mayhap I deserve it, too. I should never have divorced him to begin with, for the punishment didn't fit the crime."

There. She'd said it aloud. Acknowledged it at long last. Yet even though a burden had been lifted from her shoulders, she hoped she sounded more resolute than she felt as she met Ingrid's eyes and tried to ignore the questions in them. There was no one whom she trusted more than Ingrid.

"But you—you have no idea what awaits you in Normandy!" Morgana said brightly in a valiant effort to force her mind away from her woes. She began to tell Ingrid about Vallée de Vergers, deliberately giving her no chance to speak, until Harald came to them and begged his mother to come and watch the dolphins frolicking alongside *Wave Rider*.

They beached the *knarr* in late afternoon to start a fire beneath the great cooking cauldron they hauled ashore. Little Thor shot a deer and immediately skinned it and cut it up for the savory stew Norsemen loved. Morgana added herbs, onions and cabbage they had brought on the ship. The aroma of simmering meat and vegetables made their mouths water. The stew would have been better had it cooked for at least two days or more, but it tasted delicious to all except Morgana after days of eating dried meat.

Morgana, however, discovered she had no appetite. She could have been eating stones boiled in briny seawater for all the pleasure she derived from the little she put into her mouth. Queasiness assaulted her with each bite, so she left her food virtually untouched.

They were like a large family, these loyal men from Oslof, the two women and their young boys, and Leif and Little Thor, she thought in an effort to get her thoughts off food and its negative effects on her. She felt her throat tighten more and more as the twilight darkened to dusk, as dusk deepened to night, for this would be the last night she would spend with these, her people, since childhood. Indeed, except for Little Thor and the two boys, Morgana had grown up among these men and Ingrid.

It was one of the most difficult evenings of her life and, knowing that she wouldn't sleep, she dreaded retiring. When Leif began to tell Ingrid and Harald about Normandy, the other men gathered around to add their impressions, especially Egil the Tall as eager *skald*. Eirik sat between his father's knees, listening raptly, and looking up often at Leif.

Leif easily warmed to the subject of Vallée de Vergers, as did the others. Even Little Thor was more talkative than usual when in a group, his gaze often alighting on Ingrid as she and Harald listened, enthralled.

Quite unexpectedly, Morgana wished she could retire early, for she suddenly felt completely out of place; as if she didn't belong with these Norse any more—couldn't share their hopes and dreams, their plans. And least of all, their excitement and enthusiasm.

She caught Leif's gaze on her now and then, but he looked away when her eyes encountered his. She stood at last, needing to get away, yet knowing that nothing could mend her sundering heart. She needed a quick, clean break from Leif and Eirik, and dragging it out on this last night before they reached Reyk was pure torture.

Leif looked at her questioningly. "Do you want to take Eirik with you?" he offered.

She shook her head at his unexpected generosity, for he believed he wouldn't see the boy after tomorrow for at least six or seven winters, even if she knew otherwise.

Without another word, for she didn't trust her voice, Morgana swung away and walked toward the shore. She stood for long moments beneath the star-strewn sky, gazing

435

at the gently heaving waves that glowed silver beneath the moon's lambent glow. *Wave Rider*'s stern swung back and forth slightly with the smooth rhythm of the sea swells, her proud outline backlit by the faint celestial light. The gold on her dragon prow came alive beneath the moonlight, subduing the darker, flat purple and green, until it seemed as if portions of the dragon's head were alive, and eager to sail northward to the *knarr*'s destination.

Morgana knew not how long she stood there. She was already numb inside when she realized that the temperature was dropping swiftly and she was shivering inside her mantle. She sighed, closing her eyes for a moment, summoning her strength of will to get her through this night and the morrow.

A hand on her arm made her lashes lift in surprise. She looked up into Leif Haraldsson's shadowed face. "What do you here, Morgana?" he asked softly, pronouncing her name lingeringly, as if savoring the very sound of it.

Impossible, she thought bleakly.

"I was . . . waiting for you."

His eyes widened slightly in surprise. "Not to ask you for aught," she added quickly, "rather to tell you of the decision *I've* made."

She saw his jaw tighten, his eyes narrow suspiciously. Those golden eyes that proclaimed, according to Noor the Byzantine, that he was related to the Emperor of Constantinople himself.

"I am not your wife. I am a free woman. I have chosen to go to Reyk, as you bade me. But not with Eirik. Eirik will remain with you . . . return to Vallée de Vergers and be all that you want him to be—receive all that you would give to him and his children." Her voice quavered then, and she stilled, willing away her unwelcome weakness.

"Nei. He stays—"

Her expression turned angry, her fingers fisting at her sides. "Don't say no to me, renegade!" she said through set

436

teeth. "No mother who loved her son as I love mine could ever do such a thing to him! I see how he adores you . . . I see how he needs you, worships the ground you walk on! I may be many things, Leif Haraldsson, but I'm not completely blind, nor am I am complete fool.

"I love Eirik every bit as much as you, and *he* is the most important thing to consider here, not your damaged pride or my obstinancy. Not your distrust or my impulsiveness."

He frowned at her for long moments, unconsciously ran the fingers of one hand through his hair, then shook his head. Before he could speak, however, Morgana raised and pounded her fists against his chest once, against the healing slash beneath his tunic, hoping to hurt him just enough to make him understand she was serious. She heard his sharply sucked in breath, and was perversely satisfied. "I won't go where I'm not wanted, but neither will I keep my son from his rightful and beloved father. There's naught else to say."

"I believe he's *our* son, not yours alone."

"That doesn't mean we belong together. You put it quite bluntly at Harfleur. Two people have nothing if they don't have trust. So let it be."

"I see. That means I have no say. And what will you tell Eirik?"

"*You'll* tell him the truth. That you realized we couldn't be a family anymore . . . give him whatever reasons you gave me. Or think back to what you told him when you first whisked him away from me. Surely you've grown more clever in your explanations since then." Bitter irony infused her words.

She stepped around him then, praying he wouldn't try to stop her, for she didn't know if she could maintain her resolve if he so much as touched her.

* * *

437

Reyk was a smaller community than Oslof, and Tyra and Ottar seemed content in their new home. They were dumbstruck to see *Wave Rider* sail into their tiny harbor—and joyous to see Eirik and Morgana safe and sound.

And Ingrid and Harald! What had been happening farther south?

Morgana took Tyra and Ottar aside and explained the situation—that she and Leif had decided to go their separate ways. Eirik would remain with Leif. Tyra had narrowed her eyes in outright skepticism at Morgana, but Ottar, ever diplomatic with his beautiful stepdaughter, kept his thoughts to himself in front of Morgana.

There were only four other longhouses in Reyk, for the mountains were more rugged here, with far less cultivatable land available than in Oslof.

" 'Tis probably one reason Fairhair has let Reyk be for now," Ottar told Leif. "And Reyk needed a good blacksmith," he added with a wink. "Yet at the first sign of Fairhair's tyranny, we'll leave here and ne'er look back."

"But where will you go?" Ingrid asked.

"The jarl, Ingemar Torfinnsson, has already decided 'twill be either Scotland or Iceland. Mayhap the Orkneys." He shrugged. "We'll worry about that when the time comes." He then called over Torfinnsson and introduced the men and women from Oslof.

"You might consider Francia," Leif told the jarl, a softspoken giant with sandy hair and beard, who proved exceptionally interested in everything the others had to say about Normandy. "This is a small community, and there is much room in Rollo's new domain," Leif added.

They began feasting by mid-afternoon and carried on far into the night. Torfinnsson insisted on hosting the celebration, being not only jarl, but having the largest longhouse. The newcomers doubled the population size of the tiny settlement and the merrymaking was unlike anything Reyk had seen in many winters.

When Morgana picked at her food, Tyra said without ceremony, "You are with child, daughter. You're pale as whey, you eat less than a bird. How can you separate from the father of your unborn child?"

Morgana's jaw dropped as she met Tyra's eyes. With child?

Not impossible by any means, snickered a voice.

Heat rose in her cheeks. Of course it was possible. Hadn't Leif sired Eirik? Hakon, rather, was the one who had been unable to father a child with her. And it surely explained her moodiness, her tendency to cry for the slightest reason, her disinterest in food.

"Does he know?" Tyra asked as she beckoned to one of the slave girls who served the long table.

Morgana shook her head. "I didn't know. How could he?"

Tyra said something to the girl that Morgana couldn't hear. Nor, in those moments of brief introspection, did she care. The girl moved toward the kitchen end of the hall, swerving around two tipsy Norsemen engaged in horseplay.

"You must tell him then."

Morgana's head snapped up. *"Nei!"* Two spots of color dotted her otherwise pale cheeks. "There's nothing more to be said or done between us. Just let it be!" She made to stand, her face suddenly burning, her eyes filling. "By Odin," she gritted in an agony of frustration, "is there nowhere I can go for *peace?*"

Tyra laid a restraining hand on her arm. Her tone softened—at least as much as it could in the middle of a Norse celebratory feast and still be heard by Morgana. "Sit, Morgana, and drink some of my tea when Linnea brings it. 'Twill settle your stomach, *já?*"

"Tell no one from the ship, Mother. Give me your word. Not even Ingrid!"

Tyra gave her daughter the most imperceptible of nods,

439

but Morgana was too distraught to ask for a more vigorous affirmation.

Linnea returned quickly and set a steaming cup down before Morgana. She grabbed it with two hands, and brought it up to her mouth, lashes lowered with relief. Tyra was known for her brews—be it potent mead or soothing tea . . . *anything* that could settle her rebellious stomach, mayhap even calm her frenetic feelings, was welcome. And who knew her needs better than her own mother?

Egil began recounting the story of the rescue of Morgana and the men from Oslof by Leif and his and Rollo's retainers. The few families of Reyk were spellbound. When, however, he began to recount Leif's own capture and incarceration by the scheming Robert of Neustria and the wicked Snorri the Black, many in the crowd became angry.

A flash flood of guilt swept through Morgana, and she kept her gaze locked on the table before her. Her cheeks burned once again, and if the floor had opened up beneath her, she would have made no attempt to avoid disappearing forever.

She wanted to retire—Tyra had offered her and Ottar's partitioned-off sleeping room with its great wooden box bed. She hadn't wanted to put them out, although the offer had been tempting. She moved to stand now, propelled by churning, burning thoughts to leave Ingemar's longhouse and go to that of Ottar and Tyra.

Eirik was suddenly by her side. "Mamma?" he asked, his eyes full of concern. *"Qu'as-tu?* Are you ailing?"

She smiled through the wash of held-back tears. *"Nei,* love. Just tired."

". . . went to Rollo with the men to ask for help. She offered to pay Haraldsson's death price a hundred times over . . ." Egil was saying with well-practiced theatrics, obviously relishing having his audience in the palm of his hand.

Suddenly the crowd fell absolutely silent, and all eyes went to Morgana. She remained, for a moment, looking down at her son, taking strength from his hand in hers . . . from the love shining in his eyes. She looked toward where Leif sat with Little Thor and Harald. Ingrid was nearby with Guthrum, her expression suddenly transformed by concern.

Morgana opened her mouth to speak, feeling anticipation gather suddenly in the room like a living presence. The air fairly quivered with expectation. "I would have given anything, including my life," she said steadily, her cheeks still stinging, "for I owed him that much. But Guthrum was the one who so generously offered the buried valuables from a Frankish monastery he'd raided many winters ago. Guthrum is the hero of this story, assuredly not me."

Guthrum shook his head as he stood from a place at the table. " 'Twas Little Thor who was the true hero. He shot the black Dane through the heart with a single arrow just as the man was swinging his dagger to carve the blood eagle in young Leif's back."

A collective gasp went up from those who'd not heard the story before.

The men from Oslof began to shout and thump their feet appreciatively, and the others joined in. Morgana saw a flush creep up Little Thor's cheeks—something she'd never seen before. He glanced at Leif, as if for rescue, but Leif was watching Morgana, a closed expression on his face. His eyes looked dark from where Morgana stood, his hair deep red-brown in the shadows.

Sonja, the jarl's wife, went to Morgana and took her by the elbow. "You are pale, Morgana." Morgana felt rather than saw the woman exchange a glance with Tyra. "Would you like to rest a while?"

Morgana looked away from Leif. Eirik was still beside her, his thumb homing toward his mouth. She smiled and lifted him into her arms. She kissed his temple and said, "I think Eirik and I will sleep in Ottar and Tyra's home, if that won't offend you, Sonja." Egil had begun speaking again, honing his skills upon his captive and eager audience.

"Then Linnea will accompany you," Sonja said firmly. " 'Tis dark, and she knows well the way."

Goodbyes were said after breaking the fast. It had rained during the night, but the sun was trying to burn through the layers of mist as the morning matured and those from *Wave Rider* prepared to depart. Some of the men were rolling the *knarr* completely back into the water on log rollers beneath its stem. Others were hoisting the diamond-pattern blue and green sail.

"Remember," Leif told Ingemar and those who stood around him from Reyk, "I extend you all an invitation to Vallée de Vergers. You would not regret leaving here for a paradise."

He held Eirik in his arms, then handed him over so Tyra and Ottar could take their turns hugging their grandson. Then Sigfred and Britta hugged him, too. Britta was crying. Leif slowly walked to where Morgana stood, slightly apart from the others, where, he suspected, she was battling her emotions for rigid control. He placed Eirik in her arms and watched as the child clung to his mother.

"Be a brave lad for your father, Eirik, *já?*"

The child nodded his head, tears in his clear blue eyes, but didn't loosen his hold on Morgana. "Come home with us, Mamma," he said in a small, shaky voice. "Freki will be lonely for you . . . Hugin, too."

"Mayhap another time I will come for a visit, Eirik," Morgana managed. "Or mayhap Papa will bring you to Reyk and you can show me how much you and Harald have grown, *já?*"

442

Leif gently disengaged Eirik from his mother. He felt like a fiend. Felt as wretched inside as Morgana looked outside. And she didn't look well. Her eyes were haunted, with bruise-like rings encircling them. Two dots of color in her cheeks were the only life in her pale face.

She looked very ill, and for a moment Leif thought of remaining in Reyk until whatever was ailing her was better.

If 'tis from a broken heart, then what?

He abruptly held up a hand to the others in farewell, swung away and strode toward *Wave Rider*, where most of the others were already waiting, including Ingrid, who looked almost as distraught as Morgana.

He handed Eirik up to Ragnar, then stepped on one of the forward-most oars of the *knarr*, and vaulted over the freeboard. He immediately turned to regard those standing below him—several men who would give *Wave Rider* the final push it needed to sail away. The others stood back farther, hands shielding their eyes from the sun that peeped in and out of the slowly dispersing mist.

Morgana remained apart. She stood straight and tall, looking at him. Then he realized that she was looking at her son, for her hand raised in response to the child's wave. She looked so pale . . . pale as when he first had left Oslof after they were wed, ignorant of the fact that she was with child.

The last thought didn't quite register . . .

Until the sun briefly touched the shining swath of her hair, reminding him a second time of the sun-splashed spring morn he had gone a-viking and had sent both their lives spinning into pandemonium. And with that ephemeral flash of remembrance, he knew. He knew with the certainty of a man about to be a father . . . again.

She was with child, and didn't want him to know. Didn't want to tie him to her when his wish was to leave. Because he'd told her she had destroyed his trust in her. When he'd

443

been exhausted, disillusioned, had just looked death in the eye.

He, who was himself that paragon of trust-building . . .

"Fool!" a disdainful voice said low into his ear. "You are a fool, Kiisku-Liinu."

He didn't have to meet the man's eyes to know who spoke. Even had Little Thor not directly addressed him, he would have known. And undoubtedly, every man among his crew—and Ingrid—was thinking the same thing.

But Leif Haraldsson had never really cared what other people thought. He was his own man. And he realized in those few moments—as he watched the sun play about Morgana's hair, the quiet courage still emanating from her in the face of her final defeat—that he couldn't live without her. No matter what, living without her was infinitely worse than having her at his side. Together with Eirik. And possibly another child.

It was like reliving his leave-taking all those winters ago in Oslof, and with the arrogance of youth he may have acted hastily, foolishly then . . . but he would not make the same mistake twice.

Several men from Reyk were putting their shoulders to *Wave Rider*'s lapstrake hull for the final shove. Leif handed Eirik to Little Thor, put one hand on the freeboard, leaped over it and dropped into the water, which was up to his waist by now. He fought against the surging and receding swells, then was striding up the beach toward Morgana. For a moment, she looked stunned, then angered. Dear God, was he going to have to subdue her? He didn't dare mention what he suspected, or she would claw his eyes out and *then* run from him.

Afraid she would turn and flee, he called out in a taunting voice, "Don't be a coward, Morgana. Are you afraid to try it one more time? Are you afraid of life in Vallée de Vergers and all its challenges? Are you afraid of *me?*"

Her expression darkened further, but it didn't matter

now, because he was before her. He swiftly bent and swept her up into his arms, high against his chest, where blood still stained his tunic from her deliberate reopening of his laceration two nights before. He held her tightly against him, his face close to hers.

"Don't be a fool," she said in a low, furious voice. "I won't go with you!"

"I'm tired of being a fool," he answered. "This time I'm taking what I've always wanted and never letting it go."

He turned toward the ship and began walking. And noticed belatedly that both the people of Reyk and those aboard *Wave Rider* were cheering. The noise offered a solid screen for their less than placid exchange.

"I'm not your wife, Haraldsson!" she said, trying to kick her feet to loosen his hold. He only tightened his grip, concerned all the while about hurting her. It would surely have been easier to have slung her over his shoulder, but not in her condition.

"You cannot just take me against my—"

"You'll be my wife again. Forever. The first priest I set eyes on in Francia will wed us."

"A priest? I am not of your religion, so it won't be binding. And I'll leave again just as soon as—"

"My religion will be your religion, Morgana, my God yours—"

"I'll leave at the first opportunity!" she cut him off, her voice bordering on shrill.

"—and my land—my home—will be yours, as well."

"You can't *keep* me there!" she countered, feeling unexpectedly childish but unable to stop the angry retorts that bubbled to her lips.

"Then I'll put you in a cage—a lovely but tragic captive for all of Francia to behold." He shifted her slightly. "An example of how a Norseman deals with a disobedient wife."

She struggled in earnest now, outrage bursting through

445

her, but in vain. He staggered only once, but continued inexorably toward the *knarr*. "The more injuries you cause me, the more wounds you will have to tend on the way home."

"You high-handed . . . r-renegade!" she sputtered. "I don't *want* to go! I won't go where I'm—"

"I *want* you to go," he said into the fragrant fall of hair over her ear. His words were softer, yet no less full of conviction. "I *need* you with me. Eirik needs you. He's already lost Hilaire, who was like a mother to him. He surely cannot bear losing you, as well, now that he knows and loves you."

That reminder gave her pause, cut short her tirade. "But . . . but what of the simple woman who—"

"—would bore me to tears in no time?"

They were at the water's edge, and Leif was at a momentary loss. Could he entrust the obstinate Morgana into anyone's care while he climbed into the *knarr?* "Hush!" he said in exasperation. "I can't think!"

Ottar stepped forward then. Ragnar and Little Thor jumped into the water from the vessel above in an obvious if unspoken offer to hand her up to Leif after he'd boarded.

"Traitors—all of you!" she cried, tears streaming down her cheeks as Ottar's huge arms held her immobile.

Leif scrambled up the side of *Wave Rider*, turned and reached down as Ottar handed her to Little Thor, Little Thor to the taller Ragnar the Red, who then held her toward Leif. He picked her up beneath the arms, like a child, then before she could say a word, set her on her feet and pinned her against the freeboard behind her. "I'm sorry I had to do it this way, Morgana. I love you and Eirik, can't live without either of you! Surely you don't really want it any other way?"

"But what of trust?" she asked, her eyes avoiding his, yet falling into just as effective a trap by alighting on his lips. "You said I destroyed your trust and—"

"Then," he answered, breathless from his recent exertions—and suddenly something else, too—"we'll just have to start building it from the bottom again. Mayhap we can learn from people like Little Thor and Ingrid, *já, ást mín?*"

The moment dragged out endlessly, unspoken thoughts rife between them, but also the solid core of a profound love.

"*Já,*" she just had time to murmur with a sweet sigh of surrender before his lips finally closed over hers.

Wave Rider's sail caught the wind with a *whoosh*. It filled, and the ship drifted into deeper waters, but they didn't notice. Nor were they aware of the continued cheers of approval echoing across the widening stretch of water . . . and all around them as the late-summer sun finally penetrated the haze to enfold them in its warm promise.

Author's Note

The Norsemen (later known as Vikings) were making voyages to North America centuries before any other Europeans; therefore Leif Haraldsson's encounter with red men (who were much later mistakenly named Indians) between Greenland and Labrador was entirely possible.

The language used by the Norse characters in TEN-DER MARAUDER is Icelandic, which is closest to the actual tongue spoken by the Norsemen who originally settled in Iceland. Little Thor spoke a now defunct dialect of Algonquian, the language used by most of the Eastern Woodland Native Americans.

The establishment of Normandy was related in TEN-DER MARAUDER as accurately as possible. The Norman Conquest has long been a period of special interest to me, and after having had several of my characters in past books refer to the conquering Normans as "Vikings" (and as a derogatory term) I decided the time had come to incorporate the birth of what became known as "Normandy" in a separate story. The original boundaries of Rollo's grant are approximated only, and as time passed, he and his descendants enlarged the territory to what it is today.

And William the Conqueror was, indeed, a direct descendant of the huge and fierce Hrolf the Walker, or Rollo.